The Moscow Tape

Anyway Books® Works by John Nicholas Datesh

The Girl in the Coyote Coat (novel)*
A Need Apart (novel)*
*Same book, different title
The Body in the Bog (Novel)
The Last Three minutes (Novel)
The Nightmare Machine (novel)
The Janus Murder (novel)
The Moscow Tape (novel)

You Could Call it a Christmas Story (short)
The Pro Station (short)
The Final Equation (short)
Reruns ad Infinitum (short)
The Very First Blog Posts of All Time
(on the blog EmptyGlassFull.com)

The Moscow Tape

an *Anyway Books*® novel by

John Nicholas Datesh

**Published by
Loiseau Media**

The Moscow Tape

An *Anyway Books*® novel by

John Nicholas Datesh

Third Print Edition Published by
Loiseau Media/Anyway Books 2016
ISBN 978-1-940227-16-0
First Print Edition Nordon Publications 1980
Second Print Edition Loiseau Development 2013
Revised e-Editions by 2013, 2016
Loiseau Media/Anyway Books
e-Editions - John Nicholas Datesh, Jr. 2009

The Moscow Tape

Chapter One

The smooth-faced young man shifted awkwardly while the famous professor pored over the scrawled three-word message. Unconcerned with the contents of the note and it accompanying packet, the youth was nervous only because he was in the presence of one of the leading economists in all the Soviet Union. Dr. Alexander Mraisky was also one of the most vocal dissidents in Russia, according to the papers. The KGB man who had given him the package had warned him about Mraisky.

Dr. Mraisky glanced up from the wrinkled paper, quickly assessing the messenger. The eyes, Mraisky knew, always betrayed the stupidity of such boys. He recognized that dull, distant look instantly and dismissed the messenger as a threat to his safety. His acquaintance inside the KGB would never have selected an intelligent courier.

The Professor dug into his pocket and shoveled some money into the hand of the nervous lad. With a smile, he showed him the door and with a frown he closed it. No words, of course, never any words. For a loquacious man like Mraisky, that was particularly galling.

Even from the door, he could see out the window of the tiny one-room apartment. They would be coming soon, according to his friend, any minute. Mraisky had to admit that he was surprised. The sensitive SALT II revision talks between his country and the Americans had given him a sense of security, however temporary.

Surely, he had thought, President Brezhnev would not jeopardize such important negotiations by moving against visible dissidents. Surely.

Leaning against the window sill to study the street below, Mraisky chided himself for his own foolishness. In the Soviet Union nothing could be sure, not for a man, a Jew, who spoke his mind. To the government, internal dissent was more dangerous than all the ballistic missiles in the world.

As co-founder of the Moscow Group for the monitoring of compliance with Helsinki Accord on human rights, Mraisky was more lethal than the cruise missile that would be a major subject of the Soviet-American negotiations. For a moment, Mraisky entertained the odd picture of a forty-three year old economist being launched from an American B-52 flying over the arctic. Did the Politburo see him that way?

Where was the KGB? Surely... Not that word again.

Mraisky hefted the securely wrapped package in his hand. He already knew what it contained. His friend had explained in a separately hand-delivered note what he was to do with it. Mraisky had composed his own set of instructions for the others, ironically using the same three words his friend had hastily jotted down: "Trust no one." Hurrying down the hallway he entered the common bathroom.

Carefully lifting the thin concrete sill of the window he slipped his note under the cord tying the package and dropped the packet between the metal studs of the wall. Cheap. corner-cutting construction had won some building supervisor an extra vacation day and now it served as a conduit for the coded information guaranteed to embarrass the KGB. According to his friend, the package now nestled against the upper frame of the window below would insure Mraisky's immediate release.

He chuckled as he walked back into his room. Surely. Outside he could see three bulky men in brown military-style coats approaching the apartment building. Not the KGB? Why should the Ministry of Internal Affairs get the glory, he wondered. The men stared up at his window. Mraisky stared back. God, he had only a minute.

Quickly, he rang up Volenko. He had to tell him about the package. The footsteps scraped on the concrete landing. Where was Volenko? He could not get Elizaveta, his protégé, in time.

"Yes, Alexei, what...?"

"Shit, Mikhail. Just listen. I can see them coming for me." Mraisky did not stop to breathe, only to listen for the knock. When it came, he continued. "Please carry on for me and give my regards to Steve Klein when he comes."

"I will," the shaky voice replied.

Mraisky hung up and answered the door. The brown coat filled the door way. "Come with us," the Militia officer said simply.

"Am I under arrest?"

"Yes."

Mraisky nodded and retreated to pick up his coat. The men made no move. As he passed through the door, he wondered what would have happened if he had said "No." He also wondered why it had not occurred to him to do so until thirty seconds too late.

~ ~ ~

Amy Klein pulled the waffles and bagels out of the toaster together, humming along to the music of WRKO. She kept right on humming, well into the traffic report, before interrupting herself with a quiet "Oh shit!"

She tightened her bathrobe belt and jogged out of the kitchen down the hallway to the bathroom. The light sound of water told her that Steve was still in the shower. That meant they were both in trouble. Poking her head in the door, Amy could see the distorted form of her thirty-eight year old husband busily rinsing his curly black hair.

"No time for ceremony," she said to herself. Undoing the cord, she let the filmy bathrobe drop and sneaked into the large stall behind Steve's back. Suddenly, firmly, she pulled her body in tight against him.

Steven Klein stood stock upright. "There's been another accident on the Pike."

"How did you guess, darling?"

Turning to face her, Klein smiled. "I can always tell when you want the shower."

Amy grimaced. "At my age, Steven, I could very well want sex. I read that in a book."

"Wouldn't be the first time," Klein said diffidently. He kissed his wife on the forehead and yielded the shower. With an accident on the Mass Pike, he worried that he would be late for the meeting with Bingo Williams, the black hamburger magnate. Bingo, though ordinarily a patient man, had become increasingly edgy as the negotiations with the Soviets drew to a climax. Bingo had the chance to join McDonald's and Burger King in the Russian Plan to put up twenty-five fast food restaurants for the 1980 Olympics. Bingo Williams was damn well going to do it! It fell to Klein and his staff to get the right terms.

Well established as one of Boston's top international lawyers, Klein had few qualms about the deal. It would make Bingo Williams a lot richer and, more importantly, more famous, but it was a rather routine transaction for Klein. In his career, he had done the legal work for several, billions of dollars in international trade. In legal circles Klein was highly respected, enough to satisfy his ego. He also had money, a large house in Newton, a nice wife and two well behaved teenage daughters.

At that peak Klein had made his first honest personal commitment. He had become one of the leading spokesmen of the Boston Jewish community on the subject of human rights and of Russian Jewish repression. From the time he had first made contact with a group of Russian Jews in 1975–while lining up terms for a tractor factory–Steven Klein felt a new, compelling awareness of his own heritage. Successful himself, he realized that he had to speak for those who could not defend themselves.

The past was always on Steve Klein's mind, as was his dedication to the cause of Russian Judaism, but just now, getting to work on time occupied most of his thoughts. He decided to skip his breakfast, stopping only to pour some coffee into a Styrofoam cup on his way to the Mercedes. Once settled in the comfortable leather seat, he switched on the radio.

Amy toweled herself dry slowly before she walked to the kitchen. The tingling response made her think of Chris... She finished wrapping the towel around her trim figure hurriedly when she saw her husband, back in the house standing white-faced with the phone in one hand.

"Steve? What...?"

"It's Alex. He's been arrested."

"Dr. Mraisky?"

He spoke into the phone. "Yes. Carl? Steve. We've go a problem."

Sitting almost cautiously, Amy whispered, "Oh God."

"I just heard it," Klein said somberly. "You'd better get Chris Dunney."

Chapter Two

The bread was stale. It was usually stale, Vladimir Bellin noted, but some days he could at least get his teeth through it. His wife, Marta, had included a hefty chunk of salami along with the bread and cheese, but he had given most of that to his deputy, Bescel Radnik, as compensation for staying so late. Bellin watched in envy as Radnik consumed his soft, fresh loaf alternately with the meat. He could hardly complain. He was drinking Radnik's vodka.

Lighting a thick Havana cigar, Bellin gave up on the food. After several preliminary puffs, he asked, "You're sure you can handle the increased workload, Bescel?"

The young Deputy nodded unenthusiastically as he finished swallowing a mouthful. "If the Procurator cones through with that extra appropriation..."

"He will."

"...then I can pick up that extra man from Donetsk to handle any burden we can't." He paused to take sip of vodka from a coffee cup. "I won't be missed."

Bellin savored the over-sized cigar, which looked almost small when tucked into his broad face. "No party problems?"

Radnik grimaced. As Secretary of the Communist Party Primary in the Department of Investigation of the Moscow Procuracy, Radnik had an extra responsibility. "It's pretty minimal, Director. It's not very hard to keep our six party members quiet. Folenya is my only real problem. Since she was reclassified as eligible for our Primary..." He threw up his hands.

"We have to work with her closely on this case," Bellin said, hiding his distaste. Anna Folenya acted,zealously, of course, as KGB liaison to his Department. "It is basically a KGB problem."

"Then why do we get it?" Radnik resented having the Mraisky matter shunted onto the Department of Investigation.

Choosing his words carefully, Bellin told Radnik as much as he was permitted to reveal. "Mraisky and his Moscow Group are now an embarrassment to the KGB. The KGB mishandled the whole business. Our job is to take over the mess and make sure it doesn't get worse. That's all I can tell you, Bescel. I expect to get clearance to fill you in tomorrow, but you'll have to wait."

"If I'm going to back you up..."

"Don't worry." Feeling awkward with the limits imposed on their usually candid relationship, Bellin checked his watch.

Accepting the hint, Radnik said, "I have to go, Director. I've got a pregnant wife at home, who is gradually losing her affection for you. When I tell her about the hours I'm going to be working, I won't be able to mention the name Bellin without starting a fight."

Bellin sympathized. He had had many arguments with Marta over his hours, particularly when she was carrying "his" children. After twenty-one years, she had mellowed, some. "Good night, Bescel. Send Folenya in, will you. I may as well get this over with."

Radnik pulled his slender frame from the hard wooden chair and gathered the remains of his dinner and work. "Good luck," he said with a grin. She's been impossible all day. Because we've taken over a precious KGB operation."

"I know." Bellin re-lit his cigar. Folenya hated cigar smoke.

Appreciating the gesture, Radnik chuckled as he withdrew. "Good night." He stepped into the small waiting room his office shared with Bellin's and almost stepped into Anna Folenya.

The KBG liaison officer glared at him from her chair. She had overheard the discussion. The thought of either of them questioning evidence submitted by the KGB to the Procurator... It was hardly a wonder that subversives like Mraisky and his band of malcontents flourished where men like Bellin and Radnik exercised influence.

"Goodnight, Anna." Radnik said with a combination of embarrassment and annoyance.

"Comrade Radnik," she responded coldly. She stood as haughtily as her tiny figure would allow until the Deputy Investigator had departed.

Finally she pulled her heavy briefcase through the door. Bellin, watching her casually, observed that he rarely saw Folenya walk standing straight up–she usually had an overstuffed valise in hand. The thought made him smile, just as she struggled into the chair.

She stiffened, knowing that Bellin was laughing at her. Bellin often puffed himself up by belittling her, like so many other petty functionaries when confronted by an effective official or active Party member. Bellin, she knew, was only nominally a member of the Party.

"Vodka?" Bellin offered, knowing she would refuse. "I've read your report, Anna, and your recommendation that we go after the rest of the Moscow Group. Very comprehensive."

"Now is the time to shut the subversives down completely," Folenya declared. "Particularly now, with the evidence of Mraisky's CIA contact."

Skeptically, Bellin raised both thick, dark eyebrows. "For all Mraisky knew, it was a KGB contact."

Folenya had no response to the deliberate slur against the KGB. The KGB had discovered that the dissident, Mraisky, had received a recorded message from a traitor within the KGB itself. Because of that embarrassing disclosure, the KGB had been forced to request the intervention of Bellin's independent department.

"Did your people find the source of the message?" Bellin asked politely.

Folenya responded obliquely, "We will treat the matter internally, Director Bellin. My report summarized all of the other evidence against Mraisky and his Jewish gang..."

"I saw only about half Jews. An Azeri, a couple Tajiks. Did I miss something?"

Folenya again ignored his document. "Your department should prepare its investigation as quickly as possible. The trial must begin immediately."

Bellin frowned as he worked the cigar. "Investigations here, Anna, take time. This case will be treated like any other until I am told otherwise. More important, of course, and expedited, but with the same care and accuracy. When I feel there is enough evidence against Mraisky to justify a trial–as I'm sure I will soon–I will recommend as much to the Procurator. Then it is up to him."

His tone angered her. He spoke as if it were his duty to challenge all of the material gathered by the KGB. Bellin questioned the KGB? Ludicrous! "The priority, of course, is to make certain that these subversives do not get that message to the Americans. Naturally, you will have the complete cooperation of the KGB." She paused for a moment, sizing up Bellin's attitude toward her suggested plan of action. "If we can maneuver the subversives into a trap as well, we will have grounds to finish off every last nest of them in the Union."

Skimming her report, Bellin found little information to support her claim of widespread subversion. The KGB preferred that he proceed blindly. Folenya's "unofficial" suggestions—none of which she had ever submitted without official KGB approval—amounted to a purge of the leaders of the Moscow Group as Mraisky's collaborators. She particularly stressed the three faction leaders: Mikhail Volenko, of the traditionalist school; Nikolai Torlas, the Georgian leader of the nationalist members of the Moscow Group; and Elizaveta Krylenkev, the understudy of Mraisky himself and the major force of the Jewish faction.

He pushed the report aside with disgust. He had no use for Folenya's approach. The state had granted its people certain rights, instituted the Procuracies and installed men like Bellin to protect those rights against the Folenya's as well as the Mraisky's. "Until ordered otherwise, Anna, I will keep the subversives under close watch, but I will not arrest them just to satisfy the KGB. Present me with tangible proof of a political crime and I'll use it."

Folenya frowned deeply. She would have to recommend that Bellin himself be watched. He was clever, strong willed, but misguided. "Do as you must, Comrade."

Only one other person called Bellin "Comrade", but the name escaped him. "What does this 'message' look like, Anna? In your report, it is called any number of things, particularly 'important', 'vital' and the like. But all I really know is that it will ruin the KGB's credibility, damage state security and cost Chairman Arkilonov his medals. But I don't know what it looks like."

Embarrassed, Folenya tried to conjure a quick, acceptable excuse for the omission. The truth would hardly do: She had not herself found out until after the report had been typed. "It is a matter of security," she said lamely. "I was reluctant to put it on paper."

"I see." Bellin replied doubtfully.

"It is a magnetic tape cartridge, used in certain kinds of video recorders. Twelve centimeters by eighteen by four."

"Can it be transcribed?"

"She shook her head, barely disturbing her close-cropped black hair. "No. And no copy can be made without distorting the message code. It is a visual representation of a series of musical notes made with great precision. It is a very sophisticated mathematical cipher."

"One of our latest, I take it?"

"It is a very recent development, used only for the most critical messages..." She cut herself short, realizing too late her blunder. Unable to correct the admission, she proceeded, though with less vigor. "It was one of a dozen tapes prepared individually by the Cipher Bureau of detailing a high security matter. That's all you need to know."

Glancing out the single window of his little office, Bellin sighed at the darkening Moscow sky. It would be raining again soon. In Moscow, it was always either raining or threatening. "All right, Anna. You'd better get me a list of all the subversives. I have your dossiers on the leaders, but I'll want to know about the rest of them. Where they live, where they work, meet and so forth. I assume that you have the leaders wired already."

"Of course," she responded, insulted for herself and for her service. Top dissidents had been under electronic surveillance for years. "I will have all of that data for you tomorrow. As I state in my report, we will establish a monitoring post here in this building and step up monitoring activities."

Bellin withdrew the dossiers of the Moscow Group leaders from the report folder. He absently paged through them as he spoke. "I'll want the names and locations of the CIA operatives as well, to the extent that you have them."

"We'll take care of the CIA, Comrade," Folenya informed him. "That is beyond your scope."

He looked up from the Torlas dossier to give her a hard stare. "All right. But make it obvious. I want everyone to know that we are watching every move."

"But that will discourage...," she protested.

"That is the point, Anna," Bellin snapped. "My Job is to prevent the movement of that tape. Any trap you want to set is secondary at best and dangerous. I don't want to invite trouble."

Folenya capitulated, temporarily. The KGB would not take orders from Bellin. "Agreed."

Coming to the dossier of Elizaveta Krylenkev, Bellin found himself arrested by the large, black and white glossy of the young woman.

His raised eyebrows did not escape Folenya's notice. "Don't let her face affect you, Comrade Bellin. She is very dangerous and a half-Jew."

The photo displayed an attractive face with lively, searching, wide-set eyes. Searching? Could he really conclude that from a simple picture? Bellin looked at a second shot. Yes, it was there.

Uncomfortable, Folenya remarked snidely, "She is the most dangerous of the lot."

"Perhaps," Bellin said, for Folenya's sake, "but she will make the surveillance more interesting, won't, she, Anna?"

~ ~ ~

"It is most certainly not minor," Nikolai Torlas boomed.

Elizaveta Krylenkev held up both hands. "I'm not saying that, Nikolai."

Torlas plopped his huge body into the chair. "You may as well be," he rejoined. He looked over at his four colleagues for their nods of support. As tacit leader of the nationalities' faction in the Moscow Group, Torlas spoke for all of them. "You're the one always demanding the right to use Hebrew. And you barely know it yourself."

Stung by the insult, Elizaveta flared. "There's more to learn of my language than yours!"

Petyr Arkin moved in between the two antagonists. In the absence of Mraisky and Volenko, the host, Arkin–whose apartment was not yet bugged–had the unenviable task of chairing the Moscow Group meeting. "Your personal quarrels do not belong here. The question of nationalities' rights is settled. The Helsinki documents guarantee it and we must publicize important violations."

"This is one!" Torlas declared.

"It's not even your story, Nikolai," Elizaveta taunted him.

The corpulent novelist laughed, unable to sustain his anger. "The Union doesn't authorize royalties for Georgian language books. I can't afford to write what won't keep me fed."

Most of the group laughed, easing the tension. Arkin took advantage of the moment. "I suggest that we wait for a larger work, something more dramatic, to signify as a Helsinki violation. Agreed?"

"All right," Torlas replied, "But I don't even want to hear about another Jew's emigration rejection."

One of Elizaveta's faction began to speak, but she cut him off. "Since it's mine, I'll agree to that."

Every member of the gathering stared at her. Torlas pushed himself up with effort and crossed the narrow room to her side. "That's good. We need you here."

"It was Alexei's idea, Nikolai" He intends to..."

"He'll never leave Russia. There's too much to do here," Arkin objected. "If the strong Jews leave, who will teach the weak?"

Dismayed by the naivete of her associate, Elizaveta explained, "Of course not. But the denial will be a very clear violation of his rights to the Americans."

"And yours?" Torlas demanded.

"I hope to go," she said. It had been her only goal since the Yom Kippur war: To emigrate to Israel, to participate it the reconstruction of the Jewish nation. Perhaps because awareness of her Jewishness had come so late, Elizaveta felt it more intensely, more consciously than the others, including Mraisky. "It's where a Jew belongs."

Torlas chuckled. "It's going to come as a shock to the Ministry to find that you've been a Jew all these year without their knowledge. Is that a crime?"

Upset by the remark, Elizaveta snapped, "If my mother lied, let them go after her! I never said I wasn't a Jew." Though, she wondered, what would she have said had she been asked? For most of her life, she did not consider herself anything but Russian.

"Of course not," Torlas said skeptically.

"Please," Arkin pleaded. "Perhaps we should wait for Mikhail and Alexei."

Rolling his eyes. Torlas put his hands on his huge hips. "I told you that Mikhail said we were not to wait."

"But it isn't like either one of them to be late."

"Mikhail will be here later," Torlas reiterated. "Alexei will not be here at all."

Breaking out of her pout, Elizaveta demanded, "Why not?"

Miffed, Torlas cried, "How am I supposed to know... Mikhail talked to him, I didn't. I'm sure that if he's not coming, it is for a very good reason. Am I right?"

The others could not but agree. As they all knew, and Mraisky knew better than any, the Moscow Group could hold together only so long as he, its undisputed head, imposed his influence on all factions. Without him, there would be no Moscow Group. Only something serious would keep him away.

"Oh, my God." Arkin whispered.

Elizaveta and Torlas exchanged fearful looks. The worst had finally happened.

~ ~ ~

Mikhail Volenko stared forlornly at his friend's window. The unmistakable shadows of the KGB agents passed again across the curtained window of Mraisky's room. For two hours, they had scoured the apartment, undoubtedly looking for what he had come to retrieve.

Not a bold or brave man, Volenko had stood well away from Mraisky's building, hoping the agent would leave. He was afraid that if he went inside, the KGB would surely take him, too. It was the stuff of British spy novels, he thought, not of an ordinary man's life.

Yet, by aligning himself with Mraisky and the other dissidents, he had forfeited his claim to an ordinary life.

"Shit, Mikhail. I can see them coming for me," Mraisky had said carefully, composed enough even in his final moments of freedom to convey the needed information to him.

Under their simple code, the words meant a certain hiding place: The window of the bathroom. Simple code? It was laughable, the imaginings of boys, not of men. An even simpler code told him that it was vital for him to recover whatever Mraisky had hidden. Mraisky would never have risked calling if it were not important.

His courage bolstered some by the knowledge of the importance of this task, Volenko stepped out into the lighted street and approached the building. As he did, he could see the outlines of the KGB men rummaging through Mraisky's one room flat. Did none of them live in such award-winning buildings? Didn't they know how shabbily built such monstrosities were? For once in his long life, Volenko hoped with all of his soul that the KGB lived better than the rest of them did.

No one paid any attention to him as he tried his key to the outer door. Before he could turn it, however, the door swung open, nearly knocking him off his feet. The two KGB men who emerged helped to steady him. Volenko almost choked he was so terrified.

"Are you all right, old man?" the younger of the two asked.

"Forget him," the other said. "The Procurator's men will be here any minute. We're not supposed to be here."

After patting Volenko on the shoulder, the young KGE agent hustled after his companion. Volenko, as stunned by their abrupt departure as by their sudden appearance, stood for a moment and watched them dash toward a waiting auto and speed away.

Recovering himself, Volenko unlocked the door and stepped inside. He knew there was a small elevator half-way down the corridor, but he chose the stairs right beyond the door. The climb left him short of breath but saved minutes, particularly given the reliability of Russian-built elevators. And if a second shift of investigators–the Procurator's men, for some reason– were minutes away, every instant counted.

Volenko stole down the hallway to the first of the third floor's two bathrooms. Inside, the room was black and silent. Volenko paused, listening for an indication of activity in the hallway. Satisfied that he had a little time, he climbed up on the lower sill of the window and worked the upper one free with little difficulty. Half blinded by the cloud of dust and plaster he had released, Volenko lost his balance, almost falling through the window. Once he had cleared his eyes, he could see that he had chosen the wrong bathroom.

He replaced the sill, jamming it in place with two narrow wedges brought along for the purpose, dusted himself off and flushed a toilet. The familiar noise comforted him. No one ever questioned anyone coming out of a toilet.

The hallway was still empty as he forced his tired legs to carry him to the second bathroom. Upon opening its door, he found the light on and heard the water running in the shower. Volenko stopped dead when he saw the woman's robe hanging near the shower. He didn't dare wait, but if she finished while he was still in there...

Stilling his fear, Volenko examined the upper window sill. Perched upon the lower one, he pulled gently, freeing the wood enough to feel inside with his index finger. There was something, a package of some kind!

As he pulled the sill out the dust generated made him sneeze. The water stopped. "Who's that?" The woman in the shower demanded.

Volenko panicked. He spoke the first words that came into his head. "KGB."

After a pause, the showerer muttered, "Oh God."

The fear in her voice hastened Volenko's recovery. "Go on with your shower, Comrade. We'll be finished in a moment."

"Yes, sir." Immediately, the water started up again.

Relieved, Volenko angled the sill outward and plucked the package from inside. The note attached was clearly in Mraisky's handwriting!

With sill in place again, Volenko once again dusted himself off and went quickly out the door.

His heart pounding audibly, Volenko elected to try the elevator. While waiting, he tried to hide the package. It proved too large for his pockets, so he put it inside his shirt. Because he still wore a heavy outer coat, it created only a minor bulge.

Impatient with the elevator, he pushed the button again and, hearing no response, he pressed both up and down at the same time. When still no response or sound of movement came, he cursed and started off. He had not gotten ten feet when he heard a voice call, "Hey, you."

Volenko froze, unable to turn and answer or walk ahead. The package felt bulky and obvious suddenly.

"Hey," the voice repeated. "Do you want the elevator?"

The friendly tone allowed Volenko to look over his shoulder. It was a thin young man in a business suit, leaning out of the elevator, motioning to him.

"Yes," Volenko replied, walking back.

When he got to the elevator door, he saw them. Two uniformed Militia officers standing stolidly behind the young man. He was trapped. Involuntarily, he took a step backwards.

"Make room, boys," the man ordered. The other two complied with a simple, "Yes, Investigator Radnik."

Volenko stuttered. "I, I'm going down."

"In that case, we'll send it down for you as soon as we're finished."

Once the door had closed, Volenko sprinted down the hallway, took the steps two at a time and rushed out into the night. At that moment, he could not even think how narrow his escape had been.

~ ~ ~

Having checked on her children, Marta Bellin gently stirred her husband from his chair-bound slumber. "Vladimir, she whispered in his ear.

Bellin started, knocking the files from his lap. Marta knelt to pick up the papers, coming across the photos of Torlas, Volenko and Krylenkev as she did so. She replaced all of the papers, but studied the pictures.

"Who are these people, Vladimir?"

Bellin tried to focus on the black and white photographs and at length recognized the faces. "People you should not know, Marta."

"He is such an ordinary-looking man," Marta decided, holding Volenko's picture at arms length. "Is he a subversive?"

"To the extent that he calls the privilege of religious worship a right, yes, I suppose he is. His major crime is making noise about it."

Confused. Maria asked "Why don't you put him away...?"

Bellin shrugged and said nothing.

"The girl? Is she with him?"

Taking the photo, Bellin replied, "She is a Jew and..."

"Oh, I see. Still, she is a pretty thing, don't you think?" Marta searched her husband's eyes as he examined the photo. "Too thin, perhaps."

"Yes. She is." How odd. He hadn't noticed, but yes, Elizaveta Krylenkev was thin, hungry-looking. Intense.

Bellin felt already that he knew her. Russian father and Jewish mother. Mother managed to emerge from the Patriotic War and 1945 with a Russian identity and continued the lie, imposing it upon her daughter and only child. There reasons were obvious and good: Better a Russian than a Jew in that era. And in the present one. Did the Krylenkev girl appreciate how much easier her life had been made by her mother's deception?

Perhaps she did, now.

The Israeli war of 1967 had no apparent effect on the girl, who was just preparing for Moscow University, but almost immediately after the beginning of the Middle East war of 1973, she fell in with Mraisky and the Jewish intelligentsia at the University. She studied under Mraisky, eventually becoming an assistant Professor in his department. Joined the Moscow Group. and, only three months before, she had applied for emigration papers.

The application, of course, had been recently denied.

Elizaveta Krylenkev. A purely Russian name. That must have bothered her, as well as the designation, still on her internal papers, of Great Russian. She obviously no longer considered herself Russian, but many Jews did not. Another unhappy Jew. As far as Bellin was concerned, harmless.

"Vladimir? Will you have to arrest her, too?"

Returning the photo to its place in the file, Bellin rose and stretched his stiff arms, one of which he then put around his wife's broad shoulders.

"Arrest her?" That would be a second step toward a full campaign against internal dissent, opening the door to every petty politician and grasping bureaucrat who wanted to rid himself of a rival or a mere aggravation. He had seen it happen over and over, beginning with his village when he was eight years old. It spread like a disease, feeding upon itself until it infected every man and woman, even the children, in Russia.

The first steps were always the most dangerous. He had no intention of taking them. Unless he had to. "I hope not, Marta."

~ ~ ~

By the time Volenko reached Arkin's apartment, most of the Group had gone home. Only Torlas and Elizaveta remained, the latter more asleep than awake. Even Arkin had gone to bed. Torlas played a bizarre solitary card game from Georgia in between gulps of vodka. Carelessly, he looked up at Volenko standing in the doorway and went back to his game.

"Everyone's gone," Torlas said, diffidently.

Angry, Volenko had to resist a temptation to slam the door. "I'm sorry if it took so long to out-maneuver the KGB."

Holding out the bottle to Volenko the Georgian gathered up the cards. "You have a right to be upset, Mikhail. The others had a right to go home. These are basic human rights, inherent in the person, and are not granted by the state." He laughed.

Volenko accepted the offered vodka hungrily. It flowed easily down his throat, calming him.

"Easy, my friend. That's my own vodka, not Arkin's."

"Is Elizaveta asleep?" Volenko asked quietly.

Torlas did not modulate his voice in response, keeping at conversational level. "Yes and no, though it's more 'yes' at the moment." He looked over at her sleeping figure huddled in the Polish-made chair. Her curly brown hair hung half-across her face, softening its lines. Her posture accentuated the curve of her breasts and hips, making her appear more full-bodied than she was, more Torlas' type. Though not attracted to her, he could admire the girl objectively.

The scrutiny of his colleague did not escape Volenko. Satisfied that the fat man's eyes contained no hint of lust, Volenko merely remarked, "You may as well wake her."

"I prefer her asleep, Mikhail. Awake, she is a pain in the ass. Too much the Jew at times."

"And Mraisky?"

Torlas grinned. "Ah, that's right. He was one too. I forgot."

"Was?"

"They took him, didn't they?" Torlas asked. When Volenko nodded, he added, "We thought as much. We won't see him again."

With what he considered heroic modesty, Volenko produced the package he had taken from Mraisky's building.

He had already read Mraisky's note and knew its contents. He would let them speak for themselves. "Perhaps not."

Impressed, Torlas gave his fat man's impression of a bow. "So, you got by the KGB. You are a man of more means than you let on."

Volenko set the opened packet on the table and went to give Elizaveta's shoulder a nudge. Meanwhile, Torlas examined the object in the cardboard box. "What in God's name is it? A tape?"

"Read the note." Volenko's efforts were yielding little in the way of animation in the girl. "Come on, Elizaveta."

"Very interesting," Torlas said to himself. "Very interesting and very dangerous."

Elizaveta gradually came out of her slumber. In a half dream, she was in an economics class. On one lectern, her father lectured her on Russian history; from a second, Mraisky spoke in Hebrew. There was a third... empty.

"Elizaveta."

Impatient, Torlas snapped, "Tell her he's been arrested. That'll get..."

She started, "Arrested! Oh God!" Quickly, she was fully awake, on her feet and clutching Volenko's arms. "Is it true, Mikhail? Is it?"

He nodded.

The Georgian looked up from the note. "Is it possible that this cartridge can pull down the pants of the KGB?"

Turning to Torlas, Volenko replied, "All I know is what you know, Nikolai."

"What is it?" Elizaveta demanded. "Tell me what it is..."

"Jump, jump, jump," Torlas chided her. "We are your allies, woman. Give us a chance."

Volenko took the note from Torlas and handed it to her. "I found this in one of Alexei's hiding places. He let me know where to look just before the KGB came for him. This was all there was."

"God knows it's enough." Torlas, though an atheist, had no aversion to invoking the name of a deity in which he held no stock. It was, as he usually explained, a literary device. "It could put us all in the place where winters are coldest."

"It came with this tape," Volenko added.

Her eyes scanning the wrinkled paper, Elizaveta read the handwritten words with amazement first, then fear and finally hope. She read it a second time aloud.

"'My trusted friend, Mikhail. I will be arrested soon. I have that on excellent authority. I will have a package for you, to which this will be attached. It is a message from inside the KGB itself, a taped message. Do not try to copy it. for the code cannot be precisely duplicated by any ordinary means.'"

"'You must get this tape to the American Embassy. I was told that there, only there, is the man who can satisfactorily decode it. I was also assured that this tape, once in American hands, will make my prosecution and imprisonment completely impossible. Of this there is no question.'"

"'Trust no one. Nikolai and Elizaveta alone can be trusted among the Group. And outside of them, no one. Except 'K'. You can trust him. You must not fail. My life and the movement depend upon it. M.'"

"But who is this 'K?'" Torlas demanded. "And how did Alexei come by this thing?"

Volenko shook his head. "No matter. We do as he says."

"Elizaveta?"

She stared through Torlas. "I... He had a friend at the KGB."

"Who does not?"

Taking the note from her, Volenko tore it to shreds. "It doesn't matter! Alexei wants this tape to get to the American Embassy. That is what we must do!"

Torlas glanced out the window. "I don't know, Mikhail. The KGB will be all over us. One is already outside."

Grimly, Volenko recalled the man in the shadows as he arrived. "I saw him. We must try."

"How? I'm surely not going to walk into the American Embassy. That's technically foreign soil, Mikhail. We'd need papers for that."

"There will be Americans here for business. Reporters, of course. And with the Spartakiade..." Volenko stopped, realizing that they could not safely trust Mraisky's fate to a stranger. "'K' is our only real hope."

Torlas laughed. "Fine. Who is he, or she? Or it?"

"K"? Volenko racked his memory. A man Mraisky trusted with his own life. "Of course!"

"Who?"

"Elizaveta?" Volenko asked, shaking the girl out of her daze. "What American was closest to Alexei?"

"American?"

"Yes."

She thought for a second, but not very hard. "He mentioned that his friend from Boston would be coming soon."

Triumphantly, Volenko cried, "Exactly!"

Torlas, far less intimate with Mraisky, grew impatient. He did not like being excluded. "Come, come. Let me play, too "

"The American lawyer. Steven Klein. He and Alexei met several years ago. They have corresponded ever since. In fact, Klein has helped support us with money."

Impressed, Torlas said, "So that's where the foreign currency certificates come from."

"And he's coming to Moscow soon. Correct, Elizaveta?"

She replied, growing more excited with each word, "Yes, of course. Alexei was to meet him at his hotel. It would look all right if one of us went instead!"

Volenko and Torlas exchanged optimistic glances. An American lawyer? In Moscow on business? Who would have freer access to the Embassy?

"Is he above suspicion?"

"If anyone is."

"Ah," Torlas asked, "but will he do this?"

Elizaveta exclaimed, "He will! I know he will!"

Staring at the large tape cartridge, Volenko said, "If we can't trust him, there is no one. He must do it."

Torlas rubbed his bulging cheeks. "All right, then. But for God's sake, let's not let him know how dangerous it will be."

Chapter Three

It always amazed Andy how her pelvis moved on its own at moments of climax. Since it had not happened all that often, Andy could remember each of the times–the lurching, in spite of her efforts to be smooth and graceful, the shudder at the end of each movement inside of her. And each time, she uttered the same phrase, "Oh. Come on, come on," inserting the proper name, "Chris" in this case. Then at the last, all thought seemed to disappear before the aches of pleasure.

As Chris moved above her, she felt that moment approach, inexorably, wondering suddenly what he felt, what he thought. When it did come, of course, she forgot about him, lost him in the brief, shaking arch upward. After that instant she realized that he was still holding back, maintaining a shallow penetration. Andy tried to urge him on, but no words came out, just a feeble cry.

Then, in perfect Russian, he whispered, "Does the bus stop here?" thrust deeply into her and came spasmodically along with her second orgasm.

Once Andy regained her breath, she said, "Christopher Dunney, you are a ripping asshole," and pushed him off to the side of the bed.

Innocently, Dunney replied, "But Andrea, Klein sent me to Berlitz to brush up on my Russian."

Peeved, Andy snapped, "Not on this Russian, damn it!"

Dunney kissed her shoulder and caressed her heaving chest. "You're only half Russian and Ukrainian at that, but I apologize. All I can say is that you drilled that phrase into me and it runs through my mind every time I'm with you. You are a victim of your lascivious conditioning program."

Her annoyance drifted away before his gentle words. For all of it, he was not being unfair. Andy had used any number of trite colloquialisms to embarrass the learned Dunney. He had immediately challenged her with his knowledge of Russian and an ingratiating smile. "Four weeks, every night," Andy said offhandedly. "That was my first orgasm. And you ask for a bus."

"If that was your first, I should ask for a bus," Dunney remarked, humbled. "Fortunately, I do better with Slavic languages than I do with Slavic women."

Andy paused to wonder if she were in love with Dunney. Shouldn't she be? "You do quite nicely with both, Chris. I'd be more than happy to tour the Soviet Union with you."

Dunney sat up, leaning his sweat soaked back against the headboard. It was not an unpleasant prospect, touring Russia with Andy Wards. She had a broad, high cheek boned face, a face with character. Her body, short and solid, had character too, orgasms or no orgasms. Unfortunately, Steve Klein would get that plum and for that son of a bitch it did not mean a thing. Klein had been there–and not just to Russia. He had already done the big international deals. To Dunney, Klein's lead Associate in the Bingo Williams negotiations, the trip to Moscow has to have been the capstone to a strong, occasionally superb, five-year career in Williams, Kayle & Abelson's international department.

At first, he had been told that his crash course at Berlitz had been designed to prepare him for the actual trip. He had thrown himself into relearning his college-acquired Russian with the single-mindedness that had made him Klein's best associate. For what? After the first week, Steve had acknowledged that Bingo had refused to pay for another lawyer "living it up on Russian champagne and hamburgers." Dunney's quick re-schooling was only for the purpose of conference calls. After that, Dunney had thrown himself instead into Andy, his, and formerly Klein's, instructor. Admittedly it had become a rather satisfying substitution.

"What time is it, Andy?" He inquired absently. As she leaned over his body, her breasts moved enticingly across his groin. It should have stirred him. but it didn't.

"Seven-ten, darling."

"Darling?" The term startled him out of his reveries. "That's a bit informal, isn't it?"

It may have been a joke, but Andy was hurt, though She did not allow it to show. "Don't worry. I won't even fix you breakfast."

Self-consciously, Andy slid off of Dunney and ostentatiously searched the closet for a robe. For the first time, she felt naked in front of him. "You wouldn't want to be late for work," was all she could think to say.

~ ~ ~

Though he was the senior partner, Carl Abelson arrived at his desk at eight o'clock every morning, except Sunday. As he had gotten older, he had found himself arriving progressively earlier. No reason not to, he admitted ruefully.

By 8:45, he had downed three cups of rum-laced coffee and read the Mraisky article in the Boston Globe four times. The paper remained open over his desk. Abelson dabbed the perspiration from his bald crown with his plain cotton handkerchief. Steven Klein's noisy position on Soviet Jews had always unnerved him a bit. There was something wrong about it, for a lawyer of Klein's Stature, and yet he could hardly criticize the man without seeming anti-Semitic or pro-communist. Abelson assured himself that he was neither. He simply did not like it.

Now this Mraisky thing...

"Mr. Klein just called, Mr. Abelson," his Secretary announced. "He'll be down in a second."

"Humph," Abelson responded, stretching his long stiff legs. The International Department was on the fifteenth floor. It would take Klein at least five minutes to make it down to the thirteenth, no matter how young his legs were. Dunney, who usually beat even him to the office, was already on his way. "Let Mr. Klein and Mr. Dunney in as soon as they arrive, please."

Klein came in first and without saying good morning asked, "All right, Carl. What do you have in mind?"

"Let's wait for Mr. Dunney." He picked up the paper and offered it to Klein. "Here, take a quick look."

Accepting the paper, Klein scanned the Mraisky articles, which consumed half the front page.

"Pushed the Ayatollah's name right out of the paper," Abelson said.

Abelson's secretary knocked once and entered with coffee. three cups. "Mr. Dunney is here, sir."

Dunney walked by her, lifting his cup as he did. "Good morning Carl. Steve."

The remark drew a hidden smile from Abelson and a sudden closing of the paper from Klein. Abelson took his coffee, openly adding a touch of rum from a vest flask and said. "Sit down gentlemen. Thank you Mrs. Elon."

Once the door had closed, the only remaining founding partner of Williams, Kayle & Abelson began, "This is a large firm. One hundred and eighty-seven attorneys, a like number of paralegals, secretaries and support personnel. We are assembled to serve our clients. Our own interests come second to those of our clients, large and small. The rights of individuals, of corporations, of societies are worth nothing unless people like us are dedicated to serving them in the enforcement of those rights."

"We all must contribute whatever we can under any circumstances to fulfill the needs of our clients." Abelson paused, looking sternly at Klein and Dunney in turn. "You've both heard me say this before and I am not trying to be tedious. I have reiterated this code, if you will, so as to provide a context for our discussion. Now, Christopher, Steve will give you the facts."

Still. staring at the imposing figure of the old man, Klein stated, "Dr. Alexander Mraisky has been arrested."

Dunney said nothing. He was trying to remember who Mraisky was. The name sounded familiar.

Seeing Dunney's failure to react, Abelson added, "The Russian dissident."

Running his tongue along the inside of his cheek, Dunney nodded knowingly. He had not yet grasped the significance. Russians were arrested all the time, in Russia. So what? Hadn't that Shcharansky been arrested, as well, the year before? "Is that a problem for Bingo Burgers? It shouldn't cool business relations, at least not as long as the Administration stays off its human rights soap box."

Exasperated, Klein retorted, "Don't you read the newspapers, Dunney! Alex Mraisky is the most outspoken, most courageous man in the Soviet Union."

"And, he happens to be a close personal friend of Steven here. And there are very few people in the Soviet Government who do not know that fact."

"I see."

Calming himself, Klein continued. "I cannot possible represent Bingo Williams in the contract negotiations. My feeling is that I should withdraw from the firm for a while, but Carl, I believe, has other ideas."

Abelson shook his long head. "Bingo will not accept that and Steve knows it. Under the circumstances, I think he will agree to have Steve run the show from here with you in Moscow."

"Me? In Moscow?" Dunney asked coolly. It was what he had wanted all along. It would be his big chance for an early partnership, to get out from under Steve Klein.

"What do you think?" Abelson asked.

"I think it's a damn good idea."

~ ~ ~

While waiting to be called into the meeting with Bingo Williams, Dunney retired to the library. If he were going to Moscow, even if the trip were still weeks away, he would have to finish up his other work. The library was as good a place as any to start.

Halfway into a minor research project, Dunney heard his number paged. He hurried to the main desk and anxiously picked up the phone. It was Betty Givens, the secretary he shared with another senior associate in the Department. "Yes, Betty?"

She softened her voice noticeably as she began, "Your brother Harry called..."

His expectations deflated, Dunney replied sharply, "I've told you a hundred times not to bother me with personal calls. Take a message, please. If I want them, I'll damn well call them."

More forcefully, she said, "But it's your brother. Harry wants you to come..."

"I don't have time now," he snapped. For them he had no time, period. "Give my regrets." As an afterthought, he added, more politely, "And call Andy Wards for me. Tell her I will meet her for dinner after all."

"Yes, Mr. Dunney," Betty said sarcastically.

Dunney hung up before she had actually finished. He had barely enough time for Andy. And she, at least meant something to him. How in God's name, he asked himself, was he supposed to feel anything for his older brothers, all of whom were in high school or college before he even learned how to read?

Screw it, he thought. They could all wait until he found the time.

By the time he had returned to the international section of the library, Dunney's page sounded again. This time it was Klein.

Making his way to the conference area, Dunney checked his appearance in the mirror-surfaced wall of Conference Room H, before proceeding to B. Though whatever decision had to be reached had already been reached, he wanted to be secure in his appearance.

When Dunney entered the conference room he felt the tension. like the dampness of perspiration, permeating the air of the small, glass-enclosed room. At one end of the oblong table, Bingo Williams stood, towering over the other two men. His huge square face scowled at no one in particular. In the ten years since his retirement as an obscure football professional, Williams had struggled heroically to build a strong regional chain of fast food restaurants. He had, to Dunney's recollection, almost gone under twice. Bingo Burgers, Inc. had even spent time in Bankruptcy court under Chapter Eleven, but somehow Williams had pulled himself and his beleaguered company out of it.

To Williams, the Russian deal meant everything. It would be the crowning achievement, the international arrival of Bingo Williams. And now Klein, Mraisky and the KGB were threatening it all. The usual, easy smile was nowhere to be seen.

On either side, Klein and Abelson sat, outwardly composed. Under the table, however, Klein's foot tapped out a rapid beat. Abelson's legs were crossed at the ankles, not at the knees as when he was comfortable. Neither man had looked at Dunney yet.

"Join the party, Dunney," Bingo said quietly. "Don't worry. I already told these fellas what I think of them. I've got no quarrel with you."

Dunney casually threw his files down on the table and remained standing. "Thanks."

Williams shook his head slowly. "I like experience. That's what I hired when I came here. Now, I find I don't get it."

"Fair enough, Bingo. But you and I have worked together on this contract, so you know how well acquainted I am with it. Besides, I speak better Russian than Steve ever will."

Gently interjecting, Abelson said, "With Steve backing up Christopher here in Boston, he'll have no problem in Moscow."

Steve Klein made an abbreviated gesture toward Bingo. "We've offered to absorb the cost of an associate counsel to do the actual bargaining."

Dunney's mouth dropped open. "Who? What outside counsel?"

"None," Bingo stated. "That's bullshit. I told you I'm willing to go with your arrangement."

"Yes, but...," Klein objected.

Shifting in his chair, crossing his legs, Abelson held up his hand quieting Klein. "Bingo has imposed an extra term that you should know about, Chris. He demands that Steve say nothing, do nothing and engage in no activity in behalf of Dr. Mraisky."

Dunney shrugged. "He's beyond help now anyway, isn't he?" Catching Klein's angry frown, he added, "Seriously, Steve. What could you do for him anyway?"

"That," snapped Bingo Williams, "is not the point."

Sadly, Klein agreed. "My first obligation is to our client." His dilemma was over. He had made his choice. "Now is not the time to admit to the Russians that we are so enamored of the deal that Bingo has to change law firms simply because the Russians don't approve of my politics. It's an admission of weakness at a very strategic moment. Sending you, Chris, avoids that and at least avoids a direct confrontation."

Skeptically, Dunney nodded. If Klein's affiliation with the dissidents were so serious a problem, how could anything salvage Bingo's chances?

Testily, Bingo said, "I don't want any indirect confrontations either."

Dunney looked at Abelson. "It's just like any other conflict, isn't it, Carl? We can't represent a client whose interests conflict with another's. And Mraisky isn't even our client."

For an instant, Klein glared at Christopher Dunney. How easily he could write off a Jew. It obviously didn't bother Dunney a bit. Or Abelson, for that matter. Williams, at least, was black. Maybe he had a right to protect his own ass. And what about Steven Klein? "You're right, Chris."

~ ~ ~

Dunney yawned and put his feet up on Kline's old fashioned wood desk. He had spent a long day, prepping under Klein's watchful and disapproving eye. As it was now one o'clock in the morning, he felt justified in yawning again.

"I don't mean to be keeping you awake, Chris," Klein stated stiffly.

"Bullshit, Steve," Dunney remarked. "You love outlasting me. Okay. One more time. Everybody is happy with the idea of using Romanian hamburger; and Barclay's' will supply the credit. Rolls, ketchup, Pepsi, all of that is part of the contract. Liquidated damages have been agreed to, and we have insurance for both sides. Lloyd's, right?"

"Correct."

"All I have to worry about it siting, construction, personnel and utilities. The Soviets will build to our specs, own and lease to Bingo Burgers. If they don't like it, we'll cry racist and give 'em more McDonald's. Fair enough."

"Let me decide that." Klein could hardly argue: Dunney had it right. Only a few touches remained; most of the agreement had been clarified, in both English and Russian. Dunney had been invaluable. His facility with Russian had allowed them to work quickly and easily with the dual language contract. "You'll need a secretary," Klein said, broaching the sensitive point he had been reluctant to bring up all evening. "One who understands the spoken language well enough to take notes in the meetings."

Dunney removed his feet from the desk and stood. "I thought I could use someone from the embassy."

Klein rose also, closing the file. "No. McDonald's used one of them. I want someone we know will be ours." He had already settled on the candidate.

"Susan?"

"Hell, no. I need her here. Besides, her Russian isn't as good as yours."

"She's not my type anyway." The young attorney slipped his papers into the leather briefcase he had received at graduation from Law School. It was scuffed and dented, but he wouldn't use any other, no matter what the occasion.

Looking up at Dunney, Klein asked pointedly, "What about your girlfriend from Berlitz?"

The briefcase remained half open as Dunney paused in surprise. The last person in the world he needed in that capacity in Moscow was Andrea. "No way, Steve. We're a little too close. Too hot and cold. I'd like a secretary I can work with."

Scraping his hand over the coarseness of his unshaven face, Klein considered the problem. "Who else is there?"

Dunney grunted in reply.

"Can she type?"

"How the hell do I know?"

"I understood her to say that Berlitz was only a part time job. "

"A good way to meet business men, she says," Dunney explained, accompanying his words with a mildly obscene gesture. "If you know what I mean."

Klein knew. He knew very well. "What else does she do?"

The question caught Dunney off guard. After all that time with he   He had no idea of what she did for a living. Was that possible? "Don't ask," he said.

After a quick glance at Dunney, Klein looked at his watch. "It's pretty late. You can ask her in the morning. And that is not a request."

"I don't exactly live with her, Steve," Dunney objected.

"Who was the call from?"

"What call?"

"The one that ended 'Don't wait up for me.'"

Snapping the locks on the briefcase, Dunney feigned searching his memory. "Oh. That call. Yes, I think that might have been Andy. I could look it up."

Klein pushed his associate toward the door. "We'll pay comparable, with travel bonus, expenses, contraceptives and anything else she needs."

"You are not as naive as you appear, Steve. But you misjudge my relationship with the woman in question."

"Do I?"

"Hell yes." Dunney shook his head. "We can get her for $200.00 a week, no travel bonus."

"Get the light, will you?"

~ ~ ~

Dunney let himself in with the duplicate he had convinced–at some expense–a locksmith to make for him. The two flights of stairs took the wind out of him, reminding him of a lame commitment to take up racquetball or an equivalent. At thirty-one, he was too young to pant after either exercise or women.

The key worked smoothly, quietly, on the deadbolt, but the door creaked. Dunney edged through the narrow opening, trying to limit the noise.

"Chris?" Andy didn't even sound tired. The light went on.

Dunney threw his brief case on the nearest chair and glared at the girl on the sofa. "What are you doing?"

Andy didn't move. "Waiting."

"You didn't have to. I told you I'd be late."

Looking down at the floor, she said, "I know."

He sat at her feet on the couch, his suit coat still buttoned over his vest. As she made way for him, her robe parted slightly all the way to the top of her hip. Dunney was too aggravated to pay much attention, though he could tell she had nothing on underneath. "I'm sorry it's so damn late, Andy. Klein treats me like a summer clerk or a moron. It's hard to tell which. Want a drink?"

"No. Thank you." She reached down and closed the robe. "What are you having?"

"Vodka. Might as well get in practice." He decided to drink it straight, seizing the first tumbler that came into view. "There's been a change. I'm going to Russia in Klein's place."

Quietly, she repeated, "Russia. Congratulations."

"Thanks for the enthusiasm."

She cleared her throat and got up from the sofa. Without shoes she was tiny next to Dunney. It was a feeling that she liked, usually. Sometimes, it made him seem very distant. "I'm sorry. But I... I have to ask you something."

Dunney took a gulp of his drink. "Go ahead," he said, resigned, leaning back against the cabinet.

Her eyes opened wide, catching the light oddly as they shifted from side to side. She laughed, a one-syllable laugh. "God, you won't even touch me. Not a kiss, a hand, nothing. Oh, Chris, what's the point?" She turned away. "What's the fucking point?"

Automatically, Dunney followed her and caught her hand, which turned her around. "All right. You may as well tell me. I am here after all."

"Steve Klein called me this evening, at Berlitz." She left out the part, the old part, about Klein and herself.

Dunney took a step back. "Are you kidding?"

"He offered me the job as your secretary during..."

"The Moscow trip?"

She nodded. "My question is 'do you want me?'"

"That's not as easy a question as it sounds, Andy." Dunney hoped to stall for time while he digested this new development. "I know it seems either black or white."

"Yes. It does. Either you want me along or you don't." Andy looked for an answer in his eyes, but in the shadows there was no way to tell what the flicker meant.

"Trust me. It isn't."

"I know you don't love me, Chris. If that helps."

He had to laugh. How transparent was he? "I'm not at all sure that it does, Andy. How do you feel about me?"

She inclined her head and said, "I'm not masochist enough to be in love with you, but I'm pretty close."

"Good answers."

"Uh huh." Andy gripped his hand tighter and said, "Let's go to bed."

Dunney resisted. "Do you want to go?"

"To bed?"

"Don't be silly. I know you want to go to bed."

With a shallow smile on her lips, she replied, "Yes. Very much."

He intended to throttle Steve Klein at the first opportunity. Andy was too much of a distraction. He could feel the truth of that coming over him. "What do you do for a living anyway?"

Leading the way, Andy whispered, "Whatever you want?"

"But can you type?"

~ ~ ~

It was 3:00 in the morning when Dunney finally gave up on sleep. He inspected his face in the mirror, glancing occasionally at the reflection of the bed and Andy's curled body. It wouldn't do. Not at all.

He would have been better off with almost anyone else in Moscow. She was bound to complicate things. This trip was what he had been waiting for, and he had to be able to concentrate.

Dunney admitted to himself that he was too single-minded. He picked a project and stuck to it. Partnership was his current project and he intended to finish it off in Moscow. They had all settled on a goal of seven restaurants, at the most. Dunney intended to wangle eight or nine. Dunney, having started his career in franchising contract law, had learned how to locate two smaller outlets in lieu of one so as to produce higher overall volume. As a negotiator he had learned how to sell the concept as well.

By the time he returned from Russia, he would have shown up the great Steve Klein, exceeded Bingo Williams' expectations and convinced the senior partners that he belonged.

As for Andy... He had pretty much accepted that she was coming with him. Damn Klein. He would have to make the best of it, which might prove quite good, damn it.

Dunney looked himself over again. He was confident. Andy or no Andy. He had an extra edge. The Russians expected Klein. They knew how to deal with Klein; they were used to his style. They did not know the Dunney style. Let 'em expect the great Steven Klein, he thought. They're going to get Dunney.

Chapter Four

Sy Greenwald glanced up at the rare, clear blue sky and wiped his forehead. His step was quick and resilient as he made his way through Red Square. Hell of a nice day for the second week in June, he thought. He would have taken off his jacket, but a sharp breeze reminded him of the changeability of the Moscow temperature. Coming in conjunction with the warm sunshine, the breeze made him shiver.

After checking his watch, he accelerated his pace. The lead members of the Moscow Group had scheduled lunch with him at noon and it was already 12:10, his hotel another five minutes ahead. The three Russian dissidents were not likely to wait long for him under present conditions.

A free-lancer, associated with several American papers, Greenwald prided himself on being the dissidents' most reliably uncensored American voice. If any one newspaper refused to carry his story in full, he would simply find another. It wasn't that he had clout or a big backer. He had neither and wanted neither. Greenwald simply wrote good, newsworthy stories about the goings-on in the Soviet Union.

At the moment, the most newsworthy material centered around dissidents.

What made Greenwald increasingly valuable to his sources, however, was his uncompromising courage.

Among American correspondents, only he would meet with them whenever possible, wherever practicable. And he did not mind the cold stare of the KGB following him night and day.

The last few yards of his walk contained the usual gray uniformed obstacles. Inside the Moscow Hotel's dining room, he could see the face of the fat Georgian, Torlas, watching his progress. He gave Torlas a grinning nod and turned his attention to the seemingly loitering militiamen. He offered each one a cigarette.

One of the three men casually accepted the offer and strolled with Greenwald to the door of the hotel. He spoke very charming English. "Nice weather, Mr. Greenwald. A little bit like New York, isn't it?"

"Too cool, Sergeant. By half."

The uniformed young man stopped at the door.

Greenwald dragged on his cigarette, pausing. "Who do you have today?"

The officer smiled but said nothing. He had been assigned to the girl, which he found a relatively pleasant task. She had rather longer, thinner legs than his taste, but they looked good in her western style skirt. "Enjoy your lunch."

"Can't you join us?"

Opening the door, the young man scanned the lobby. In the far corner, he spied the expected KGB agent. "It's not my job, Mr. Greenwald."

The reporter followed the other's eyes and nodded. "Maybe someday you'll make KGB."

With a disapproving expression, the militiaman said quietly, "Who needs it?" He ground the cigarette against the wall of the hotel and put the butt in his pocket. "End up in Kabul?" He then returned to his post, striking the pose of an off-duty serviceman.

The deliberate stance made Greenwald laugh. He wondered if the passersby were taken in by the deception. He knew, of course, that it was not intended to fool him.

Once inside the lobby, Greenwald strode to the desk to check for messages. Finding none–he had expected something on his latest Mraisky piece–he shot a look over at his KGB shadow for the moment. The tall, thin man, easily in his mid-forties and, therefore, probably demoted, did not bother to affect disinterest, glaring back instead.

When Greenwald started toward the dining room, the KGB officer moved with him. Not a single pretense, the reporter mused.

Assuming his seat at the table, Greenwald silently greeted his lunch companions. Torlas, the novelist, had begun to lose weight and now subsisted mostly on vodka. Volenko remained as even-tempered as usual despite the obvious surveillance. Elizaveta sat on the edge of her chair, leaning into any conversation intensely. When she saw Greenwald's member of the KGB take the table next to them, she scowled.

"Only the one today," Greenwald said in Russian.

Wearily, Torlas said, "Everyone has gotten the message.

Have you been by the American Embassy lately, Sy?"

Greenwald nodded. "The extra security is very generous."

"Izvestia's reason," Volenko interjected, "is not very convincing, is it?"

"I haven't seen anyone stoning the Ambassador lately, Mikhail, though I would consider it myself if he were still in town." Greenwald waved at a waiter and motioned his order for a martini, his usual. "I'm a little surprised actually that there's so little reaction to the Ambassador's so-called trip."

Elizaveta, still staring at the man sitting alone at the next table, snapped, "He should have left weeks ago."

The reporter placed his hand on her arm. He had grown fond enough of Elizaveta Krylenkev to care about her opinions. "It isn't all that easy, Elizaveta, and don't pretend you don't understand that."

"In your country, politics is too complicated," she retorted.

Archly, Greenwald responded, "And yours is too uncomplicated. That's what this is all about."

Resolutely, she set her jaw on her right hand, saying nothing in return. Her dark brown eyes betrayed her skepticism. Elizaveta did not respect Greenwald. He was a typical American: He only had his own interests in mind, even as he aided their cause. He helped Mraisky because it made him important and paid well. It galled her to be dependent upon such a man. All she could think of was the need for a true friend, a man like Steven Klein, who was due in Moscow shortly.

She had expressed her thoughts often enough to let Greenwald know what lay behind the look in her eyes. It did not hurt him, though it bothered him, because he knew she could not understand him.

"What have you got for me today, Mikhail?" he asked, turning toward the Russian. "Anything good circulating?"

Volenko cast an involuntary look out the window, where the three uniformed men remained. "We are all afraid," he said in his careful English. No one had written privately circulated manuscripts in several days. He had himself actively discouraged it. They wanted the pressure off when Klein came to town. Even the meetings with Greenwald would have to stop after this one. The KGB was too well aware of his CIA connection. Not that that mattered; the surveillance was comprehensive and open.

Greenwald wrinkled his nose. "Good enough. I'm still waiting to hear what the Post thought about that last article on Mraisky. I can plug in the one on you, Elizaveta, tomorrow."

She started. "No!"

"No?" Puzzled, Greenwald examined the faces of all three dissidents. Each wore an individually screened look. "What is it? You thought it was a good idea at the time."

Volenko relieved the young woman of the need to respond. It had been largely his decision anyway, one of few lately to gain unanimous support from the Group. "It is not the time."

"'Low Profile' I believe it is called," Torlas spoke as though only interested in the terminology.

Stunned by the change in attitude, Greenwald exclaimed, "Low profile! What happened to all that idealism, all that courage? Shit! I didn't think you three would let them get to you, too!"

Having lived for days under increasing tension, Elizaveta snapped out of her chair. "How dare you! If you Americans..."

"Stop." Volenko's voice had an immediacy to it that stopped them both. A public row would not help their position at all. They were already being shunned by their usual American and foreign contacts. The purpose of the KGB had been fulfilled: The Moscow Group was completely cut off. The message that could save Mraisky and ultimately the dissident movement still lay in its hiding place in Elizaveta's apartment. Any more unusual interest could put them in prison.

"Christ," Greenwald continued quietly. "I have the interview right here. You didn't seem hesitant then." He reached into his pocket and fingered the recording. To make his point he pulled his hand clear and opened it to show the table.

Before he could complete the motion, his hand was clasped shut. He looked up in shock. The stern face of the man from the KGB bore back at him. "Let me have that, please," the man said. It was not a request.

~ ~ ~

Shifting his weight from one foot to the other did not help. Bellin rubbed the base of his back as he stepped toward the front of the line. He hated spending his lunch hour buying specialties to suit his station in life. Certainly he was Director of Investigation for the Moscow Procuracy, but did he need film for his wife's Japanese camera? He doubted it.

He would rather have spent the hour in the Sundonovski baths, downing three or four drafts while relaxing. God knows he needed it. His meeting with Procurator and the Procurator General would begin in ten minutes. Mraisky, always Mraisky. He should have stayed in Volgograd where he belonged.

"Bellin," the clerk cried, "I knew you would be here today."

"Film, Lena, Always film."

"Didn't I warn you about that camera?" Lena had watched her sixtieth year drift away with no remembrance, no souvenir. She considered Bellin's camera the height of silliness.

"It was for my wife," Bellin explained as he dug out the necessary rubles. "Do you have four?"

"Three's the limit. It was a small shipment. A lot of foreigners in Moscow these days," Lena said matter-of-factly. "You should try the bread lines, Bellin."

Hiding a moderate feeling of satisfaction born of having subordinates to stand the line for him or his wife, Bellin nodded. "Three's fine. I only have two children."

With the Fuji film stuffed in his suit pocket, Bellin began his walk back to the Procuracy. He put his mind off of the meeting to come, letting himself enjoy the bright June day. Bellin liked summer. He spent as much time as possible on the tiny plot of land he had just beyond the city's limits. His dacha was larger than most, a two-room cabin on thirty-five square meters of ground. His tomatoes never ceased to raise the envy of Zhoronov, the Procurator, who could grow almost nothing himself.

Mraisky had kept him from his dacha for two weeks. Bellin had begun to sincerely dislike the whole idea of Mraisky.

The Militia guards grinned as Bellin Jogged up the step of the Moscow Procuracy. The senior of the two spoke. "Did you get your film, Director?"

"Forty-five minutes worth," Bellin declared going through the double doors. Was that any way to measure a material object? He wondered. Having lived in Volgograd, which got very little in the way of frivolous consumption goods, Bellin knew that neither minutes nor rubles served as an adequate measure. Only the ability to get them mattered.

His footsteps echoed as he walked down the marble-floored hallway. The Procuracy, a holdover from tsarist times, had been built without regard to expense or utility. It was a prestigious place to work and Bellin enjoyed that fact. He owed Zhoronov a great deal. Without him, Bellin would still be in Volgograd, or certainly Kiev. His advance to Leningrad and ultimately to Moscow came from the confidence and good grace of his superior, Sergei Zhoronov.

Zhoronov stood outside of the conference room, waiting for Bellin. A compact, bullet-shaped man, the Procurator of Moscow worked his stiff arms back and forth across his body as he watched Bellin walk toward him. Even at five foot seven, Zhoronov could not find the proper sized clothes. Everything looked too small, too tight or too short. He had no waist, no hips and no shoulders. Though not bald, he had a nearly shaved head, because he felt that he looked more appropriate that way. He shot Bellin a short grin and jerked his subordinate's hand up and down.

"The Procurator General," Zhoronov announced, "is awaiting our arrival. He is new, so don't let him bother you. I'll do most of the talking Vladimir."

Bellin shrugged, and followed Zhoronov into the conference room. He needed none of this bureaucratic politics. The Procurator General merely wanted a piece of the credit for Mraisky.

Dmitri Feuchinko sat at the end of the room, gnawing his fleshy lower lip. The long-time friend of the President of the Soviet Union looked to Bellin about the same size as a bear. He did not look exactly stupid, only a bit dull. He was neither, as many of his contemporaries had learned.

A purely political appointment, Feuchinko had spent his first six months in office scrupulously avoiding any entanglement with the district Procurators. He knew his limitations. Although he had been trained as a lawyer in the Stalin era, he had never used that skill, still less cared to. Before even trying it out, he had learned that the law was difficult to follow in the Soviet Union. As Procurator General for the whole of the Soviet Union, he had decreed only one policy: "Do what you feel the Party would require, unless the Party, through me, tells you differently."

The Mraisky affair was one in which the Party had a very distinct policy, he knew.

"Sit down, my friends," Feuchinko boomed. "This meeting is an informal one. No need for notes or speeches."

Zhoronov motioned to Bellin, almost imperceptibly, to sit. He remained on his small feet, standing next to Bellin's chair. "Procurator General Feuchinko, this is my Director of Investigation, Vladimir Bellin. He is handling the Mraisky investigation personally."

"Good, good," Feuchinko said, his big, shaggy head nodding. Though well over sixty-five, his hair had retained a touch of its original brown among the dark gray. Coupled with his smooth-skinned face, it made him appear fifteen years younger than he was, more vigorous and industrious. "You have a good record, Bellin. Excellent. Started in Volgograd, didn't you?"

"Yes, he did." Zhoronov answered. "The Mraisky investigation is well under control."

"Comrades," Feuchinko began without pomposity, "Our mutual problem is the KGB. Chairman Arkilonov himself came to me yesterday warning of the grave problems involved. He wasn't very diplomatic about it, but, then, he never is." He grimaced at the reminder of the acrimonious discussion. "He has obviously made an ass of himself, but doesn't want the Americans to know it. He's very influential–I can help out there–but you two must see to it that Mraisky is handled properly and quickly, before any adverse information reaches the Americans."

"Hasn't the KGB found the infiltrator yet?" Bellin asked, to a frown from Zhoronov.

The big man raised his broad shoulders and cocked an arm at the elbow. "I doubt it. He would have told me," he said, referring to the Chairman of the KGB, Vasili Arkilonov. "He has promised full cooperation which, for him, is unusual. Bellin, you have an important responsibility. That message, whatever it is, would be very damaging, according to Arkilonov. He insists that he cannot allow the prosecution of the Jew if it falls into CIA hands. He did not bother to explain. He never does. I've known him for years. But he is always very serious. I believe him."

Zhoronov, still standing, said, "I will have to proceed on Mraisky very quickly. To limit the potential, then."

"Absolutely. Arkilonov said that if Mraisky were put away, the problem would disappear. Don't ask me how. In any case, as soon as possible. Don't wait as long as usual." Feuchinko did not know how long "usual" was, but he knew that the Procurator commonly waited for public furor abroad to dissipate before holding the trial. "He suggested that we not worry about the ravings of the Americans."

Skeptical, the Procurator of Moscow asked, "Does that have the appropriate approval?"

Feuchinko looked from one man to the other. "Yes. I got a confirmation this morning. Press it."

"It will be our pleasure," Zhoronov said.

Bellin kept his annoyance to himself.

"Excellent," Feuchinko said, pushing himself up. "I have confidence in both of you."

As the three men left the stuffy room, Feuchinko asked, "By the way. Is he guilty?"

Zhoronov gave Bellin a sign by tilting his head. "So far, I would have to say yes. On all counts."

A twinkling in his eyes, the Procurator General said, "They usually are."

~ ~ ~

Anna Folenya was sitting in Bellin's office by the time he reached the third floor. Representing Arkilonov, she was the last person he wanted to see. He resented the pressure of the security agency and its intrusion into his job. The Mraisky mess was their doing, not his, and now they would not allow him to do his work.

As for Folenya, she had proven over the months to be the antithesis of Bellin. Cooperation between such disparate personalities lay beyond the bounds of practicality. A prize member of the Young Pioneers and the Komsomol, she had been well taught as a girl in the virtues of Communism. She still boasted of her first several denunciations, though Bellin had since learned that none came to anything. On the other hand, he, as a villager, had had no time for historical and political philosophy in his youth. Or now.

Sitting, Bellin conspicuously placed the three boxes of Japanese film beside his telephone. He knew it would offend Folenya and her artless eyes confirmed his expectation. In a way, he admired her stoic sense of dedication to the revolutionary spirit, a sense he lacked. He did not expect the ultimate revolution soon and he doubted that his life would contribute much to its inevitable course.

Folenya viewed the Fuji film boxes with disdain not comprehensible to Bellin. He underestimated her. She understood his desire for material comforts, even empathized. Her main concern was not the Director's materialism: That was central to existence, Marx had said. What galled her was the time he had wasted to get it. An hour in line probably, for what? Hadn't he better things to do?

"We have arrested an American journalist," she stated.

Alarmed, Bellin demanded, "Arrested? In God's name, why?"

"Not arrested, in fact," she said, backing off, her tone less matter of fact. "Merely detained. Greenwald."

Thoroughly familiar with Seymour Greenwald's file, Bellin relaxed. A fairly insignificant journalist, Greenwald had no newspaper, broadcasting, or wire service behind him. His so-called detainment would go unnoticed once he was released. Greenwald had, to be sure, enjoyed the company of the dissidents too often for Bellin's taste, spreading their self-serving tales among the American press. Still, Bellin did not welcome Greenwald's expulsion. He had hoped to contain the anti-dissident campaign and each move should make the next one easier. "Was it necessary, Anna?"

Folenya tossed a small tape cassette onto his desk. "Not as it turned out, Comrade Bellin," she admitted casually. "Our operative saw him reach for this and moved to prevent any kind of exchange."

Nodding, Bellin said, "It's better to avoid the transfer if possible. I agree. But with this in-hand…"

"It would have seemed strange not to keep him a bit," she replied to his unfinished question. "Besides, he has published seditious lies about the Soviet Union. That's enough to justify our action."

Grimly, Bellin examined the small plastic object. "I don't read American newspapers."

"It is part of my work."

"Norelco? Is that the Dutch?"

Anna Folenya took the cassette, checked the name and returned it. "Phillips, yes. Serviceable."

He grunted. Serviceable? He would have given a great deal to possess such "serviceable" conveniences. Even for his office, he had been refused for dictation equipment. The clerks took truly miserable dictation; consequently he spent most of his time editing his own reports.

A trace of triumph filtering through her voice, Folenya produced a Norelco tape player from her briefcase, while asking, "Would you like to hear it?"

Studying the hard, aggressive woman, Bellin wondered how she would have been in a normal job. In sex, he mused, she would have been intolerable. "Not right now, Anna. I would appreciate it if you would leave it."

She deflated instantly. Then, the deliberation of his denial angered her. "I need it."

An ingratiating smile playing on his lips, Bellin corrected her. "I am the one who needs it, Anna. The tape is part of my investigation. Your superiors are all over me to get it moving ahead." His message clearly enunciated, Bellin relieved her of the machine, marveling at its light construction. "Where is this reporter, Greenwald, in case I want to interrogate him?"

Already too upset to enjoy her second surprise, Folenya let it out without hesitation or pleasure. "Downstairs."

Having made his points, Bellin felt compassion for her, sparing her further. "You anticipate me too well, Anna. For a liaison officer, you are invaluable to this department." He stood and circled the desk, carrying the Norelco and its tape. "I'll return these as soon as I am finished. Unless the Procurator needs them for evidence."

"Yes, Comrade."

"Which I doubt," he added, heading through the door.

~ ~ ~

As the ancient elevator grumbled down to the first floor, Bellin examined the buttons, pressing each in turn. The last one on the right caused a plastic hatch to flip dramatically open. From a quick look at the interior, he figured out how to insert the cassette. The little door shut, the machine indicated nicely what to do next. With tolerable English, he had no trouble with the buttons.

The first voice he heard, a man's, he did not recognize. Greenwald, he supposed. Following its well-phrased Russian questions—one of which eased Bellin's mind considerably because it revealed the Greenwald preferred speaking largely in Russian—a female voice spoke with its characteristic impatience. Elizaveta Krylenkev, he had learned, had little time to waste on petty conversation. He had monitored enough of her conversations in the past weeks to have grown accustomed to her pacing and intensity.

"I am fluent in English," her voice stated. "French, Italian and Hebrew, if you prefer."

Slightly embarrassed, Greenwald's voice replied too quickly, "Definitely Russian." Then he tried to explain. "I can more easily compare your speech to the others, that way."

"As you wish," she came back, tolerance showing too obviously.

Bellin chuckled. How difficult she was! Would Greenwald have laughed, also, had he known that the girl had only learned Hebrew three years before? Perhaps not. Greenwald, Bellin knew from the KGB file, was not much of a practicing Jew.

When the elevator opened, Bellin switched off the Norelco and walked up the high-ceilinged, marbled corridor. Without asking, he had assumed that the American was being "detained" in the usual place. Since the Procuracy had no real holding area, a row of dingy, empty offices served the purpose. If they were intended to be oppressive, the rooms succeeded. Bellin always felt closed-in himself.

The American reporter sat quietly in the first of the rooms. The cubicle had no other furniture in it. Bellin had to scavenge a chair from a nearby assistant's office. Greenwald watched Bellin the entire time with neither word nor expression.

Once he had jammed the off-sized door shut, Bellin took his seat opposite Greenwald. He held up the recorder and asked in Russian, "Is this yours?"

"No," the American responded. "Nyet. I speak very good Russian."

Continuing, then, in Russian, Bellin took an apologetic tack. "Mr. Greenwald, we are very sorry about this."

"The KGB threatened to withdraw my visa," Greenwald informed him. He was concerned–once arrested in the Soviet Union, almost anything could happen–but not panicked. It seemed most likely that he would simply be sent home. "I would like to stay."

Bellin filled his cheeks with air and then deflated them gradually. "This interview with the woman, Krylenkev, what does she have to say?"

Calmly, Greenwald replied, "Haven't you listened to it?"

"Not yet."

"You should. It will help you understand the dissidents... Is that word acceptable?"

"To me? Yes. Dissent in this country is permitted, Mr. Greenwald, despite you write about us," Bellin said. "It is looked down upon as uncreative, but not in itself a crime. Publication of a libel against the Party or the State, however, is a serious offense. Even for you."

"Spare me, Comrade Bellin."

Bellin shrugged elaborately. "If it were up to me, I would only send you back to New York for a while."

His head cocked and surprise in his voice, Greenwald said, "They told me that it was."

"Was?"

"Up to you."

Bellin felt some surprise himself. He had fully expected that the usual authorities would make the decision, since it was really more diplomatic than criminal or political. Yet, it did bear directly upon his efforts to contain the dissidents. No American journalist would chance contacting the Moscow Group for a while after the expulsion of another of their number. And since several American journalists had suffered similar fates as an expression of Brezhnev's displeasure with the American press' response to the Mraisky arrest, Bellin clearly had a free hand with Greenwald. He might as well use what was given him.

~ ~ ~

The gray-and-red uniformed Militia paraded up and down below as Senior Staff Secretary Harmon Kyle sipped his brandy. Activity at the American Embassy had dropped away to nothing since the departure of the Ambassador.

Kyle, left in charge of the place, had officially very little to do, but he intended to do it with style. Caviar and brandy made a perfect supper.

"Extra protection," he scoffed aloud. From whom? The Russian people, by and large, wouldn't know where the building was located without guidance from the Kremlin. Protection from Americans. That was their goal. Intimidation and annoyance served as adequate tools. Traffic at the Embassy had completely dried up since the imposition of the heavy protective watch.

Across Smolensk Square lay the American-oriented International Hotel, with at least thirty Yanks in residence. Yet not one of them had made the one-hundred-yard jog over to the Embassy. The reason was not unfathomable and evidence of it began to unfold below, at the gate as Kyle watched and placidly drank.

One of the staff, John Winker, an economic attaché, patiently endured the ordeal of questioning by the guards. Though they recognized him on sight–he did not live on the grounds and passed them every day at least twice–the guards grilled him in their usual manner. Occasionally, the Militia patted down a "suspicious looking character" even a woman. After this "protection" was in place, the President instructed the Ambassador to return to Washington for discussions on the "situation."

What were they looking for?

Just then, the Cultural Exchange attaché entered the suite. Seeing Kyle at the window, an intent look on his face, the attaché asked, "Someone held up?"

Without turning, Kyle replied, "It's only Winker, Tom. He went out for a walk."

Thomas Simpson laughed. "I know. I saw the parade that formed as he left." Incredulous–at the time–Simpson had observed three uniformed men and one plainclothes KGB'er hustle off after the harmless Winker. "I've got some dope on this shit, finally."

Interested, Kyle left the window and resumed his place behind the Ambassador's desk. Since Simpson was also with the CIA, he had let the younger man handle most communications with the agency. "Washington? Or here?"

Simpson wrapped his long thin legs around the cushioned wooden chair before addressing the question. "This came from the very top, Harm, Director McDeamon. You may be in charge of all of the people in Moscow, but you may not be."

"Yeah. Those bastards are always skulking around with a special, secret, big deal, spy ring." Sometimes the CIA brass disgusted Kyle. He had his ass on the line all the time and they trusted him no farther than they trusted the KGB. "Did one get nailed?" He hoped so.

"Not yet, but the KGB is working on it. It seems that an inactive plant in the KGB decided to come to life without telling anybody first. He stumbled onto something, they figure, and made a move on it. The KGB is supposedly crapping in their pants over this."

"Interesting." Kyle mentally checked his agents. "Who was the contact? It didn't come through here."

With a sly look coming onto his face, Simpson hesitated. He wanted the maximum impact. "Dr. Alexander Mraisky."

The news had the desired impact. "Mraisky? Oh, my fucking God."

"The KGB assumes that Mraisky got the word to his cohorts in the Moscow Group. That's why they've shut the dissidents off."

"And grabbed Greenwald."

"He was the only American I know of who's been chummy with the Group since the KGB and Bellin gave every security man in town work for the summer."

Kyle gulped the rest of his brandy, half the snifter. "Do our people know what it is?"

"No. They aren't even sure they want it. For now, we're supposed to take a vacation. Stay away from the dissidents in particular. I told Washington your orders of a couple days ago."

"How close can we get with the Militia's guards and the KGB at everybody's keyhole?" Kyle snapped, directing his annoyance not at Simpson but at the dunderheads in Washington. "Are the boys laying low?"

"Very."

"When the KGB catches the quarry, I don't want any of our agents going with him. Steer everybody clear of new contracts until further notice."

"The word from the KGB is that we're supposed to behave," Simpson stated. "If we don't they'll pull in most of the ones they know about. McDeamon says to go along, not to jeopardize our whole network for one lousy piece of intelligence."

Tapping his nails on the polished mahogany desk top, Kyle ran the facts through his brain. They were obviously talking about something big; otherwise the KGB would not have been so obvious. It would have been a coup to get the word from the prematurely-activated plant, but if he failed, his career would be over. Even the biggest steal of the century would not balance that kind of risk. "All right, Tom. Get the word out. To our people and to the KGB."

"Right. What about the dissidents?"

"When we don't lift a finger to help our dear friend, Greenwald," Kyle said, "they'll get the word."

Simpson nodded, rose and left the room excitedly. Kyle leaned back in the high backed chair and reached into the lower book cabinet for the brandy bottle. The Ambassador's decanter was three quarters empty anyway and the bottle was a hell of a lot closer.

Pouring the heavy liquid into the snifter, Kyle considered the dilemma of the dissidents. They had really significant information. Probably in the form of a coded tape, the KGB's current vogue. They could not understand it, could not transfer it to microfilm, could not even transcribe it. And now, they would not be able to so much as cough in the direction of a CIA operative, assuming they even knew any, which he seriously doubted.

That asshole Greenwald hardly qualified as a CIA contact or courier. He was just a newspaper man willing to trade anything for a few tidbits he could have gotten through leg work. Kyle would hardly miss that son of a bitch. He would be a good medium to get the message across to the KGB and to the dissidents.

Kyle dialed the Press Department of the Embassy. "Hello, Tony. About that friend of yours, Greenwald? I think we weaken our voice by using it too much. Tell the Russians that, tell them we won't protest this time since they have been so polite about it. Next time. Okay?" He gave Tony Emmery a chance to express her opinion. "Hell, no. I won't either."

And so, he thought, slipping the phone home, that was that.

~ ~ ~

Elizaveta trudged up the three flights to her flat near the University. Despite the shocking arrest of Greenwald she had had to teach three hours during the afternoon. In the absence of Mraisky, she had a load and a half, plus her paper to finish. God, she was tired.

Had Greenwald been arrested only at noon? It seemed so far away, so unreal. So unnecessary.

She could scarcely recall the horrible white, rubbery texture of Greenwald's face as the KGB agent took him away. A moment before, the reporter had been so full of bluster. Elizaveta had not stopped shaking for over an hour.

Volenko's news had only made it worse. Greenwald had CIA connections, she had learned, but they had not helped him. By five-thirty, the American had been put on a plane back to America. The Americans had not even protested!

The Americans had turned their backs on them. In her room she held the key to the salvation of Mraisky and yet...

She had tried praying, but her prayers all seemed too like a resignation. Action was demanded, not prayer.

"We must wait," Volenko had said firmly.

Waiting required strength, Elizaveta knew. Four thousand years or four days, waiting also demanded character.

Did she have enough of either?

The door to the apartment pushed open. Had she forgotten to lock it? Had the KGB searched? Elizaveta panicked. The tape!

She could not move. Every hope she had was bound up in the piece of plastic. If the KGB had found it, Mraisky would be finished; she would never leave Russia; it would all be over. In paralyzed anguish she raised her eyes...

Squarely above her, jammed into a crude hole in the plaster, it glared out at her: A tiny television lens!

She laughed, releasing all of the tension in an explosion of relief. They had not found the tape. It was safe. They were all safe! Watched by the KGB, but safe.

She could wait now. For a while, at least, she would wait.

~ ~ ~

When she laughed, Bellin laughed. It was supposed to be obvious, but how obvious was it? He wished that he had the other camera operative, so that he could see what kind of job they had done.

He watched her as she prepared herself for prayer. Every motion was so uncertain. He realized that she had still not mastered the art of praying, at least confidently. It was absurd.

He liked her for it.

Chapter Five

As Dunney and Andy strapped themselves into the Concorde seats, the Senior Steward crouched beside them. "You have a call. Mr. Dunney."

Dunney, his trip already delayed three times for various reasons, growled under his breath just loudly enough for Andy to hear. "What now?"

She touched his arm, and remembering their bargain, quickly withdrew it. They had not slept together for several days and would not do so during the trip. They would be at the same hotel, but on different floors. She felt the attitude of her former lover exceeded good sense, but allowed him his way. If only because she had no choice. "I'll save your seat."

Stalking off down the aisle of the plane, Dunney wondered what Klein had come up with this time. The first delay developed out of a drafting error in the Russian translation. Then Bingo Williams decided he wanted to use smaller sized patties in the double hamburgers than in the single. The Romanians refused and now the beef used would be imported from, of all places, Florida.

The third delay arose when Klein developed a case of nervous exhaustion. Dunney knew his stuff, but Klein's support was part of the deal with Bingo Williams.

God only knew another postponement would put Dunney into the hospital. He had found the emotional build-up to departure intensifying each time it neared. As it was, he could hardly sit still.

The Steward led him to a phone on the jetway platform, hitting the appropriate button as he handed Dunney the receiver.

The voice on the other end, of course, belonged to Klein. "Bad news, Chris."

Dunney said nothing aloud, but cursed a string of college-level terms to himself.

"Barclay's has suddenly declined the letter of credit terms," Klein explained, his voice still somewhat shaky. "They're talking about another twenty base points."

"Screw 'em, Steve. That's Moscow's problem. They wanted Barclay's'. I'll take Credit Suisse any day."

"Not enough time. You were going to Barclay's' anyway, Chris. They aren't too happy since the Russians dropped that truck parts deal after the Afghan coup, leaving them with only half as much profit to work with. As they told me, 'Two letters with the Russians are cheaper than one.'"

"Damn politics," Dunney snapped, referring to the U. S. Senate's recent condemnation of the Kremlin's backing of a military coup in Afghanistan. That move, in turn, led the Russians to eject five American journalists and cancel a much ballyhooed deal with International Harvester for another truck-parts plant. "It's a good thing that this deal is too small to cancel."

"We sweet-talked Barclay's down to fourteen. Bingo and the Russians have agreed to split that much. I thought you should know."

Annoyed that so much had been done without him in so short a time–he had left the office less than eight hours before–Dunney doubly resented Klein's professorial tone of voice. He intended to get the bastards down to ten. "Okay, Steve," he said, evening out his voice. "Say good-bye to Amy."

The last was a dig. Both men knew of Amy's attraction to Dunney, though only Dunney knew what had come of it. Klein's hesitation reflected acknowledgment of the insulting implication. "Have a good trip. Don't overwork Andrea."

Touché, Dunney thought. They were even and he felt better for it.

Dunney's blue-and-gray striped suit caught Andy's eye as he passed through the jetway into the Concorde. She could not help but admire him as he walked toward her, a preoccupied smile on his well-defined, if thin, lips. Though a shade under six feet, he always looked taller to her and the Concorde's low ceiling exaggerated the illusion. His solid shoulders filled his suit just right and played off well against his waist, hips and strong legs.

Andy felt the usual pangs when she saw him from a slight distance. At ten feet, she found him irresistibly attractive, all the more since she had slept with him. It gave importance to his movement, to each part of his body. knowing how they worked when he made love to her...

As he came closer, however, the fever ebbed. His face became his dominant feature and that never helped. Not that Dunney did not have a perfectly acceptable face–he certainly passed muster in her opinion–but its expressions licked warmth. His eyes could be, and had often been, chillingly neutral. The way he had of looking it her from a slight angle, one eye half closed, always bothered her. The one time, the only time, they had made love in full light still haunted her. He had watched her, off to the side like that, as if examining her, playing on her emotions, her movements, everything.

The rest of his face was misleading. It tended to be soft, his face rounder than most, his skin paler and more rosy. His nose was not important by itself but coordinated well with his lightly browed eyes and an unusually thin mouth. Dunney's hair varied from sandy to brown depending on the season. It also had a maddening tendency to be always in place.

When he had settled again in his seat, she asked, "is everything all right, Chris?"

"I suppose so. You remember our friends Barclay's Bank? They wanted a bit more, because some third-rate coup canceled another deal which had helped get us the good rate in the first place." He patted her leg absently. "Klein's taken care of it." That son of a bitch, he thought.

~ ~ ~

The customs official studied the American couple's papers. They were not married. For a moment, she wondered if they should have been. The man had an impatient arrogance about him that annoyed her. Indeed, most Americans passing through her station acted the same way. For her, doing what she did every day, day after day, haste had no value. Rather, she concentrated on the people, their possessions, quirks, their hairstyles, everything that might be different about them.

Dunney tugged at his earlobe, waiting for clearance. At another station, people sailed through in minutes. Already, his agent had taken fifteen. He gave Andy a look and found her too outwardly composed to be of much solace. For Christ sake, he had things to do!

The instant she had first seen Moscow from the air, Andy had fallen speechless. Until that moment, she had not believed it would actually happen, that she could actually end up in the capital of the USSR. Moscow, the capital of her father's country–in a sense, at least. She reveled in the attention showered upon Dunney and herself by the personnel, watching it from without as in a dream. She knew that Dunney's arm held hers but she did not feel it.

Dunney felt for the Winston's in his suit coat pocket. Klein had recommended that he have several things along to "encourage efficiency" among the various civil servants with whom he would have to deal. The inexpensively plated lighter suddenly felt heavier in his shirt pocket, the pen-flashlight clanking against it noisily. He had other gratuities packed in his suitcase, for use later, ranging from perfume to calculators.

The clerk slowly stamped the various documents. The young man looked better in the photo than in person, she mused. Black and white did him justice, softened the look in his eyes. She was surprised to find his weight to be one ninety-two in American pounds; he looked a bit lighter than that. No, not with such thick shoulders, perhaps. Undoubtedly on the strong side for an American lawyer. Most of them concentrated their development in their asses. Not this Dunney fellow.

His hand growing itchy, Dunney casually took a cigarette from his pack of Winston's, making a show of offering the most prominent remaining one to Andy. When she had ignored him, he shrugged, placed the pack on the counter and checked every pocket for his lighter. Discovering it in his shirt, he laughed at his own forgetfulness. The cigarette lit, he deposited the lighter next to the cigarettes.

None of his actions escaped the notice of the clerk. She marveled at the subtlety of his execution, admired the way he used his hands. She also admired the cheap little lighter. In Moscow, it would cost a fortune. Only she could never get one. Only the hard currency stores had such devices on hand. The other stores had few and only the bureaucrats, and only the cream of them, would get a chance at one. It would have been very nice to have that lighter. Not that she smoked–it was an expensive and undesirable habit–but the butcher... She would be the first in line for a month.

Turning back to Andy, Dunney let his coat sweep the lighter and the cigarettes off of the counter. With no one noticing they fell at the clerk's feet. After a moment's hesitation, she stooped to pick both objects off the floor. The lighter got lost somewhere between the floor and the counter, but the cigarettes made the trip unimpeded. Her butcher did not like American cigarettes.

~ ~ ~

All three of them had made the trip to the International Hotel. Torlas and Volenko would act as the decoys, while Elizaveta made the contact. Of them all, it was hoped that Klein would best recognize her. Torlas, of course, was too obvious for the KGB to miss; Volenko too nondescript for anyone to recall.

"The plane must be in by now," Volenko whispered, as they strolled with deliberate aimlessness in the square. Their plan was simple. When the limousine from the airport arrived with the foreigners, mostly Americans, the men would choose two or three persons to approach for conversation. Elizaveta, too, would pursue at least one American, but she would also make contact with Steven Klein. She had spent hours memorizing his face.

The KGB could hardly keep count of every American in the lobby.

One by one, they headed for the hotel, each trailed by uniformed Militia officers. As usual, the soldiers remained outside, leaving the plain-clothed KGB to pick up the dissidents when they entered.

Making themselves obvious, as they always did, the men of the KGB provided the trio with unexpected hope. Only two were on duty, one very young and inexperienced at that. The pair had a careless look about them, even jovial. The youngster went so far as to give Elizaveta his version of an ingratiating smile.

The three converged near the elevators. They did not want the KGB on its guard, or well positioned for the entry of the Americans. Only when the people began to arrive would each go his or her separate direction. With only two men, the KGB would not be able to watch them all. Torlas and Volenko would act first, drawing the two men after them. That ploy would leave Elizaveta free to seek out Klein.

They had little time to wait. The courtesy car from the airport rolled to a stop within minutes of the dissidents' entry. Seconds later, Americans poured into the lobby. The group of thirteen or so, included several suited businessmen; four young men carrying AAU athletic bags along with their suitcases; an elderly couple and a young woman with a man in a three-piece suit.

Torlas moved his bulk off first in the direction of one of the athletes, a lean black with a trim afro. Volenko liked the look of the elderly couple, who stopped at the door. With them, they took the KGB men.

Having examined the crowd for Klein, Elizaveta found herself drawn to the young, business-like couple heading straight for the desk. The man had a determined look that impressed her. The girl was faintly attractive in an American way. Everything about the man appealed to Elizaveta. He used long, purposeful strides, keeping his arms from swinging too freely. His mouth seemed clamped shut, flexing his facial muscles in a way that reshaped his roundish face. In the eyes she saw a kind of intensity missing in the people around her. After a beat or two, Elizaveta walked directly up to the man, now standing at the desk.

"No, as a matter of fact," he was saying in Ukrainian accented Russian. "It would not be in my name."

When the desk officer ignored him the American reacted immediately. "I told you that there is no Christopher Dunney on your list."

Touching his arm, Elizaveta stepped halfway in front of him. Her English came out warm and soft. "Don't bother with him, Mr. Dunney. Let me help."

He shot her an inquisitive eye, one that remained on her face for a disquietingly long time. Then he glanced up and down. He smiled back. Using English, he said, "If you would, I'll buy you dinner for a week."

Something thrilling ran through Elizaveta, which she quickly dismissed. She turned to the desk clerk who was busy and then back again. The feeling came back immediately.

"Chris?" the woman with Dunney interrupted, intentionally. "Is something wrong?"

Dunney was slow to react. The Russian girl had his immediate attention. There was something in there, he thought. He would like to have the chance to look for it. Andy's voice finally intruded. He broke away from Elizaveta's eyes. "No. We didn't make the reservation in my name. Steve's is more familiar here. If I have a chance to explain it to them..."

"Please allow me," Elizaveta suggested.

Her Russian sharply expressive, Andy said, "I am perfectly capable, thank you."

The tone nearly brought an equally sharp reply from Elizaveta, but it reminded her instead of her main purpose. She looked quickly for Torlas and Volenko.

Volenko had sequestered another of the black runners near the dining room. The Georgian had one of the businessmen by the arm walking across the lobby. Faithfully, the plainclothesmen followed wherever they were led.

Elizaveta searched desperately for Klein. He had to have arrived. They knew that Klein had made a reservation for that night, noting his arrival time. It was the only flight direct from London. That flight had just come in.

With Andy lecturing the desk attendant, Dunney's eyes sought out the Russian girl. He hadn't far to look. She stood just behind him scanning the crowd with apparent dismay. From the rear, she appealed to him as much as from the front. She had close fitting jeans, of all things, accenting a nice set of legs, ending in solid, if mildly too broad, hindquarters. The hips gave way rather abruptly to her waist, which in turn anchored a gently curving back. She was not dressed as most Russians were, in formless, uninspiring dresses. This girl looked more like an American, or a European imitator, than most Americans. Perhaps, he thought, it was that home-away-from-home look that she had...

"Can I help you?" he asked.

Elizaveta spun around at the sound of his English. She had expected Klein's face. Dunney's helpful face was a palatable substitute. "A friend," she began before discarding the approach. Instead she asked, "Is that all from the London flight, Mr. Dunney?"

"I believe so. It wasn't quite full. This was all of us coming to this hotel. If that's what you mean."

He watched her expression collapse. She seemed disappointed to the point of tears. Not normal disappointment either.

"A man?" he asked.

She evaded the question. Torlas and Volenko were running out of Americans, looking panicked. "I have to go."

Dunney caught her by the arm, holding her back. "I'll have my secretary ask at the desk for you. How's that?"

"No!" she whispered.

"Come on," he insisted. "Just tell me. I'll find out. Very subtly. Don't worry. He'll be my friend, not yours. Okay?"

His voice soothed her fears. She liked his touch, his closeness. "I was supposed to meet him."

"You'll make me jealous," Dunney said, half meaning it. This was a very desirable woman, vital, immediate. "His name is...?"

She decided to whisper it.

Dunney stepped away instinctively at the sound of Klein's name. "Jesus Christ."

From the desk, Andy called, "It's all right, Chris. We can have Klein's reservation."

In a horrible moment, Elizaveta realized the truth. Christopher Dunney had replaced Steven Klein! The man on whom all their hopes rested, upon whom Alexei's life may have depended... Steven Klein was not coming.

It wasn't fair.

She glared at the substitute, the man who so attracted her just minutes before. She suddenly hated him. It just wasn't fair!

~ ~ ~

One of the television monitors flickered. The technician played with a couple of dials, to no avail. He tried his fist on the cabinet. The picture stabilized. Volenko, talking with yet another businessman, came back into focus.

On the one beside that, Bellin easily found the Georgian bullying the only white athlete in the American party. The lower two monitors were oriented in useless positions, including the dining room. He searched for the girl.

For fifteen minutes, he had observed them. Radnik had called him as soon as the dissidents entered the hotel. It had been a fascinating experience.

Volenko, Torlas and Krylenkev had hugged one corner of the lobby, glancing nervously at the overacting men from the KGB. Though dressed in street clothes, the agents had taken pains to wear easily identifiable KGB dress.

Bellin had laughed out loud at the outrageous manner displayed by the "secret" police.

Folenya, who had accompanied him to the monitoring station, had stormed out of the room. She deeply resented the way Bellin had ordered such members of the KGB to display themselves. The added effrontery of his laughter proved too much for her. Curiosity, however, had overcome her and she returned at that moment.

"Welcome back, Anna," Bellin said, his eye searching the monitors for the girl. "You haven't missed much."

"Nothing." Radnik agreed, cheerfully.

Keeping an empty chair between herself and Bellin, Folenya sat down. Bellin had had a row of comfortable chairs installed behind the technicians panel. He valued his comforts above his duty to the State. Still, it would increase the hours, she could tolerate monitoring the activities of the criminals.

Bellin puffed his cigar in her direction, watching the flagging Volenko scurry from one American to another. The American waved him away at first, but the Russian followed like hungry mongrel until the American gave up and stopped to chat. Hardly the portrait of a dangerous traitor to the Party and the State.

If Volenko scurried, Torlas lumbered when he moved at all. He was having more success, however, for he had a writer's ease with words and more gall than his colleague. Unlike Volenko, he had actually had difficulty shedding one American to seek out another. Several times, he had taken his leave, only to be frustrated by a quicker moving American tourist, who apparently took him to be a local attraction.

Bellin had lost track of Krylenkev in all of the activity, which was, of course, the point. First, she had held her ground as the others led the KGB observers off with them. Then she had fixed upon a youngish, serious-looking American couple, the man in particular. The man and she had talked a bit while she grew increasingly nervous. How openly she had searched for her companions! And yet, having found them, she searched even more avidly. The American offered help, she whispered and both came away shocked.

It was a strange drama indeed. "Why no sound?" he asked the technician. "I thought there were microphones."

The technician turned to answer, but Folenya cut him off. "We tried that. It's too noisy. The mikes are not directional."

"I can't help feeling that we are missing too much," Bellin lamented. "I have no affection for silent pictures, Anna. Can't we do better?"

Folenya bounced off her chair and played with a couple of dials. A cacophony of voices boomed through the speakers.

"You've made your point!" Bellin called above the noise.

She resumed her seat without comment. Inwardly, she enjoyed her little revenge. Let him laugh again, she thought.

A stern look toward Radnik quelling a disguised smile, Bellin changed the subject. "Do we know who these Americans are?"

Before Folenya could answer, Radnik pulled out a sheet of names. "This is the passenger list."

Cigar in mouth, Bellin ran down the names. Meaningless to him. One of them, however, had importance to the dissenters.

"I have," Anna Folenya began, "the Americans who have reserved rooms at this hotel. Most Americans stay there, since it is across the square from the American Embassy."

Frowning, Bellin said, "That was quick."

Proudly, Folenya explained, "The KGB gets this list every day. I knew it would be important."

His eyes did not travel far down the sheet. "Klein." Suddenly he was angry. The reservation date was more than three days before. "How long have you had this?"

"Only a few hours," she replied defensively.

He almost threw it at her. "Look at the name Klein. He's had a room reserved there for days."

Folenya grew frightened. She had no idea who Klein was or what his name meant. All she knew was that she had had the information for a number of days and had deliberately withheld it to check each name. There was no one important, no CIA operatives. She had to check. It was her duty, especially since Bellin was so lax, so sympathetic to the subversives. "But, I..."

Bellin ignored her, his attention riveted to the screen. Klein was nowhere in sight. Surely, he was the target! Where was he? Had they managed to get him out of range of the cameras? Had he changed since that last picture taken with Mraisky in 1977? In God's name!

"He didn't come in!" Radnik exclaimed.

"What?" Bellin tore the list from his deputy's hands, cutting Radnik's thumb in the process.

As his chief surveyed the paper again and again, Radnik silently sucked on his thumb. Had anyone else acted so rashly, Radnik would have been enraged. He was used to Bellin, however, and was only a bit surprised. Bellin rarely lost his genial nature over anyone else's mistakes, with the acceptable exception of Anna Folenya.

"I'll have to have this verified," Bellin said, still not looking up. "But I feel better. Klein is going to be trouble."

Folenya, regaining her balance, asked, "Who is this Klein?"

"A sympathizer of Mraisky's," Radnik replied, for the preoccupied Bellin. "He's a leader of Massachusetts Zionists."

The term caught Bellin's ear. A loathsome term used to describe a hated group, "Zionist" carried unpleasant connotations for Bellin and every Russian, including many Jews. "Don't use that word around me, Bescel. Unless it applies."

"Yes, sir."

Folenya pursed her lips at Bellin's demand and at Radnik's compliance. All Jews, she knew, were Zionists. Deep down. Otherwise, they were not Jews. Bellin definitely bore watching.

"I've accounted for most of these people," Bellin informed them. "All but five. Five of the passengers on the London flight, who are Americans, are not staying at the hotel. At least, they have no reservations. Of those who have reservations, only Klein did not make the flight." He was disturbed. Why should he be disturbed? He ran over the passenger list again.

"Boston," he read aloud. "Two passengers were from Massachusetts." And so was Klein. Had the American lawyer used another name? Hardly likely. A coincidence then?

On the monitors, he saw that Krylenkev had joined her companions in the middle of the lobby. The small-looking threesome formed a pathetic knot, forlornly isolated from the Americans crowded around the registration desk. They all stared in one direction, toward the far end of the desk. It was like a play, a poorly acted television play.

Huddled together, with agents of the KGB seemingly in their orbit, the miserable creatures could not pretend anymore. Someone had shattered their hopeless hopes, their too obvious plans. With their eyes they savaged the villain.

Bellin followed the line of vision, easily from one monitor to the next. There they stood, apart from the other Americans vying for attention of the clerk. The man and the young woman with him stood oblivious to the stares of the sad little band, waiting for their luggage to be brought in from the limousine. He was tapping his foot, folding and unfolding his arms, as he talked off to the side without looking at his companion. She hardly listened, drinking in the richness of the hotel lobby atmosphere.

Volenko and the others had expected an ally. Had they only been set back by a day or two? No. Klein was not coming, Bellin knew. The drama told him that much. The American lawyer had sent a substitute: A diffident, sharp-eyed, young man, cool and probably indifferent to others' causes.

But he was speculating, Bellin warned himself. He could be wrong. "Bescel."

"Yes, Director," Radnik came to attention.

"See that American couple? The one just now getting their luggage?"

"Yes, sir."

Bellin rose, tense, stiff. "Find out what room they get. Make sure that the cameras are activated."

Radnik swallowed with difficulty. Bellin's voice had a tougher, harder, sound than usual, intimidating even to his chief assistant.

Without another word, Bellin crushed his cigar against the wall and stalked out of the room.

While he still had the Americans on the monitor, Radnik reached for the phone. He dialed quickly. "Desk? Do you see the American couple off to your left?" He watched the clerk glance off in their direction. "Getting their bags? Yes. What room do they have? Separate? His, then. Six-one-eight." He shot a look at Folenya, who hopped down to the panel and then nodded. "Good."

Radnik gestured to the technician. The borrowed KGB officer pushed two buttons and flicked one switch. One dormant monitor sprang to unstable life. With a careful turn of a dial, the room came into sharp focus. Room six-eighteen.

~ ~ ~

"What does it matter now?" Elizaveta demanded petulantly.

Volenko dabbed at his forehead with the damp handkerchief. His spirit had ebbed since Elizaveta's announcement about Klein. Perhaps she was right.

Swallowing his entire glass of vodka, Torlas waved for attention. Once he had it, he said, "Mikhail merely asked if you got the room number. As it mattered enough for him to ask, it matters enough for you to answer. In our own little group, each of us can decide what is important. I, for example, have always found your emigration program to be an idiotic demand." He had to stop her objection with his stubby hand. "But, I'm equally secure in knowing that you could care less about Georgian autonomy."

"You're damn right."

"Fine. If we cannot allow each other the privilege of differences of opinion..."

Sternly, Volenko corrected him. "Right, my friend. It is a right, not a privilege."

Tapping his forehead, Torlas sighed. "I will never get that straight."

"Elizaveta," Volenko explained, his energy stirred by the discussion, "Our only hope lies with this American."

"I'll deliver the tape myself," she retorted.

"Didn't they search you the last time," Volenko said, "even before you reached the Embassy wall... What if you had had it with you?"

She had to admit that such a plan would be too risky. As a trial, she had attempted to visit the Embassy several weeks before. Without papers or special permission, she had been told, no one could be allowed near the building. Even at that, she had suffered a superficial pat-down designed to reinforce the point. A similar attempt by Volenko yielded the same results.

"I doubt he would get past them either," she said, feeling her anger toward the American interloper growing again. "He's not important enough."

"With Embassy instructions," Torlas interjected, "an American will get in. He may be searched, but he'll get in."

"And none of us can," Volenko said quickly. "Were we to so much as ask the Embassy, the KGB would stop us immediately. Without an American, there is no hope. What is the room number?"

Reluctantly, she gave it to him, "Six-eighteen."

Volenko immediately flagged a waiter. "You have a guest here, in 618. A Mr. Dunney. Please have this invitation sent up to his room immediately."

The waiter nodded, took the note and left the table. On his way out of the room, he glanced at the nearest plainclothesman. The KGB officer quickly rose and left the room. A minute later he returned.

Volenko had not bothered to be clandestine. He knew there was no point.

~ ~ ~

His preemptive call to Andy out of the way, Dunney reread the note from "the girl in the lobby." She wanted to meet him, alone, for champagne. It was only natural; after all, she knew Klein. Dunney laughed. Did Klein have a woman in Moscow? Klein?

Dunney dressed casually, forgetting the tie and wearing only the vest. He hoped, at least, that he looked casual. One of his basic bargaining rules was to avoid making someone important know that you felt they were important. It only added strength to his, or her in this case, position.

Not that this Russian girl was particularly important, of course, but he found something about her interesting. While Dunney considered himself a poor judge of female character–with ample evidence to support him–he assessed mutual attraction well. Besides, he had only Andy in Moscow and that, under the circumstances, was hardly satisfactory.

Hair half-combed, breath Colgate-freshened and beard untended, Dunney set off for the dining room of the hotel. He felt a sense of adventure unlike any encountered in his normal pursuits. Though he resisted it, Moscow's strange, faintly exotic atmosphere colored everything. It was the capital of Communism, that dreaded, mutant orthodoxy which threatened to conquer the world. For all of that, it maintained its eastern imperial buildings alongside its new structures, and fostered an intelligentsia amid a generally peasant mentality.

Perhaps that was what made the girl so attractive. She was the first well-put-together Russian he had met. An honest-to-God Russian woman, but one he might relate to without becoming involved in philosophical differences or doctrinal cant. She wore blue jeans after all, and had the uncommon sense to approach him first, twice.

Andy had been quite upset, though she said nothing.

Dunney skipped the elevator, which made enough noise to sound unsafe, and took the stairs. The wide, elegantly banistered staircase spoke for the whole hotel. It had an almost regal appearance at first. The carpet was a rich wine and cream color with thick piles. The woodwork had a hand-carved look to it. At each landing a crystal chandelier lit the way. Upon closer inspection, however, he noted that the carpet had lost its life and grown threadbare at the edge of the steps. The woodwork was chipped and dull, even dusty. Much of the glass in the chandelier had a cloudy appearance and much of it was simply missing.

For all of its shortcomings though, the hotel had its own air. It was the aristocrat bearing up and adapting to a still new way of life, doing its job without much understanding or help. There was an honorable feel to it, a stoic diligence. The hotel, he realized, reminded him of Carl Abelson's adaptation to the likes of Steve Klein and himself.

The lobby exuded the same ambiance, but Dunney did not pause to enjoy it, crossing quickly to the dining room. The once elegant hall had been altered substantially, in the name of socialist efficiency. Fluorescent lights adorned the high ceilings, inexpensive, oft-changed cotton cloths covered metal tables. Underneath the thin legs, a solid brown, woven carpet barely cushioned the footfalls. Only the two-story high windows betrayed the legacy of nobility.

Beside one of them, Elizaveta sat with two men.

Dunney pulled out the vacant chair, across the table from the girl, but remained standing for introductions. In Russian he said, "My name is Dunney."

None of the three smiled. If anything, all became more grim. "We all speak English, Mr. Dunney," the oldest said. "I am Mikhail Volenko. My colleagues are Nikolai Torlas…"

The fat man mumbled something unintelligible in English.

"…and Elizaveta Krylenkev, you have talked with."

"Your champagne," Elizaveta said, indicating a glass in front of her. She started to hand it across to him, but rerouted it through Volenko.

After a sip, Dunney asked her. "Weren't we supposed to be alone?" He tried the name. "Eliz…"

"Elizaveta," she said, offering him no shorter version. Her mother had used "Vetova", but Elizaveta hated the sound of it. "What we have to ask is important."

Dunney studied his champagne. As of yet, he had no idea who these people were or what they wanted. He had to be careful not to compromise his position in Moscow. "I may not be able to answer you. All right?"

His words crushed Elizaveta's last struggling hope. This American, she concluded, would not help them. He was afraid to even listen to them. "We should not have bothered you, Mr. Dunney."

He did not want to alienate Elizaveta, but Dunney's suspicions doubled upon hearing her dismiss him because of his reasonable hesitation. "Let me explain what I meant. I represent a client, a company. I came here to talk to your government on his behalf. I can't afford to say anything which might jeopardize my client's relationship with your government."

The beefy Georgian laughed and said, "It is not our government. We are its subjects, but it is not our government. "

Dunney almost said "shit" out loud. He wanted no part of this conversation.

"We are members of the Moscow Group," Volenko said. "Do you know of it?"

He wished he did not know of it. Until Steve Klein had hit him over the head with it, Dunney neither knew nor cared about the so-called Moscow Group. "You're the human rights people. You and…" With a glance at the agent, he suppressed the name on his tongue. Mraisky. "An associate of mine is familiar with you."

"Steven Klein?" Volenko asked.

"He's the one." Dunney felt as reluctant to mention Klein's name as Mraisky's. God damn it, what had he gotten into?

Elizaveta stated, "We had hoped he would come."

Christ, what if he had? Bingo would have gone to the dogs. "Steve was ill." He weighed every word. How much dare he say? "I came in his place. To finalize some commercial arrangements with your… the Soviet government. I'm sorry, if you're disappointed."

Looking to his two companions, Volenko said sadly, "We are. Very much."

Rising, Dunney looked directly at Elizaveta. When her eyes met his, they were filled with emotion, mostly anger, but not, he guessed, only that. Tears brimmed, threatening to run off. She sniffed once and fought to hold her mouth at the level. It was a display of a rare presence, of control and quite possibly courage. Unfortunately, such character made her too risky for him.

"It is late," Dunney said. "I would like to do some work before going to bed. I hope you will excuse me."

Elizaveta turned away, leaving one clenched hand on top of the table. Frustrated anger, directed toward the criminally indifferent American, coupled with a betrayed hatred for the weak Klein challenged her self-control. She could not face Dunney, or the others.

Accompanying Dunney to the doorway, Volenko said only, "Thank you for meeting with us, Mr. Dunney."

"My pleasure," he lied. He looked over at Elizaveta who was shrugging off a smile from Torlas. "I couldn't very well turn you down."

Volenko followed Dunney's eyes . Perhaps it was not over. "Enjoy Moscow, Mr. Dunney."

"I'm not here for that, Mr. Volenko. I've got a job to do. I won't have much time for enjoyment."

Ironic words. Volenko thought. It was the same for them all.

~ ~ ~

"His secretary," Radnik told Folenya, as they monitored Room 427. It had taken him three phone calls to the hotel to establish her location and activate the connection. "Are you sure it's worth it?"

Folenya, still blurry-eyed from her unscheduled nap in the rear of the room, watched the smudge that was Dunney's secretary move across the monitor screen. Offhandedly, she said, "I would not have had her moved unless I thought it important. The American may spend time in her room." Most Americans were like that, she added to herself. A dying, depraved society, American supported lasciviousness on a scale beyond the imaginings of normal people. "If Dunney is to be watched, we have to have this room covered as well."

"Logical," Radnik agreed. It did not bother him observing the attractive young American woman. He had, in fact, found her innocent undressing stimulating. She had a very un-Russian body, at least in his limited experience. As he followed her movements–she paced endlessly, a long, satiny nightgown clinging to her–he decided that he preferred this KGB-type investigation to his usual interviewing and report reading. His wife would not appreciate his assignment; he would not upset her by telling her about it in detail.

The American woman stopped for a moment hovering over the telephone. She picked it up, replaced it, picked it up again and finally requested Room 618. Impatiently, she kept beat with the rings, tapping her foot. After thirty seconds, she rolled her eyes toward the ceiling. The phone in Dunney's empty room kept on ringing.

"Why doesn't she give up?" Folenya asked. She hated to see any woman, even an American, make a fool of herself over a man. "Can't she see that he's not there?"

Radnik, sympathetic to the subject, said easily, "Not everyone has the KGB's capabilities, Anna."

Folenya intended to report the insolence of the Deputy to Bellin in the morning. She preferred the observation of proper formalities and would demand it again from the Director's subordinates. On her note pad, she recorded this, the fifth occurrence of the use of first names. She despaired, however, of making her point directly with Radnik. He had already ignored her once.

At the same time, she made a note to comment to Bellin on the unprofessional manner of Deputy Radnik in conducting the observation of the subject Americans.

More than once, Folenya had seen Comrade Radnik lose control of himself during the monitoring of the American woman. Men could not disguise the physical manifestation of their urges. Radnik certainly had failed in that regard. In the KGB...

"Chris!" the American cried, startling Folenya.

"He's finally back," Radnik announced, a bit disappointed. Now, the girl could finally go to sleep; what would he do for entertainment? Dunney was dull.

Folenya barked at the technician manning the monitoring panel, "More sound!" To Radnik, her words were equally sharp. "Silence yourself, if possible, please."

Used to the KGB liaison's outbursts, Radnik only smiled to himself. Anna Folenya had emotion bottled up in her, he thought, ready to be loosed by the right man. It was a foolish thought.

On the screens, Dunney loosened his vest, while the girl awaited his reply. Radnik could tell that the call perturbed the American. What if he had known that the girl had made a trip down to his room while he was in the dining room with the Moscow Group?

"Andy," Dunney began "I asked you not to..."

Apologetically, Andy interrupted, "I had to, Chris. They moved me."

"Moved you? What are you talking about? It's after midnight."

She continued to speak in a rush. "The desk said I was in a room reserved for someone else, and that I had to move tonight because they..."

Dunney's growing smile broke into laughter. "Hold it, Andy. Calm down."

Andy looked surprised at either his words or his laughter. "I just wanted to tell you. I'm sorry if I bothered you!" With that she slammed the receiver down and stood staring at the phone.

When Radnik chuckled, Folenya shot him a critical look. She did not hold it long, however, her eyes returning to Dunney's monitor. She, at least, had work to do.

Dunney was giving the telephone receiver a stare of curiosity. He let his hand drop to his side, shaking his head. Out loud, he said, "So, where the hell are you, you dumb broad...?" He returned the receiver to his ear, thought better of it and hung up. After removing his vest and shirt, he went to the small bathroom.

Folenya called, "Get that."

The technician made two simple movements and another screen lit up.

Radnik gasped. "The bathroom?"

"This is completely monitored," the technician explained, without turning.

The fish-eye lens from above terribly distorted Dunney's body as he first used the john and then stared into the mirror. When he left, the technician killed that screen. Dunney's walk over to the bedroom of the suite forced a camera switch–the main room had three normal view cameras–and the activation of the fish-eye-lensed camera in the bedroom.

"Don't show off to Comrade Radnik." Folenya said reprovingly.

"It's always useful," the technician replied in a vaguely superior tone, "to keep in practice, when nothing is happening, Comrade Folenya."

Anna's pencil wrote the technician's name on her pad and ran a sharp line through it.

In the bedroom, Dunney dug into a drawer and pulled out a pair of pajamas. He held them up as if they were foreign objects and then threw them on the bed. For several seconds he just looked at the bed, or the pajamas or both. He returned to the dresser's top drawer and pulled out a large flask.

Dunney headed out of the bedroom and went directly to the phone. "This is Dunney, in 618," he said slowly, in Russian. "You moved my secretary tonight. Miss Andrea

Wards." He unscrewed the flask's top while waiting and took a long drink. "427? Four-Two-Seven. Very good. Thank you."

"Humph," was Folenya's only reaction.

Keeping his smile to himself, Radnik concluded that, perhaps, this American was no so dull after all. As Dunney left, and shut the door to Room 618, Radnik said, "If she doesn't have a thick Polish robe, you can turn off Room 427, my friend."

Folenya frowned, took up her pencil and waited to see the telltale bulge appear in Radnik's trousers.

~ ~ ~

When Andy opened the door to his knocks, Dunney could see that she had not turned her lights off and, presumably, had not yet gone to bed. The bright glow that surrounded her as she peered through a generous crack in the door, filtered through her hair like a gentle aura. Suddenly, he found himself feeling very awkward.

"Yes?" she asked tentatively. There he was, his shirt hanging outside his suit pants, the neck open the top two buttons. On his face he wore a sheepishly warm expression. Her anger waned, desire and its accompanying apprehension waxing in its place.

He offered the flask. "A hotel room warming party?"

Andy responded by opening the door full to let him in. When he had passed through, she closed it quietly, hesitantly, fearing that they would not stop if they started. She pressed her hands tightly against her waist and tried to suppress the feelings coming on too fast. "I'm sorry."

"Do you have glasses in this place?"

She pointed to the bathroom. Waiting until he came back out, she said, "I shouldn't have hung up on you."

Dunney examined the glasses, shrugged at the film on them and poured a bit of bourbon in each. Handing one to Andy, he stood facing her a few feet away. "You have too much character, Andy. People with character don't take insults, however innocently inflicted. I came here to apologize. Mostly." He offered his glass for her to touch in silent toast, his mind and pulse racing.

Andy accepted the gesture and watched him as she drank. He was looking back. "Mostly?" God, she thought. Had it already started? "That has a dangerous sound."

"I wasn't drinking to that," he objected grinning.

"I think I was."

Magic words, Dunney thought. She wanted him as much as he wanted her. And the hell with everything else! He put his arms around her, felt her respond warmly, supplely. The first kiss was a shallow, brief one, the second went on for almost a minute.

Dunney broke off the kiss and rocked backwards awkwardly.

Holding him loosely, Andy asked, "Are you all right?"

Dunney shook his head, more to clear his mind than to reply to the question. "Too much champagne," he said. Champagne? "On the plane, you know."

She looked at him askance. "It tastes like bourbon. Have you been drinking without me?"

Lying, he said, "Just a small one. In my room. But I'm not drunk, Andrea. If that's what you think. I don't have to be plastered to apologize when I'm wrong."

Feeling her body calming down, Andy released him. "We were both wrong, Chris." She decided that the truth would help them both. "All I had really wanted to do was tell you I had moved. But I got lonely, just thinking about you lying around up there. When you weren't there, I got worse. I know what we agreed to, but a girl can get that way, you know."

Character, he mused. She had it. That was what he found so attractive. Just as he did in the Russian girl. His body relaxed. He would not make love to Andy. Not that night. Lust and character don't make a good mix. Only one at a time.

~ ~ ~

"Americans talk too much," Radnik observed. He felt mildly ashamed of how the two Americans' abbreviated love scene had affected him. He found that he was not excited as much as he was put off by his own intrusion. Like a schoolboy, Radnik had felt stirred and embarrassed and crude.

"Humph," Folenya answered, in disgust. Comrade Radnik had no control over himself at all, she knew. She had watched him. She had watched him the whole time. And she knew.

Too embarrassed to look at Folenya, Radnik slumped in his chair. His mother would have killed him. And his wife! Of the technician, he asked, "Is it always like this?"

For the first time in hours, the KGB engineer swiveled in his seat. Both screens had grown dark as the subjects retired for the night. He looked upon Radnik sympathetically. Hadn't they all started out the same way? "No, Sir. Most of the time, it's empty rooms, snoring, reading, showering. Sometimes, it is more than that."

The technician glanced over at Folenya, who was still bent forward in her seat, her nostrils flared. To him, she was absurd in refusal to admit that she, too, was new to monitoring the lives of others. There was nothing wrong with being new at it or being affected by it. "You get used to it, Comrade Radnik," he said. "They don't know it, so it doesn't bother them."

Only slightly mollified, Radnik said, "I suppose."

"We are supposed to watch them," the engineer added. "And so we do. They are just people." He spun back to his complex electronic board, surveyed the various screens and yawned. That would pretty much do it for his shift.

Chapter Six

On his third day in Moscow, Dunney arranged an appointment at the American Embassy. The second day had been consumed by a scouting trip around the city and its Olympic site. In his opinion, the Soviets had placed the Bingo Burger restaurants in positions decidedly inferior to the other fast food operations. As the Embassy had played a major role in assisting the competition, Dunney hoped for some help from its personnel for Bingo's as well. Before leaving, however he made one important call.

"Hello. Steve. I would like you to do me a favor."

Klein answered noncommittally. "What did you have in mind?"

"Give Bingo a call," Dunney began. "I think that he should call a news conference later today, tonight, in your case. Have him announce..."

"Chris," Klein interrupted, "No announcements until this contract is signed. Carl and I feel very strongly about that."

"Just give me a second." Having anticipated Klein's objection, Dunney had fully practiced his argument, with Andy's help. He glanced over at her as he spoke. She nodded and smiled hollowly in return.

"Steve, I looked over the sites yesterday. They are miserable. I am afraid that the competition may have retaliated against Bingo for horning in over here. Either that or the Russians are setting us up for bargaining purposes."

"Damn. Let me get my map."

Dunney spoke quickly. "Don't bother. You can't tell from the map. What counts are streets, traffic flow and crowd orientations. We'll have hundreds of thousands of people waking within twenty yards without seeing the places. I want them where the crowd flow changes momentum; where it stops for a light, not after the light; right before turning a corner, not a block later. The point is that we are going to need some pressure."

"Go on." Klein was obviously reserving judgment, but was no longer hostile.

"If Bingo will simply announce that he is negotiating with the Soviet Union on this deal and is getting along well enough without our current administration's help. He might use some of that preacher rhetoric he puts on so nicely. Tell him to lay it on that the Soviets love their black brothers. That may get us the President if we need him. My guess is that it will also put the Soviets publicly on the spot."

"Perhaps," Klein replied, considering with Dunney's plan. "I think you may have a good idea."

Dunney swallowed his aggravation at the use of the word "may." Klein knew the scheme would work perfectly, but would not admit it. That did not matter, Dunney had called Carl Abelson to sketch it out only half an hour before. "The Russians will think twice before being too tough. Bingo Burger is only over here because it's a black enterprise. And this place will be crawling with African dignitaries a year from now."

"I'll talk to Carl about it immediately."

Rolling his eyes, Dunney said, "Good. Tell Bingo not to let me down. So long."

As he hung up, Andy got up and stretched. "You didn't mention the other call."

"To Abelson? I guess I forgot." Dunney was feeling good, as good that morning as he had felt badly the day before. When he had seen where the Russians intended to set Bingo Burger Restaurants, he had felt sick. Even before coming to Moscow, he had feared placement problems, but nothing like what he had found. And he had so boldly planned to increase the number of outlets! Now, he would be lucky to hold the price. Out of the long melancholy evening reviewing the problem, he and Andy had devised a purely political solution. Bingo's biggest asset, aside from an excellent TV personality, was his race. Dunney hated to play such a game, but if he did not, the Russians would send him back to Boston thoroughly beaten.

He had no intention of being bested, not by Brezhnev himself.

"Finish your coffee. Andy. I want to shake up the Embassy a bit." Already on his feet from the phone call, Dunney bounced lightly on his toes, itching to move.

Andy, in an attempt to calm him down, sipped the thick Turkish coffee. From the window she looked down on the square. "Why are there so many soldiers in front of the Embassy?"

More to hasten their departure than to look, Dunney joined her. Below them, the moderately busy square had a surprising complement of uniformed soldiers milling about directly in front of the Embassy. "Christ, so there are. I have no idea."

While they watched, someone tried to enter the Embassy without stopping. He did not succeed. Two of the soldiers slipped quickly between him and the gate. After a brief conversation the individual departed huffily.

Dunney and Andy exchanged surprised looks. "Christ, is that normal?"

Leading her from the window by the arm, he said, "You're the Russian."

"Ukrainian. And only half at that."

He squeezed her arm in recognition of their private joke. "Check with the front desk while I call the Embassy. I'll be there in a few minutes." As an afterthought, he added, "Don't forget your papers, or whatever they call them."

Uncomfortable for the first time in Moscow, Andy said quietly, "I have them," and left the room. Out in the hallway she stopped for a moment to collect herself, before heading for the elevator.

Dunney wasted no time in raising the Embassy. It took him several minutes to reach the man in charge. "Hello, Mr. Kyle?"

"Yes, Mr. Dunney," the Senior Staff Secretary replied pleasantly. "What can I do for you?"

"I am in Moscow representing…"

"Bingo Burgers," Kyle cut in amused. "Yes, I know. Your firm's Mr. Klein is well known hereabouts. Is there anything we can do to help you and the American hamburger?"

His annoyance at Kyle's manner lasted only as long as he forgot the view from his window, which was not very long. "I had hoped to come over for a visit, as you know, but I've noticed that the Russians have posted…"

"So they have, Mr. Dunney," Kyle said, continuing his habit of interrupting. "For our protection. From all of the demonstrators. "

Confused, Dunney began, "I haven't seen any."

"How odd. Neither have I. But never mind. I will meet you at the gate. That won't save having your briefcase examined," Kyle warned. "Without diplomatic papers, you're subject to whatever crap they have up their sleeves."

Dunney glanced toward the window. He couldn't see the soldiers from that angle, but he felt nervous about them all the same. "I'd like to cone over now, if I could. I'm at the…"

"Yes, I know. Your office told us. See you in about ten minutes?"

"Fine," Dunney said, glad to have the conversation ended. He already disliked the Senior Staff Secretary. Many people had the habit of completing sentences which others have started, but Kyle simply interrupted with appropriate responses. It made Dunney feel that he was always a step behind. Unused to such situations, Dunney did not operate well in them.

Uneasy about both the soldiers and Kyle, Dunney pulled on his suit coat and departed the room. As usual, he took the steps rather than the elevator. It was almost the only exercise he had had in Moscow.

Andy stood at the front desk, staring out one of the hotel's high windows. Dunney's appearance at the top of the stairs made her feel secure for the first time in minutes. She wanted to clutch him to her, but fought off the notion. It was just as well: She did not want him to know that she was shaking.

Trying to smile reassuringly, Dunney said. "Kyle at the Embassy will meet us at the gate. He said to prepare for a search."

Her stomach queasy, Andy related the information given her by the desk clerk. "They're in the Militia, which is like the regular police, I think. Supposedly, the government posted them there to protect the Embassy. Supposedly crowds have reacted to American criticism of Mraisky's arrest."

"Mraisky?" Dunney asked. "That figures."

"I asked if anything had happened and he said no."

Exhaling a sigh, Dunney put his arm around her waist. The contact helped. "We might as well get it over with."

The square, despite its geometrical appellation, ran twice as long as it measured in width and had a slight bend in the middle. Their hotel stood just to one side of the break, while the Embassy was across the square on the other side of the angle. In the middle, there was a small monument of some kind, about ten feet high. A number of other governments' embassies and other official-looking buildings lined each side of the square.

The sun, though not yet very high, warmed the air enough to overcome their chills. A gentle, inconsistently warm and cool breeze made the late June day feel like spring. Sparsely populated, the square was dominated by the Militia squad posted in front of the American Embassy.

His eyes fixed upon the uniformed men, Dunney nearly walked into a tall black, dressed in a red-and-white trimmed blue track warm-up. "Hey, Mr. Dunney," the young man called as he hopped out of the way, "You should be more careful of your fellow Americans."

Clinton Thomas, the senior sprinter of the American Spartakiade team, a holdover from the 1976 Olympics, continued to jog in place as he spoke. "Nice day for running." Although the Spartakiade was only a dress rehearsal for 1980, Thomas trained every day, usually at the University.

"Sorry, Clint," Dunney said, taking a second or two to remember the runner's first name. They had met briefly several times in the hotel lobby since the night of their arrival. "Where are your friends?"

"Everybody's out at the University stadium. I got up late," he admitted, his smile seeming too big for his thin face. "I'm going there in a couple minutes. You going to the embassy? Shit…" He stopped when he remembered Andy's presence.

Nodding Dunney asked, "Have you been over?"

"First thing. We were supposed to report first thing. Those damn Ruskies'd make you strip in mid-January if you had a hand in one pocket." Clinton laughed, pointing to the small USA emblem on his jacket. "Who'd they think we were? Chinese?"

Andy and Dunney both laughed with him, said good-bye and took up their walk again. The guards watched them the entire way, converging at the gate. Behind them, Kyle leaned casually' against the metal bars.

Speaking in Russian, one of the older, more imposing soldiers stepped out in front of them. "Your papers please. We cannot let anyone pass who is not American with business inside." He spoke in a gruff manner, as if he did not expect to be understood. Andy's Russian response obviously bothered him and he switched to English. "Come on now, let's see your visa."

"They're here to see me," Kyle said from behind. He waved a piece of paper in one hand.

The guards ignored him, or more properly, further ignored him. After surveying the papers, the commander of the handpicked unit looked them over again for a few minutes. His orders were to make the passage as difficult as possible without going beyond the outrageous. From Bellin himself.

Another guard asked, in Russian, for Dunney's briefcase and Andy's purse and file case. Three of them made a show of rummaging through the belongings without actually looking for anything. Then they handed them to a fourth man, in a different uniform, who hardly seemed to look, but whose KGB-trained eye would have picked up the one object he was searching for. He knew of all the places to hide the tiniest objects, including micro photographic film; a tape cartridge he could spot in seconds.

Once finished with the purse, the KGB officer ran his hands quickly up and down Dunney's body. He turned to Andy and asked, "Have you objections?" in English.

Snapping in Russian, Andy said, "Yes, but not to you're being a man."

He nodded and proceeded with his almost unnoticeable pat-down. His touch was feathery and oddly genteel.

Kyle cursed, crushed the paper he was holding and hoped it would end there. "Come on in, folks. Just think how safe and secure you're going to feel."

As Andy, repulsed and yet thrilled by the mystery, passed Kyle, she asked, "Can't we protest this?"

The Senior Secretary gave her a once over and dismissed her as too young for his taste, too innocent. Kyle had long passed the stage where innocence attracted him. Having been in the CIA for twenty years, he was repelled by the idea of violating innocents, either psychologically or sexually. Protest? "Young lady, we've about protested ourselves out. This has been going on for weeks. Our protests just waste paper." For the right kind of woman, Kyle would have written a very long, very futile protest, but for this secretary... "Sorry."

Kyle's attitude did not escape Dunney. Uncooperative on the phone, Kyle would be only a bit better in person. He had watched Kyle size up Andy in a glance and knew what the verdict had been if not the reasoning. Dunney made his turn come next. "I'll take care of the protesting myself tomorrow, Mr. Kyle. We'll be meeting with the All Union Construction Undersecretary. He won't pay attention, but I'll make some noise."

Andy fired a sharp look his way, but Dunney continued, "In fact, I expect to have problems on substantive matters as well. Your help may not hurt."

Kyle, attracted by the even-toned bravado of the younger man, spent a bit more time looking him over. Dunney had a solid, slightly too recognizable build, with an acceptably good looking face. What Kyle admired, however, was the hard determination in it. Kyle laughed to himself. He had been in the business too long, falling automatically into the CIA analysis of a man. He separated his job from himself briefly and decided that he, surprisingly enough, liked Dunney. Maybe that was what he could have been.

Nodding to Dunney's statement, Kyle led the two into the Embassy and off to a small parlor. "Let me call our junior economic man, Winker. He was involved with the other fast-food people when they were here. Perhaps he can help you."

Waiting for Winker, Kyle found himself wondering if, perhaps, Dunney were not from Washington, there to check up on his operation. Since Mraisky... Winker answered and Kyle put the thought away until later. "Johnny, I've got the Bingo Burger people down here. Do you suppose you could drop down and talk to them?"

As usual, the shy Winker did not even answer. He never refused a request, so an answer was hardly necessary. Kyle often wondered how timid Johnny Winker ever got a chance for such an appointment as a Moscow attaches. The word was that Winker's father knew the Secretary of State, but hadn't the Secretary even seen Winker? That would have been enough to exile the guy to Luxembourg.

Panting, Winker came through the door and stopped to smooth his ruffled hair. When he saw Dunney and Andy, he took a small step backwards. He blinked twice and said in his small voice, "I thought you were Klein."

Dunney stepped forward offering his hand. With Winker shrinking back, it took him several steps to reach the man's limp hand. Hiding his repulsion, Dunney said, "Steve couldn't make it. My name is Dunney. I was senior associate on the Bingo Burger matter."

A long, skinny finger scratching his forehead, Winker looked at Dunney through the fingers of his hand. He then played with his thin mustache as he spoke partly obscuring the words. "Bingo Burgers. Six restaurants. Using Florida beef now, aren't you?" He used his high pitched laugh. "Oh, that made them mad."

Impatient, Kyle suggested, "Sit down, why don't you. I'll have some coffee sent in. Excuse me." Hastening to the door, Kyle slipped out. He could not abide Winker's mannerisms around strangers. What kind of man was he? He would order them coffee personally, his only excuse for leaving.

Inside the room, Andy took a well stuffed chair, while Dunney used the sofa for himself and his map of Moscow. Winker hovered over the map, his long narrow head bobbing as if his neck could not adequately support it.

"Mr. Winker, did you do much in the way of intervening in the negotiations of the other companies?"

Pursed lips turning blue, Winker ran through his mental files. "Some, mostly administrative. You'll meet your share of red tape here–Pardon the expression–but we were told to keep hands off. I think those companies contributed to the Republicans." Winker laughed again.

"What about sites? Did you see them?"

"I did go around with their representatives, but I wasn't much help. Nobody was too happy about locations, as I recall. The Russians made quite sure of that."

Dunney breathed a sigh. He did not know how to feel. The Russians had executed an unexpected bargaining maneuver, assuming that was what it was, which might frustrate his ambitious plans. At least he knew that it was intentional and could be countered with tough negotiating. "Did they get some changes?"

Smiling, Winker said, "Changes? For every single site. But it cost them. The Soviets had no intention of leaving the restaurants where they had sited them, I can assure you, Mr. Dunney."

Pointing to his map, ticking off each of the six, red-marked sites for Bingo Burgers, Dunney noted, "These spots are horrible."

Winker's pale blue eyes opened wide. He straightened, looking rather tall and considerably less frail. For an instant he had a hard-edged look on his face. "Son of a bitch."

Dunney started at the strong tone of voice. "What is it?"

Winker had already darted over to the phone. "Sondra, bring me my McDonald's file number three. Thanks. Oh, and get Kyle in here as well." He turned to look at Dunney first then Andy. His gaze going back to Dunney, he exhaled, making his body collapse to its usual state. "I'll explain in a minute."

After about three minutes, the coffee, Kyle and Winker's secretary arrived together. "What is it, John?" Kyle demanded, not quite civilly. "I was in the middle..."

"Screw job." Winker said. "Here, look." He pulled a small map of the Moscow area from the file. Setting beside Dunney's large map, he said, "Take a look. Yours are blue triangles."

Andy rose and joined the three men as they compared maps. It was immediately obvious to her, as it was to Dunney. Kyle merely said, "So what? It's different."

"Christ," Dunney cried, "Those sites are ten times better than the present ones!"

"Why?" Andy asked Winker.

"Mr. Dunney, hadn't you seen an overall site map before?"

"It was to be settled here. The Soviets sent us a list of what they wanted, but only for discussion purposes. It was a pure bargaining matter. We thought we'd be better off waiting until the last stages. I guess we blew that."

Winker waved his hand. "No, no. It would have been something else. Don't worry about that."

"Why?" the annoyed, confused, Kyle demanded. "Why the fuck would they fuss with it?"

Without a moment's hesitation, Winker glanced at the date of his small map. Perhaps that was it. "The date."

"Which date?"

They all looked at Winker, who avoided all their eyes. "I got this map long before Mraisky was arrested."

Dunney felt his stomach muscles flex. "Shit. Not him again."

"We all expected Klein," Winker said. "Apparently so did the Soviets."

"I'm screwed," Dunney said barely audibly. Or was he? He was not Klein, after all. Klein was behaving in Boston. Maybe the Russians would realize that Klein would not engage in any pro-Mraisky activities. God, he hoped so! "Mr. Winker, you have been an enormous help."

Shaking his head, Winker stared at the maps. Sometimes the perversity of fate went beyond his imagination. How vital they all thought it was, Bingo Burger Restaurant's locations. Jesus Christ. A man's life hung in the balance.

Winker looked over at the bored Kyle out of the corner of his eye. He knew that Kyle was thinking about the arrest of Mraisky, too, but only in terms of what it had done to the CIA network in Moscow. Dunney, obviously was only concerned with what it did to his chances of making a good show for the folks back in Boston. The girl, she was with Dunney and probably identified with his goals.

The hell with Mraisky! Winker had his own thought on that. Mraisky meant something to him, something much different from anything the others would have suspected.

The lecture had run on automatically for the first forty- five minutes. No one had dared to ask questions and Elizaveta was thankful for that. Now, however, she faced an inquiry by one of the second year economic students, presenting her with an insuperable problem: She had no idea what she had been saying prior to the question.

If only she could wiggle out of the dilemma, she could let the group out early. She pretended that she had not heard the question clearly, giving her time to think.

"Yuri, I'm sorry, but would you repeat the last part of your question."

Yuri Morozova, one of her favorite pupils, recognized his teacher's increasingly common difficulty, concentrating on her own lectures. He simplified the question. "All I really need to know," he said, "is how the need for capital is eliminated in a socialist economy."

Quickly, she made a note that Yuri Morozova was to get a 100 for his day's performance. He had, reduced his complicated question to near idiocy. "It is not eliminated, Yuri. But, as all capital is the product of the labor of a collective society, it need not be identified directly. The beneficial use of the capital element, in all cases, follows to the collective. All right?"

Yuri nodded.

"Let's move on next time," she intoned, "To the allocation of capital in Britain as opposed to the United States.". With that she closed her notebook and stepped away from the lectern. After flashing Yuri a thankful smile, Elizaveta fled through the rear door of the hall.

The economics building was only a few hundred yards away and the path was, fortunately, uncluttered with students. With two lectures already that morning, she had had enough of students for the moment. The rare brightness of the day helped to restore her somewhat. It was not enough to raise her spirits from the depths, which they had hit the night before when four of the members of the nationalities faction ended their connection with the Moscow Group. Without Mraisky, the Helsinki Monitoring movement was dying, dragging the emigration effort with it. Although Elizaveta had managed to drive the specifics of the last few days out of her consciousness, the general depression they generated remained.

Once in the Economics building, she signed in and headed straight for the elevator and her office on the fourth floor. It took all of her strength to pass Mraisky's former office. It was now occupied by a rather limited colleague who had not waited a week after the arrest before claiming the prestigious office as his own.

Between Mraisky's old office and her own, she passed the division secretary's desk. The affable older woman, Vasiliev, gave her an unusually somber smile. "You have company, Elizaveta," she said loudly. Then she added in a whisper, "From the Procurator's Investigative Office."

Her knees weakened at the announcement. She had been half expecting the KGB or the Procurator to call her in, but it had been so long since Mraisky's arrest that the dread had largely abated. As she rounded the doorway and saw the back of a man's head, she suffered it with renewed intensity.

"Can I help you?" she asked assuming the seat behind her narrow desk.

Bescel Radnik squinted, frowned his approval and sat back in the hard backed chair. He had seen her on the monitor only the one time and wanted to compare her two appearances. From the distance of the camera, she had looked quite pretty, in a Russian way. Now, closer, Radnik recognized the Jewish elements of her features, which gave her a complicated, interesting face.

Elizaveta felt uncomfortable under Radnik's scrutiny, not knowing whether it was official or personal. Not that it mattered, for he was the enemy.

"My name is Radnik. Elizaveta," he said informally. "I'm in the Department of Investigation, for the procurator of Moscow. We are looking into the matter of Alexander Mraisky."

"I see."

Radnik pulled a small notebook out of his suit coat and laid it on the desk. Conspicuously, he searched for his pen, allowing the girl time to see that the pad was half filled with information about her. When she had finished, her face a bit whiter, he spoke again. "Now, you worked with Dr. Mraisky, both here at the University and in his agitation activities," he stated, reading from the notes. "The Moscow Group for the Monitoring of Violations of the Helsinki Accord on Human Rights. That's quite a long title."

"It's descriptive," she said defensively. "Our group simply helps the State by pointing out the failure of lower officials in putting its policies unto effect."

"Very noble," Radnik replied. "The KGB felt that Dr. Mraisky used his role in the Moscow Group to subvert the interest of the Soviet State and the Party..."

Upset by the mere statement of the lies, she broke into Radnik's sentence. "That is absolutely ridiculous! He loves this country!"

Calmly, Radnik commented, "One may love Russia without agreeing with the Party."

"Exactly!"

"But to do so," he went on, "indicates either counterrevolutionary tendencies or madness. Now, which would you say applies to Dr. Mraisky?"

The smooth, conversational twisting of her words horrified Elizaveta. What had he led her into saying? Could any of it be used against Mraisky? "I did not say that," she said carefully.

"What does 'exactly' mean?"

She said nothing.

"The Moscow Group had CIA connections..."

"It most certainly did not!" Elizaveta felt penned in, frightened, helpless.

Radnik's voice maintained a gentle level, incorporating an occasional ironic note. "Mr. Seymour Greenwald has had CIA contacts for several years and he is not alone among the Moscow Group's many American friends." Radnik stretched the truth for the sake of convenience. It had, ironically been a constant source of irritation for the KGB that the Moscow Group's CIA support had been negligible. "Dr. Mraisky is also charged with the publishing of liable against the Party and the government; generally seditious writings circulated privately in Moscow and publicly in the West; obstruction of Soviet foreign policy; obstruction of domestic policies and a number of other things. Do you have any information that would tend to support or refute these charges?"

Dazzled by the array of legal, semi-legal and a-legal allegations, Elizaveta could not find words sufficient to use against Radnik. All she could say was, "You know it's not true."

His task largely finished, Radnik rose and closed his notebook. "That is for a court, Elizaveta. I am burdened with investigating the KGB's charges for the Procurator. Often, we find that the KGB is overzealous, but rarely is it completely wrong. I will come see you again. Perhaps, you will have something for me then. Until this is over, I would suggest that you avoid any involvement with the agitators of the Moscow Group. A number of your associates have already withdrawn and wisely so. If you were to be called as a witness, you would be more effective if the Procurator could present you as a loyal, diligent citizen."

Nausea churned through her. "Please go."

"Otherwise," Radnik concluded, "You would do more harm to Dr. Mraisky's cause than the most vigilant member of the KGB. Good day, Comrade Krylenkev." He turned to go and then added, "I attended part of your first lecture this morning. With you in this department, I am sure that Dr. Mraisky will not be missed."

Radnik said the final words with cheerfulness he did not feel. He had not intended to be too hard on the young woman, but she had not reacted as expected, evidencing more reserve than the file indicated. It could be a rotten job some days.

Once the investigator had left, Elizaveta pushed herself out of the chair. Measuring each step she walked out of the office and into the hall. If she were to be sick, she would not let them see.

~ ~ ~

Taking a break from his deep involvement in the Mraisky investigation, Bellin took over an interrogation of a Militia complainant in a minor theft case. With the brief file spread out in front of him, he waited for the officer to make his appearance.

The preliminary investigation by his investigator, a youngster named Velnavich, indicated that the accused had been the victim of an arrest-happy militiaman on the lookout for petty violations. The alleged victim had expressed uncertainty as to whether his East German watch had been lost or stolen. The accused, a factory worker of modest means, was found in the vicinity with the watch, though he claimed to be looking for the owner. The officer insisted in his sketchy report that there had been no witness, but Velnavich came across at least one individual, a shop clerk, whose statement tended to verify those of the accused.

As the uniformed officer took the chair opposite him, Bellin ran over the dossier on him.

The man, named Andreanov, cleared his throat.

"Andreanov, thank you for being on time." Bellin began politely, "You are aware of the case we are to review?"

"There are many arrests in a day, Comrade..."

"Bellin."

The man's face went pale at the name. "Director Bellin are you...?" The Director himself! Andreanov thought, worried. "But this is a small matter, Director."

"Not at all," Bellin replied, "Our task in this department is to generate enough facts to allow the Procurator to prosecute an individual if necessary. And to drop a case if unjustified." He put emphasis on the latter choice. "The rightful prosecution of all crimes is important to the

People so I like to keep touch. I'm sure you know what I mean."

"Yes, sir," the nervous Andreanov answered. Hadn't his evidence been enough? Had he made a mistake?

"According to your record, Andreanov, you lead your section in arrests."

He only nodded. Sweat began to bead on his forehead. He could receive a reprimand from the likes of Bellin!

The discomfort of Andreanov indicated to Bellin that the thirty-eight year old officer knew that he had overstepped, or under-investigated. The file told him that it was a chronic problem. "Does it surprise you, Andreanov, that my investigator found a witness to corroborate the claim of the accused? How about that?"

"I am surprised, sir." Surprised and horrified.

Peeved that such a mindless fool had escaped his department's sanction, continuing to wreck his personal havoc, Bellin bore down on Andreanov. "He was there when you arrested this worker, not fifteen meters away. Do you care to see a signed declaration by that clerk?" He shoved the paper in front of Andreanov. "Note the last few lines first, please. 'I was not approached by the officer. Neither was anyone else that I saw.'" Bellin glared at Andreanov and continued. "The statement says that your 'thief' had bent over within the view of the clerk and subsequently asked if anyone had reported a lost watch. Does that sound like a thief to you, Andreanov? Does it?"

Verbally battered, Andreanov looked at the floor and whispered, "No."

"Did you so much as ask for witnesses, damn it?"

"Not very loudly perhaps."

"Do you realize that you could have deprived society of a good worker if this man's record is accurate, and of an honest man, a rarity these days? What kind of security officer are you?"

Andreanov dared not say that he considered himself a fine officer, in spite of his mistake.

Bellin shut the file and wrote 'dismissed' on the cover. "I am not going to ask for a reprimand. Not this time. But I intend to mention your sloppiness and if I see your name come up again on a questionable arrest, you will have to get used to shop duty. Is that clear?"

"Yes. Director Bellin."

"Get back to work." Bellin watched the humbled Andreanov exit quickly but felt no satisfaction. Though now the officer would take his responsibility to the society a bit more seriously, Bellin worried about the laxity of his own people. Surely, this unconscionable arrest had not been Andreanov's first. He would have to use the case as an example.

He studied the pile of cases, trying to find another which indicated a similar pattern of abuse. He found only black market charges, monetary violations, a homicide or two with weak evidence, but nothing obvious. Leaving the files behind, Bellin made his way to Velnavich's cubicle, indicated that the other interrogations were all his and retreated to his office.

Radnik, just returning, called to Bellin from down the hall. Bellin ignored him, closing the door to his own office. The young man was the last person he wanted to see, thanks to Folenya. He hoped Radnik would take the hint.

The knock on the door eliminated that hope. "Come in."

Puffing, Radnik entered and flopped into a chair. "I tried to get you in the hall…"

"Catch your breath, Bescel." That would give him time to construct his bad news.

Radnik took a couple deep breaths, holding each for about ten seconds. "I finished with Krylenkev, sir. Who should I interrogate next?"

"What did she say?" He had to be careful not to lead Radnik on too long.

He breathed in again. "Nothing much. I was surprised. She should have burned my ear with all that Jew rhetoric, or something. She didn't, but I got the message across."

"Good "

"Not that it'll stop her. At least I don't think it will. I'm not sure that we can intimidate her." Radnik recognized the expression on Bellin's face. "Did I do something wrong?"

With the question presented so directly, Bellin had no choice but to respond directly. "Bescel, I have transferred you off of this investigation."

"What?" Incredulous, Radnik could not even begin to think of reasons.

Bellin shrugged. The Mraisky case was just like that, he wanted to say, everyone interfering. "Folenya submitted a report which included a recommendation that you be pulled. I laughed at her at first, which was a mistake. The Procurator himself made the final request, with pressure from the KGB."

It was a nightmare, Radnik thought. Folenya! The KGB. The Procurator. What had he done to them? "I don't understand."

"The report criticized you for a lack of detachment." Bellin said, without elaborating. Folenya's report was fairly specific if indirect in it accusations. He could have resisted Anna or the KGB, but not Zhoronov. His orders had to come from someone. "There's nothing I can do, Bescel. The KGB is very sensitive about Mraisky, the dissidents and the Americans."

"But what about my shift?" Radnik was due to monitor the American's hotel again that night. "We don't have any replacements for tonight."

Bellin clenched his teeth. It had to happen sooner or later. "I will take this shift." Then he started to laugh.

Perhaps that was the best way after all. "Be patient, Bescel. If Anna had to deal with me, she'll beg for your company."

Radnik did not laugh. He had been victimized by the KGB and Bellin had done nothing. But what could he have done? In a way, though, he would not miss surveillance duty. "I have to admit, sir, that I did not enjoy monitoring the Americans."

"If you let it show, Bescel, then you know why Folenya wrote it up. She emulates the KGB mentality, where everyone is very matter of fact about it. It's like any job," Bellin said. "You have to get used to it."

"I suppose."

"Now you'll have time to supervise the Department for me during this Moscow Group business. Why don't you concentrate on the nonpolitical cases. Folenya won't bother much with those. Her special interest is in the anti-Party activities, and Mraisky occupies most of her time right now. "

Accepting his orders without a word, Radnik departed. Bellin wondered if their special relationship would survive the strain of Radnik's ignominious transfer. He knew that the young man had done nothing wrong. Perhaps, he should have resisted with more vigor, but he had enough trouble opposing the KGB and Folenya's anti-dissident demands. Radnik was a temporary–he prayed–casualty of that struggle. There was a good chance he himself would be the next.

~ ~ ~

The Second Secretary for Agriculture shook his head. Beside him, the Second Secretary for Construction gave Dunney a vacant stare.

"All I ask," Dunney reiterated, "is that the sites be restored. Restaurants in the locations you have allocated to us now would be useless to you."

Sarkat, Construction's representative on the negotiating team and its spokesman, looked at the maps once more. "We are certain that the current sites are superior."

Fortunately, Dunney knew no particularly strong Russian oaths. He found his opponents very frustrating. One minute they wanted one thing, the next another. If he left Moscow with the present arrangement, he would be laughed out of the firm. Yet the Russians seemed unwilling to budge. "Gentlemen, if you don't want to serve the visitors, then why bother? Ninety percent of the people here for the games will never even notice these Bingo Burger Restaurants. Why build them at all?"

Curtly, Sarkat replied, "We have chosen locations which we, repeat we, consider most appropriate. We are willing to guarantee volume if that is what you want."

The first movement in an hour of discussion. Dunney felt relief swirl around inside him. He nodded to Andy to make sure that she picked it up and recorded the offer.

"That is very generous, Secretary Sarkat. Very generous. A volume guarantee would almost make those sites acceptable. Almost." Dunney knew that anyone in the world would have been satisfied except for Bingo Williams. And himself. "But, Bingo Burgers is more interested in doing the job for you than it is in guarantees."

Sarkat's face did not reveal his shock. He had fully expected the American to fall into the neatly prepared trap. A trap that would allow the Soviets to take full command of the negotiations. Sarkat had one order from his superiors: Neutralize the American lawyer Steven Klein. By putting the American in a deep hole, Sarkat had hoped to accomplish the objective subtly. He decided to try the ploy, however defused, anyway.

"Mr. Dunney, you can have these sites you say are better, if you will do the same."

"Guarantee volume?" Dunney was not surprised, but acted it. "You can't be serious, Mr. Sarkat." He calmed his voice ostentatiously. "Bingo Burgers would never ask your country to guarantee anything, and would not expect to be asked to do so itself. But if it is volume that you are worried about, we can solve the whole problem by using this composite plan."

At his signal, Andy produced a third map. As she spread it out on the table, Dunney admired his own handiwork. The map of Moscow had ten red crosses on it, three of which were in spots designated by the recent Soviet map, three of which were from Soviet's master original and four others placed where Dunney knew they would do the most good.

"This is completely different," Sarkat declared. "You have too many."

Dunney gave Andy another sign and she handed out drawings of the proposed restaurants. "These are a bit smaller than the originals submitted and about thirty percent less expensive to build. Seating space is about twenty percent less in each, but totaled there is more than the original proposal."

"Moscow cannot support so many small restaurants after the games are over," Sarkat objected.

"I realize that. Three of the units are knockdowns, which can be disassembled and added to the others to increase long-term space. It's a natural solution."

Sarkat looked at his colleague who shook his head. "Out of the question."

"There must be some appeal to you."

"Mr. Dunney, we must ask you to respect our choices."

Somber, Dunney asked, "In exchange for what, Secretary Sarkat. You have unilaterally established the sites. That is contrary to the express terms of the letter of intent. I respect your judgment, certainly, but I do not agree with it. If you respected Bingo Burger's judgment, as I have presented it to you, then you would be willing to discuss a compromise."

Christ, he thought, he was not a diplomat. Why not just come out with it? "Gentlemen. I'm willing to listen to anything you have on your minds. Bingo Burgers and," he stressed this part, "my firm are willing to entertain anything, to reach a satisfactory agreement. Anything."

"Our government is not inclined to deal with or through persons or organizations which are outspoken in their attitudes against our country." Sarkat placed both hands flat on the table. Having failed at subtlety, he went ahead with bluntness. "Your colleague, Mr. Klein, has put us in a difficult, very sensitive position."

Carefully, Dunney recited the words that he and Klein had composed in Boston. "I can assure you that Mr. Klein is only interested in seeing our client's agreements completed and signed. He is not clear in his understanding of your country's policies, but he is no longer involved in publicly questioning such policies."

The two Russians exchanged smiles. They stood up and collected Dunney's new map. "Give us a few days to review this new proposal, Mr. Dunney," Sarkat said, happily shaking the American's hand. His job had been saved. "If what you say is true, I think that we can make quick work of our negotiations."

"Good." Dunney gathered his papers, waited for Andy to do the same and led her out the door. "Please let me know as soon as you have studied the proposal."

Sarkat ushered Dunney and Andy out the door and into an official Muskovitz limousine. "Your flexibility is much appreciated, Mr. Dunney. I only wish that your government were so sensible."

"That's their business, Mr. Sarkat, not ours," Dunney said, as he closed the door. "Good-bye."

As the car pulled away, Andy made a face at him. "God, you crawl gracefully."

"Andy, please." Dunney did not need her criticism or anyone else's. He had merely done what he had had to do.

"It was disgusting."

He did not respond, but inside he mustered all the necessary arguments. It had been Klein's decision; the client comes first; he had a job to do, period.

Seething after being quiet so long, Andy could no longer contain herself. She had admired Dunney before, been attracted by his drive. Now, it was different. "Christ, how could you grovel like that. I thought that you were proud if nothing else."

His eyes hard and narrow, Dunney clipped his words. "If groveling gets the job done, I grovel. If you were my client, you can be damned sure that you'd demand that I kiss every fucking ass in town."

"Bullshit."

"We represent Bingo Williams, damn it. Represent! Do you understand that word? If Bingo doesn't give a shit for Mraisky, then I can't either. The same goes for Klein."

"Then he's an asshole too!" Andy turned away in a huff preferring the stark scenery outside.

Dunney grabbed her by the arm and jerked her around to face him. His nostrils flared and his jaw muscles worked as he said, "He's a damn professional. He's a great lawyer. Who the hell are you to criticize Steve Klein? He's a top man in his field, God damn it. I'll be lucky..." In the middle of the statement, Dunney stopped. What was he doing defending Klein?

"Andy," he began again, quietly this time, "please try to understand what my position is."

Rubbing her sore arm, Andy glared at him. She had no intention of understanding. "I don't know what you want, Chris, but you go ahead and get it."

For a moment, they looked at each other and then away. During the rest of the trip to the hotel, they said nothing either to one another or to the silent driver.

Clouds had begun to gather, threatening rain, darkening the sky. The temperature perceptively dropped even during the tense drive. By the time the limousine had reached the hotel and unloaded its passengers, the wind had picked up as well. Andy hurried inside without waiting for Dunney.

Dunney studied the sky, annoyed with the appropriateness of the sudden shift in its character. Just like Andy and his relationship, he thought. But how sudden had it been? Clouds take time to form, the temperature change was the result of a frontal movement that took days to reach them. Nothing happened without preconditions, without a suitable gestation period.

He turned around, looking for Andy and saw that she was already at the desk of the hotel. With a final glance at the weather, Dunney swung through the door and joined her. "Any messages for Dunney in 618?" he asked in hasty, slightly garbled Russian.

"I already asked," Andy responded in English. She handed him the three notes and headed for the elevator,

"If you need a secretary, give me a call."

Dunney watched her as she waited for the elevator. Without a sign of recognition in his direction, she stood there impatiently, shifting from one foot to the other. It took the elevator a long three minutes to open and remove her from the lobby.

He turned his attention to the messages. The first was from Winker, at the Embassy, requesting a report on the meeting with the Russians. The second, from Klein, was a confirmation of the arrangements for Bingo's speech. When he saw the third, Dunney's eyes opened wide.

"Please phone E. Krylenkev at the following number as soon as possible," it read in sturdy-handed Russian.

"A phone?" he asked the clerk.

"It is easier to use the one in your room, sir," the clerk responded, "They are all new."

"Thank you," Dunney said, as he strode to the staircase. "Thank you very much." He glanced quickly at his watch. Five fifteen, fairly early. He might still catch the enticing young Russian. He did not feel like whiling away the evening alone. And it promised to be a cold, rainy night.

~ ~ ~

The tiny reels spun wildly under Bellin's watchful eye. Folenya beamed as the Director stopped the rewind and played the tape over again. She felt that, finally, the so-called dissidents were going to make their move. Bellin would have to admit it and bring them all in. That would trigger the complete obliteration of the Helsinki watch committees, all over the Union.

The first ring had activated the recorder attached to the American's phone. Then came his hollow sounding voice, "Come on," exhorting the slow Russian phone service in English.

"Yes," was the response after eight rings. "Department of Economics, Moscow University."

Dunney's Russian reply was a firm, unexcited. "I would like to speak to one of your people. Elizaveta Krylenkev."

Without a word, the party who had answered left the line, which caused the recorder to stop, as indicated by the click on the tape. Immediately, a young woman's voice came in, "Elizaveta Krylenkev. Who's calling?"

"Dunney," the American's voice said simply.

The girl's voice quivered with nervousness. "Oh, Mr. Dunney," she said in rapid English. "Thank you for returning my call. I wanted to apologize for the way I acted the former day. At the hotel?" She was clearly tentative about the whole thing.

Bellin shook his head in disbelief as he listened. Were they really going to be so foolish? God, he hoped not. He could see in Folenya's eyes that she craved such a blunder.

"... enough so that I hardly noticed," Dunney was saying. "I appreciate your calling, but an apology is hardly necessary. I would like the chance to see you again under less crowded circumstances. My offer of the champagne still stands."

"Stands?" Although there may have been a moment's reflection on the idiom, her recorded voice chipped in immediately with, "Oh, yes. That's very nice of you. Is tonight too soon?"

Dunney's voice seemed to lose its even beat. "Too soon? That would be fine. What time? Can I pick you up?" The words came in a rush, but it may have been due to the voice-activated method of recording.

"Perhaps you could meet me," she replied anxiously. "We go a nice restaurant near the University all the time. You might enjoy seeing the way we aborigines eat."

"Dinner then? I can be there by seven, eight, whenever you like." Dunney sounded accommodating, without being pliant. "That is, assuming I can get a cab."

After a two-syllable laugh, Elizaveta said, "Eight is probably safer in that case. Just give the driver this address: Twenty-eight Vladivostok. It's called 'The Shashlik.'"

"Twenty-eight. Fine. I'm very happy we'll have a chance to talk."

"Me, too," she said. "I will wait for you there, Mr. Dunney."

"Chris," the American replied. "But we can sort that out at eight o'clock."

"Eight o'clock. Good-bye."

"Good-bye."

The tape played on. "Desk," the next voice said in Russian.

Dunney's voice instructed, "I will be going out this evening. If my secretary calls for me, please have her call me in the morning about nine."

"Yes, Mr. Dunney."

Bellin did not wait for the conversation to end, turning the machine off with a jabbing index finger. His lips pursed, he looked over at Folenya. She was too damned excited for his taste. "What do you think, Anna?"

"It will be tonight."

"I doubt it, but perhaps, they are more desperate than expected. They don't know how far along we are with the Mraisky case..."

"Not far enough." Folenya interrupted.

He indulged her with a smile. Folenya was becoming more and more difficult. She had maneuvered to replace Radnik as secretary of the Communist Party cadre in his own department. Coupled with her KGB position, that post gave her the clout to seriously interfere with his investigation.

"Anna, can you arrange to have the KGB send some plainclothes men to that restaurant?"

"I have already notified them. Six agents will be at your disposal. Four men and two women to make it look better," she informed him, proud of her efficiency.

Bellin lit a' cigar and thought about the potential problems. "Make certain that the table that the American and the girl get is properly placed."

"Absolutely."

"And post one uniformed KGB agent inside," he added quietly.

Folenya bolted out of her chair. "What? That'll give it away! They won't do anything!"

Trying to look thoughtful, Bellin said, "Not inside, no. But we have to keep the pressure on them. And it must be obvious. Then they will ignore the fact that when they leave, they will be surrounded by plainclothes KGB. You must have a cab there to pick them up with another of your men in it. If it seems, once inside the cab, that they are free from surveillance, then the girl will make the move."

Impressed with Bellin's logic, Folenya's face broke into a smile. Perhaps she had misjudged him. "I will make the arrangements right away."

Once Folenya had left the room, Bellin crushed out his cigar. It did not taste quite right. Stale or something. He lit another, slightly more satisfied. He just hoped that the girl knew a KGB stiff when she saw one.

~ ~ ~

"The KGB is right," Elizaveta remarked ruefully. "You both belong in asylums." She kicked a stone across the street.

Neither Torlas nor Volenko smiled. It was not, and had not been meant, as a joke. "We are very serious, girl," Torlas growled.

She snapped back, "I made the call, didn't I?"

Wearily, Volenko placed one hand on the shoulder of each. "Keep your tempers." He grimaced. "We left your office, Elizaveta, to avoid eavesdropping. Now you two want to shout in the streets."

After a moment, the other joined him in a smile. Torlas slapped his back with a "so we did," while Elizaveta squeezed his hand gratefully. The tension under which they had been living for a month eased a bit.

"Do you want me to sleep with him?" Elizaveta asked, her voice emotionless, her stomach tightening.

Grimly, Volenko replied, "If it comes to that."

"He's an American," Torlas joked. "It's bound to come to that."

She thought of herself as she had last viewed her reflection. Physically, she was nothing special, not like the kinds of women Americans liked. And in bed... Russian men were not like American men. The American would probably laugh at her. "I have to get him to want me first."

Torlas interjected, "We have given you the strategy, tactics are your department." After a sidelong glance at her, he added. "Mikhail and I have confidence in you."

After looking around them, Volenko confirmed that the KGB agents were far enough away to be out of earshot. "But it may not be wise to give in to him right away."

"Even I know that," she shot back. Did they think she liked the idea of giving herself to the American? If it hadn't been for the sake of Russia's Jews...

"There it is," Torlas announced pointing across the street to a small blue-painted storefront. "It doesn't look like a place of intrigue, does it?"

Taking a deep breath, Elizaveta started toward the restaurant. Volenko restrained her. "One thing more."

More? How could they have more planned for her and the American? She felt the weight of both men's eyes as she looked from one to the other. They appeared so horribly somber that their mere expressions frightened her. "Go on." she said.

Reluctantly, Volenko reached inside his pocket. He kept it there a second, pausing to give Torlas an inquiring glance. The Georgian nodded. "Nikolai has suggested a secondary plan." He took his hand from the coat and clasped hers.

Elizaveta opened her hand slowly, timidly. "Oh, my God." she whispered to herself. There is her palm lay a hundred rubles worth of hard currency, worth unimaginably more than normal rubles because they could be used in the special luxury stores. Elizaveta had not see so much "valula" since the day Mraisky had taken her to buy the blue jeans.

Volenko quickly closed her hand for her, hoping that the KGB had not seen too much. If they suspected, the trap for Dunney would never come off.

"It won't be difficult," Torlas was saying. "Just insist on paying for the dinner, the champagne, anything. Then tell him that you need some rubles in exchange for your hard currency. He won't even think about it."

Clasping both her hands, Volenko stared deeply into her wide eyes. "And then, if we must, we will blackmail him."

"Mikhail!" she cried, "You can't..."

Volenko clenched his teeth. He felt about it as she did, but he had no choice. "We must."

Chapter Seven

The back stairs at the Procuracy were dimly lit and treacherous. Bellin should have known better than to try them without a light, but he was preoccupied. Radnik, stung by his "demotion" and his loss of the Primary Secretariat, had suddenly quit. As Radnik had claimed, Folenya's report to the KGB had gotten to the Party as well. Radnik had actually been forced to resign the Party job by higher Party officials!

"There's no point in fighting, Vladimir," Radnik had angrily declared. "What good is your damned department if the KGB's running it..." Storming off, Radnik had refused even to say good-bye.

Bellin missed a step and almost tumbled down the second half of the narrow stairway. He caught his balance with the aid of a splintering handrail, which would cost him the effective use of his left hand for a week. The initial pain shaken off, he proceeded more carefully. Tightening the light bulb dangling above him at the foot of the stairs, Bellin shed light on what was a servants' hallway in tsarist days. As he took in the familiar hall, he chided himself for his rage at Folenya and "her" Party. How badly Russians must have lived if such a place was considered relatively luxurious by the workers and peasants? For all their faults, the Party fanatics worked very hard in the tradition of Lenin and his Bolsheviks.

After the revolution, the servants' quarters had been converted into a firing range. Few, if any, of his subordinates used the firing range and Bellin discouraged its use. He had usurped it as a private preserve. Shooting relaxed him, that often-felt jolt against his shoulder, the tingling in his arm, the smell of powder, the all-encompassing roar of the gun. In his village, Bellin had been one of the older boys and, therefore, one of those trained to use the few antiquated firearms not requisitioned for the war. He had first used it on a man at the age of nine.

Bellin unpacked his pistol, carefully unwrapping the gauze surrounding it. He removed the carton of bullets, set down the box and entered the firing range itself. With the door closed, the room was completely dark. For a few minutes, he remained in the darkness, forgetting everything that had come before. It was a trick he had learned early and had refined in the army security branch. It only worked for him now down in that secluded, darkened room; nowhere else could he maintain that kind of concentration.

The placement of the feet, shoulder width, came naturally still, after all the years away from formal training. He flicked the switch which activated the system.

After a moment's delay, a light bulb blinked on, illuminating the target for an instant. It was one of ten, each of which lit up one of the silhouette targets on the wall ten meters away. The bulbs lit in a sequence which Bellin knew so well that he often fired before the light flashed. It was a bad habit, a very bad habit, particularly when transferred to actual situations. One had to know what the target was and what part of it to hit.

Another bulb flashed and still Bellin stood without raising the gun. He had to compose himself. Radnik's resignation had caught him completely unprepared. The third light went off. Bellin cursed, positioned the heavy pistol in both hands, leveled the barrel and waited. When the fourth went off, so did Bellin's gun. He had aimed at the right arm, but, of course, would not know if he had hit it until afterward

His body timed the wait, though he was not conscious of it. His teeth tightened their grip on his cigar, crushing the tobacco. The smoke, with nowhere else to go, drifted thickly into his eyes, bringing them to tears. The next light came and went to the sound of two cracks of the gun. The left shoulder and left thigh. Was that right?

Bellin spit out the cigar and most of the loose tobacco. The sixth bulb came more quickly, but he was ready, firing one bullet, aimed he thought afterward, at one of the feet.

Seven and eight were almost together, getting one shot each. Bellin knew that he had fired eight before the lights had come on. The response was automatic. Again, he cursed.

With number nine, he fired noticeably before the light showed him where to shoot. When it lit the target, he could tell, but he lost the second needed to shoot the tenth and final target while illuminated. He had missed the light emptying the clip into the completely dark target.

"A fucking bastard!" he growled out loud. Bellin slammed the pistol down on the top of the support ledge and glared at the unseen targets.

Damn it! Why did Radnik quit? Bellin would have helped him ride out Folenya's storm. Radnik was his best. The only one who had any sense of, any feel for, the job. He and Radnik thought alike on the responsibility of being a Procurator's Investigator. Without them, the Procurator could not know, even if he wanted to, when a KGB man went too far. They had a mandate to keep things reasonable and honest. Radnik had been proud of that responsibility.

The room sprang to life, fluorescent tubes flickering to life in the ceiling. Bellin spun around and took a half step toward the intruder. A stunned Anna Folenya took a corresponding hall step back. Her eyes were fixed on the large gun poised in his hand.

"What do you want?" he snapped.

"It's good," she said, her voice weak, "that you keep up."

Bellin did not move. "What is it, Comrade Folenya?"

Folenya gulped at the title of address, which Bellin had almost never used with her. "It's the American and the woman, Krylenkev."

"What about them?"

"You said you wanted to be informed..."

He looked at her with unrestrained hostility. Bellin could have watched her die without remorse at that moment. "Not by you, Comrade," he retorted, pushing past her.

Shaken by the brutal shove, Folenya leaned against the wall and looked forward toward the target area. "Nice...," she began, conciliatory. When she saw Bellin was gone, Folenya gathered herself and went to inspect his targets. She had heard rumors about his marksmanship and, now, she wanted to see if he was, in fact, any good.

She started from the left, the first, and walked sideways to the left. "Ha, missed the first two," she said under her breath. The third he had almost missed completely. The fourth, only the right arm at the elbow. In the fifth, the shoulder and the upper leg. Squarely inside the target, but hardly dangerous shots. Six, the foot. What kind of shooting was that?

By the seventh and eighth target, however, Folenya began to respect Bellin's aim. Seven had a bullet square in the intestines, while eight showed one clean hole in mid-forehead.

So did number nine. Very nice shooting, she thought.

Mentally, she ran over Bellin's file, a growing file she knew by heart in every detail. She was not really surprised that he could handle a pistol. Bellin had been a member of an elite army security guard assigned to top ranking generals. He had undergone rigorous training, which, though he had never had to put to the test, he had obviously retained. He, and the others like him, could hit any part of the body if given time to aim. If not, of course, they had been drilled to shoot to kill. For a man like Bellin, it had been a reflex.

As she examined target number ten, Folenya wondered how much of that hard core training the Director had retained. Very little, she assumed, considering his soft living and easy understanding manner. Yet, he could still shoot. That tenth target was really quite impressive. The new target paper had suffered multiple entries in a two-inch square area dead in the middle of what would be the head. It made for quite a dangerous looking hole.

~ ~ ~

The Shashlik Restaurant, Dunney found, lay only a few minutes' walk from the main part of the University where the cab driver ran out of gas. The driver had gotten out with Dunney nonchalantly, said, "It's over there," and flagged another car. After putting in his request for help, the cab driver looked at the American and added, "It happens. The gage is not very accurate."

Dunney hesitated. The other car had not yet left. "Do you need help?"

The cab driver chuckled. "They will go for me as soon as you are inside." He came closer and whispered. "The KGB."

"What?"

"There are so many of them, they have to do something."

With a parting glance at the KGB car, Dunney set off for the Shashlik Restaurant. Perhaps, he thought, he should have expected it. He was dining with one of Mraisky's compatriots. The feeling crept in on him that he had made a serious mistake. He was not dealing with a private company in Moscow, but the government itself. He should not have been socializing with its opponents. "Socializing?" he asked himself. Poor choice of words.

Still, he decided not to turn back, if only because he had no transportation. Riding with the KGB did not seem a viable alternative.

As he neared the Shashlik, he quickened his step to keep pace with his racing pulse. Admittedly, he had known that the girl was a dissident when he had accepted her invitation to dinner. Indeed, it had only made her more attractive, the invitation more alluring. To stop now would serve to make him look foolish, nothing more. He could not back down now that he was thirty yards from the rendezvous.

Settled, Dunney slowed down, straightened his tie, shifted his vest and ran his hand through his hair. He checked his shoes, flexed both hands and cleared his voice. Only the latter made him aware of what he was doing. "Laugh at yourself, Dunney," he said. "Before someone else does."

The facade of the two-story concrete building was a peeling blue storefront, with large, partly broken windows covered by lean white curtains. The name, The Shashlik, was printed crisply on the wooden door. It meant, according to the cab driver, something the rough equivalent of a shish kabob. From the outside, it presented little promise. The few places in which Dunney had eaten in Moscow had been the show places of the city designed for foreigners. Squaring his shoulders, Dunney prepared for a new experience. Perhaps several new experiences.

He gently turned the handle on the door. Nothing happened. He tried again. It was locked. For a moment, he did not quite know what to do. Finally, he knocked, lacking an alternative. He scanned the street to see if anyone had noticed his strange act and found it sparsely populated. Even the KGB had deserted the area.

About to knock again, Dunney found himself looking into the broad, forbidding face of a doorman. A bouncer? he wondered. The doorman shook his head at first, but after looking Dunney up and down rudely, he grinned and opened the door. In a gruff, but genial Russian, he said, "I'm sorry, sir. We are booked and I didn't notice that you were American."

"Common mistake," Dunney said in casual Russian. It was, in fact, a mistake he had not yet encountered in the whole of Moscow. He often felt like Clinton Thomas in his red, white and blue track suit. "I was to meet a young lady here tonight, I'm sure she has reservations."

The doorman waved away the comment about reservations. "We have plenty of room. One meal over our quota won't hurt." The man was thrilled to have an American businessman in the restaurant. Motioning for Dunney to follow, he led the way out of a small, square entryway, decorated mostly with coat racks. Beyond that lay a large floor with a long plain bar on one side, a stand on the other and a dance floor in the middle. Tables and chairs filled the rear and the semi-circular balcony of a second floor.

"Dancing after nine o'clock," his guide mentioned as they walked by the bandstand. "American music," he added happily. "Elton John, Rolling Stones."

"Very American," Dunney agreed.

Once they had gotten back among the well lit tables, he picked out the girl, Elizaveta Krylenkev–he was getting good at it–sitting alone at a table, but hardly isolated. All around her, the tables were full, though a good part of the restaurant was empty. It was hardly surprising to

Dunney that the place did so little business, with the damn door locked.

"This is your girl?" the doorman asked when Dunney stopped at Elizaveta's table. An American businessman with her? There would be no dancing for them, he decided. When he saw her eyes widen as the two exchanged one word greetings, however, the doorman changed his mind. "Perhaps," he said to himself.

"Pardon?" Dunney asked.

"Dancing, nine o'clock," he said simply, grinned, and went back to his position near the door.

He left in his wake an awkward pause. Dunney, still on his feet, could not figure out a way to sit down gracefully.

It was a distorted view from his perspective, but, Dunney thought, a damn nice one. She wore a thin red sweater over one of those ubiquitous print blouses and tucked into a pair of new blue jeans. By American standards, at least, she looked the part of a college girl. She had pulled her medium brown hair back behind her ears and secured it there with a pair of gold-tone clips, beyond which it exploded into hundreds of tight curls. With her face inclined upwards, the lines of her jaw and narrow chin were accentuated. Her mouth was slightly parted in a smile that pulled the upper lip just to the top of her teeth. The nose, rounded at the tip, was otherwise straight, short and a touch broad, sloping toward very rounded cheek bones. Above that lay her wide-set, glistening brown eyes.

The sum of the parts, he decided did not equal the whole effect, beauty.

She knew he was studying her and felt a tightness grip her as she watched his expression. He had a gently rounded face, with the remnant of American boyishness in its hint of an upturned nose, half smiling thin mouth and excited, darting eyes. What did he think of her? His expression betrayed no disappointment, but...

"Aren't you going to invite me to sit down?" he asked in light Russian, finally breaking the brief, but intense, silence.

She responded in English. "Is that American?"

He brushed his lower lip with his little finger. "Yes, I guess it is," he replied in American idiom, sitting down. "We'd better settle the language question first, Elizaveta."

The perfect pronunciation of the name forced her to smile. "Names first. Yours is Christopher?"

Dunney caught himself before saying that everyone called him "Chris." His full name sounded far better, coming as it did in her mingled British-Russian accent. Oddly enough, he had never liked it much before. "Yes. Your English is excellent, Elizaveta. Is it as hard for you as Russian is for me?"

"I have taken it since I was a girl, along with some others. English has always been my favorite." She blushed. "After Hebrew."

It had not yet occurred to Dunney that Elizaveta would be a Russian Jew. But, of course, Mraisky was. And she knew Klein.

Seeing his expression change, Elizaveta suddenly regretted the gratuitous mention of her adopted "native" language. As quickly, she reacted against the regret. "Is something wrong with Hebrew?"

Recovering, he said easily, "Hell, yes. I don't speak a word of it. I think I'd prefer either Russian or English, if you don't mind."

Was he making fun of her? she wondered. It did not matter if he were. He would not be able to in Russian. "English is a strain for me."

"Russian it is," he replied immediately, in Russian. "But you'll have to make allowances. Don't leap to the conclusion that I am a bore based on what I say. Give me a chance to correct it. Agreed..."

Even in Russian, he was a facile talker, she fretted. "All right."

"Good. Now, do they have champagne in this place?"

"No. Just wine and vodka," she said, gesturing to the lone waiter.

Dunney feigned disappointment. Actually, he was rather pleased. "We can go for that later."

The opening appeared so suddenly that Elizaveta stuttered. "I... I would like to pay... I mean, I want you to be my guest."

"Don't be silly."

Anxiously, she put her hand on his. "Please." Aware of the contact, she withdrew hers abruptly. "I was very rude to you. And you're a guest in Moscow. Please."

Dunney felt embarrassed. What was the polite thing to do, in Moscow? "Elizaveta, I appreciate your offer, but you really shouldn't. I'm on an expense account and..."

"It's not important, the money. I would just feel better. You can get the champagne." She queasily felt for the valula in her pocket. "One bottle will cost more than this whole meal," she added forcing a laugh.

After thinking it over for a minute or so, studying her anxious face all the while, Dunney gave in. If he had his way, it would not be their last meal together. "This time, all right. But in return, I want to decide how much champagne offsets this dinner. One night's may not be enough."

Something in his voice frightened her. No, it was her response to that voice that worried her. He was being wonderfully kind to her. Maybe he would help their cause without...

The waiter suddenly appeared beside her, prompting Dunney to ask, "What do you recommend, Elizaveta?"

He let her order, listening to her nervous voice, enjoying her mannerisms, drifting away from his last mental caveat: His career, his whole life turned on this Moscow trip. What would the Russians think of this wining and dining of a Jewish dissident? What would the firm think? And Klein?

She grew more animated, her voice less wobbly, as she ran through the several courses. From time to time, she looked over at him for approval. It didn't matter: She had it. He had no idea what she was ordering him. It could have been anything. He knew nothing about native Russian dishes. As the waiter left, he asked with a mock plaintive tone, "What are you getting me into, Elizaveta?"

"Just an average Muscovite dinner, Christopher. I'll warn you about anything dangerous before you eat it."

"Thanks." He looked around the restaurant. "Is it always this empty?"

"The Shashlik? Oh, no. It will get crowded later, but it is near the end of the month," she explained. "I ordered wine..."

"Hold it." Dunney interrupted. "I don't understand what you meant about the 'end of the month' What has that to do with how crowded a place is? Are people out of money?"

She gave him a blank look for a moment, before saying, "They would exceed their quota for meals if they did not limit reservations. That's all right once in a while, but to do it consistently would make the planners raise the quota."

The waiter, an old man with a mild limp, brought their wine, in a finger-smudged carafe. The two glasses, one of which had a crack in the base, had the cloudy appearance of inadequately washed glass. The waiter left it to Dunney to pour, which he did to a level less than halfway up the glasses.

"Is something wrong?" she asked observing his reluctance to fill the glass. "We can drink as much as we want."

With an amused nod, Dunney pushed the level of the wine near the brims. He decided that it might be prudent to leave any toasting to Elizaveta.

"We have to drink to something," she said, hesitant to propose anything. They had such different customs. That gave her an idea. "To diversity of cultures."

Raising his glass to hen, Dunney added, "And to their free exchange." Their glasses touched quietly and each drank watching the other. Dunney felt that the ice, which should have been broken by that first drink, had barely begun to melt. "Have you always lived in Moscow?"

The suddenness of the question jarred Elizaveta. It recalled the abrupt manner of the Investigator from the Procurator's office. She did not like questions, for there was always something behind them. "Yes."

Her monosyllabic answer to a simple question alerted Dunney to drop his interrogative style. His natural inclination was to get answers quickly, to challenge and verify them when he got them. It had never served to augment his popularity. Consciously, he took another approach; he did not want to scare this girl off before he had the chance to know her. "I haven't seen as much of the city as I would like to have, but so far, I like it. It's an exotic mix of old and new, isn't it?" Trite and harmless, he thought.

The obvious switch in Dunney's manner put Elizaveta more at ease. She remained tense enough, however, trying as she was to please the American. To win him. To betray him. The wine helped soothe her nerves and she resorted to it often, refilling it as he looked on.

"You've been busy, Christopher?" she asked swallowing the first gulp of the second glass with difficulty. "I remember you said..."

"Forget what I said that night," he cut in. "Please. But, yes, I have been busy." He took several minutes describing what he had been doing since arriving in Moscow, who he worked for and what he hoped to achieve. "It's not earthshaking, Elizaveta, but it is my first real professional opportunity."

The way he had presented it, Elizaveta felt a certain excitement about his work. He was taking on the Soviet government, meeting it as an equal, arguing with it. Trying to fool it. Suddenly, she looked at him with a measure of respect. "Can you really do that? Make the government agree with you?"

"If I am any good, Elizaveta, I will convince them that they need Bingo Burgers restaurants." He smiled. "And I think I am."

He spoke almost casually about facing up to the greatest government on earth. Elizaveta had never heard such an attitude in all of her life. They all had hoped in opposing the government. Hope. But Christopher Dunney had that and more. He had confidence. She knew then, that if she could make him see, he would help her.

"In any case, that is what I do," he said. "I already know a little bit about you, but not as much as I would like to." Dunney stopped there, afraid to press her too hard. "But you don't have to tell me anything, if you don't want to. I probably wouldn't understand any of it anyway. Would I?"

~ ~ ~

The dinner between the Krylenkev girl and the American, Dunney, had proved singularly uneventful, much to Bellin's satisfaction and Folenya's dismay. They sat side by side in the monitoring room listening to the conversation through a microphone miraculously placed on the table itself.

"A thin disk," Folenya had reported, "under the tablecloth."

In any case, the listening device allowed them to eavesdrop on the entire meal, including the clanking of plates, the tapping of flatware and the thud of fall carafe of wine squarely on top of the sensitive disk. "No problem." Folenya had announced proudly, as proved to be the case: The mike went on working perfectly.

After it became clear that the music now being played by a live band would effectively drown any conversation, Folenya stopped taking notes. She was still convinced that the exchange would take place and was crushed that she and Bellin would not be able to hear it happen.

Bellin had his feet up on one of the chairs, which he had shifted around for the purpose. He puffed away on his fourth cigar of the evening as he listened to the music and the occasionally shouted phrases of Elizaveta and Dunney. At the same time, he kept an eye on the monitor keyed in on Andy Wards' room. The American girl had left not half an hour ago for, what the KGB told them, was a walk around the square.

His main attention, however, focused inward where he mulled over the bits and pieces of personality revealed by Dunney, Elizaveta Krylenkev and, for that matter, by Andrea Wards. Though uneventful, the two hours of monitoring told him things about the people involved, things that the dossiers could not.

The conversation between Dunney and Elizaveta started slowly, as the two of them searched for safe topics. Certain taboos were established immediately. Her Jewishness; her cause; his colleague, Klein; his relationship with the Wards girl. The few times those topics arose by mistake, one or the other reacted strongly either offensively or defensively.

With the second carafe of wine loosening them up, they revealed themselves to each other, to Bellin, subtly but generously. Elizaveta told Dunney minor stories about her parents, which plainly indicated a strongly emotional relationship currently skewed toward rejection of the mother. She went to greater lengths to express her philosophy, of the human need for moral guidance, and her desire to play a role in providing it, which, as she put it, necessitated her emigration from the Soviet Union.

Dunney, for his part, gently queried her about her childhood, giving some of his own to prod her. Though she consistently repulsed the effort, Dunney persisted, giving Bellin a fair reading of Dunney's own.

Raised in Boston, Dunney had been the youngest of six children, the youngest by seven years. The closest sibling to his age was the sister, Cathy, while all his brothers had been far older. By the time, Dunney started school, his brothers had already gone off to work or to college, while the sister had apparently recently made the transition to adolescence. If Dunney had been left in the cold, however, he had grown used to it. The rest of the American's talk centered upon how he was going to carve out a place for himself in his profession, a profession that, he had made clear, meant nothing in particular to him.

It was not much, of course, but coupled with the dossiers he had–the one on Dunney had grown considerably since the hiring of an American private detective–the information would help Bellin anticipate. And that was the nature of the game. Bellin had to move before they did, to discourage them if possible. The KGB continued to emphasize how important it was to prevent the document, the tape, from falling into American hands, but that insistence seemed tainted by the growing intrusion of Folenya into his Department's affairs. Folenya, wanting more to crush the dissidents than to stop them, seemed to have powerful elements in the KGB and the Party behind her. He dared not give her and her backers an excuse.

Movement on one of the monitors caught his eye. The American girl had returned to her room. She was not alone this time. A tall thin black man, attired in one of those American track uniforms followed her, tentatively, into the room.

Beside him, Bellin heard Folenya express disapproval. "What's the matter, Anna?"

"Americans are disgusting," Folenya replied harshly. "Disgusting."

Addressing her expectations, Bellin said, "Anna, nothing has happened yet. Look, she is just offering him a drink. Give us some more sound."

The technician leaned forward and Andrea Wards' voice spoke over the sound of the Shashlik's music. "All I have is vodka, Clint. Is that Okay?"

"Fine," Clinton Thomas replied, standing nervously in the middle of the room.

Her back to him, Andy asked, "Do you always run around in the middle of the night?"

Thomas smiled and did a little step, "Hey, it's safer here than Watts." He laughed and she joined him.

"As long as you don't attack the embassy." She held a couple of small glasses and a pint of vodka when she turned back toward him.

Thomas took his glass when offered and sat down when she did. "I was kind of wondering if that's what you were doing out there. You know, maybe you like getting searched."

The comment brought a look from Andy that made Folenya cough. "I was feeling a little lonely, that's all," Andy said.

"I didn't have much to do myself." Thomas took a hefty gulp of vodka and leaned back, trying to relax. "It was nice to run across another American out there."

"I can't tell you how much I agree with that." Noticing that Thomas' glass was near empty, she asked, "More?"

The athlete drained the rest of his vodka and held out the glass. "Why not? You're buying."

Andy stood up and got the bottle. She sat down again right next to Thomas, very close, and leaned over to fill the glass again. "Here you are. You can have as much as you want." After she had put the bottle down on the floor, she ran her hand over his thigh. "You have such long, thin legs, Clint. How do you run so fast?"

A rhetorical question, Bellin thought. He re-lit his cigar and took a few lame puffs. By the time Clinton Thomas had run his hand all the way up the inside of the girl's leg, Bellin said, "All right. We don't have to watch everything."

"What?" Folenya demanded. "We're supposed..."

"Kill it," he ordered the technician. "It does not serve our purpose to watch people making love, Anna. Besides, our main business is with Dunney and the Krylenkev girl. Give us more volume on that one."

~ ~ ~

Simpson's scrawl was all but unreadable. Kyle squinted, held the paper to the reading lamp and finally gave up. He said to the ambassador's secretary, "Show him in, whoever the hell it is."

Kyle checked his watch. It read just after nine. He balanced the pile of intelligence reports on one knee while he reached for his snifter on the floor. The brandy trickling down his throat helped him to forgive the imposition of the later caller. The fellow had come from State on a diplomatic visa, that much Simpson's note had made clear.

The door inched a sharp shadow across the carpet of the Ambassador's study. A mumbled direction from the secretary preceded the further opening of the door. The visitor stood outlined in the doorway, his feet spread more than shoulder width. All very mysterious, Kyle thought with contempt.

"Mr. Kyle," his voice said quietly, "how nice to see you again."

Not moving, Kyle swirled brandy in the glass. "It would be nice to see you, too. Unfortunately, it's dark in here."

The figure approached with an even stride, an attaché case swinging loosely at his side. "May I sit down?"

Kyle motioned to the seat opposite him. The intentional intrigue of his guest had begun to annoy him. "You're from State?"

As he sat, the man said, "Yes." Once the light hit his face, he added, "McDeamon decided you needed an aide."

"Mac what?" Kyle almost dropped his snifter, at the mention of CIA Director's name. As it was he spilled most of the contents on his jacket. "Greenwald?"

"At your service," Greenwald said officiously. He had never liked Kyle and enjoyed putting him on.

"I thought they'd thrown you out!"

"The Ruskies? Oh, they revoked my visa as a reporter. But then Mac got me a new one through State."

Kyle made a variety of gestures before being able to put together the words. "McDeamon? We should he want you here?"

Greenwald made a show of opening his diplomatic "pouch" and handing several documents to Kyle. It proved very satisfying to him to put the overbearing CIA operative in his place. "I'm an important man. Isn't that the gist of it?"

A speed-reader, Kyle scanned the pages gleaning the needed information in a minute. "Not really." The documents related nothing new. The Administration was having increasing difficulty juggling Save-Soviet-Jewry pressure, Senate efforts to scuttle the SALT Revision talks and reelection plans. "All this crap over Mraisky? Christ, who cares?"

"The President," Greenwald replied. "Does he count?"

"Mind your manners, Greenwald," Kyle snapped. "You're still under me in this country. Understand?" He read on, turning. "Jesus. Now they want to arrest a couple KGB boys working out the Soviet Embassy. 'For exchange potential' Amateurs."

Eying the brandy, Greenwald asked, "Do you have any more of that, or is the stain there the last of it?"

Trying to control himself, Kyle laughed. He was a pro, after all, and could get along with anybody the amateur McDeamon sent his way. Besides, it was funny, his spilling the brandy. He got up and poured Greenwald a drink. "Sorry we couldn't make some noise in your favor, Sy. When your visa was pulled. But Washington didn't want any further contact with the dissidents by Company men. If we had lifted a finger, it would have looked suspicious and might have damaged Mraisky's chances."

"What chances!" Greenwald scoffed. "You can't seriously think he has a chance. Washington doesn't harbor any illusions."

"No."

Sipping the brandy, Greenwald raised his eyebrows. "This is very good stock. Does the Ambassador know who's raiding his cellar?"

Kyle did not answer. The Ambassador was the last person in the world who worried him. Instead, he contemplated the new development. What earthly good could Greenwald or he do Mraisky? Everyone knew Mraisky was cooked, why send Greenwald to Moscow? Was he more than he appeared? "I take it you're my resident Mraisky expert."

"Dissident expert," Greenwald corrected him. "I know all of the top people in the Moscow Group. Mac wants me to distill any information you get on either Mraisky or the rest of the Group."

"And how do we get it? We can't get within a hundred yards of those people now without marrying into the KGB."

"I thought you had."

Kyle sighed. Greenwald knew too much about his operation and he did not like it. McDeamon had taken a mighty big chance with the CIA in Russia. Greenwald, after all, was a reporter. "The KGB has a very select group working on the dissidents. And the top people from the Militia, operating under the Procurator's Department of Investigation, are all over the place. I have never seen anything like it. They are intentionally scaring us off. It's no trap. The word is simply 'stay away' and that's what we're doing."

Draining the snifter, Greenwald remembered his own experience. "Yeah. I got that message myself."

"But you're back."

"Only until Mraisky goes on trial," he said ruefully. "Once that happens, I'm pretty useless. Got any more brandy?"

Kyle sprang up. The conversation livened his evening, as shop talk always did. He was more generous the second time around with the brandy. "The word at the KGB is that the pressure is on the Procurator of Moscow to get his ass in gear. Bellin, he's the Director of Investigation..."

"I met him."

"Really? He's a good one, they tell me," Kyle said. "The folks at the KGB think he's playing politics with this case. Either that or he's just anti-KGB."

Conjuring the Russian's face in his mind, Greenwald dismissed both possibilities. "He's just careful. What were you saying about him?"

"Oh, that's right. They say he's dragging his heels. The Procurator doesn't like to indict without Bellin's okay, but he may have to this time."

"Does Mac know that?"

"If he reads his mail."

Troubled, Greenwald rose and paced for a minute. It made no sense. Why the haste? The Soviets had taken months to bring Shcharansky to trial. Some of the others still had to come up. Why hurry Mraisky's? Clearly, they had no confession, because Bellin was not satisfied. Maybe Bellin was dabbling in politics. No, Greenwald did not like that scenario. Bellin had seemed genuinely uninterested in palace maneuvering.

"I don't get it, Kyle."

"Neither do I," the CIA man replied smiling. "So what? If we're supposed to know, we'll find out. Until then, relax."

Glaring at his briefcase, Greenwald said, "I can't quite yet. Is the economic attaché, Winker, around?"

Surprised, Kyle stood. "Winker? John Winker? What do you want with him..."

"When Mac gave me all this shit, he had something State wanted me to give Winker. He didn't know what it was."

"That's a laugh. Mac an errand boy."

"He did not like it. Grumbled something about bureaucratic stupidity."

"Typical of a bureaucrat," Kyle replied, half amused. "I wish to hell we had a pro in that job again."

Typical pro, Greenwald thought. He knew that Kyle and

the other career men in the CIA disliked McDeamon for his political purpose as head of the "Company", which was to "clean it the hell up". Greenwald had found McDeamon a compelling personality with the right ideas for the job. Mac was a skeptic, without being cynical. Kyle, on the other hand, was too cynical to question his own motivation. Perhaps he had to be.

"Winker lives off-grounds." Kyle explained. "I suggest you wait until he comes in tomorrow morning."

"Mac said State wanted this package of data delivered immediately," Greenwald said. "How tough is it to get around?"

Shrugging, Kyle tightened his smoking jacket. "I'll have one of the cars take you. It's not far, but there's no point in fighting with that patrol out front any more than you have to."

"Thank you."

Kyle put his hand on Greenwald's shoulder. "Listen, Sy. I'm an old hand at this business. We old hands sometimes get annoyed with amateurs. Don't let it bother you. Okay?"

Though he did not expect to be in Moscow long, Greenwald knew that friction between Kyle and him would make it seem like an eternity. He could put up with him for a while. "Fine."

"Good. Now, you deliver Johnny's package," Kyle instructed. "and hurry back for another bottle of brandy."

With a nod, Greenwald went on his way.

Using the phone, Kyle ordered the car for the reporter and waited at the window until it had left. Damn strange, the way Greenwald turned up. He wondered briefly what in God's name he could have so important if it were going to Winker. Nothing happened overnight in Winker's business. Economics? Bullshit, pure bullshit.

He turned his mind to more significant matters. "Now, which brandy should I open next?"

~ ~ ~

By ten, the Shashlik had livened up to a point at which another couple joined Dunney and Elizaveta at their table. No conversation was necessary and none was possible. The band, an assortment of youngsters with western-looking instruments. including at least one electric guitar and an eight-piece drum set, boomed its music in increasing decibels. The dance floor, situated directly in front of the band, supported over two dozen gyrating couples in close quarters.

Breathless and nursing a headache, Dunney pulled Elizaveta off the floor in the middle of a strange Russian version of an ABBA tune from three years before. On the way back to the table, he almost lost her twice. Before they sat down again, he pulled her close to him and shouted in her car, "Let's get out of here," in English.

To his surprise, she shook her head. She had originally refused to dance at all. Dunney, though not fond of the activity–he had acquired the skill only to establish himself at firm social gatherings–had insisted. And now, she did not want to quit, despite the fact that she was not particularly enjoying it. "Come on, Elizaveta. I'm getting..."

Elizaveta jerked away and sat down resolutely. If they were to leave, then she would have to pay for the dinner. She was not ready for that, not yet. She nudged the second male at the table, indicated the dance floor and left Dunney to his own devices.

Alone at the table, the other girl having disappeared into the ladies' room fifteen minutes earlier, Dunney watched the crowd gobble up Elizaveta and her new partner. Across the room, he noticed several couples heading for the door. He decided that if Elizaveta wanted to stay and dance with just anybody, he could at least grab some fresh air.

Fighting his way through the jumping, wriggling dancers, Dunney made it out the door in less than two minutes. He let the doorman know that he would be back and escaped through the door. No sooner had he emerged from the restaurant, than a cab squealed to a halt and offered him a ride to his hotel.

"No, thanks. Not at the moment." He thought with a tinge of annoyance of Elizaveta and her new-found energy and added, "But if you're around in a few minutes..."

Hurriedly, the driver said, "I can wait."

Giving the man a small tip, Dunney strolled off down the street, enjoying the solitude. He went so far as to light one of the Winston's he carried to hand out to Russian functionaries to encourage their cooperation. Normally, Dunney did not smoke, but on that occasion, the moment seemed right. His first two drags took him a couple blocks away.

"Pardon, Sir," a heavily accented voice said in English. "Can I bum one of them?"

Startled, Dunney turned to find a familiar man walking up behind him. He was from the table right beside Dunney's. "Why not?"

The Russian accepted the Winston and bent forward for the light. "I saw you go. I needed a rest from the sound."

"I know what you mean."

The two of them walked on together. "You are American. Mind if I practice English?"

Not pleased to have company, Dunney nonetheless accepted the burden of the ambassador of good will. "Sounds like you don't need much practice."

Brightening, the interloper introduced himself. "Gregor Vasiliavich Fedranoi."

"Christopher Dunney."

The man, Fedranoi, offered his hand and squeezed Dunney's hand firmly. He was an average looking Russian fellow, average height, weight, complexion. Even in the dark, however, his face betrayed a certain level of alertness beyond the normal. For the first time, Dunney wondered if he had been followed.

"Nice girl," Fedranoi said. "Your girl?"

Remembering that Elizaveta was not an ordinary Russian girl by any means, Dunney kept his reply short. "She's a good dancer."

"Ah."

Having traversed a third block, Dunney stopped, puffed twice and began back. "Going back in?"

Fedranoi smiled and fell in beside him. "You are missed," he said, pointing ahead.

In front of the Shashlik, Elizaveta stood looking quickly first one way, than the other. When she saw the two men, she took two sudden steps and stopped. Behind her, one of Fedranoi's companions peered out of the door.

Dunney kept his voice expressionless. "Looks like you were missed, too, Gregor. You'd think that with all of those people in there, we'd be able to get a few moments' peace, wouldn't you?"

In an entirely different tone, Fedranoi retorted, "Some of us are much more noticeable than others. An American, for example, will always stick out in a crowd." His rough accent gave way to perfect English diction.

Elizaveta waited impatiently for Dunney's return. She had initially panicked over his departure. Once she had seen him, down the street, she had felt better. As he and the other man approached, however, her sense of fear returned. It was the man from the table near them. Had he followed Dunney? Or had Dunney gone out with him? By the time both men came into the light of the restaurant's window, she was sure that the other man was with the KGB.

Uncertain, Elizaveta rushed into Dunney's unprepared arms and kissed him. "I was so afraid you'd left me."

Dunney's automatic response was to enclose her, pressing her to him. Considering that her action was what he had hoped for ultimately, he decided to kiss her back. She stiffened at the touch of his lips. "Not in public. Elizaveta," he said, in mock embarrassment.

She shot Fedranoi a look and turned back to Dunney. "Can we go for a walk?"

"My legs are going to get pretty tired," he objected. "But, all right. Excuse us, Gregor."

Fedranoi said, his accent back in full force, "By all means."

As they retraced his earlier steps, Elizaveta whispered "He's KGB, I know it."

Dunney put his arm around her waist, glancing back suspiciously. "He's watching," he whispered back, even though Fedranoi had gone inside. "Relax. Make it look convincing."

Elizaveta arched around to look, saw no one in sight and broke away. "You're making fun of me."

Holding his hand out to her, he said, "Not at all. Come on." When she did not respond, he shrugged. "Okay, but you kissed me first. Now in the United States…"

"I only did that so we could get away from him."

Dunney laughed. "All right." He ostentatiously put his left hand, the one towards Elizaveta, in his pocket. "Why did he follow me out like that, Elizaveta?"

"You're with me." Perhaps, she thought it was best to talk about it, to avoid the currency change. "Christopher, you know I'm not a very desirable person for you to be with. "

"That's a double question."

"You know what I mean, though." His statement flattered her and she felt faint warmth spreading, coloring her face. "I am very serious."

Dunney sidestepped a bit closer to her. "I know you are, Elizaveta. You're a very serious woman."

Talking to him proved hard. It was so easy. "You said the other night that you didn't want to jeopardize your business. Being seen with me…"

"That might hurt, yes. I've worried about that."

Elizaveta stopped and faced him. She felt his eyes holding her own. Automatically, she placed both hands against his chest, neither pushing nor pulling, or perhaps doing both. "You don't want to help us, Christopher, and you can only hurt yourself. I think we should go back."

She turned to go, but Dunney held both her hands.

"Christopher, listen to me," she said sternly. "I have things I have to do. Dangerous things. Things the government won't like. Everything I believe in… If you are an intimate of mine…" The thought slipped out, but did not embarrass her as she had thought it would.

"Even an acquaintance will be compromised. It isn't fair to you."

How could someone so lovely compromise his efforts? It was unimaginable. Unimaginable, but true. "It isn't fair to my client, perhaps. Don't worry about me."

Elizaveta tore her hands away from him in frustration. What was she doing? Worrying about being fair to him? He did not care at all what happened to her, to anyone! Her hand felt for the valula in her right hand pocket. She would have no trouble going through with it now.

"Come on, Christopher," she said, hiding her anger. "You must go now."

"Elizaveta..."

"Please. There's a cab. I'll pay..."

"Don't be silly. And what about our champagne?"

She ignored him. "I will pay the bill as we agreed." Elizaveta remembered the offer of champagne, and all of its romantic overtones. She also remembered the second part of her task: To seduce the American to her cause. She softened her voice. "The champagne. There is champagne at your hotel, isn't there?"

"Yes, there certainly is."

Elizaveta walked more closely beside him. "That is convenient," she observed warmly. "But, Christopher, you must let me pay for our dinner. That is my only condition."

~ ~ ~

The technician flicked the switch controlling the camera in Room 468. No one appeared in the small living room. "They're still in the bedroom, Director Bellin."

Bellin checked his fly before sitting down. His only break from Folenya came when he used the john. Settling back into his chair, he decided to take advantage of the facility more often. "Turn it off."

Taking her usual voluminous notes, Folenya made a sound of disapproval.

"What is it, Anna?"

"We should at least tape it."

"For the love of God, Anna, why?" Bellin asked. "It's enough that we observe such activities when necessary."

"It is necessary," she pouted.

Sharply, Bellin replied, "I make that decision, Anna."

Folenya said nothing, keeping her derogatory thoughts to herself. As Primary Secretary, she would have the right to question such a decision, to bring it to the attention of the Party hierarchy. There was no question in her mind that Bellin was not pursuing the dissidents vigilantly and would not do so without pressure from the KGB and the Party. Now that she had Radnik's old job as Primary Secretary, Folenya knew she had the ears of both and could afford to wait until Bellin proved, overtly, just how soft on the dissidents he was.

After a minute, she said, "The American and Krylenkev returned while you were out."

"Has that blasted music stopped?"

The technician answered, "This is the last number before a ten minute break, Director."

Relieved, Bellin resumed his feet-up position and re-lit his cold cigar. "My ears are killing me."

"We have to turn up the volume to hear the conversation." Folenya reminded him gratuitously. "Certainly, we cannot afford to turn that off."

Bellin blew smoke in her direction in response. He had fallen into a fairly neutral mood since rebuking her earlier and dismissed her jibes. "There are such things as filters, my dear Anna. I'd've thought that the KGB would have them."

"We do," the technician noted. "In fact I have one on now. They just aren't effective enough when the music is so loud."

As they all strained to listen, Elizaveta shouted over the music, "Any minute now, we can leave. I told the doorman to send the waiter. When the music is over."

The band swung into what was obviously a finale of the set. The drummer burst into a thunderous solo ending with a loud thwack. Dropping the sound level, the technician nodded. "That's it for now."

Swinging his feet to the floor, Bellin leaned forward in anticipation. He wondered what the two subjects had discussed while outside the restaurant. Perhaps, Anna had been right and they were about to make an exchange. He heard Folenya shift positions as well and forced himself to appear relaxed.

The waiter's voice was the first one to come through. "Your bill, sir."

"Come back in a minute," Elizaveta said.

After a pause, during which the waiter must have left, she said to Dunney, "Oh, dear. This is higher than I thought."

"Don't worry, Elizaveta, I have plenty of..."

"No, no. I have money, but I have to have it changed. They won't take this."

"What?"

"Hard currency."

Bellin sat up, took the cigar out of his mouth and listened intently.

"Do you have enough rubles, Christopher?" Elizaveta was asking. "If you change these for me, then we can go have the champagne."

What was she doing? Bellin jumped out of his chair and took up a place beside the speaker.

"I can use this in those special shops?" Dunney asked.

"Waiter," the girl called. "Give me a hundred for this."

"Can't I just...?"

"No," she cried. "Remember our bargain."

"Yes." the waiter asked. Bellin could detect a certain tension in his tone.

"There," Dunney said, finishing his counting.

His mind racing, Bellin sought reasons for the girl's insistence that Dunney convert her valula into regular money. Such a transaction was illegal! And yet, she had done it out in the open. She had conducted an illegal exchange right in front of the waiter. How idiotic!

"That's for your trouble," Elizaveta told the waiter.

Immediately, the waiter voiced a refusal. "No, thank you, Comrade. It is my duty to serve you. Please, I want nothing for..." His voice died off as he obvious fled the table.

A glance at Folenya told Bellin what he already knew. She was studying Bellin, waiting for his response.

Why had she done it! Bellin ran the sequence over in his head. An exchange of Valula for regular rubles? It was a crime to buy valula except through the government. Suddenly, Bellin had it.

"Anna, have your people pick them up!" he ordered. "Right now. I don't want them to so much as get into that cab."

Upset, Folenya waved her hands "no", too excited to speak at first. "No, no, Bellin! Give them a chance..."

Bellin cut her off loudly. "To what? Make that exchange you were so sure of! It won't be tonight, Anna. Not tonight."

"It will be. Just give it a chance. In the cab."

"Contact the agents at the restaurant," Bellin instructed the technician. "You're connected with one of them aren't you?"

The KGB technician hesitated, his eyes on Folenya.

"Do it. Now," Bellin commanded evenly. "The American has broken the law. And I want her as my witness." He turned on his heel and headed for the door.

Folenya nodded to the technician and left after Bellin. She caught up to him in the hallway. "Comrade Bellin, it's nothing. You could have arrested them at any time. That conversation was recorded. Why not give her the chance to hand over the tape? She was going to do it, couldn't you see that?"

Coldly. Bellin stared into her silence. She could be such a fool in her militancy. "You can't see it, can you, Comrade Folenya? It was played out right in front of you and you can't see it."

His criticism hurt her, though she did not understand what he was talking about. What had she missed? It was a minor violation. Next to what she expected to happen, it was almost pitiful.

Contemptuously, Bellin stalked off. "I will be in my office. Notify me when the American and his blackmailing Jewess are brought in." He turned for a second and added, "And I don't want to be interrupted before that. Understand, Comrade. Not by you, not by anyone."

By God, he thought as he stormed down the corridor, he had to stop them!

~ ~ ~

The black Embassy Lincoln glided down the dark street, Greenwald pensively observing the row houses as they went by. John Winker lived in a rooming hotel at the end of the narrow road. It was a cramped neighborhood, one set aside for some of the foreigners who had to live in the capital for one reason or another. Greenwald had known several members of the press who had taken residence in that area, freelancers like himself mostly. Freelancers who had no lucrative connection with the CIA.

When the limousine halted, Greenwald checked the number on the hand-painted sign above the door. Grabbing his briefcase, he opened the door and slid out. He pulled his suit coat a little tighter. It was now late enough for a chill to return to the summer air.

Thirteen steps, Greenwald counted, led up to the main door of the three story house. Built before the revolution, the building showed its years and its superior construction. The solid wood of the door, its paint scuffed and chipping, muffled his knock. Instead, he tapped the glass on the one side. At one time, perhaps, there had been a bell operated by a button in the now empty brass faceplate.

Getting no response, Greenwald tried the cheap handle and pulled the door open easily. Inside, he crossed the worn throw rug and stepped down into a dimly lit foyer. A hand-printed list had Winker, J. set two thirds of the way down, in Room 2B. The interior door, too, was unlocked and led Greenwald to an old fashioned, bannistered staircase.

After taking the first flight, Greenwald discovered that he had another flight to go. Whoever had put the house together had apparently been enamored of the French system of giving the second floor first floor status. On Winker's floor, two of the bulbs had burned out, leaving the work of lighting the high-ceilinged hall to their two weak companions.

Greenwald passed Winker's door without realizing it and had to retrace his steps. His rap on the door brought a sudden thumping from the inside, but nothing else. His second try succeeded in soliciting an unbolting of the door, in three separate spots on the frame.

"Who are you?" a voice said from inside.

Puzzled at such precautions, Greenwald hesitated.

"Who are you?" demanded the same voice much more insistently.

"Greenwald, I'm with State," he said. "I've got a note from Washington for you."

"I don't know any Washington," Winker snapped.

Greenwald laughed. "DC, for God's sake. The State Department."

Winker eased the door open three inches and assessed Greenwald through the gap. "Come in."

To Greenwald's surprise, Winker was a timid, caved-in little creature. Perhaps his precautions were advisable from the look of him. "Thanks. Sorry to disturb you so damned late, but State said it was urgent."

Winker gave him a quizzical look. "Urgent? Maybe they think so."

Scanning the room, Greenwald learned one thing about Winker: He was an incredibly orderly fellow. The few pieces of furniture gave the impression of mathematically precise placement. His magazines were perfectly squared in their piles. The set of file cabinets in one corner were closed and had nothing on the tops of the individual units. He even had ashtrays, clean and bright, angled perfectly on each end of his rectangular coffee table. Through the door, Greenwald could see a tightly made bed. Yet there was a tension between the room and Winker's slovenly posture and shambling walk. It made Greenwald wonder if there were not some woman hiding behind the door to the bedroom.

"Well?" Winker asked. "Is it all right?"

"Pardon?"

Padding over to his tidy desk beyond the open door, Winker picked up his glasses. "Nothing."

Greenwald laid his briefcase on the coffee table, crouched down and snapped open the locks. The noise made Winker jump, but both men pretended to ignore it. The small, sealed pouch in hand, Greenwald straightened. "This is it. I hope it was worth the inconvenience to us both."

Skewing his mouth, Winker accepted the leather bag. After staring at it for a few seconds, he smiled. "I'm sorry, Greenwald, I just get edgy when someone knocks on my door these days."

"I see."

"They're picking on us, what with the Mraisky protests and all."

Keeping his sense of irony to himself, Greenwald simply agreed. "So I hear. Wouldn't you be better off in the Embassy?"

"I like it here. The Embassy? I don't know. I don't like to live where I work. I suppose that's it."

Taking note of Winker's continuing anxiety, Greenwald shut his valise and prepared to go. "I don't think there's supposed to be a return message. If there is, I'll be at the Embassy tonight and tomorrow. For several weeks actually. Maybe longer."

"Welcome to the team, Greenwald."

They shook hands. "Sy."

Winker's head bobbed up and down in preoccupied concurrence. "Thank you. Sy. I'll talk to you tomorrow."

Greenwald said, "Good-bye, John," and went out the open door.

"Good-bye." Behind him, Winker shut the door. Carefully, he reset the dead bolts and turned his attention to the pouch. The leather, he knew, covered several layers of aramid fiber weaved into an almost impenetrable fabric. He worked the small rotary combination lock gently. That done, he went to his desk and removed a bobby pin marked by a series of nicks. He counted to be sure. Seven and three. It was the proper key.

The pin inserted in the lock, he twisted hard. The lock fell open and he unwound the wire. That done, he took out the vial of acid to avoid triggering it by mistake. Only then did Winker open the inner part of the pouch. Inside was a single slip of paper.

The vial of acid in one hand and the note in the other, Winker sat down at his desk and began to decode the message. For him, even, it took an hour. A long, eye-straining, back-breaking hour for John Winker, one of the world's premier cryptologists, to filter through a code he already knew, one he had himself created.

As any good cryptologist does, Winker deciphered the entire note before actually reading it. He rubbed his eyes, blinked three times and focused on the small letters he had written in under Mac's.

It was a short note. To the point, Winker thought. "Get the hell to the Embassy. Or you're dead."

Winker set the note in a stainless steel container and broke the nodule of acid over the surface. Watching the paper disintegrate amid noxious fumes, Winker turned his mind to the destruction of his belongings. How long would that take? Ten minutes? Half an hour?

Before he got started, Winker unlocked a small drawer in his desk. From a false bottom, he removed a small leather box. Inside sat three of the pills, the strong ones. The ones he had on him weren't strong enough, not sure enough.

"Get to the Embassy." he repeated, half amused at Mac's naivete If the Soviets were on to him, it was too late. He was already dead.

~ ~ ~

His guts twisted into a tight knot. Dunney sat in one car between two of the plainclothesmen, one of whom was Fedranoi. In a second car, Elizaveta suffered a similar fate. He still had not learned what he had done, but he suspected, or rather hoped, that the Soviets were only trying to intimidate Elizaveta. She was, after all, a dissident. And a Jew–the Soviets concentrated on Jews.

What really had him worried, however, was the expected side-effect of his "arrest." Surely, he had blown away any chance he had of a coup in dealing with the Russians. Possibly, probably, he had destroyed his opportunity to continue as Bingo Burgers' negotiator. He would have to return to Boston in disgrace, guilty of compromising Bingo's interest in favor of a long shot at laying a girl he had just met. Not just a girl: A Soviet Jewish Dissident! Christ, he knew better than that!

In one evening, Dunney had destroyed his career, his life, everything. It was too incredible to believe.

When the car abruptly stopped, Dunney looked around him. Yes, it was all real. Fedranoi elbowed him in the ribs as if to remind him. The man to his left slid out of the car as Fedranoi shoved him again to get him moving. Dunney complied with difficulty, realizing only when he stood again that he was wearing handcuffs.

"Oh, My God," he said softly. If only Klein could see him now. Or his family.

"Follow me," Fedranoi commanded.

Before they started up the stairs of the building, the second car screamed to a halt. Elizaveta emerged sandwiched between two tough looking women. Dunney recognized the taller of them as the woman seated next to their table at The Shashlik. Christ, they had been watched the whole time!

"Let's go." Fedranoi barked again.

As Dunney turned away to follow the KGB agent into the Procurator's Building, Elizaveta felt her shoulders droop. It was a queer feeling, a detached observation. The KGB had beaten them, she thought. How illusory hope was. The KGB had followed every move, knew every step. Getting the tape to the Americans, freeing Mraisky, holding the Moscow Group and its satellites together, getting to Israel, it was not destined to be. It had been a cruel, idiotic joke anyway: That she thought she could become a Jew after twenty years of being nothing.

The female KGB agents bullied Elizaveta up the stairs. Not far ahead, Dunney and his escorts stood in front of the elevator. The door opened and Fedranoi held it until Elizaveta and her captors caught up. Dunney avoided

Elizaveta's eyes and she, after a fleeting look, did the same. It was too humiliating.

When the door opened again, another woman stood waiting. She surveyed the two prisoners critically, frowning deeply.

"Where do they go?" Fedranoi asked.

"Follow me," The woman said petulantly. "Director Bellin intends to interrogate them himself.

"All right my friends, you heard Comrade Folenya."

After a short single-file march down the corridor, Folenya motioned the party to a stop. "Wait here."

When she had disappeared, Fedranoi growled, "Officious bitch," to the nods of his companions.

Several loud if indistinct words came from Bellin's office and Folenya emerged with his orders. "He wants the girl first."

Dunney and Elizaveta exchanged glances. Each managed a smile.

Folenya took Elizaveta to the door alone, knocked and let the girl in.

His cigar out, Bellin sat, elbows on desk, staring at Elizaveta. He found her still more compelling in person than either on the monitor or in photographs. She was frightened, but trying very hard not to show it. "Sit down, Miss Krylenkev." Once she had done so. Bellin took a minute to relight the cigar. He wanted the extra time to study her.

"You don't look dangerous," he said. "Are you?"

"No." She might have wanted to elaborate, but even the monosyllabic negative strained her throat.

"Your American friend, Mr. Dunney, is trouble. You know that, don't you..."

"Trouble?" Elizaveta gathered herself together. "Mr. Dunney has done nothing."

Bellin smiled knowingly. "Of course not. But you have."

"Me? What?"

"Elizaveta, that's a strange name for a Jew. It's Russian."

"Yes."

"Of course, your father was Russian," Bellin went on, demonstrating his knowledge and indirectly his power. "Elizaveta, the currency exchange at the Shashlik was entirely your idea. Not Mr. Dunney's. He was doing you a favor. Well, perhaps not a favor, because he hopes to get you into his bed and you made the exchange a condition. Didn't you?"

During the entire disclosure by Bellin, Elizaveta was breathless. He knew everything! She felt close to being sick, as she had when the other Investigator had…

"In any case, you knew what you were doing. And he did not. You are the guilty party, but that isn't the point I want to make." He rose and slowly walked around the desk, finally taking a seat on its edge directly in front of her. When he leaned forward, he could see tears begin to form in her eyes. "The point, Elizaveta, is that I know why. And the corollary to that is: It won't work."

His speech finished, Bellin went to the door and called out, "Send in the American."

From behind the girl, Bellin admired her. She kept her head up, her shoulders fairly straight, her back erect. One or two motions with each hand wiped away any incipient tears and a cough cleared her throat in ease she had to speak.

Dare she face Christopher, Elizaveta wondered desperately, if Bellin told him? That she betrayed him in order to force him into doing what he had refused to do? He would hate her! And she could not justify herself to him. He would never understand. She feared his eyes, the hate they would convey. "Please, don't tell him," she heard herself say. "Please. Not until I've gone."

Bellin touched her shoulder gently as he walked by her, to resume his position behind his desk. Of course, he had to tell Dunney.

The American entered, his hands dangling down in front of him, still handcuffed together. Bellin shook his head, although he appreciated the effect was significant. Dunney had a chastised look on his face. Without leaving his desk, Bellin shouted. "Anna! Get someone in here to get those manacles off Mr. Dunney."

He lowered his voice to speak to the American. "I'm sorry, Mr. Dunney. The handcuffs were a bit excessive. Have a seat while we're waiting."

As soon as Dunney had taken the chair next to Elizaveta, Fedranoi hustled in, told him to stand up again and undid the handcuffs. The entire operation lasted twenty seconds. The mere absence of the hard metal restored Dunney somewhat. Bellin, lounging back in his chair, a huge Havana in his mouth, looked almost like a businessman. Dunney began to feel comfortable for a man whose career was over and who faced God knows what in a Russian prison.

"I wanted an opportunity to speak to the two of you together," Bellin began easily, looking off in another direction. "Elizaveta is already aware of this, Mr. Dunney, but perhaps you are not. And she obviously could use a refresher. Moscow, a great city, is very small in many ways. The KGB helps keep it that way. Nothing you do escapes its notice. That is as it should be, of course, and as long as you or anyone else act properly, you may take comfort in its vigilance. But if you are careless, like tonight, or worse, the KGB also knows that. It is an obvious point, but worth making." He let his eyes fall first on Dunney, then Elizaveta and finally back to Dunney. He debated whether to reveal Elizaveta's motives at that moment. He decided against it.

"Elizaveta, wait in the hallway... No, wait in my waiting room. I want to speak to Mr. Dunney alone."

She got out of the chair with difficulty, her eyes glued to Bellin's. "Thank you," she said in a half whisper, relieved. Yet, still she would face Dunney after Bellin told him the truth. Perhaps she could make him see, if...

Bellin looked Dunney over once again, slowly, letting his dominance sink in. The tactic had a curious effect. The longer he took, the more scornful became Dunney's demeanor. "Well. Mr. Dunney. You are in an embarrassing position. You've come to Moscow to deal with our government and yet you have no reservation about violating our laws."

"What laws, Director Bellin?" Dunney asked carefully. His ignorance put him in a weak position and he found it very uncomfortable. "So far, I am unaware of my alleged crime."

"Are you?" Bellin suspected as much and opted to keep the American in suspense. "Suffice to say that it is serious."

"If you say so, Director Bellin." It was going to be a game of some sort, Dunney recognized. A game of very high stakes from his point of view. What about Bellin's stakes? "Of course, it will be much harder for me to confess."

A very nice, unexpected response, Bellin thought, gaining some respect for the American lawyer. "I won't ask you to confess, Mr. Dunney. It's not necessary. Would you like a cigar?"

"No, thank you, but I would like to smoke. I have some cigarettes..."

"American cigarettes?" Bellin asked, choosing another cigar for himself. "By all means."

Dunney reached inside his coat and produced the package. After pulling out a Winston, he leaned forward to accept Bellin's offer of a light. Once he sat back, Dunney tossed the cigarette pack on Bellin's desk. Bellin took it up and examined it.

"I am not a lover of American cigarettes," Bellin said, returning the Winston's to their place at the edge of the desk.

"Try them sometime." Dunney did not move to recover the cigarettes. Would Bellin take the hint? Could the Director be "influenced?"

Ignoring the offer, Bellin ignited his long thick Havana. "Mr. Dunney, you are an American in a strange city. You would like our government to cooperate with you. We must ask some consideration in return."

"Naturally."

"I don't have any desire to see your mission here jeopardized by what is a technical matter, one that is more the blame of your young friend than yourself." He shook his head. "No one gains by that. Don't you agree?"

Waiting for the hammer to fall, Dunney said, "Yes." What would Director Bellin demand? Money? Information about Elizaveta? A better deal for the government in his negotiations?

Bellin allowed Dunney time to speculate about what would come next. He pretended to be thinking over his alternatives. Finally, he said, "All I ask of you is this: Do not place our government in an awkward position. It is very important, especially during this period of strained relations between our country and yours, that you choose your Moscow acquaintances with discretion."

Dunney stiffened. "Do you have anyone in particular in mind, Director Bellin?" He heard his voice reflect his growing anger. Christ, the man may have been saving his career! He lowered the volume and the pitch. "I have made the acquaintance of only a few people. Outside of the KGB, I mean."

Hiding his smile, Bellin nodded. "I realize that, Mr. Dunney. You have been very busy with your business and that is as it should be. If you keep that in mind, I'm sure you will be fine."

"Are you suggesting that I avoid politically undesirable individuals?"

His stare fixed on Dunney's face, Bellin nodded again. "Good sense, Mr. Dunney. I rely on your good sense."

Calmly, Dunney looked back at Bellin. "I am an American, Director Bellin. We have kind of an exaggerated feeling about this kind of thing. We are so used to freedom, that sometimes we have trouble abiding by the dictates," he stated, emphasizing the last word with a beat of hesitation "of any government or any person. It's not an intentional thing–what the Soviet government does and what it wants are its business–but we Americans can't shake what we're used to. Understand?"

Bellin pushed himself out of his chair with both hands on the desk. Once up, he kept his hands flat on the desk and bent forward. "Mr. Dunney, I understand and I want you to understand me. You won't go anywhere in Moscow where you can't be seen. You won't do anything that I won't know about. You won't see anybody, anybody, I am not aware of. Now, what you do under these circumstances is not just your business, it is also mine. All of it. You are not clever enough to avoid that and I am not dumb enough."

Controlling his anger at Bellin's threats, Dunney rose and tipped the cigarettes toward Bellin. "You know, these damned things can kill you." He laughed once. "And I still smoke a pack a day."

Transferring his intensifying glare from Dunney to the Winston's, Bellin noticed how white the knuckles on his left hand, the one next to the cigarettes, had become. He wondered how much of his annoyance showed in his face. Finally, he stood erect. "In Russia, Mr. Dunney, we call that killing yourself. A very foolhardy thing to do." He shook his head and said. "You may go, for now."

"Good-bye, Director Bellin."

"Good-bye, Mr. Dunney?" he asked. "Not at all. Good night."

Dunney went to the door where he paused to say, "Is even that appropriate?" Without waiting for a response, Dunney exited and closed the door firmly behind him.

In the unlit waiting room, Elizaveta anxiously stood to greet him. For a moment, they said nothing, then Dunney took her arm and said, "Champagne is better after midnight, I understand."

Hearing their muted voices through the door. Bellin crushed his cigar out and threw it in his wastebasket. There would be hell to pay if he were wrong.

~ ~ ~

For the first time in his life, John Winker feared the dark.

He knew that McDeamon's warning was not an empty one. He had been expecting it. The rumor out of the KGB–the one about the infiltrator and the message smuggled to Mraisky–had worried him from the first. Certainly, there were hundreds of foreign agents in the KGB, not just his ultra-secret twelve, but rumor encompassed the probability that the agent was one of his.

And now, of course, he knew for sure. One of his men– one of those quiet, dormant agents, the identity of whom only he, Mac and a couple of Mac's predecessors knew– one of those men had broken the only rule they had: Do nothing until activated by Winker. How had it happened? It didn't much matter to Winker. Idle speculation did not appeal to his mathematical mind, particularly at that moment.

His neighbor's dog pulled on the chain suddenly, nearly yanking Winker's arm off. He needed an ostensible reason for leaving his apartment and settled upon the dog owned by an elderly Italian diplomat in the building. The fool had thanked Winker profusely when the American volunteered to take the animal for its walk. It was unlikely that he would see the dog again.

When the dog stopped and crouched, Winker heard the footsteps not far behind him. He wished he had not requested the Embassy car to meet him so far down the street. It seemed a ridiculous precaution. If the KGB knew, it knew. Did he expect to fool them with his silly dog-walking act?

The dog yelped as Winker jerked its leash to get it moving again. The footsteps were getting too close and made no sound to indicate hesitation. In an involuntary reflex, Winker twisted his neck around to see the face of his enemy.

To his shock, it was a woman. In her arms, she carried a stuffed laundry bag. Winker started to laugh in relief. He even allowed the dog to stop again.

Down the street, he heard the noise of a car braking to a sudden halt. The Embassy car! Once inside he might be safe. If only he could make it to the car! Would the KGB stop an embassy car? Perhaps, but it would be nice to get inside.

After the animal had finished sniffing its handiwork, Winker led it away. He would be able to send it back to the Italian from the embassy. As he neared the car, he even allowed himself a hushed whistle.

As he came closer, however, Winker realized his mistake. It was a short, stubby, ugly thing, not the long-hooded limo owned by the embassy. Desperately he looked all around him. Squinting he made out the long outline of the limousine a block further down the road. Between him and the Embassy limousine sat the single ominous automobile, an insurmountable barrier to his safety.

All four doors opened at once. Before anyone stepped out Winker started to run, still clinging to the leash. The small dog barked as it and Winker raced toward the car. Behind him, the woman shouted something in guttural Russian but he did not understand it over the pounding of his heart and the yelping of the dog.

Somehow, Winker reached the car before the men inside on the sidewalk side could get out. Mustering all of his force, he slammed the doors, kicking them securely closed while the passengers screamed in rage. That took time, cost valuable seconds. Worse, the dog slipped between his legs and made a quick escape impossible. He finally dropped the leash, but still had to kick it free.

The agents from the other side of the car were now out, circling around the front. The woman, shouting and running, closed in from the rear. Winker hesitated. The sidewalk ahead was blocked by two dark figures hundreds of pounds heavier than he. As he turned toward the woman, he saw the gun, with a long blunt silencer affixed to the front. He shrugged and stood still.

In Russian, one of the men said, "That's better, Winker."

As they reached him, Winker struck out at each man's face with his middle fingers protruding. He hit his mark perfectly. One man went down, the other spun, crying in pain. At the instant the opening appeared. John Winker bolted through it, his eyes on the open door of the Embassy limousine.

"Stop thief!" came a female-voiced cry from the rear.

Unconscious of the effort, Winker felt his legs churning, heard his feet pounding the ground. For that second he felt like the heroic running back everyone wanted to be.

Winker did not hear the shot, of course, though he heard the "umph" from the woman as the pistol recoiled. Neither did he feel any localized pain, just a general agony.

The next step he took Winker's front leg collapsed and he tumbled forward, rolling for several yards before ending up sprawled within a dozen feet of the limousine.

The agents from the KGB got to Winker fully ten seconds before the driver from the embassy. One of them violently turned Winker over on his back, placing a palm on his chest. Frantically, He searched the neck for a pulse, then the body for its wound. He found the large hole in the left shoulder. Forcing open Winker's mouth, he jammed his nose against the teeth. There it was: The sweet smell of nutmeg, the scent the Americans often used to cover the odor of their strongest poisons.

While the agent thoroughly conducted a physical search of Winker's body, the woman walked back to where she had dropped her bag. When she returned to the KGB vehicle, she opened it, displaying its contents. "He stole it. My friend lived in his building and he stole it from her. Silverware is very valuable."

The limousine driver shook his head in disgust. He gave the woman and the other a contemptuous sneer, spit within an inch of her shoe and walked away. Winker had no family, nobody who cared about him, not in the Embassy, not in the US. The driver knew that no one would say much.

Finishing his search. the KGB agent rocked back on his heels. "It's not here."

The woman shrugged. "Was it supposed to be?"

"No."

"Why did they want him then?"

Standing, shaking each leg out, the agent replied, "I didn't ask." He stared down at the scrawny, harmless looking dead man. Vaguely, he wondered what had happened to the dog.

~ ~ ~

"I'm sorry, Mr. Dunney," the night clerk said in perfect English. "The restaurant is closed."

Dunney issued an exaggerated sigh and said, "I had promised this lady a bottle of honest Russian champagne. What about room service?"

The very sound of the term made Elizaveta nervous, but she was bound to go through with it. She might as well get the sex over with. Pulling close enough to Dunney to feel his warmth, she whispered. "Rubles."

Nodding, Dunney dug into his pocket and produced a wad of rubles. Peeling off an ample amount, he put some in the clerk's ready hand. "All we need is one bottle. I can supply the glasses in a pinch."

Feigning thoughtfulness, the clerk decided, "Yes, for an American guest, champagne is always available."

"Room…"

Winking, the clerk said, "I know your room number. 618. The champagne will be right up."

His hand on the small of Elizaveta's back. Dunney escorted her into a waiting elevator. "You don't mind?"

"No, Christopher. I've been looking forward to it." It was not quite a lie.

By the time they had reached the sixth floor, strolled down the familiar hall and entered the room, Elizaveta felt that detainment by Director Bellin was a pleasant experience in retrospect. She was no raw virgin, she told herself, and this was no different from her other encounters with lovers, casual and serious. Only it was. She intended to use her body to get something from Dunney. Nothing else.

No sooner had they entered than a boy arrived at the door with a bottle of champagne in a bucket and two fine crystal glasses. Dunney gave the boy a generous tip and sent him on his way.

The bottle reminded Dunney of something. As he worked the cork loose, his eyes examined the room, looking for bugs or places to hide them. He had no expertise in such matters and found the exercise frustrating. He knew that Bellin could hear them… Hear? Didn't he also say "see"? Did Bellin have cameras in his room? Son of a bitch, if he didn't! Even though he could not see any hint of a camera, Dunney was absolutely certain that there was one. Maybe more.

He poured the champagne with a flourish, confident that Bellin would see it. "How about a toast?" he said to Elizaveta. "To just the two of us. Okay?"

Elizaveta smiled, oddly warmed by the words. "I think that is very nice."

Their glasses touched and they sipped the champagne together, their eyes meeting over the rims of the shimmering crystal. After the first sip, Dunney led Elizaveta to the couch. She sat very near the end, leaving just enough space for Dunney.

Taken aback by her enticing maneuver, Dunney hesitated, but only briefly. Things rarely went so smoothly for him and considering the kind of day, he had had... But perhaps they both needed a release from the pressure. In one movement, he sat down, placed his arms around Elizaveta and brought her even closer. The touch of her body, so much of it, sent a bewildering rush through him.

Elizaveta felt an internal shiver from the pressure. Quickly, she recalled why she would make love with Dunney. The shiver came again, almost a quaking the second time. She wondered if he could feel it. Was it obvious?

Automatically, when he put down his glass, she put hers down as well. Had her breathing grown deeper or was she imagining it?

With a motion made easy by her cooperation. Dunney brought Elizaveta's body around for a long, deeply penetrating kiss. He caressed her back, pressing her to him as he did. From that point, they both knew it was inevitable.

~ ~ ~

The bedroom camera produced an oddly unerotic view of Dunney and Elizaveta's lovemaking, Bellin mused. The limited foreplay in the living room seemed more interesting. The microphone, turned to very high volume, picked up very little in the way of the usual sounds of passion. It was a remarkably quiet act, in contrast to Marta's and his.

The American's outright defiance of his direction to stay away from the girl worried Bellin. How far would that attitude take Dunney?

Folenya squirmed in her seat next to him. For all her criticism of Radnik, she could barely contain herself, Bellin thought. He considered that ironic but not particularly amusing.

On the speaker, Dunney's "shit!" came out as a loud grumble. Bellin motioned to the technician to reduce the level.

As the American rolled off to one side, Elizaveta rolled with him. "Christopher?"

His voice conveying peevishness, Dunney answered, "So much for that," in English.

"I'm sorry," she said quietly.

"For Christ's sake, why? You were doing better than I was."

"I didn't know…"

Dunney stretched over to her and kissed her on the forehead. "It was a long day, Elizaveta. We Americans suffer long nights after long days."

Elizaveta said nothing, but sniffed several times.

"It's all right. If you'll give me another chance."

Her voice cracked and was barely audible. "As many as you want, Christopher."

Dunney put his hands under his head, staring at the ceiling. seemingly straight into the camera. He blinked, narrowed his eyes and cocked his head to one side. His eyes suddenly widened and a sarcastic smile spread over his face. "You're a very desirable woman, Elizaveta. Thank God."

Bellin could almost feel Dunney's eyes boring into his own through the video monitor. He had found the camera!

Elizaveta's voice reflected her confusion. "Thank you, but..."

"Oh, it's just that Director Bellin," Dunney explained without moving, "told me to avoid undesirables." He laughed. "Perhaps, I shouldn't see him again."

His face flushed. Bellin clamped down on his cigar and stomped to his feet. Dunney had gone mad! He was virtually challenging the Russian people, the Soviet government. It was insane, dangerous, ultimately destructive! How far could the man go? Bellin's whole strategy rested on Dunney's unstable shoulders. If the American acted rashly, it would be the end of civil security for Russians for a decade. There would be no brake on the excesses of the Folenya's and her petty ilk.

"Don't be a fool, Dunney," he heard himself say.

~ ~ ~

It was so damned obvious! Did Bellin think he was blind? Dunney's rage doubled on the thought of the insult. He knew that Bellin and his mindless crew were at the other end of the protruding lens. He wanted to leap up to the tiny opening and twist the lens, give them a better view.

He felt Elizaveta snuggle closer to him and reflexively slid his arm under her neck and shoulder, clutching her tightly. Her breasts moved against his side as she breathed. She lay one leg over both his, nestling her damp pubes on his hips. Though his concentration remained on the camera, Dunney felt himself stiffening. Oh, yes, he thought. That was more like it.

Elizaveta was taken by surprise when Dunney tore the cover from the bed. She did not know how to react. Feeling like a total failure earlier, she had resigned herself to uneasy rest. When she hesitated, Dunney powerfully pulled her over on top of him. He pushed her up by the shoulders and held her there, his hands working her breasts against the rhythms of her heaving chest.

Back on her heels, astride him, Elizaveta raised herself in response to his firm hand pressure. Releasing one hand from its position on her breast, Dunney cupped her underneath for an instant, sending shock waves through her. Then he positioned the head of his rigid shaft just inside her and for a moment her legs weakened at the sensation. Both hands on her hips. he forced her down on him. The sliding, stretching, liquid movement burned everywhere.

As she threw her head back to cry, to close her eyes in a wrenching pleasure, Elizaveta saw that Christopher was pleased, too, his eyes fixed far away, beyond their room. She wanted it. She wanted it to work. She wanted Christopher to love her. Then they could do it together.

Chapter Eight

"It's Mac, Harm," Tom Simpson had said. Kyle heard the voice say the same thing over and over again. Grave. Shaken. "About Johnny."

Greenwald sat slumped in the love seat across the Office from him. He cradled his head in his hands. Simpson, as usual, said little as he oversaw the scrambler, his face ashen. And there Kyle sat, outwardly calm, pondering the impact of the news on the Central Intelligence Agency operations in Russia.

"The Soviets shot one of our Embassy people," McDeamon repeated. "An economics attaché? Who?" After a pause, Mac's voice conveyed resignation. "Winker?"

"It just came through," Kyle said, taken aback that Mac picked Winker. He hadn't bothered with the name. It should have been unimportant to Mac that the economics attaché who had been shot down by the KGB on the streets of Moscow was named John Winker. It should have been unimportant to Kyle as well.

With seeming effort Mac said, "If it gets any play and is related to Mraisky, we won't be able to contain the public reaction. Take my word for that." As an afterthought, perhaps, he asked, "This guy, Winker. He wasn't a Jew, was he?"

Kyle responded in the negative.

"That's something anyway."

"Will we protest, Mac?" Kyle asked mildly, hiding his agitation.

"Yes. That is the minimum." With a grim note in his voice, Mac added. "The Secretary has another meeting with Gromeko, tomorrow. He might mention it."

So, Kyle thought bitterly, SALT would continue in spite of Mraisky's indictment. In spite of Winker's death.

"One more thing," McDeamon concluded tightly. "The President wants some kind of counter-offensive, Kyle. Have you gotten anywhere on that project?"

"It'll be on your desk tomorrow morning," Kyle responded vehemently. "Full profiles. You can take your pick." Kyle was angry, unprofessionally angry.

Mac had last word. "Our intelligence is that the KGB is insisting on a quick trial and a showy trial. We may not have much time."

Son of a bitch, Kyle stewed. The Soviets could fry the bastard for all he cared.

~ ~ ~

His back aching, Dunney rolled over on his side, facing a sleeping Elizaveta. She lay on her back, her smooth, glowing face inclined half toward him. Until he cleared his eyes by rubbing them with a thumb and forefinger, Dunney could not make out the expression she wore. When he saw it, he felt a twinge of disappointment.

Her lips were pursed, the eyelids closed just enough to tightly to crease her forehead. It was not the peaceful, satisfied expression he would have liked to have seen on a woman he had made love to three times during the night, each time, he told himself without pride, better than the previous one.

He remembered the camera and Director Bellin at its other end. Glancing up toward the ceiling, Dunney reassured himself that it had not melted away into the same warmth which had absorbed his awareness of it.

He hoped that Bellin had not been insulted by his preoccupation with other matters. Had they watched the whole time?

After the first time, they had not presented much of a spectacle, preferring to remain under cover, as it were. As a pornographic exhibition, he mused, it may have flopped at the KGB, but he could still feel Elizaveta's breath searing his skin. The effect, he noticed, retained its potency.

Raising himself on one elbow, Dunney checked his clock on the dresser at the foot of the bed. He could not make out the exact time, but neither hand had reached the nine. It was early yet. He looked back to Elizaveta, her lips now parted and moving slightly.

Unable to resist such an enticing, and moving, target, Dunney reached over, his hand on her stomach, and kissed her on the mouth. She responded, still asleep, with a hum of acceptance and an opening of her mouth. Dunney's tongue gently used all of the space made available and then withdrew. As he backed off some, she hummed again and whispered a name. "Christopher."

Christopher. How easily he had gotten used to her saying that. How right it sounded even when she was asleep. Dunney quickly quashed his idiotic thoughts. In a few days he would be gone. In a couple of weeks at the outside, he would have returned to Boston. To Boston, and what else?

The "morning romantics", he thought, amused at his weakness. He had heard about them, if not experienced them. Ordinarily, he awakened with the women and nothing else: No regrets, no promises, no intentions, no hopes. Alter a shower, either at his place or the girl's, he would change and head for his office cubicle down the hall from Klein's.

And get to work. How romantic could he be when he had to spend his days and most of his evenings with cold black letters on harsh white paper; demanding, often ugly people; and money, usually in the millions and always in the hundreds of thousands? How romantic could he have been when every move was scrutinized for mistake; when failure and error were presumed; and worth had to be proven beyond doubt? Dunney had never had much room to operate and no room for failure.

What room did that leave for…?

Elizaveta stirred beside him, kicking him with one foot as she repositioned her legs to accommodate a half turn of her shoulders. The impact brought an unintelligible verbal reaction from her lips and a half opening of her eyes.

Seeing Dunney smiling over at her, Elizaveta was unsure whether she was not still in a dream. Everything remained blurry and sluggish. She tried to talk, but managed only a pair of nasal hums. It sounded a little like music to her.

The warmth of Dunney's kiss helped rouse her, enough to want more. She held his head, drawing herself up to meet him. "Good morning, Christopher," she said in English.

Before Dunney could respond, his room phone interrupted the conversation. He gave Elizaveta a quick kiss on the nose and rolled out of bed. He almost answered the phone nude, but took along a robe in deference to the cameras.

"Chris?" It was Andy using a tentative voice.

"Hold it, Andy." Dunney said, taking a second to don the robe. "Good morning, Andrea. Nice of you to call."

"Chris, please. I only called to tell you about the newspaper." She spoke in quiet urgency. "I think you should see it."

"Pravda or…?"

"Pravda. I'll bring it down."

"No, Andy. Thanks, but I'd rather you didn't. I'll have the desk send one." He kept his tone level and cool. "Do we have any appointments today that I've forgotten about?"

She paused. "No, but..."

"Thank you. I'll talk to you after breakfast."

"I thought we could..."

"Good-bye, Andy."

Dunney rang the front desk.

"Desk," a familiar voice answered. "What can I do for you, Mr. Dunney?"

"Have breakfast sent up, please. My usual, twice. And a copy of Pravda."

"Very good, Sir."

In a way, Dunney was upset with himself for failing to learn what it was that Andy wanted him to see. If it were not on page one, he might never find it. Unfortunately, the mere sound of her voice had set him off. How quickly things turned, he mused. How close had it come that Andy, and not Elizaveta, might have ended up in his bed that morning?

He began to return to the bedroom only to find that Elizaveta had emerged wearing the shirt he had worn the night before. It was like a God damned movie, but it seemed perfectly natural.

"Your secretary?" she asked. "A girl named Andy?"

"Andrea." he explained admiring her legs as he leaned against the door jamb. A bit heartier than his usual taste, but they worked well in proportion to the hips he had come to like so well.

"She's not coming for breakfast?"

"No."

The reply oddly pleased Elizaveta, pleased, yet worried her. She was not sure that she could handle too much more time with Dunney. Sooner or later she would have to say something about the Moscow Group, about Mraisky. She dreaded that moment, agonized over its inevitability. "I have a class at ten."

"You're too far away, Elizaveta. Come over here."

She shuffled into his arms, shirttail flopping provocatively. For a moment, they simply held each other. When they parted, Dunney suggested, "Why don't you take a shower? I'll wait breakfast for you. Hard rolls don't get cold."

After exchanging a brief kiss, she went off to the bathroom and he started to the bedroom. A knock at the door caused him to reverse his field. Expecting room service, Dunney opened the door without hesitation. The unexpected, in the usually pleasing form of Andy, stood sheepishly before him.

"Jesus..."

Andy took one look at him, his tousled hair, his memory-stirring smell, and fell back a step. Something inside of her went empty. She handed him the paper and said, "In case they don't have one."

Dunney made no move or sign of welcome. He wanted her to go away. He chose to make it obvious. "Thank you, Andrea."

"I'm sorry." Without another word, Andy gave him half a wave and left. She felt like running, all the way back to Boston, but she managed an easy stride as far as the elevator.

Long before she had gotten out of sight. Dunney closed the door. Her intrusion had bothered him far more than it should. He decided to leave until later the question of "why." Instead he opened up the copy of Pravda and searched the front page, in vain, for something of interest.

"Was that your secretary?" Elizaveta, wrapped in a towel, had come out of the bathroom once she was certain that Andy had gone. She felt a twinge of dislike for the attractive American who acted as if she owned Christopher.

Reluctant to admit it, Dunney said, "She wanted to drop off the paper."

"Really?" Elizaveta doubted such an innocent motive. "Is it important?"

"I didn't find anything on the front page. I suppose it could be inside. I'm expecting an item on a speech my client made yesterday."

"Your client. All you ever speak of is your client," she said peevishly. Perhaps, she should be working on his strange relationship with his client. "Is your client a woman, too?"

Dunney laughed, a laugh with no sound. "A woman? No, my client is not a woman. Not this one."

"You have others... You are so single-minded about this one, the one who sent you to Moscow." A woman, she thought. She would have every right to be jealous of such a client. She, of course, had another reason to dislike his client: That client, and Christopher's dedication to him, was all that stood between Christopher and her cause. "Will you have any time for anything else?" she asked coyly. "For me?"

"Nights?"

She shook her head violently. "No. I want more than that from you." The unintentional irony of the statement struck her and she felt the need to correct it. "I'm sorry, Christopher. I don't mean to ask anything of you. Last night..." It was so complicated suddenly!

The unexpected anguish which colored her face and changed her mouth into a frown, brought Dunney to her side with a reassuring hug. "Last night, Elizaveta, is not over. We can stretch it out for days." But no more than that, he recognized, saddened by the admission. Some things deserve to last longer.

Elizaveta said softly. "I had better take my shower." Absorbing a second hug from Dunney, she longed for it all to be over.

Dunney let her go, watching her as she walked. Once the bathroom door shut hint off from her, he reread the front page of the newspaper, from the bottom up. The story about Bingo's speech, assuming it had even made the paper's front page, would undoubtedly be near the bottom. The top columns were devoted to more important news, such as...

His eyes widened as Dunney saw what he had glanced over just minutes before. How could he have read it and not have read it? It was the lead story! Several other columns were directly or indirectly related to it. God, how narrowly his mind sometimes worked!

It was not exactly a surprise. Pravda, Izvestia and other papers had carried denunciations, increasingly strong, each of the days he had been there. But no, it had really begun.

He stared toward the bathroom door, his mind paralyzed. What should he do? He could hear the water running. Should he tell her now? Should he wait? And what of himself? Of his own position?

His thoughts raced back to Bellin. The not-so-veiled threats about Elizaveta, her friends and himself. Did Bellin mean what he said? With Elizaveta in his room, in his shower, in his bed, he had thrown everything back in Bellin's face. How would the Soviet government respond?

Dunney threw the newspaper across the room. The failure he had seemingly escaped the night before–his first major failure since he was a boy–now seemed all the more imminent for having been so recently avoided.

And she was still there!

Not that Elizaveta was the cause. He knew better than to blame her. Or even Bellin. He knew who was at fault: Christopher Dunney! He could try as hard as he wanted, God damn it, but he would never make it!

And yet, he was only incidentally involved. Elizaveta was personally entangled in it.

Dunney wrenched the bathroom door open to a cloud of steam. He plunged in without taking an extra breath and felt his way to the shower curtain. Tearing it aside, he startled Elizaveta with his unintelligible shout.

Realizing that she had not heard, Dunney ducked into the water, turning the handles hard. Dripping wet, he returned her quizzical look with a single sentence.

"Elizaveta, they've indicted Mraisky."

Stunned, she swayed backwards, nearly losing her balance. But for Dunney's reaction, she may have fallen. He lifted her completely out of the bathtub as she clung to him. Dunney steadied her. "You had to expect it," he said gently. "You had to know it was coming."

"No, no, no," she cried. He missed the whole point! "Oh God, Christopher. Oh, God, we have so little time." That was the hideous part! They wouldn't let her wait! They wouldn't give her time.

Her reaction frightened Dunney. Would they come to arrest her too? Surely, that wasn't what she meant. That wasn't possible! What would he do then?

"Hold me, Christopher. Help me," she begged him.

~ ~ ~

Upon hearing the news from his relief man, a fuming Bellin stomped up to the Procurator's suite. He did not bother with the formality of waiting while Zhoronov's personal secretary buzzed his superior. Bellin was through the door before the Procurator had touched his intercom switch.

"Do you have an explanation?" he demanded loudly.

Sergei Zhoronov had anticipated Bellin's reaction. He had known the Director too long to expect anything but fury. Calmly, he pushed out his chair, rose and went over to his most valued working asset. "Feuchinko gave me no choice, Vladimir."

"Is he running your office now?"

Zhoronov replied, "To the extent he wishes to, yes. Just as I would yours, if I felt it necessary."

"Perhaps you should, Procurator," Bellin suggested harshly. "Apparently, you prefer the KGB's report to my own."

"No." Zhoronov glanced over his shoulder at the thin negatively slanted report from Bellin's Department, sitting, as it was, beside the bulging, damning file from the KGB. "We do not have enough reliable evidence to convict Mraisky of all the charges."

Throwing up his hands, Bellin asked, "Then how can you expect to...?"

"I'm doing as I'm told, damn it!" Zhoronov snapped. "How long do you think Feuchinko can hold off Arkilonov? The KGB will not wait any longer, Vladimir! Period. They want Mraisky's trial begun tomorrow..."

"Tomorrow? That's absurd! With what?"

"You don't think he's guilty?"

"Of course he's guilty!" Bellin knew that Mraisky was guilty. He had known it at the time of the arrest, KGB or no KGB. "But, Sergei, I can't give you adequate proof. The KGB sources are all for hire. You know that as well as I do."

"They will have to do."

"Doesn't it matter?" Bellin asked quietly. He knew the answer. Radnik had been right. "No, of course not." Beaten, and exhausted from the long night's duty, he collapsed into a chair. "Not when it serves a higher Party interest."

With a half smile, Zhoronov said, "You sound like you do not believe that. That's dangerous."

Waving away the comment, Bellin replied, "What the Party wants is its business, not mine." The comment sounded strangely familiar. "I just don't see the point of having a Procurator if his responsibilities are to be usurped whenever it pleases some ass in the KGB."

Zhoronov, who shared his friend's feelings, said nothing.

"Does he at least get a lawyer?"

"No lawyer in Russia will touch Mraisky. The two or three who expressed interest suddenly lost interest when the Legal Union began an investigation of their authority to practice. "

"I see."

"Mraisky has agreed to defend himself. In writing, as usual."

Bellin's rage began to wane, lapsing into impotent frustration. He was tired, more than anything. Perhaps he would take the rest of the day off. Why not? Mraisky's prosecution was being handled so well by the Party and the KGB, they hardly needed him. He would merely get in the way, which perhaps was the upper limit of his responsibility in any case.

Zhoronov patted Bellin's sagging shoulder and returned to his spot behind the desk. "I delayed the trial at least a week, Vladimir. Possibly two, although I doubt I can hold the KGB back that long. Do you know that the Party Primary in the Procuracy has a new Secretary?"

"Here too?" Bellin shuddered, thinking of Folenya.

"Don't tell me that Radnik is out in your department?" Zhoronov was dismayed. He himself found his newly vigilant Communist Party Primary Secretary a tremendous burden. What could Bellin think of his? "What happened?"

"Bescel resigned."

"Oh God, why?"

"Not the Secretariat. His job."

"Folenya?" Zhoronov had seen her infamous report.

"And she was appointed interim Secretary," Bellin added with complete disgust.

The Procurator winced at a tightening in his chest. There was obviously no point in even trying to delay Mraisky's trial for more than a week. The KGB and the

Party were leaving nothing to chance. For the first time in his career, Zhoronov feared for his position. By the time the Mraisky affair ended, the Procuracy could easily be under the control of one of the organizations it was to oversee, the KGB. Before that could happen, of course, he and Bellin would have to go.

All he could say was, "Don't oppose her, Vladimir."

~ ~ ~

Anna Folenya stood in front of the small mirror in the women's room across from the monitoring station. Her eyes had trouble focusing on her image. If Bellin did not act soon to precipitate action on the part of the dissidents, she would have to. She had been up for three nights running, monitoring the activities of the dissidents and the Americans. Without the pills, she could barely keep her wits about her.

And that was necessary. Bellin could not be trusted. The Director, she knew for certain now, was soft on the dissidents. His intention, reflected in the various orders he had given all along, had clearly emerged the previous night: He was interested only in preventing the transfer of the message to the American completely, rather than forcing it and using the justification for destroying the entire Moscow Group. Why else would he have been so angry at seeing the American and the Jewish slut together after he had earlier warned them to stay apart.

Using her hand for a cup, Folenya swallowed two of her stimulants. She gagged on the second, but managed to force it down eventually. While waiting for the pills to take effect, she used the commode, or tried to. More complications she did not need!

Recovering her vigor, Folenya returned to the monitoring room to claim her papers. Her requested back-up from the KGB had already arrived. An experienced older woman from Surveillance, she would not mind the carnality of the current task, probably not even notice it. For Folenya, the depravity of the Americans and of the dissident whore grew increasingly depressing. The sooner they were neutralized, the better she would like it.

"Comrade Folenya," the replacement said, "I have something for you".

Folenya took the sealed folder, nodded and left the room. The cover was stamped "Secret. No Disclosure Permitted." Impressed. Folenya retired to the women's room to examine its contents.

After breaking the seal, she carefully slid the document out. She had seen very few "secret" papers in the past and did not want to mar this one in any way. The top page read:

"Highly Secret. No Disclosure of contents Permitted. Case Number 897-3484576, Mraisky, Alexander, Isaac,"

Fighting off the suspense, Folenya slowly read the pages in silence. The first two included background on the Mraisky arrest, which of course, she already knew by memory. The third page summarized the various degrees of "interrogation and admission" involved, which was limited, due to the intervention of Director Bellin–Naturally!–Nothing of value had been gained through Mraisky himself.

With page four, however, the report began a revelation of major importance.

"Through the inquiries made by the Political Branch, a certain Valerianovich, Tsoril Tsorilivich was located and identified as the last contact of the subject prior to his arrest. Valerianovich, age seventeen, made delivery to the subject minutes prior to such arrest. The witness testified that he had been requested to deliver a small package to the suspect by a member of the Cipher Branch of the KGB." They had found the traitor!

"Such member has been identified, arrested and interrogated. The following admissions have resulted:

1. Such member was the party who sent a package to subject;
2. Such member warned subject of his impending arrest;
3. Such member had intended such package to reach, through subject, the American CIA;
4. Such member was affiliated with the American CIA;
5. Such member intended such package to reach, through subject and his colleagues, an American CIA operative by the name of John Winker;
6. Such member worked under the auspices of such CIA operative John Winker and knew of no other CIA operatives.

Such member did not survive interrogation. CIA operative, John Winker, shall be apprehended and interrogated."

The report ended upon that ominous note, except for an addendum handwritten on a note pad. "CIA operative, Winker apprehended without opportunity to interrogate. The message cartridge was not on his person, nor in his flat. Presumption that tape has not reached Americans remains operative."

For five full minutes. Folenya sat staring at the report. They had the proof! Mraisky and the Moscow Group were in direct touch with CIA infiltrators of the KGB! She would have given anything to have been allowed to wave the truth under Bellin's nose, but she could not.

It did not matter, though. Bellin would discover the truth soon enough, she knew, at Mraisky's trial. All of the denunciations, all of the slanderous writings, all of the witnesses on which Bellin had worked so hard were meaningless. They had proof of Mraisky's–of all of the dissidents'–treachery. And with it, they had proof that Bellin was at best a fool. At worst...?

~ ~ ~

Elizaveta barely noticed Volenko when he sneaked into her lecture as she went through the final sequences. Torlas, however, she could not have missed. He had to open the door all the way to fit his corpulent body through. Behind him, she could see the KGB "shadow".

"No questions today, class," she said.

A hand shot up in the rear of the room. There was something disquietingly insistent about it and Elizaveta ignored it. Finally, a voice cried, "Why isn't your traitor friend here today?"

She hesitated. The strident question was repeated, in several voices the second time. As another repetition began, Elizaveta repressed her urge to reply. Instead. she collected her notes and immediately left the podium. Simultaneously, Torlas and Volenko existed via the front door.

The three met around the back of the lecture hall, as the students streamed out the front. Volenko clasped her hand, patting it over and over. Torlas stood, his fat legs widespread, his big arms folded over his chest, glaring at the members of Mraisky's former class.

"His own damned students!" she hissed.

"Elizaveta, you knew it would come to this," Volenko said, calmly. "We all did. It doesn't matter what they say."

"What matters," Torlas cut in abruptly, "is how you and the American got along last night. You missed our get-together at midnight, so I assume that you slept with him."

She reacted before thinking, her hand quicker than her mind. The slap staggered Torlas, more from the surprise of it than the force of the blow. Elizaveta pulled back when she realized what she had done. "I'm sorry, Nikolai. I didn't mean..."

Torlas, recovered from the shock, laughed. "You were right to hit me, my dear girl. I was being a boorish

Georgian. It's just that Mikhail and I have been discussing…" He looked at Volenko's horrified face and elaborately clamped his own hand across his mouth.

Turning to Volenko, she asked, "What were you two discussing?"

Volenko released her hand, freeing both of his to gesture. "It is important, Elizaveta. Did you?"

Almost proudly, she declared, "Yes. Three times. And I will again tonight."

Clapping his hands together, Torlas smiled broadly. Cheerfully, Volenko asked, "He likes you?"

"Yes. Very much." Christopher had said as much, she recalled, just as they parted in the hallway.

"Enough?"

All pretense of bravado dissipated at the sound of the one word question. It was one of the questions she had been asking herself since leaving Dunney's side. One of the easier. "I don't know. I don't even know how much is enough for what we want, Nikolai. He would not walk me into the square, but he begged to see me tonight." Begged? Asked politely. Firmly. "Christopher is…"

Torlas slapped Volenko on the back. "Christopher!"

Volenko stole a critical look at the girl. He was worried about her. Her vulnerability had become one of his chief concerns. "What about the currency exchange?"

Elizaveta went pale. She saw herself in the KGB car, wedged between the two agents. "The KGB arrested us."

"What?"

"The KGB? My God."

"They were sitting at the next table. Mikhail. Nikolai, they were all around us!" She calmed herself to continue the story. "We were taken to the Director of the Procurator's Investigative Department, named Bellin. He told me that he knew what I was trying to do, what we were trying to do. He knows everything."

"What about the American?"

"Christopher did not say explicitly, but he hinted that Bellin warned him to stay away from certain 'undesirables.'"

"And so he should," said Torlas lightly.

Volenko issued a heavy sigh. "He defused that plan, then."

"Yes. Intentionally."

"Is he that smart?" Torlas asked, skeptically. "I had one of his men contact me. He didn't seem particularly acute."

"Hmm." Volenko, having received a visit as well, did not share Torlas' dim view of Investigators in general. Besides, Director Bellin was clearly different. He had detected the scheme from its outset. Knowing what was coming, Bellin had moved in quickly to prevent the dissidents from gaining a hold on Dunney. Volenko was worried. They were no match for such an adversary.

"We have very little time," he reminded them. "The trial will begin any day."

"And it won't last long," Torlas added. "Only long enough to make a show of it."

"Elizaveta, you must spend every spare moment with the American. You must make him need you."

"But he has his secretary." She knew that something existed between Dunney and the girl, Andrea. It had been obvious in his eyes.

Thoughtfully, Volenko mulled the problem over. "Then you must make yourself more desirable."

"Stop it!" she cried. "Either he accepts me as I am..."

Sharply, Torlas said, "This is not a love affair, damn you. This is our whole movement. He doesn't have to do anything. You have to make him want to... to want you. That may sound nasty, Elizaveta, but we're out of alternatives." He lowered his voice to a whisper. "We have to get that tape to the Americans. Your American is the only way. Don't forget that."

His hands on her shoulders, Volenko looked deeply into Elizaveta's glimmering eyes. "You are a very desirable woman. Make it easy for him. Do whatever he wants, before he wants it. In and out of bed. If he becomes dependent upon you, that may be close enough to be confused with affection. The proper moment will present itself to you. It will still be only a chance, but you will have to take it."

Torlas had one additional suggestion. "He is an American. Americans are overly proud of their reputation as a free people. Liberty. Justice. We know that they are just words, but the words are important just as in religion. Use those words. Speak with him in English and use those American words. Start blending them with yourself, your cause, and Mraisky's plight."

"Nikolai is right, Elizaveta. Speak to his American vanity."

She stared at the two men. It was awful to hear them speak as they were. She did not want to hear any more. "He is not like that. Let me get to know him." Was that too much to ask? she wondered.

Somber, Volenko said, "There isn't that much time, Elizaveta."

~ ~ ~

Procurator General Dmitri Feuchinko stepped up into the press gallery and motioned Greenwald forward. When the American hesitated, Feuchinko grinned proudly and insisted. "Come, come, Mr. Greenwald," he boomed in Russian. "This is a newly designed court room. The show place of Soviet law."

Greenwald stared up at the massive Procurator General, a man he knew to be an intimate of Brezhnev himself. It was an intimidating sight. Feuchinko stood framed by the doorway, blocking Greenwald's view into the room, which might have contained a dozen KGB agents for all Greenwald knew.

From the shattering moment when he learned of John Winker's death at the hands of the KGB, Greenwald had had waking nightmares about what kinds of fate lay about Moscow for him. After all, he was a CIA agent now. And Winker had been. And Greenwald had been his last visitor.

In spite of his paranoia, Greenwald had no second thoughts about accepting Feuchinko's invitation. As a "former" reporter, he could never pass up the chance to observe Mraisky's trial. Never.

Greenwald took the steps one at a time, angling by Feuchinko, who tried to shift some of his bulk aside. The press gallery had twenty-four seats, in two rows, each with its own headset. Beside each seat sat a telephone. He tried the chair, finding unusual comfort in the Russian cushions. In front of him a huge glass panel stretched the entire thirty feet of the wall, giving all seats a perfect line of sight into a modern courtroom below.

He placed a hand on the phone. "Does this go to the pool room?"

Feuchinko. towering over him, nodded. "It's hooked up to a speaker in the American press' room downstairs. You have free use of it at all times. It is plugged into your earphones, here," he explained, showing Greenwald the headphones.

"Very impressive."

"Thank you."

Greenwald studied the courtroom. Obviously as new as Feuchinko had claimed, it appeared virginal. The judges' bench, large enough for five judges, had dark inlays in its blond wood. To one side, the prisoner's box sat removed from the other parts of the courtroom, stigmatizing its occupant. The Procurator would work out of a bench in front of the judges, but slightly off center, away from the defendant's area.

"Why are there two sets of witness areas?"

Craning his neck unnecessarily, Feuchinko considered the question. "Ah, yes. One is for the State, the other is for the witnesses of the criminal."

It figured. Nothing was left to chance in the Soviet system. "You can put on quite a slow with this courtroom," he observed, choosing his words.

Arching one eyebrow, Feuchinko replied, "Why do you think we built it?" He followed up with a deeply resonant belly laugh. "But enough of that, Mr. Greenwald. I promised to introduce you to the Procurator."

"Will you excuse me an undiplomatic question, Procurator General Feuchinko?"

Still smiling, the big man shrugged to convey the impression of "but of course."

"You know that I am a reporter, primarily, by occupation. And that my visa had been lifted. Why have you invited me to represent the American press?"

Feuchinko's face took a serious cast for the first time since Greenwald had met him. "You are known to be a friend of Dr. Mraisky. You have written some of the harshest words against our government and in favor of those few who, for whatever reason, criticize the Party. That makes you the logical choice."

"How? You've just described a very prejudiced reporter. "

"Exactly, Mr. Greenwald. Exactly."

~ ~ ~

As the American President's press secretary read the official Administration statement. Vasili Arkilonov downed his third cup of scalding, black coffee in the half hour since his lunch with Feuchinko. The relayed radio signal was annoyingly weak, fading in and out on the White House Press Conference.

Arkilonov checked his watch. The hastily called news conference had produced a modest statement. In a way, the Americans seemed relieved about Mraisky's indictment. There was, of course, the other news.

"...of us in this country and particularly in the Administration regret that so great a human being as Dr. Mraisky should be treated so cruelly and summarily by the Soviet government. The charges lodged against Dr. Mraisky include what we in the United States consider to be the exercise of natural rights endowed upon all men and women by our creator."

The crowded room apparently responded to the words with disapproval. Snorts, jeers, laughter, groans came over clearly.

"...anything that we can to win freedom for Dr. Mraisky," the press secretary concluded. "All right, I'll take a few questions. Make them good, though. I can't spend all morning on this."

Arkilonov nodded, satisfied. It was going well.

The opening question was, "Will the President call off the Secretary of State's secret talks with the Russians, or will he pretend that Dr. Mraisky doesn't exist?"

"Assuming the Secretary is conducting secret talks, I cannot comment upon them," the Press Secretary said lightly. "And the President is very much in Dr. Mraisky's camp."

"Follow up."

"Yes."

"What can the President do to help Dr. Mraisky?"

The young man's voice faltered. "The President is employing every diplomatic device at his disposal to express this country's support of Dr. Mraisky and his personal entreaty that Dr. Mraisky be freed."

A woman from the LA Times was recognized next. "How much pressure can the President put on the Russians if he is going ahead on SALT?"

"The President feels the human rights are of primary importance in his foreign policy. He does not feel that it is wise to compromise his demands for human rights by tying them to politics." The last few words were shouted over a rising moan of protest. "You cannot bargain human rights!"

An identifiably black reporter spoke to another question. "Do human rights include the right of this country's black community to be represented in American business?"

"Emphatically yes. I assume you refer to Mr. Bingo Williams' speech last night? The President will see that minority business is well represented among American companies both in Moscow and everywhere overseas as well as in the United States, including giving personal support to Mr. William's venture."

With that question answered, the reporters settled down. Arkilonov did not relax. The moment approached. Now? He bent forward as a reporter from a Chicago paper got the call. Yes. "Does the President have any comment upon the brutal murder by the Russians of an American supporter of Dr. Mraisky?"

The KGB Chairman did not move, listening carefully. He detected no hesitation in the Press Secretary's voice. If anything the young fool sounded confident.

"The President expresses sorrow at the death of John Winker..."

The statement was never finished. For two minutes, the room was obviously in an uproar as it emptied of reporters.

They had not anticipated so viciously worded a question, a deliberately inflammatory juxtaposition of two unrelated incidents. Arkilonov smiled. Of course not.

Chapter Nine

"I must say, Mr. Dunney," Sarkat admitted, "that in the week since your client's rousing speech, several African governments have praised our even-handedness."

Dunney concealed his impatience, as he had for six full, frustrating days. "As they should." The Russians had gotten all of the mileage out of his ploy; he had gotten nothing. Certainly the spreading furor over Mraisky's indictment back in the states had completely overwhelmed the Administration and neutralized the affect of Bingo's speech domestically. The Russians had somehow turned even that against him. "But in the meantime, you have offered even worse locations than when we began our discussions."

Sarkat, familiar with the argument, had his familiar response on the tip of his tongue. "We want Bingo Burgers Restaurants to be a showcase, Mr. Dunney. The sites are all chosen with maximum exposure to the African peoples in mind."

The smile on his lips belied Dunney's feelings. "Exposure, yes, but Bingo Burgers may not sell a single meal in those spots. Television cameras can't eat. And people cannot get to these locations easily. I hate to discuss this same point again, Secretary Sarkat, but you are being uncooperative to say the least."

"My government's policy..." Sarkat shrugged. The argument requiring no restatement. He was as frustrated as Dunney, perhaps more so. The American's judgment on site location had proven superior from the start. Sarkat desperately wanted the negotiations completed so that construction could proceed. The concept of American fast-food restaurants to handle the huge Olympic crowds had originated in his ministry and he was proud of it. Without such a plan, the Soviet Union would appear foolish, incompetent. He had slaved on the project for a full year and a half. And now, the Party, the government, everyone was telling him to stall Dunney until the end of the Mraisky trial. Sarkat could only thank God that the trial was due to start the following morning. Sarkat did not enjoy taking orders directly from Arkilonov's lackey.

"Mr. Dunney, you must understand," Sarkat began, drawing upon the recommended explanation, "I am in a very difficult position. Our governments are not on the best of terms. If your President were not daily denouncing our country, I could take a more agreeable approach. But as it stands, I cannot afford, my government cannot afford, to be overly accommodating."

"We are talking hamburgers, Secretary Sarkat," Dunney declared, exasperated by the monotony of the conversation. "Not human rights or nuclear warheads. It is not a sign of weakness to put a hamburger stand in the right God damned place!"

Harshly, Sarkat responded, "You are hardly in a position to complain. Surely the delay in our negotiations has proven most pleasant for you."

Stung increasingly by Sarkat's references in his relationship with Elizaveta, Dunney chose to withhold comment. Sarkat knew only too well every move he made and did not hesitate to use that knowledge against him.

Sarkat also knew, for Bellin knew, that Dunney had not slept much during the past week. Even Elizaveta's comfort was a torment. Even? No. She was the source of it, the embodiment of it, the agent of it. And yet he could barely tolerate their separations. He had, in one short week, developed a need for her akin to addiction. It was a physical need. Hopefully only a physical one.

Even then, as he sat opposite Sarkat, he could feel himself against her, her legs wrapped around him. It was an incredible and very dangerous irony. His career already jeopardized by his relationship with her, was further dependent upon his keeping her out of his mind.

But then, the President did not exactly help matters. Each day his condemnations had become more sharply worded, more emotionally delivered. The Russian press ignored him, thank God, but everywhere else, the President's attacks on the Soviet persecution of Mraisky dominated the front pages in every other newspaper he had seen. And yet, somehow, the SALT revision talks seemed to continue.

As did the hamburger talks. "Off the record, Sarkat," Dunney asked after a long silence, "What do you want? Can we go anywhere under present conditions?"

The Russian stared at Dunney. His instructions made no mention of how far he should go, how candid he should be. Sarkat, empathizing with the American, decided to level. "Under present conditions? It depends on you, Mr. Dunney. Not your President, or the others. The climate is bad, yes. But it will remain so until the Mraisky matter is settled."

"I see."

"I am not finished," Sarkat sighed. "The problem is that you show no respect for my government's concerns. They won't let me concede to such a man. It is a matter of honor."

"How do I show the proper respect, Secretary Sarkat?"

Sarkat pushed his lips. "A rhetorical question, Mr. Dunney. isn't it?"

Dunney rubbed his eyes and let his hand fall onto the table top in resignation. "Shall we meet tomorrow?"

"I am at your disposal."

"Same time?"

"Until tomorrow." Sarkat, who carried very few papers, rose and left the small conference room.

Taking his time, Dunney put his things together and closed his briefcase. He had no answers. He knew what he had to do, but he had no idea how to do it. Or even if he could.

~ ~ ~

"But if the trial starts tomorrow," Folenya insisted, "they must try tonight. You can not want them to recall Dunney."

Bellin ran his finger around the dark bag below his left eye. The view in the mirror that morning had unsettled him for the whole day. Had he aged so in just one week? His reflection appeared well over fifty. Ten of those extra years he credited to Folenya and her constant harping. His only consolation was that she looked even older than he did.

Tonight. Yes, Anna was right. That was why he wanted rid of Dunney. He had gone so far as requesting the KGB's assistance in making Dunney's firm aware of his compromising affair with the girl. Folenya, ever alert, had helped block it.

"Anna, my primary concern is preventing the Americans from getting the tape. That is what your people asked me to do. It's more important to stop that than to trap a few dissidents. Do you want me to take the chance that the message will get through just to have the chance to arrest the girl?"

"Of course not. But there is no element of chance involved."

Bellin was too tired to argue. "All right, Dunney stays." First Sarkat had insisted that Dunney remain, now Anna. Bellin would have preferred to call the American law firm and tell them directly what Dunney was up to in Moscow, and he would have done it a week earlier. No, he kidded himself in thinking that. Dunney, a known, relatively predictable quantity, was better than some newcomer he would not understand.

In the week he had covered Dunney, Bellin had grown familiar with Dunney's reactions, his moods, even his lovemaking techniques. If Marta had not been so puritanical underneath, he would have tried one of them himself. Of course, he had gotten home only twice all week at night; he had seen far more of Dunney and Elizaveta than he had of his own family.

He had also seen more of Anna Folenya than he cared to. Relieved of the duty to conduct the pretrial investigation, Bellin had elected to spend his evening and nights monitoring Dunney, Elizaveta and the other dissidents, of whom there were few still active. Ordinarily he slept during the morning, on the couch recently installed in his office compliments of the KGB. This particular morning, Folenya gave up her own sleep to badger him about his suggestion that Dunney go back to Boston.

"Vladimir Bellin, you need sleep," Folenya said in a superior tone. Her excitement about the coming evening, coupled with the four pills, would keep her going all day. She knew that Elizaveta would enlist Dunney that night. Folenya felt confident that it would all happen in Dunney's room, because there the girl had her greatest power over the American. Then, the KGB, which she had alerted, would sweep in and arrest them both, message cartridge in hand, the whole transaction recorded on video tape.

With that evidence, the Moscow Group could be finally obliterated, the track for Communism cleared of another pile of bourgeois debris.

"Are you all right, Anna?"

"What?" she asked, startled by the sound of her name.

Bellin smiled knowingly. "You need sleep as much as I do. Anna. Neither coffee nor pills do the trick."

Stiffening, Folenya retorted, "It will be over soon enough. Then I'll sleep."

"Certainly one afternoon will not…"

Folenya bounded out of her seat. "I am perfectly fine, Director Bellin. I intend to be there to watch you." She blushed at her outburst. "I mean, to watch them. I want to take part."

"Well," he said, amused at her slip of the tongue, "if you want to watch me, I will make it very easy for you." He pushed out of his chair and strode to the couch. "I'll be right here."

Before he could plop down, his phone rang. Bellin retraced his steps and answered, "Bellin."

It was the Investigator on watch in the monitoring station. "Director, the girl, the American? She just placed a call to Boston."

Bellin frowned. "Who?"

"Steven Klein."

Hanging up the phone, Bellin looked at Folenya, who stared back with wide, pupil-dilated eyes. If he knew women… "Come on, Anna. This may be important."

The two operators discussed the problem briefly, and put the call through to Boston a second time. Andy nervously shifted the telephone from one ear to the other. Though she had become used to Soviet phone inefficiency, she was not in the mood for it at that moment.

Finally, the Boston operator succeeded in establishing an adequate connection, eliciting a sleepy "hello" from a neuter voice.

"I have a call from Moscow for a Mr. Steven Klein."

"Moscow?" The voice was identifiably a woman's. Andy had never spoken to Amy Klein and had never wanted to. Fortunately, she did not have to as the operator was interposed between them.

"Who is it?" Amy asked.

"A Miss Andrea Wards," the Boston operator replied crisply. "From Moscow."

Andy detected no hostility in Amy's voice when she repeated, "Andrea Wards? Just a minute." Obviously, Mrs. Klein did not know about her husband's momentary lapse of fidelity. Andy felt somewhat relieved, but that only served to underline her anxiety about making the call in the first place.

During the pause that followed, Andy waited impatiently, her mind irrepressibly reliving the past week: her excitement: Chris' increasing coldness toward her, her self-indulgent manipulation of Clint Thomas; the gnawing loneliness she felt when Chris was with Elizaveta; the anger finally.

"Hello, Andy?" Klein's voice startled her.

Clearing her dry throat, she said, "I'm going to come back. Steve. Tomorrow."

"Come back?" Klein asked. "Andrea, please. Dunney needs someone intelligent..."

Her voice, strained, she interrupted, "There's no point. We cannot work together." She paused, weighing words. "It's my fault. Chris is getting alone fine without me now."

"Do you want to explain that?" Klein had obviously noticed the sarcasm that she had not hidden. "What do you mean?"

"Does the name Elizaveta Krylenkev mean anything to you?" Andy asked coldly. She caught her reflection in the mirror. God, her eyes...

"Yes." Klein sounded shaken.

"Well, it does to Chris, too. He's with her night and day. She can handle his translating chores, along with everything else, a hell of a lot better than I've been able to." How harsh it came out.

"How long?"

"All week."

Klein said nothing for a moment and then asked, "Would you please stay, Andy. And keep me informed."

"Spy on him?" Andy demanded, staggered.

"Keep me informed. I cannot trust Dunney's judgment unless I know on what it is based."

Adamantly, she said, "I will not spy on Chris. Period."

"For his own good..."

"I don't care about his own good, damn you. What about me? Jesus, nobody gives a shit about me! And I'm tired of it. I want to come home."

Conciliatory, Klein said, "All right. It's up to you, Andrea. You're there, and understand the situation better than I can. All I can say is that it will help if you would stand by..."

"No."

"It's up to you," he repeated. "Thank you for the call."

"You're welcome, I'm sure," she retorted. "Goodbye." She hung up before Klein could say a thing, hating him for his demand. How low an opinion did he have of her?

Andy struck out at the phone, knocking it to the floor. Slowly, she returned the receiver, her composure returning with the help of the mirror. Her eyes were not hard. It had been an illusion. They were just red.

~ ~ ~

Afternoon fading into evening, Dunney thought, as he closed the curtain over the head of the bed. When he turned around, propped up on pillows, he found Elizaveta leaning in the doorway. His robe draped all over her made her look small. Innocent. Vulnerable.

"Am I keeping you?" she asked lightly.

"Yes, you are. I should be working."

Elizaveta stared at him for a moment and then sat on the edge of the bed. "Why do I always feel that I am taking you away from your work?"

"Irony suits you." Dunney decided not to tell her how much irony, at least not directly. "Work. My work is important to me. In the United States, there are three ways to make it: Luck, birth and work. I've never been lucky. God knows I've never been lucky. Birth? More bad luck."

"It's a sad story," she said mockingly.

"Accidents always are."

Elizaveta reached for his hand. "Christopher, I'm sorry."

"I lived through it."

"But you can't know that kind of thing. Can you?"

Dunney thought back. A mother aged thirty-six; four brothers nine to sixteen years older; a sister seven years older. He laughed. "I suppose not. It was good anyway. It made me work, on my own. That's still my greatest limitation."

Pulling herself up beside him, Elizaveta rested her head on his shoulder. "You're learning."

His arm nestled her closer. "How about that?" That first night, had he tried too much to do it alone? Had he always? Perhaps, because with Elizaveta, now, it was completely different. He returned the subject to its original course. "Everything that I have spent all this time working for...?"

'Yes?"

"I could have it by the time I get back to Boston..." He felt her body grow rigid, but went on. "If I don't screw up here."

She did not want to talk about his going back. Or about her affect on his assignment. "Please, Christopher."

"I'm screwing up, Elizaveta."

Because of her, she knew, though he kindly spared her that much. What did he know? What of her? Her friends would hardly speak to her. She had jeopardized everything by pretending that time would make it better; make him love her enough to want to help her.

She had pretended she had not fallen in love with a non-Jew. She had lied to herself, to Mikhail, to Nikolai for a week! "Please," she protested. She wanted to lie just a little longer.

"They don't want to deal with me," Dunney admitted, unburdening himself. If he could not, then there was no point in going on anyway. "Your government doesn't like my choice of company. Of course, they don't know you the way I do."

"I understand. Do you?"

"What do you mean?"

She looked deep in his clear questioning eyes. "Do you understand what we are against now? Now that it is focused against you. Can you imagine what it is like to be a Jew in this country? You are just associating with one."

"I'm associating with an activist..."

"To be a Jew is to be an activist!" she snapped. "It's what I want to be! What I must be!" Elizaveta yanked loose and stalked out of the room.

Watching after her, Dunney experienced the absence of her. He found the empty bed disquieting, pulled on a pair of slacks and joined her in the living room. She sat curled up on the couch, head down. Dunney sat next to her, near but not touching.

"Elizaveta, you've told me what you want to be and what you think you must be, but not what you are."

Her eyes widened, she stared at him. "It doesn't matter. Life is a process. Toward something. I know where I'm going."

"You know I can't go there with you," Dunney said uncomfortably.

"But you must help me!" As she finished the exclamation, she pulled back physically wanting to recall the words.

Angry with her for demanding his aid, he glowered at her. "Don't use the fact that I have feelings for you,

Elizaveta, to make me do something I cannot do. That would be a mistake we'd both regret."

Earnestly trying to repair the damage, Elizaveta begged, "Please, Christopher."

Dunney misinterpreted her plea and responded harshly, "No."

Elizaveta rose and walked to the window. Out in the square, the Militia continued its ceaseless watch over the US Embassy. She thought of the tape cartridge hidden in her apartment and what it meant. It meant that Judaism would gradually die in the Soviet Union and that she would die with it. Christopher certainly would understand that. "If you loved me…"

"It wouldn't change a thing!" he declared, imposing his own ending on her sentence. "I know, because, I do love you. But I made a promise to myself a long time ago. That I would make it. That I would do something that anyone would recognize as success. And I am too close to fuck it up!"

"Elizaveta, I know that what you want is just as important to you as this is to me, but I cannot get any further involved in your… in your life than I am now. What's the point? You want to be a good damn Jew and I can't be. So, please, don't ask me to help you."

Disheartened. Elizaveta tugged the belt of the robe tighter. "Is there nothing we can do?"

"I don't know."

"Do you want me to leave? To stay away?"

"Of course not," Dunney said emphatically, adding quietly, "But what choice is there?"

Elizaveta turned quickly and disappeared into the bedroom, leaving Dunney to his thoughts.

He had done what was necessary. Life was full of hard decisions and he had made plenty of others. This particular one had been harder than most, emotionally if not logically, but it had finally been made. He would get over it. A partnership could salve a lot of wounds.

The bedroom door opened revealing a fully dressed Elizaveta with his bathrobe on over everything else. "May I keep this?"

Off the couch, Dunney took a couple of steps while eying the robe. "It looks very nice on you. Yes."

She took off the robe and folded it carefully into the string shopping bag she, and every other Russian, always carried. She smiled sadly, walked up to him and kissed him tenderly on the mouth. "If you want me to come back, Christopher, I will."

Caressing her thin arms, he shook his head. "If I thought that, Elizaveta, I wouldn't let you go. You know that."

She kissed him again and said, "I know. Good-bye."

"Good-bye."

Dunney walked her to the door and out into the hall. He waited until the elevator had come and gone, taking her from him. A very neutral feeling possessed him as he reentered his room. Not until he reached the window did the neutrality of the feeling reveal itself as emptiness.

He looked around the room. For the first time, he saw how bare it was, how truly empty a room could be. It was as if he were seeing it from the outside.

From the outside. "Bellin!" he cried, spinning around looking for the camera. "Bellin, God damn it! Are you satisfied now?"

~ ~ ~

The dull green car ran its third consecutive traffic signal, at the speed of sixty-eight kilometers per hour. Though not overly fast, the speed drew annoyed stares from pedestrians and a few curses from people backed off by its horn. No one knew, of course, that the car belonged to the KGB.

A KGB car, Bellin thought, as he lounged in the back seat and watched the borrowed KGB driver negotiate the streets. "Weren't there any Department cars?"

The driver replied, "Yes."

"Then why are we in this one?"

After swerving around a third turn, the driver said, "Comrade Folenya has had this one standing by all day. She called after you did and suggested that you use this car. Since it was ready."

"It's enough to make one walk," he mumbled.

"Pardon. Director?"

"When we get to the hotel, drop me in front and wait." Bellin figured that if he did the job right, he could go straight home. "It shouldn't take long."

Dunney's calling out to him had been the signal, Bellin felt. The American had come to think of Bellin as all intrusive. Would he not, then, consider him all knowing? Bellin had, in addition to his ability to relate the entire sequence of Dunney and Elizaveta's parting, another piece of ammunition: The call made by Dunney's secretary to Boston.

Bellin had his tactics worked out, but understood that flexibility of response would serve him better than a rigid plan. He had developed a confidence that he could react properly to Dunney. His anticipatory level in that regard had reached an uncomfortably high plateau. Uncomfortable, because he began to worry that Folenya could anticipate his moves just as well as he anticipated Dunney's.

If Folenya remained a step ahead of him, trouble was inevitable.

As the car pulled up in front of the hotel, Bellin composed himself, shunting thoughts of Folenya to his unconsciousness–he knew they were always there of late–and concentrated on Dunney. His American would be extremely agitated upon seeing him, but controlled. Dunney would not want Bellin to have the satisfaction of seeing the true state of his emotions. Resentment would most characterize Dunney's manner, but even that response would, for once, be muted. One response Bellin hesitated to predict: Dunney's reaction to Bellin's significant disclosure, his wedge.

Bellin had never before entered the international Hotel, but he felt familiar in its lobby, although it looked different from what he had grown to expect from the cameras. The people in the lobby, including himself, looked less like laboratory mice and more like human beings. He resisted an impulse to glance over his shoulder at the most often used camera. Folenya would make a note of that kind of thing, he knew.

At the desk, he displayed his credentials and told the clerk to relay any calls for him to Dunney's room. The clerk, mildly intimidated by the Director of Investigation, nodded in small, quick movements. Bellin indicated Dunney's message box. The clerk hurried over to the boxes and back, unfolding the note for Bellin as he handed it to him.

Without reading it, Bellin folded it between two fingers and waved it at the clerk. "I will deliver this to Mr. Dunney. Thank you for your assistance."

In the privacy of the elevator–private except for the usual camera–Bellin looked at the note that Elizaveta had left behind her. He evaluated the contents and placed the paper deep in his suit coat pocket. Now was not the time for Dunney to hear that she loved him. In a few minutes, no note would convince Dunney of that anyway.

Bellin checked his breast pocket for the package of Winston cigarettes. On the way to Dunney's room, he lit one and took a long drag. The cigarette would set the stage.

Two solid raps brought the sound of shuffling feet, a growling "Who the hell is it?" and the "shit" accompanied the opening of the door. Glazed eyes met Bellin's through the free inch wide crack. "Who...?"

The shock of recognition forced Dunney's eyes open and made him swing wide the door. He managed to close his mouth after a second. Then he smiled grimly. "Well, I'll be damned!"

Responding in English, Bellin gestured with the cigarette. "May I?"

After a laugh, Dunney asked, "Do you have to ask?"

"Yes. This is not truly an official call."

Dunney looked Bellin up and down, critically. "No? Then, by all means." Once Bellin had passed him, Dunney recalled what was wrong. "Where's the cigar?"

Pleased with the American's observation, Bellin produced the Winston's. "I know you don't smoke, but would you join me?"

It was too much like a nightmare, Dunney thought, amused and repelled at the same time. His picture of Bellin was not complete without the big cigar. Yet here was the face he had visualized so often while sleeping and awake, with the Winston's he had himself supplied. "No thanks, Director Bellin. But I'm glad you accepted my little present."

Calmly, Bellin said, "Ah, Mr. Dunney. I had begun to think that you had forgotten our talk. I am gratified that you remember the incident if not the substance of it."

A spark of anger fired inside the American. He had Bellin's words burned in his mind and Bellin knew it. Dunney battled the emotion and won. Bellin had seen what had happened with Elizaveta and had probably come to gloat. Or worse. Dunney wasn't about to help him.

"I would have thought by now, Director Bellin, that you'd be calling me Christopher."

Intentionally. Bellin let his eyes drift up toward one of the cameras. He tried to make it subtle. It was not lost on the American. "Curious. Perhaps you could help me out, Christopher. You ordinarily use 'Chris'..."

"I allow particularly desirable people to use my full name, Director Bellin." Dunney turned toward his small bar. "What about you? Since this isn't really 'official', why don't I call you something informal? Drink?"

Folenya would hit the ceiling, Bellin thought pleasantly, but he had to maintain appearances. "Thank you."

"Mostly I have vodka, of course, but I brought alone some prize Kentucky bourbon," Dunney said, setting up two glasses. "For gratuity. You know."

"I will take the bourbon if we may speak in Russian," Bellin said jovially. "English makes me uncomfortable."

"You Russians love to barter." Pouring a stiff drink for each, Dunney threw away the remnants of his earlier drink. It reminded him to go slowly. He had had another good one since Elizaveta's departure. "In the US, we buy and sell."

Bellin took the drink and, satisfied that it was not overly much, gulped it down. "Interesting flavor, Christopher. Is it popular in your country?"

"Oddly enough, not as popular as vodka," Dunney replied, jarred by Bellin's precipitous consumption of four ounces of neat Rebel Yell. He could ill afford to keep pace. "Another?"

Smiling, Bellin shook his head. "It is not official. But it is serious. Besides, I hope to see my wife tonight and she would not appreciate the obvious effects of too much drink."

"Don't you see your wife often?" The remark stuck Dunney as so peculiar that he could not restrain his curiosity. He had also not thought of Bellin as a husband.

The slip, Bellin told himself, was purposeful. "Not for a week or so. She works during the day," he explained amiably, "while I have been very busy at night."

My God, Dunney thought. The son of a bitch was admitting to his face that he had spent the nights watching Elizaveta and him! Shaken more than angry, Dunney wondered, Didn't Bellin realize what that meant? "I hope she appreciates your coming home tonight," he said, trying to keep his cool. "Not everyone will be so lucky."

"I am sorry, Christopher," Bellin said, deciding that he had to proceed. The conversation about his family life seemed out of place. "Under different circumstances..."

"Didn't you enjoy it? Director Bellin?" Dunney asked bitterly. The man's hypocrisy was too much to bear without an occasional outburst. Still, he managed to reassert control. "I'm sorry. I suppose it is your job."

"Duty, Christopher. It is my duty."

"That's a dirty word in America those days. It covers too much and not enough."

"In America." Bellin took a puff on the cigarette, having forgotten that it was not a cigar. He followed it with a deep drag and a slow exhale. "Perhaps, that is your problem."

"It's not mine," Dunney retorted. "You should know that after tonight."

Bellin settled back into the couch and crossed his legs. He looked up at Dunney, a sympathetic expression playing on his face. No, he admitted, it was not an act. "I admire you for what you did. It was unwise to become involved with her initially, but wisdom doesn't play a part in love."

"Love?" Dunney objected.

"A general term." Bellin elaborated, "It is close enough. Perhaps I should have said 'emotion' or 'relationships'. I apologize if I offended you."

Scratching his eyebrow, Dunney sat on the arm of the chair cornering the sofa. "It's moot now."

"You will be finalizing your negotiations soon?"

"Oh God, Bellin, what do you think?" asked an exasperated Dunney. He finished his drink in two swallows. "Right now, I just want to get the hell out of your damned country to a place where I can take a crap in private. Yes, I found that one too, after she left. I wanted to see the face of a man... And there it was." He stood up and went back to the bar. "You're thorough, I'll give you that. Another?"

Quickly, Bellin got up and walked over to Dunney. Another might help, though he had better not drink it. "Short."

"Don't swallow it like a Cossack," Dunney said. "It makes me nervous." Was it the effect of the liquor or Bellin's kindly matter-of-fact outlook on his total invasion of Dunney's life that prevented his hating the man?

Once the drinks were sparingly refreshed. Dunney asked, "Okay. Official or not, what is it?"

Holding off a desire to drink, Bellin began, "There is something you should know, Christopher."

"Tell me."

Their eyes met, each studying the other's. Dunney did not believe for a minute that Bellin was about to do him a favor for nothing; the Russians, he recalled, love to barter. Would they barter love? A play on words only, he told himself.

Bellin had to adapt to Dunney's mood, to his expectation, yet he was unsure as to what either was at that moment. He detected the suspicion easily enough, but what else was there? A trace of hope, trust, confidence in what he had to offer seemed to shade Dunney's skepticism. Dunney, he felt, would believe him, accept what he was about to say, but only if he offered it in exchange for something. His mind sought what Dunney would perceive as Bellin's need.

He had it. It would be complicated and potentially dangerous, but it would work. Lighting another cigarette, walking to set his drink on the table, acting reluctant, Bellin fashioned the approach. He could feel Dunney's impatience, betrayed by the clicking of his tongue. Finally, he was ready.

Dunney, tapping his fingers noiselessly on the glass, braced himself for Bellin's disclosure. He fully expected it to hurt and to outrage him at once and he wanted to be ready.

"It's not a pleasant role I play, but," Bellin said facing away from the American. "Before I start, you should know that I will inform Secretary Sarkat that you are no longer in touch with the Moscow Group. That simply is. It has nothing to do with what I am about to say."

Dunney nodded slowly, suspiciously.

Bellin laughed as he turned back around. "Sarkat wants those hamburger restaurants. Our government wants them more than ever, now that the Africans are watching your client's progress."

"Fair exchange."

"The important matter, however, is the one which has involved my Department. It is an unusual thing for me and for my Department, Christopher," he explained honestly. Bellin had no liking for the task, to be sure. "It became our duty because the KGB felt it more appropriate that we handle it, since it also involved certain members of that agency."

"I see."

"Dr. Mraisky. as you know, has been arrested not only as a subversive and propagandist, both of which he is in a way that strikes some of us more than others, but also as a collaborator of your country's CIA. He is that, as well, Christopher, I assure you."

"Elizaveta doesn't think so," Dunney observed, using her name aloud for the first time since she had left.

"She cannot admit it," Bellin said, again with sincerity. "But she knows better. She knows better because either she or one of her colleagues in the Moscow Group is in possession of evidence of that fact."

"What?" The information stunned Dunney. "You can't be serious."

Bellin closed his eyes and shook his head. "That they have it, yes. Perhaps, they are not fully aware of how Mraisky obtained it. That is possible."

"Are you saying that it came from the CIA?"

"So I am informed."

"By the KGB."

Somber, Bellin went on, "The KGB is reluctant to proceed, because of the embarrassing source of the evidence. The CIA, you see, has infiltrated the KGB."

Unimpressed, Dunney remarked, "They infiltrate each other all the time."

"Perhaps. But this particular infiltrator communicated certain information to Dr. Mraisky–of that I have proof–and he conveyed it to his associates, though we do not know quite how."

Dunney began to worry about Elizaveta. Did she know what she was involved in? Could her blind dedication to her cause, to Mraisky have compelled her to work with the CIA? God, they could put her away forever!

Sizing up Dunney's introspective look, Bellin assumed that the American had accepted the facts related so far. "The KGB, of course, wants that information back. It is apparently a coded tape in a cartridge. The Procurator needs it for his case against Mraisky."

"And you?"

The individual incentive, Bellin mused, how American. He fabricated an "American" answer. "This is a very big trial for my superior. The government wants a very strong showing against Mraisky and will reward those who make it strong."

Satisfied, Dunney said, "Go on."

"The members of the Moscow Group–Elizaveta and her two friends whom you met your first night in

Moscow are the leaders now that Mraisky is in custody-believe that the information in their possession will help Mraisky's cause if it gets into the hands of the CIA. They have made a number of feeble attempts to do so themselves, but we have seen to it that it is impossible."

Glancing toward the window, Dunney asked, "Are you responsible for that?"

"Yes." Bellin hoped his candor was having its intended effect, for he was taking a chance in revealing so much. "The information may be useful in Mraisky's behalf, as an exchange factor, as an embarrassment, I don't know. From the KGB reaction, I am inclined to think that they would prefer the Americans not have it." He was telling Dunney only what Elizaveta would tell him herself, but he worried nonetheless. With Folenya undoubtedly watching, he could only go so far.

"Why are you telling me this?"

"I will tell you in a minute," Bellin said carefully, hoping to avoid alienating Dunney now that he had him where he wanted him. "We knew, you see, that the Moscow Group desperately wanted to get to the CIA. We took every possible step to cut them off from everyone they trusted. And we succeeded. Except for one thing. There was one man they trusted above even their most frequent contacts."

"Well?"

Bellin paused a long time, because the real point would come next. "A friend of Mraisky. An active American Jew. A man who supported Mraisky with gifts of money..." He let the information sink in.

It did not take Dunney long. "Jesus! Klein."

"Yes."

Staggered, Dunney tried to put the pieces together. His arrival at the hotel. the greeting by Elizaveta, the conversation with the three of them: It fit. It fit too well. "They expected Klein."

"And he did not come," Bellin added pointedly. "He did not come. The one man they knew would be willing to risk everything to help them, to help Mraisky, to act as a courier for them, that one man did not come. You did."

All of the images of the week, the feelings, the words, everything fell into place. It fell into place in the abstract. It moved too fast for Dunney to digest it fully, to feel its impact.

Relentlessly now, Bellin continued, his voice quickly stabbing home its points. "We expected Klein as well. We were ready for him. But not for you. We understood that you would be the logical substitute, the only substitute considering the time involved. We simply did not know how you would react, or whether Elizaveta and her colleagues would risk dealing with a complete stranger. Of course, we had you followed. Of course, we monitored every movement. But it was not until the night at the Shashlik that I knew. Christopher."

Dunney's eyes, feeling each wound Bellin had inflicted. swung toward hint, uncomprehending.

"It's an old trick. Probably Torlas' idea, he's the novelist. The KGB loves it. I've thrown out more trumped up currency violations than you can imagine." Bellin said with an unfelt ease. He shared some of Dunney's obvious pain. He had lived with him too long not to. "When I caught on, I had the two of you brought in immediately. I could not afford to allow her to keep that leverage against you. I wanted to take the plan and strip it of its effect before anything could happen."

Trumped up currency violation. The phrase whined inside Dunney's head. "She set me up."

"Torlas' idea. I'm sure," Bellin said, trying to control Dunney's reaction. "Once that had failed..." Bellin let his sentence end without an explicit conclusion. Dunney would draw his own.

Seen in the harsh light shed by Bellin, Elizaveta's actions and words looked cold and ugly. Set next to the warm, dimly lit memories he loved, it was too overpowering to ignore. Dunney was too well accustomed to betrayal to deny it. He had grown too used to Bellin's veracity to doubt his truth. But he did. Somehow, Dunney's mind resisted, his normally cynical, suspicious mind resisted. "Let's get to the why."

Pausing to evaluate Dunney's response, Bellin took his time with a third cigarette. He made it seem important that he wait until he had several long pulls of smoke in and out of his lungs. Dunney had rejected his accusation, as he should have, even though it was largely true. The reaction proved surprisingly cool and Bellin did not know why or what he should do, if anything, about it. He decided to press ahead, make his pitch and save a kicker for the end.

"All right. The 'why' I want you to be prepared for her request, if it comes. If it does not, then I'm an ass and that's fine. If it does come, then you will have to help either her or me."

Dunney watched Bellin smoking, aware that it was theatrical, a prop. "What about neutrality?"

"Neutrality is for those who have nothing to gain. I am prepared to offer you something in exchange for your help, in lieu of neutrality, which will do nothing for any of us."

Feeling cold creeping along every blood vessel in his body, Dunney acknowledged the offer with a hard smile.

"If you will accept the tape from Elizaveta when–if–she asks you to aid her, and you hand it over to me, I will convince Sarkat to give you whatever you want. Anything."

"That's a generous offer."

"It is a fair offer."

Though not seriously entertaining Bellin's plan, Dunney was curious. "What happens to the girl?"

"I don't know."

The candor of the reply shook Dunney's faith in his skepticism. Bellin had only so much to give him and that made the Director seem more credible than ever. "I think you should go now," Dunney said quietly.

Satisfied with his work to that point, Bellin agreed. "Yes. Marta, my wife, is waiting. Think about it. Christopher. Just in case."

"It won't come up."

Bellin shrugged as he walked beside Dunney to the door. "Perhaps not. I think it will, but I hope for your sake that you are not faced with the decision."

"Thanks." Dunney marveled at Bellin's ability to appear concerned. There had to be some sincerity... "I appreciate your concern. Good night."

"Good night, Christopher," Bellin said as he went through the door Dunney held for him. Once he was a couple steps down the hall, he turned and came back. "I meant to mention this earlier. Your secretary called Klein in Boston and told him about you and Elizaveta. Spite, I suppose. I will suggest to Sarkat that he speak directly with Klein and assure him that the problem has been cleared up."

Was it true? Dunney's stomach tightened and his breath hung up in his lungs. Bellin knew everything! He was everywhere. Why should he lie? Why should he tell the truth?

Holding for a beat, Bellin added, "I'm getting used to you. I don't want you going back to Boston just yet. Not if I can put you to good use." Bellin gave Dunney a smile and said, "Good night, Christopher."

Once he shut the door. Dunney tried to erase his new doubts. He knew the feeling he shared with Elizaveta. Shared? It was too real, too sure. Bellin had to be lying. And yet...

Striding through the lobby, Bellin knew that he had done well. He had not expected to feel glad, just satisfied. Somehow he did not feel even that. He took out another

Winston and paused to light it. Taking advantage of the moment to look around him, Bellin saw many familiar faces. The businessman and his wife checking out he had seen the day they checked in. The two black American track stars were jogging in place, as they always did when waiting for one of their colleagues. The third who joined them, he recognized as the young man in Andrea Wards' bed. Bellin felt embarrassed.

Outside, the car pulled up to meet him. Before he got in, he looked up in the direction of Dunney's room. Sixth floor.

There he was, Dunney. standing at the window, looking down. At him. Bellin waited. Dunney let the curtain drop finally, leaving only his silhouette. Bellin dropped the Winston, crushed it with his foot and climbed into the car. "I want to go back to the office," he said. How could he expect to feel satisfied? he thought. How in God's name could he have expected to feel satisfied?

~ ~ ~

Ten fifteen PM. Greenwald stared at the LED readout waiting for the next minute change. Twelve hours to the entrance of the three judges, signaling the start of the trial. They would be judges in name only. One of them was a holdover from the Shcharansky trial the year before. They would take the evidence and... ignore it.

According to Feuchinko, the Procurator of Moscow had scheduled only two days for the Mraisky trail. "A complex case." Feuchinko had said, winking.

The courtroom below him was dark and only his cigarette lit the press booth. Why didn't they hold it that way? In the dark. The bell on his phone rang quietly twice before he picked up the receiver. "Greenwald."

"We're ready for the test, Sy," stated a voice on the other end. Greenwald did not recognize it offhand, though he knew most of the gang gathered in the press pool room for familiarization. "Sy, you there?"

"Yeah, yeah. You control the general speaker levels from the console. Everybody can use headphones if they want. They control volume on their sets. Okay?"

Thirty or forty news hounds mumbled in the background. All had expressed both surprise and dissatisfaction over Greenwald's good fortune. All that paled, however, when they found that the US news services had only one reporter in the booth, while France had two and Ethiopia had its own. The Soviet press, of course, had space in the gallery of the courtroom itself.

"Give us a level, Sy."

Visualizing the mockery to come, Greenwald slipped into the cadence he had used with rewrites. "The Trial of Dr. Alexander Isaac Mraisky. Lenin Prize winning economist begins tomorrow morning at ten fifteen AM, Moscow time. The trial will last as long as necessary to make the point. Have you got that?"

"Where's your objectivity, Sy?"

"Read Pravda for objectivity," Greenwald grumbled. He slammed the receiver down, not because the remark insulted him but because the remark was correct. "Where's your objectivity, Greenwald?" he demanded of himself. "You used to be a fucking pro."

Perhaps he could reach Feuchinko, call off his acceptance. Everyone would be better off with another reporter, a real reporter handling the pool. Christ, he wasn't even a reporter anymore. He was a spy. And maybe responsible for the death of one man already. Winker's.

McDeamon had denied that, but Greenwald still wondered.

The lights began to flicker as the fluorescent starters warmed the tubes. Squinting, Greenwald saw the guard outside gesturing. Greenwald went and opened the door. "What is it?" he asked in polite Russian.

Nervously, the guard replied, "I would like to lock up the courtroom now."

Greenwald looked out over the dark room now slightly illuminated by the lights in the press booth. Lock up the courtroom? He liked that expression, in this case at least. It was the one thing that made sense.

~ ~ ~

"You have been avoiding me," Volenko repeated gently.

Elizaveta put her head down and watched her feet on the pavement of the square. "Yes. I was afraid he wouldn't respond."

Volenko looked at her, feeling ashamed that he had put her through such a trial. Yet, there was no choice. "So, you waited. Has it improved?"

"That's what I wanted to tell you. He said no." She sighed and raised her eyes to Volenko's. "He doesn't want to see me anymore, Mikhail."

The contained anguish of her voice told Volenko much more than the words. Her response to Dunney's rejection had become almost purely personal. He should have expected it; perhaps he had and had just not admitted it. "Are you in love with this young man?"

"How can I be?"

Volenko put his hand on her shoulder, stopping her. "I didn't ask that."

Her eyes evading his they drifted back to the hotel, and its sixth floor. "My feelings are irrelevant. He does not care about our cause, Mikhail or me. That's what matters." She counted the windows. "Christopher has a goal, one that conflicts with ours... He cannot see me or help me. That's all."

"Is his job that important to him?"

Elizaveta gave the question a shallow shrug. "His life is important to him, more than mine. And mine is more important to me. My life and his do not mix. I am a Jew, Mikhail, he is not. That's reason enough."

Skeptically. Volenko said, "Only to one who thinks so."

"No." If Christopher were a Jew, she thought, he would naturally understand and help her. Wasn't that the way it was? "I don't know."

They walked on again, ignoring a slight drizzle and the watchful eyes of the three men trailing their footsteps. Aside from the three agents and a solitary embassy guard, only a jogging Clinton Thomas provided company in the lonely square. Thomas recognized Elizaveta from her link with Dunney and Andy. He angled away from Volenko and her, perhaps discouraged by two of the agents following them. Clint circled them, limiting himself to an unfriendly stare.

Noticing Thomas' attention, Volenko asked, "What about him? Do you know him?"

The question brought back the memory of her awkward meeting Clinton Thomas while dining with Christopher on a night earlier in their week together. Quickly she pushed the disquieting scene from her mind. "No. I met him once."

"We can't trust him?"

Angrily, she said, "I told you, I don't even know him."

Anticipating her response, goading her to it, Volenko had to concede, he said, "Then it's Dunney or no one." He followed with a sigh of resignation. "Is there any chance he will see you again? Tonight?"

Horrified, she cried, "Tonight!" She could not face him again that night. Not after what he had done to her! "No!"

As forcefully as possible, Volenko took her by the shoulders and jarred her. "Don't you know what tomorrow means? Tomorrow is the end. Without Alexei, there is no movement, no Moscow Group. Helsinki will be only a town in Finland again. There will be no Israel for you, ever."

In disgust, Volenko tore his hands from her. "Not that there is any point, but Nikolai left for Georgia this afternoon."

"Oh God, Mikhail! No."

"Well, of course," he said harshly. "What did you expect? They've been dismantling us piece by piece. Without Alexei's prestige, we are nothing. I am nothing. Nikolai is nothing and you are nothing."

"I don't care about me."

"Then get up there and beg him!" Volenko ordered, forcing the words through clenched teeth. "Forget yourself, forget your pride, Elizaveta. Forget that you may love him. Make him see."

"He won't listen!" She backed away from Volenko's staccato commands. "He doesn't care!"

"Not about you, perhaps. But tell him what you are fighting for. Tell him! And remind him that he is an American! They are so proud of themselves. Let him show why!"

"Mikhail," she pleaded, confused, frightened. She had no one to turn to. Mraisky was in prison. Nikolai... Christopher. She wanted to cling now to Volenko, but he pushed her away. "Please."

His voice growing harder, Volenko said, "Go and do what must be done. Tell him everything. Beg him, threaten suicide, murder. Make him." He turned on his heel and stalked away.

After several steps, his anger cooled, but he suppressed the inclination to look back. What had to be done, had to be done.

Elizaveta could not bear to watch Volenko abandoning her. It left her no alternative.

The drizzle intensified into a steady rain, driving even the KGB operatives to cover. Elizaveta stood completely alone. She wiped the rain from her face and brushed her wet hair back off her face. In a steady stride, she walked back to the hotel. She saw no point in hurrying.

~ ~ ~

Her bags almost packed, Andy heard a knock at her door. Nearly midnight. She hesitated answering. She did not want to see Clinton Thomas... And there was no one else... Chris? No. Surely, he had no time for her.

Refusing to hope. Andy went to the door and opened it all the way. Her heart jumped when she saw Dunney standing in front of her. It plummeted when she noticed the expression. His mouth set, his eyes shining cold, Dunney wore the look of an adversary, not a lover.

He said nothing, but walked past her into the middle of the room. Seeing the bags on her bed, he strode over to them and jerked both open. He grabbed the first article on top, looked at it and then threw it back. His head recoiled in what Andy knew to be a sarcastic, silent laugh.

"Chris," she began. "I'm sorry..."

Turning, he asked, "About what? Leaving? That's fine with me." He left out the other thing, the one Bellin had mentioned. He wanted to hear that from her.

"Yes. And more." Andy knew that she had to tell him. But she couldn't.

Impatient with her, Dunney demanded, "What?"

Andy realized suddenly that he knew. Now she had to tell him the truth. "I called Steve Klein."

"That's an expensive damned call."

"I told him," was all she said, all she could say.

"About Elizaveta?"

"About the two of you. I'm sorry."

The anger went out of Dunney. He now knew that Bellin had not lied. Everything was true... Andy had betrayed him. Had Elizaveta?

Seeing the abrupt and complete change in Dunney's mood. Andy took an involuntary step forward. She forced herself to stop. "Chris, I know what I've done is unforgivable

Dunney shrugged. "It doesn't matter now."

"I know it's my fault," she explained, "but you hurt me." When he did not react, she added, "That doesn't matter either, does it?"

Without looking at her, Dunney walked out of the room. His mind could not handle Andy, Klein, Bellin and Elizaveta at the same time.

Andy left the door open a long time. She finished her packing except for the clothes she would wear traveling the next day and the nightgown she wore. She could not help looking out the door every few minutes. She felt ridiculous, leaving it open as it was, especially with her in a nightgown.

For all of that, Andy could not bring herself to close it.

~ ~ ~

When he returned, Folenya was on the phone, smiling. Bellin glanced at the monitors and instantly appreciated why. Elizaveta Krylenkev was just emerging from the ladies' room off the lobby of Dunney's hotel, her wet hair combed back behind her ears, her clothes streaked by the rain.

"You're sure," Folenya said. "They exchanged nothing?" Her grin faded. "She did nothing else in the restroom?" Looking at Bellin as he stood in the doorway, Folenya stopped. "Thank you." She saw no point in Bellin benefiting from her efforts. He was supposed to be home.

Annoyed, Bellin asked, "Did you expect her to check her pockets for the tape, Anna? With one of your clumsy agents in the stall next to her?"

Still holding the phone, Folenya's hand dropped to her side. She glowered at Bellin. His performance with the American had enraged her. The friendly manner Bellin had displayed, the feeble attempt to bribe Dunney, the drinking. The entire sequence convinced her that Bellin could not be trusted to pursue the American and his traitorous whore with the proper determination.

Expecting him to adhere to his stated intention of going home to his bourgeois wife, Folenya had set in motion an attempt to encourage the exchange. She had given direct orders to the Militia, in Bellin's name, to stand down their obvious guard in front of the embassy. The equally obvious KGB agents following the Krylenkev woman dropped out of sight, replaced by covet operatives. Had she been able to think of any other of Bellin's precautions, she would have reversed them as well.

But now he was back!

"It was worth the try," she said avoiding his eyes. "Under tension, the guilty make mistakes."

"Ha! So do the innocent." Bellin moved closer to the monitors. "She is back sooner than I expected." He removed another cigarette from the pack, looked at it suspiciously and discarded it in favor of a cigar. "Where is the American?"

"He was with the American woman. He will be back any minute."

Watching Elizaveta cross the lobby self-consciously, Bellin said, "He'd better hurry" though he preferred that the two miss each other. It would be better if they never saw each other again.

Dunney's door opened on the screen covering his room. The technician ran a rapid cutting sequence from one camera to another. The fourth camera position yielded no picture. "He's disabled the bathroom camera," the technician announced for Bellin's benefit.

In spite of the seriousness of the moment, Bellin smiled. The American had understated his "finding that one" before Bellin's arrival. Dunney, he decided, had character. More soberly, he thought, that made Dunney dangerous.

Dunney stood in the doorway, his face a tightly drawn map of frustration and defeat. He forced his hands deeply into his pockets. From one of them he pulled a ball of paper, at which he stared with an intensifying anger. All of a sudden, he hurled it across the room, very hard. He turned and kicked the door closed.

For the next several minutes, Dunney stood stock still, his face turned away from the camera. The technician was too busy switching from lobby to elevator to the sixth floor hallway cameras following Elizaveta, to cut to another angle on Dunney. Bellin silently cursed Folenya for all of the new cameras installed. He wanted to see Dunney's face.

Once Elizaveta had begun her hesitant walk down the hall, the technician switched to a camera optimizing the view of the impending doorway confrontation. He used her knocking to calibrate his sound level. Ultimately, it sounded as if the knock were in the monitoring room.

Having so recently been in Dunney's hotel room, Bellin could not help feeling Dunney's seething presence. As Dunney finally approached the door, Bellin himself took a step forward. When Dunney's hand shot out for the door knob, Bellin's almost moved to stop him. Though he knew who lay beyond the door. Bellin stopped breathing at almost the same moment as Dunney.

He looked over towards Folenya once he had realized what he was doing. She had not noticed and was still transfixed by the monitor.

The only part of Dunney's expression visible from the camera angle, was an eyebrow pinched down on his narrowed right eye. Elizaveta's reaction, however, told enough about Dunney's face. She swallowed hard, unable to speak though her mouth parted in an attempt. Her eyes were large and moved rapidly back and forth, fearful.

Dunney spoke first, but only after a long silence. His voice was flat, unemotional. "I didn't expect to see you."

His words seemed to free up her own, for they came in a rush to accompany her motion toward him. "I had to come, Christopher. I know I shouldn't have, but where else am I to go? I can't go home. It's not home anymore. I can't stand to stay there."

Dunney backed away from her embrace. "You shouldn't have come, Elizaveta," he said coldly.

The tone of voice shook Bellin. Had Dunney already rejected her? He could make her desperate. "Get her out of there," he said to himself.

Deflated by Dunney's icy reaction, Elizaveta turned away, almost leaving. She apparently thought better of it and simply closed the door. "Christopher, there is something very important for me to tell you."

Bellin clenched his hand into a fist and thumped the table. It was too late for anything else now. His mind turned to only one question: Did Dunney have too much character?

~ ~ ~

Dunney hesitated only because he preferred not to look Elizaveta in the eye when he said what he planned to say. If Bellin were right, of course, goading her on would not have been necessary, but Dunney felt either unsure or spiteful. Perhaps both. Without asking, he left her at the door and fixed them both a long drink. Finished, he leaned over the glasses. "Before you say anything, you may as well hear this."

"Christopher…"

"No, listen," he said before she could get beyond his name. "Steve Klein, he knows about you. And me. Andy called him. There's no point in starting up again, Elizaveta, I'm finished here anyway. Klein'll pull me out tomorrow."

Elizaveta listened, her latent hopes crushed. She could no longer delay or hope for a tomorrow. She had him only a few more hours. Tempted as she to run to him and hold onto him, she knew that she could not. Time enough remained for one thing alone.

Her own voice sounded horribly hollow, artificial. "Then I must beg you to listen to me. And to believe that I say it only because I have no choice."

Dunney faced her, realizing that he had to see her tell him. Words without expressions, without the beauty that still entranced him would not suffice. He had to give her full reign to prove or disprove Bellin's accusation. He offered the drink, which she took reluctantly, and sat down. "All right, Elizaveta, I'll listen. I will, but only because of my feelings for you. Remember that."

Elizaveta felt the color drain from her face, along with it much of her resolve. He seemed to want to hurt her. Or was that her own guilt? She steeled herself. "You know my feelings for you. I know you do. I don't know anymore what yours are for me, but it doesn't matter. In a way, I think it would be better if you had none."

His response was a long, airy sip of bourbon. If what he expected were true, then he agreed with her.

Only slightly disappointed by his silence, she continued, "The Helsinki movement is dying. Since Dr. Mraisky's arrest, the factions have split and the government has dispersed us. My friend, Nikolai Torlas–the fat one with me the night we met–he was forced to return to Georgia this afternoon. Our Group has not had a meeting in weeks, because of the KGB and because all we can do is quarrel. Christopher. without Alexander Mraisky, we can be scattered like dead leaves."

"All we want is a little of the freedom you Americans can forget about every day. I don't even know what it means, most of it, only that we must fight for it."

Unsympathetically, Dunney said, "What you really want is to emigrate, Elizaveta. Why not just say that? You've said that was what you felt you had to do. Emigrate to warm, safe Israel."

She nodded. "Yes. I am a Jew, Christopher, and that's where I belong."

"I've heard it," he snapped.

Now without illusions, Elizaveta went directly to her point. "We have information that will help Mraisky, Christopher. If we can get it to the American Embassy..."

Bitterly, Dunney heard Bellin's words in place of Elizaveta's. He no longer felt emotion, no anger, no disappointment, no pain. He could look at Elizaveta in an impersonal, dispassionate way. Whatever feeling he had had for her–and he now knew its potency from its absence–the feeling was gone.

"... only you can do it," she was finishing. "We need you, Christopher."

Clinically, he observed, "Then you did set up the currency business to trap me, I take it."

His knowledge caught her off guard. She had not yet admitted that she had deliberately set out to win his aid. "Christopher, believe me..." she tried to say.

Dunney, however, had only paused. "And for a week, you catered to my every physical whim." He drained his glass and set it down quietly. "I admire you, Elizaveta. You are, in your own way, a very noble woman. Not many women would barter their bodies for principal."

"It wasn't that simple, Christopher," she offered in a whisper. "You know that."

Ignoring her hushed denial, Dunney ventured to the window. He gazed into the square, across to the embassy. How little she wanted from him. A shot walk, a light cargo... The Embassy. It was virtually unguarded.

Dunney did a double take. He looked at Elizaveta, revealing nothing, and then at the ceiling for the cameras.

So, Bellin was not at home. The son of a bitch was still watching. He must have known that Elizaveta would be hack. Was he that damned sure Dunney would play his gain and take the offer of "career triumph" in exchange for Elizaveta and her cause?

"What is it. Christopher?" Elizaveta, worried by his preoccupation with the ceiling, joined him at the window. Even a glance reminded her of the fact that she had failed to recognize earlier. "God, the Guard."

"Bellin's cut it down, Elizaveta," Dunney explained matter-of-factly, "because he knows I won't help you. He was so sure that he told me everything you did, everything you would do to get me to take your tape cartridge." He nodded at her staggered reaction. "Yes, Elizaveta. Bellin told me all about you. Not an hour ago. He told me you would come back, pleading for help. He told me about the currency shit. He told me all about our well-plotted affair."

Squeezing his arm, she cried, "Oh God, no. Christopher."

Dunney let her dig her nails into his skin. He barely felt it. He stared hard, mercilessly, into her brimming eyes. At the last minute, he left out the part about the deal Bellin offered. He didn't know why, but suspected superficially that he just wanted her out of his sight. "I haven't any regrets. We had our nice little fucks. I ruined my career for it, but what the hell. You didn't exactly get what you were after either." He added a shrug and pulled away.

"We put on a good show, at least," he said as he reached the door. "Bellin got his kicks, too."

Her mouth formed the question "what", but she did not get the word out.

Scornfully, Dunney asked, "You mean you didn't know? Innocence in such a conspirator?" Looking at Elizaveta's face, a face no longer capable of holding a single expression for more than a moment, he felt a stirring of anger. He was angry with her for her vulnerability and naivete and with Bellin for hurting her. "Look around you!" he shouted in English. "The place is lousy with cameras."

He moved to her, dragging her by the arm into the bedroom. Pointing to the ceiling's protruding lens, he cried, "What do you think that is? He's been watching from the very first night."

Hoarse, she asked. "You knew?"

Her reproach, however unjustified, shamed him. He should have told her. It was her business as much as, or more than, his. Why had he hidden it from her?

"Oh. Christopher." Elizaveta, her reserves gone, sat on the bed and wept outright. She was not only rejected, but humiliated, by the man she loved. She may as well have died there, in front of him. There was nothing left.

As he towered over her, Dunney consciously battled his feelings. He had to run her offenses over and over in his mind, growing more distant with each replaying. Once he had removed himself enough, he put his hand on her shoulder. "Elizaveta, I'm sorry."

Hearing only the sounds and not the words, she shook her head and tried finally to stand. Dunney's firm muscles, ones the nuances of which she had learned so well, pressed against her as he supported her. Elizaveta's only physical awareness was the touch of Dunney. She did not seem to taste or hear anything. She did see the door open, the corridor unfold. By that time, she could hear her voice say, "Thank you."

Elizaveta recovered herself fully only with the stinging contact of the early morning rain. She thought of the Embassy Militia... If she had had the tape, she could have... Then she saw that they had only been fools. She turned toward his window, not expecting him to be looking.

He was. First out the window and then he looked back inside. Then out again. At the guards scurrying into position in front of the Embassy gates.

Walking toward a single cab, she was grateful that he had even gone to the window. Not that it mattered anymore.

Dunney's earnest question confirmed what Bellin wanted to know. "Bellin," Dunney asked, "what the fuck are you doing?"

He did not feel it necessary to wait for the call from the Militia commander. The guards were back in place.

Bellin directed his attention back to Folenya. "Anna, why?" He already knew the answer, of course, and did not expect her reply to convey anything new.

Defensively, Folenya stated, "You told me you were going home. When the Krylenkev woman returned, it was a critical situation. I felt it necessary to act."

"To encourage them."

"Of course, Director Bellin!" she exclaimed, her patience at an end. "You want the evidence for Mraisky's trial, I want it for the rest of them. Don't play the fool, Vladimir."

What a strange time to call him by his Christian name, Bellin mused. Folenya's nerves must have been stretched taut. "Anna, I don't want that evidence for any reason. It is my duty to bottle it up. Your people have only told me that it is vital that it not reach the Americans. And even then, only until after Mraisky is out of the way. Please let me do my duty."

Coldly. Folenya retorted, "Your duty goes beyond that. You must help us wipe out the subversives."

"Anna. it's not..."

Suddenly livid, Folenya screamed at him from two feet away. "You're as much as one of them! You support them with your tolerance!" Spent, Folenya rushed from the room.

Bellin felt the eyes of the technician boring into his back, but in turning could not catch him at it. Resuming his seat, Bellin silently watched the monitors.

After two more hours of almost mindless viewing, Bellin had seen the American girl phone and bed down with her black sprinter and Dunney drink himself to sleep. The infrequently used camera in Elizaveta's tiny room flickered so badly he had ordered it turned off.

Finally certain that Dunney had been neutralized, Bellin prepared to leave for his own home. He had waited, too, to be sure that Elizaveta had fallen asleep. Within a few minutes, she had called a name that, while barely audible, was clearly "Christopher."

~ ~ ~

The knock woke Volenko, who had fallen asleep in his chair. He went quickly to the overhead light, switching it on to provide light for the doorway. Careful not to wake his brother's family, which shared his apartment, he whispered as he let Nikolai Torlas inside.

"Come in, Nikolai, let me get my coat."

Torlas shifted his considerable weight from one foot to the other, a waiting habit he had acquired through years of waiting in winter cold for Moscow buses. "It's late, Mikhail, to be walking about in the rain."

"Less suspicious than having your conversation overhead," Volenko replied, referring to the microphones planted around the apartment. Once he had his raincoat on, he led Torlas out of the apartment and down into the dimly lit street.

Squinting in the light rain, Torlas located his KGB agent. It made him feel more secure to know where his "shadow" was. "So, Mikhail, welcome me back," he said with a laugh.

"Did you call from the station?"

"No, no. I've been in Moscow for hours. I didn't go beyond the first stop."

Volenko's mouth dropped open. "You what?"

Patting his friend on the back, Torlas admitted, "It was a fraud, Mikhail I just did it for effect. Effect on Elizaveta."

Momentarily angry, Volenko said, "What about me?"

"You are not a convincing liar, my old friend." Torlas winked. "Did my 'departure' have the intended effect?"

Disgusted, Volenko remarked, "My father told me never to trust a Georgian. I should have known better."

Torlas laughed, amused at the effect that his ruse had on Volenko. "It is nice to be missed."

Volenko vowed never to reveal to Torlas how shattered he had been upon seeing his train leave the station. "Missed? I missed your KGB tail more than I missed its dog."

Knowing better, Torlas let the comment pass. "And Elizaveta? Did she…?"

"I admit that it had some impact on her, though I don't know how much." Volenko acknowledged inwardly the usefulness of the ploy. "It helped."

"She went to him?"

"Yes."

"And?"

Making no effort to hide his resignation, Volenko answered, "She would have called me. I'm sure. As upset as she was Elizaveta knows the seriousness." He had waited and waited, falling asleep until Torlas' own phone call, and sleeping again until Torlas arrived.

Nodding, Torlas agreed. "She would have called you, Mikhail. She has no one else."

"What of us? Dunney was our last hope."

Torlas issued a great sigh and patted his bulging stomach. "I have given it much thought. We obviously need a plan."

"You always were the master of the obvious." Volenko's spirits were worsened by Torlas' light-hearted tone. "Well?"

"I said we 'needed a plan,'" Torlas replied crossly, "I didn't say that I had one."

"Nikolai, we are down to the last day or two," Volenko reminded his erratic friend. "The note with the tape was very explicit. We have to get the message to the Embassy before the end of the trial. Now, either we have a plan or we don't."

"We don't," Torlas said flatly.

They walked along together in dismal silence. The realization had come at last. Nothing else could save Alexander Mraisky, the movement, themselves.

Torlas said it first. "A suicide run."

They walked on a few feet nodding their heavy heads until it hit them simultaneously. Their suddenly hopeful eyes met as their thoughts coincided. A suicide run! Of course!

"Elizaveta," Torlas said, grinning.

"Elizaveta," agreed Volenko.

~ ~ ~

Wakened for the fourth time that night, Marta shook Bellin awake. He awoke with a start, his face gleaming with sweat, his arms jerking in a gesture or reflex. After a moment. Bellin gained control of his senses and lost the memory of his dream. "Marta?"

"You keep swinging your arms, Vladimir," she said, "as if you are trying to fight off someone or something. My lip is swollen."

Tenderly, Bellin searched for the sore spot until she winced. He could feel that her usually soft, thick lower lip was hard on the left side. "You were better off when I wasn't here."

Marta responded to his remark by kissing him lightly on the forehead. "Lonely, Vladimir? Is that better off?"

He gathered her to him, relishing the feel of her. He was reminded that he had collapsed on the bed the minute he got in. It did not measure up to what he had intended as he rode home. The contact, however, began to rouse him, completely, a fact not lost on his wife. She gently massaged his erection to its peak, while sliding the cotton gown up to her waist.

His mind lost in the too long missed pleasure, Bellin felt his wife sliding upon him, guiding it between her widespread legs, inside her. Marta's breasts rubbed against his own chest. He lost the minutes, enveloped in sensation after sensation. Before he knew it, he had Marta's shoulders in his hands, pressing her upwards. He supported her with his hands massaging her breasts until she had thrown her weight backward.

The resulting wrenching seized him in a spasm of sensitivity which coupled with her rapid downward thrusts to spin him to the back-stiffening border of pain and pleasure. Slow, undulating movement buried him deeply, high inside her body. Pressing himself up hard against her, Bellin jerked the uncontrollable trigger again and again and again.

The woman groaned and collapsed on top of him fighting for breath. Her throaty groans continued drowning his thoughts. Bellin drifted, his eyes neither open nor closed, seeing and not seeing.

It was in the ceiling, above and below. A tiny glass projection into his world, its barrel pointed obscenely at him. Someone looked through at him. He knew who it was... He was either asleep or not, dreaming or actually seeing a camera lens stiffly protruding from the sky. His eyes wide open in the dream or in the darkness.

Bellin closed his eyes and preferred it to be in a dream. The camera, the woman. The American.

Chapter Ten

Sitting quietly beside Kyle, Greenwald counted off the minutes it took to reach the Moscow Courthouse and Justice Building. He had stalled as long as possible–it was already 9:35–before the Senior Staff Secretary piled him into the Embassy limousine, coming along for company.

The rain of the early morning had washed Moscow clean, leaving its streets a glistening gray and its sky a rare crystal blue. With the sun grinning brightly halfway to its zenith, the day was ironically cheerful. Greenwald's depression only deepened in response.

As the limousine made its final turn, onto the boulevard leading to the courthouse, Kyle observed, "In a way, I can't believe it's happening."

Greenwald said nothing, though he agreed.

"I thought for sure that they would delay it. I have never seen such a fast damn move into a court here. Shcharansky took months. This has been a week from indictment and only a month from arrest. Christ, it bothers the hell out of me, Sy. I don't mind telling you: This is no ordinary show trial."

"No." Greenwald had lived through several of them, including those of Shcharansky and his associates. Had he had the same ominous feeling then as he had about Mraisky's fate? No. He had begun to fear that Mraisky's sentence would be the first death sentence handed down since Stalin's day for a political crime.

Kyle was less concerned about Mraisky's fate than he was about its affect on his people. Ordinarily, he felt confident of his projections, this time he could not even guess. His sources told him that the Revision of SALT had top priority, that the Soviets would let nothing prevent the talks. And yet, Arkilonov had used all of his clout to pressure the Moscow Procurator into rushing Mraisky to trial in the face of a tidal wave of Save Soviet Jewry sentiment in the US. Furthermore, he had word that the KGB knew full well that the FBI intended to grab a couple of its agents–and didn't care! Did the Soviets intend to accept the exchange of the agents for Mraisky? He could not believe that, not with Arkilonov riding roughshod over the Procurator to put Mraisky away. But why? Why so much emphasis on Mraisky? It was maddening!

"Do you think your pal Bellin will be there, Sy?" he asked, searching for some, any, clue. Bellin's involvement remained a mystery. His Department of Investigation was encroaching on KGB operations as never before at the very moment Arkilonov was moving against the Procuracy.

Oblivious to Kyle's intent, Greenwald snapped, "Screw Bellin, damn it. You know this is a KGB operation."

"Okay, okay, Sy." Kyle worked another angle. "Have you met the Procurator? I mean of Moscow?"

"Yes." Greenwald could recall mostly the leering face of Feuchinko, the All Union Procurator General during the brief introduction. He had a better idea of the Moscow Procurator from seeing Zhoronov in action and sensed that he had talent. And a sense of urgency about his position.

"I don't suppose the Procurator would let anyone else handle Mraisky," Kyle wondered aloud. The pressure on Zhoronov must have been tremendous. "Or is that up to the KGB, too?"

Greenwald grunted and nodded at the thought. "The KGB." His mind ran back to Winker lying on the street bleeding. "Why did they release those pictures this morning?"

"Pictures?" Kyle shuddered. "Oh God. You mean Johnny's... It was idiotic." He had forgotten–purposely?– about the callous issuance of the official pictures of Winker's body. To all foreign news services! "Thank God, it's still night in the States!"

"It's going to make the morning editions," Greenwald said flatly. "And then look the hell out."

"Why can't they leave the bastard alone? He didn't have a damn thing to do with Mraisky or anyone else!" Harmless Johnny Winker, Kyle thought, barely spoke even to him. He had his agents working overtime to find the reason why Winker had been set up the KGB. Burglary, bullshit!

His hands cold, Greenwald wondered aimlessly what the packet he had given Winker contained. "Are you sure...?"

"God damn it, Sy, I run the God damned CIA in this God damned country! If Winker had anything going, I sure as hell would have known about it!" Kyle reasserted his professionalism. "Winker was clean. Just about the only guy in the embassy who is."

Both men stewed over the exchange as the Limousine cruised through the final blocks of the trip. Traffic remained light, with no abnormal activity around the courthouse. The rumors of a demonstration had had no merit after all. Passersby did not so much as give the courthouse a glance as they went about their normal business. Pravda, Izvestia and the other papers had made only passing reference to the trial, though denunciations of Mraisky dominated the editorial pages.

"Don't they know?" Greenwald demanded.

Kyle twisted to check both directions. "Maybe they don't care."

A pair of impassive militiamen stood by the doors as Greenwald stepped out. He flashed his authorization card to their approving nods and hustled up the steps. Kyle reached over to shut the car door, his presence ignored by the guards. From his position, he could see Greenwald all the way to the top of the steps and through the doors of the building. Several other men rushed inside along with Greenwald, but made no sign of recognition.

Kyle sat back and stared ahead of him. It was simply incredible. Perhaps the biggest trial in decades and hardly a stir. Did the Russians want it both ways? Mraisky and SALT? How could the "Human Rights" President allow it? The Senate?

Having waited by the windows inside the building, Greenwald watched Kyle's limousine glide into the sparse traffic. He needed the moment to collect his thoughts. He did not want to walk into the pool room with his mind hazy or dwelling on Winker.

From behind him, the voice boomed, "Mr. Greenwald. You have come." As before, Feuchinko sounded inordinately pleased to see him. Combined with everything else, Feuchinko's sunny greeting filled Greenwald with horror.

The bear-like Procurator General was dressed in his finest Polish-made suit. For the first time in his life, Feuchinko carried a trial valise. His smile beamed as Greenwald turned. "Our little affair is about to begin. I worried that you would miss the opening statement."

Greenwald assumed, with difficulty, his cool professional demeanor. "Hardly, Mr. Procurator General. The opening statement sets the tone for the trial."

Winking, Feuchinko agreed, "Indeed it does, Mr. Greenwald. This trial will be no exception." He increased the size of his grin and said, "I must go now. Perhaps we will meet later, after the opening session."

Amazed at Feuchinko's insensitive cordiality, Greenwald stumbled off toward the pool room. He detoured to the men's room. There, he bumped, literally, into several American reporters.

"Sy, old boy!" the first one said, pumping his limp hand. "We were worried about you."

A second chuckled. "Like hell, Cory. You'd give your wife's left tit to have Sy's place in the booth."

"True enough."

"Sy, what about those pictures? Dynamite, don't you think?"

"You mean Winker's?" the third chimed in. "It's front page stuff at the Post. I can tell you that."

"Our bureau chief said the wire's going to give it priority."

"Sy, you're with State now? How're they taking all this?"

"It's blown SALT out of the water, for good. Don't you think?"

Greenwald looked at each reporter in turn, envying their innocent zeal. Would he ever have it again? He shook his head, partly in response to his own question and partly in answer to the last question. "This trial is all that counts, gentlemen. If Mraisky goes to Siberia, SALT goes with him. That's a personal evaluation, not an official one."

"Good quote though," Jim Cory enthused.

"Can't make up his own."

Despite himself, Greenwald joined in the laughter. "I've got to go and check the booth, guys. I'll catch you later."

The hearty good-byes followed him down the corridor until he turned to take the stairs to the press booth. The murmur of the public gallery situated on the mezzanine level between the courtroom and the booth reminded him that this was, for all its importance, only a social event. The real trial was over; Mraisky had already lost. He had only to report the display of a carefully written fiction. This courtroom show was the denouement, the afterword of that moralizing known as Socialist Realism.

By the time, he had reached the booth, Greenwald had overcome most of his reservations. Taking his seat, he nodded to the other foreign press representatives whom he knew, even smiling as he greeted old colleagues. He found himself able to chat briefly with the Japanese correspondent next to him, without distress. He kept his eyes on the courtroom below, becoming increasingly engrossed in the movement of the players into position.

A herd of Procurator's witnesses were guided into their pen on the left side of the room by a bailiff. The defendant side, of course, remained empty. At the Procurator's table, Feuchinko stood talking to a nondescript, middle-aged fellow dressed in a formal gray suit. Feuchinko seemed undisturbed by the absence of the Moscow Procurator, whom Greenwald had known was to try the important case himself.

Thinking nothing of Zhoronov's absence beyond that observation, Greenwald waited impatiently for Mraisky's appearance. He checked his watch three times in a minute before deciding to contact the pool. Quickly, he ran down a few preparatory remarks and started in on Feuchinko's casual study of the witnesses. Midway into his description of the various witnesses, the door on the left side of the Judges' podium opened.

The bailiff announced the judges by name and relative rank and stepped aside. Three business-suited men entered, filed behind the bench and surveyed the courtroom. Exchanging satisfied smiles, the three men took their chairs. The bailiff ordered the defendant brought in.

During the pause. Greenwald detailed the judges, reading an official biography handed out in the booth. The chief judge, though a seventy-year old stalwart of the judicial system, had never heard a case in Moscow. His seat was ordinarily in Kiev. The other two, both in their mid-forties, were veterans of the earlier dissident trials.

When Mraisky finally appeared, Greenwald was speechless at his appearance. The hunched accused looked far from the prize-winning economist in his dirty prison uniform. His thin hair had been closely shaved, in the manner of convicts in the Soviet Union. He had his hands manacled in front. The impression was undeniable: Mraisky looked like a common murderer.

The senior judge motioned to the Procurator's bench and sat back to listen to the opening comments of the Procurator. Greenwald's eyes shifted to the man standing to speak. Feuchinko? Where was Zhoronov?

"I will have the honor," Feuchinko intoned, "of representing the people, Comrades, with the able assistance of the Procurator of Moscow, Boris Ivanovich Toliskorn. We shall prove that the accused..."

Every reporter in the press booth froze. Not a word was spoken as they digested Feuchinko's remark about Toliskorn. Greenwald did not bother to consider the implications as he broke the terrible silence.

"Zhoronov is out! There's a brand new Procurator here in his place. Not an assistant! Repeat, not an assistant. They've canned the Procurator on the morning of Mraisky's trial!"

Now that the others had begun shouting into their phones, Greenwald leaned back, his curiosity overwhelming any sense of foreboding he had carried into the room with him. Toliskorn? Toliskorn. He leafed through his bio fact sheets and came up empty. He looked through them again with similar luck and decided to try the pool.

"Who's got anything on the Procurator? Name, Boris Toliskorn."

After a long minute the response came from the pool moderator. "Nothing, Sy."

"Nothing? That's impossible! This is one of the biggest damn things anyone has ever tried."

"I'll try the book, Okay?"

The "book" was a compendium of every Soviet official above the local level Greenwald waited, watching Toliskorn rise to continue the introduction to the case.

The voice on the other end cracked as it said, "You aren't going to believe this."

"Come on damn it! Is he in there?"

"Yes. He's right in there. He had just jumped to Feuchinko's staff about four months ago."

"What was he before?"

After a long breath, the moderator said, "Personal assistant to Arkilonov."

"Arkilonov?" Greenwald gasped. "Mr. KGB himself."

~ ~ ~

Dunney's hangover was not his worst and he had largely shaken it by the time Sarkat's Muskovitz picked him up at the hotel.

"Good morning, Mr. Dunney," the Second-Secretary said.

Adjusting to the oddly uncomfortable seats, Dunney said, "Good morning. I like your idea."

"About viewing the sites? I'd like to take advantage of our chance to agree while we still have it."

Heartened by Sarkat's change in attitude and by the absence of word from Klein, Dunney silently nursed his once-dead hopes for a major coup. The Secretary, anxious for a coup of his own, had made it clear that he was again authorized to proceed. Unless Klein intervened, Dunney knew that he would leave Moscow with the original deal intact. The question remained as to whether he could improve on it. Without Bellin's "help".

"I received the call about eight this morning," Sarkat explained, as the car sped toward the stadium area. "I would say that you have made an impression on Director Bellin. Mr. Dunney. He went to great effort to convince the proper people that you were concerned about Russian opinion. I am, consequently, free to make whatever agreement I feel is in the best interest of the Olympic effort."

"Fine."

"Shall we return to our original proposal?"

Spent from the previous night's difficulties and wasted by the effects of the bourbon, Dunney felt his patience ebb. "Let me play it straight, Secretary Sarkat. There's only one way for me to go and that is to have a number of units equal to our competition."

"Twelve?" The Secretary, as weary as Dunney of the entire frustrating process, could not hide his surprise. The American Embassy's economic attaché–what was that name?–had indicated that Bingo Burgers wanted eight or nine maximum. "Impossible! That's double our allotment for you."

Archly, Dunney asked, "Why should a man have fewer outlets than his competition just because he is black?"

Sarkat stared at Dunney to see if the American were remotely serious. When Dunney smiled, Sarkat felt free to chuckle. "Is that a pressure tactic, Mr. Dunney?"

"I'm offering you a Public Relations bonus, Mr. Secretary, which your government would be shortsighted to pass up." Dunney pulled from his valise a report given him earlier by Sarkat. "You have heavily skewed your attendance to Africa, Black Africa. This city will be crawling with them. Where do they go to eat?"

"Shall I guess?" Sarkat laughed. "Twelve?"

Dunney's mind processed Sarkat's response: Amused but not completely negative. He saw his life falling back on track. He would make it to partner, all right, in spite of his lapse. Partly, in fact, because of it. The stall by

Sarkat had given him the kind of frustrating time which always spurred his imagination. It had been bottled up inside him, only bursting loose at six AM that very morning. Hung-over, exhausted and looking for a way to get back at them, Dunney had concocted his proposition.

He did not need Klein or Bellin to swing what he wanted.

"I will agree, Mr. Dunney, to seven stores."

Dunney's face fell.

Reacting to the change in expression. Sarkat added, "With square footage equal to McDonald's overall. One extra square foot to make Bingo Burgers the largest chain in Moscow!"

"No!" Dunney exclaimed. "Square footage doesn't mean a damn thing! No one will notice! Units, damn it, that's what counts. You can count them. Everyone will see that. It has to be obvious!"

The departure from Dunney's normally self-contained manner puzzled Sarkat. He had not expected Dunney to be satisfied, for he knew that the American preferred multiplicity to size, but he had hardly anticipated such an outburst. Perhaps, Director of Investigation Bellin knew Dunney as well as he said he did.

Fuming partly at Sarkat and partly at himself, Dunney did the best he could to keep quiet. Failing that, he endeavored to control his voice. "Secretary Sarkat, I apologize. It's simply that you have to understand fast food. Access is more important than space. That's an essential marketing aspect of it. And for PR, nothing is better than having a Bingo Burger on every damned street corner. You and I have a once-in-a-lifetime chance to really do a job for both our sides."

"Which," Sarkat added cynically, "will help each of us, Mr. Dunney. As individuals."

Dunney's silence affirmed Sarkat's accusation.

While the American was in a vulnerable state of mind, Sarkat let Bellin's words speak for themselves. "When there is something you want badly and something else you cannot use but which another wants, you would be a fool not to deal." He let the complicated statement sink in and then said, sympathetically, "You are asking too much; Bellin is asking too much. Being the broker was not my idea."

Quietly, Dunney said, "You know the whole story?"

"I know what Director Bellin has told me. And what I have observed. Together that is very little." Sarkat knew mostly that the KGB and the Party had been explicit in his orders: Play along with Bellin. "I don't know what it is you have to trade, Mr. Dunney, but I suspect that it is the woman."

Dunney nodded unconsciously.

Sarkat recalled the final thing Bellin suggested he say to Dunney. "Bellin doesn't think you will do it."

"What do you think?" Dunney asked examining Sarkat.

The Secretary shrugged. "We have time. We may as well see the twelve sites you have in mind. We should be prepared for even the remote contingencies, don't you think?"

~ ~ ~

Bellin bit off the end of his cigar and spat it at Zhoronov's feet. "Deputy Procurator General? Hell of a prestigious title, Sergei."

Zhoronov, his hand resting on a stack of personal files, ignored Bellin's remark. He surveyed his office one more time, checking for photographs, knickknacks, books and the like, which he wanted to take with him to the Kremlin. There was no point in arguing with Bellin, who would never understand. A man could not oppose the individuals with power all of his life, he had concluded upon receiving Feuchinko's so-called offer. He was moving up. What was wrong with that?

His only regret was that, finally, his old friend Bellin could not come along.

Bellin fumbled with a match and then a second before lighting the cigar. "Who is this Toliskorn?"

"An assistant of Feuchinko's," Zhoronov answered, leaving off the part about Toliskorn's KGB career. The important part. "He's not as particular about proof as I am, Vladimir. His background will make him want to rely on the KGB's evidence. If you insist on verifying every detail, he'll have you out of Moscow. Feuchinko and he made that very clear."

The impact of Zhoronov's removal finally struck Bellin full force. With Zhoronov gone, his department would not have the support required to check KGB personnel excesses. His entire function would be stripped of its value to the State. Without a Procurator calling the Folenya's to account for their mistakes and abuses, KGB operatives would become difficult for the Party to control, even for Arkilonov.

Bellin knew, of course, what had caused it: Zhoronov had not prepared the Mraisky case fast enough to suit the KGB. And that was his fault, for he had refused to certify enough KGB evidence for Zhoronov's standards. "Sergei, I'm sorry about this."

"Don't be," Zhoronov replied quickly, hoping to avoid a display of emotion. "It wasn't your fault, Vladimir. It wasn't even mine, to hear Feuchinko's side. He had Toliskorn working independently and he was ready. My thoroughness, you see, deserves to be employed at a higher level." He stopped, aware that bitterness had begun to creep into his voice.

Cradling his forehead in one hand, Bellin blew a discouraged sigh. "You will do some good, no matter how high up you get, Sergei."

"The first project I am supposed to have," Zhoronov said sarcastically, "is the supervision of a uniform standard of proof among the Procurators. A low one, if I'm not misled by Feuchinko."

Reluctantly, Bellin had to agree. "Investigators may as well retire."

"Not you, my friend. Feuchinko and Toliskorn have plans for you."

"Oh..." Bellin had no desire to work with either man or collaborate in their plans to dismantle his department."

"They did not admit anything, but I surmised that once the Mraisky business is over and the Helsinki movement is fragmented, the KGB will be sweeping up every dissident it can lay its hands on. But they will need a provocation."

"Why? Why do they need a provocation?"

"I get the impression that not everyone in the Politburo is convinced that the benefit will exceed the difficulties we'll have with the American and European public over such a campaign. They will have to be convinced."

Bellin thought of the taped message that Elizaveta and the rest of the Moscow Group clung to so desperately. From what he knew, it would serve very well as the pretext for their own extermination. Why didn't they see that? Not only would dissidents be swept up, but once the KGB agents began to move unimpeded, the nation would suffer the worst, most debilitating repression since Stalin's last days. It was a horror he had not, would never forget. He had always viewed it as his duty to help prevent a recurrence.

Zhoronov slapped Bellin on the shoulder, hoping to cheer them both with unfelt heartiness. "Don't worry, Vladimir. We'll see to it that nothing too outlandish happens."

If it wasn't already too late. Bellin thought of Elizaveta.

~ ~ ~

"Her classes have been canceled," the department secretary informed Volenko. "The Procurator wanted her on call as a witness."

"A witness?" Volenko examined the paper she handed him. The Notice of Availability had been signed by a Toliskorn, under the title of Procurator of the District of Moscow. Though he did not recognize the name, Volenko could see that the document had the official look. But why had Elizaveta gotten one when neither he nor Torlas had been called.

"Is she at home, then?" he asked.

The woman seemed surprised. "She hasn't even called, Professor. I assume that a notice was sent to her home as well." Reluctantly she added, "Elizaveta could use the rest."

If she were called, Volenko thought, she would hardly have much of a rest. "Thank you for your trouble."

"I hope she'll be all right if she comes back to teach."

The secretary and Volenko exchanged glances as each realized the slip of the tongue: The word "if" instead of "when" put things in their proper, if disquieting, perspective. Volenko knew as well as the department secretary about the rumors circulating concerning Elizaveta's unfortunate relationship with Mraisky and the Moscow Group, and its probable consequences.

Volenko hurried from the Economics building, crossing the University grounds without making his planned stop at the Psychology Department. He waited several minutes before the right subway arrived, flanked by two KGB agents, each about ten feet away. The three of them mounted the same car? Once inside the train, Volenko, as he had often done recently, forgot all about his constant companions.

The only thought on his mind was that he had to find Elizaveta. He and Torlas had worked out a plan in which she would have to play the major, if unwitting role, but she had to be convinced to take part. After their argument of the previous evening, Volenko had no assurance that Elizaveta would even speak to him. Particularly, if Dunney, the bastard, had further humiliated her upon her return to him.

How curious people were? He had himself become convinced during the past week that the American had fallen enough in love with Elizaveta to answer her plea. Little flashes of joy in Elizaveta coupled with a complete refusal to detail her relationship with Dunney–in the few chances he had had to talk with her–indicated clearly that she had made herself fall in love with him. The odd part–aside from two people developing such feelings so quickly even under such dangerous, oppressive conditions–was that Volenko had never suspected that it could happen. If he had, he would never have allowed it to go so far. Elizaveta's emotions had clouded her mind, fine enough under normal circumstances, but normal circumstances did not prevail.

Which led him to the plan. It was not–and Nikolai agreed–a very sure plan and certainly not a very honest one. Yet, they had no choice. Elizaveta would, in time, forgive them. If he knew her at all, Volenko knew that she would fall into her martyr role almost automatically. What worried him at the moment was that she had already.

He and Torlas wanted Elizaveta to act as a martyr. Timing, however, was important... No, it was the essence of the plan. Elizaveta, Torlas and he had to be coordinated among themselves and had to coordinate with the progress of the trial. If Elizaveta had been hurt too badly by Dunney, she would possibly decide to move on her own. And she had the tape.

The tape. Volenko saw the large cartridge in his mind and wondered vaguely what is contained. What message could have such power as to humble the mighty KGB, the omnipotent Soviet state? Volenko did not know, but he did not for an instant doubt Mraisky's word that it would do so. It had to get to the American Embassy before the verdict.

Ringing Elizaveta's bell, Volenko got no response. He tried several more times before checking to see if her watchful agents were present. One of them lounged in plain clothes on a bench in front of the building, while the other, in uniform, stood nearby reading a newspaper. Volenko knew, therefore, that Elizaveta had to be in. He breathed a deep sigh of relief.

He fished the key she had given him on the night they had hidden the tape under the shaky base of the sink stand. Letting himself in the building's outer door, Volenko went to the small elevator, which proved still out of service after six months. Resigned to the steps, Volenko took his time, due more to hesitation in confronting the girl than from fatigue. What state would she be in and how would he handle it?

His knock on her door produced no results, but he continued for several minutes. Finally, he used the key again and opened the door enough to poke his head inside. He could see her standing, her back to him, at the window. She gave no hint that she heard him come in.

"Elizaveta," Volenko unintentionally whispered.

She lowered her head slightly, paused and turned around. "Mikhail," she said sadly, "I'm sorry. I should have called you." Closing the prayer book, which Mraisky had given her to further her religious training, Elizaveta went over to Volenko and took his hand. She led him to one of her two chairs, while saying, in a mournful voice, "Christopher turned us down, Mikhail. And me."

Sitting forward in the chair, Volenko squeezed her hand earnestly. "You mustn't give up, Elizaveta. That's not your people's way."

She smiled and looked at the book. "He gave me this. 'To make you a better Jew, Elizaveta' he said. Has it, Mikhail?"

"I am not in a position..."

"Am I?" she demanded, a note of harshness in her voice. It had gone when she spoke again. "My mother never even mentioned prayer or observed the Sabbath. Father, of course... He was a Russian. And so am I."

Withdrawing her hand, Elizaveta opened the book to the passage she had been reading. "By now, I should have read these passages a thousand times, Mikhail. I don't even remember this one." She laughed. "Last Sabbath? I won't even admit to myself what I was doing, what I was thinking."

Her melancholia began to annoy Volenko, who had lived through too much to indulge her any longer. "Elizaveta," he said sharply, "you listen to me. Childishness is not the response we need from you today. Let's get this over with. Are you in love with Dunney, or aren't you? If you are, then you are entitled to be hurt. If not, your pride is the only problem. Alexander Mraisky is on trial for his very life and only you and I can help him. It's difficult and it's horrible, but adolescent musings will not help."

Elizaveta simply stared back at Volenko. Did he deny her her misery?

"Answer my question," he ordered her, peevishly. She was not the only one under a strain, he thought. Why should he have to shoulder hers as well as his own? "Do you love the American or not?"

She had decided that much earlier. "No." The mere verbalization of it convinced her otherwise. "How can I?" she hedged. "He doesn't care about me."

"All right." Volenko, softening a bit, began to implement his strategy. "You love him. He does care about you, Elizaveta. He must. He spent a very long, very important week with you. He is not in Moscow to romance you. He is here on business with the government. Correct?"

The familiar edge of bitterness crept back into Elizaveta. "Yes. Business. It is his God."

"And why has he not been doing business? Because of you. The government was using you against him. And him against you." Volenko kept his eyes on hers, forcing her to accept his points. "Face it, Elizaveta. The government doesn't care about me or about Nikolai Torlas. We're harmless. We've always been harmless in this country. It's you and Mraisky and the rest of you. It's the Jews, damn it. The Jews are the only cohesive group around which to build a movement. Jews have their own sense of unity. You have it, because you feel it. You don't have to understand it, just feel it. And you know you do. It's that unity which has kept the Jews alive for four thousand years. It is that unity the Party fears. That is what they want to crush."

Battered by Volenko's words, and echoes of Dunney's, Elizaveta broke down. She wanted to feel that sense of unity. She wanted to believe that she felt it, to know for certain. Was it supposed to be so hard? Or was it automatic in a way she could not know? Elizaveta was terrified that she did not honestly feel it all. Not the way she felt about him.

Volenko watched her weep, hoping that his assault would create some measure of good out of the pain it had inflicted. He could not comfort her while she cried, for doing so would undercut his purpose. All personal regard had to be forgotten. Elizaveta had to recognize her cause as paramount. He would then try to redirect her dedication to the Jewish cause, her despair in losing Dunney, her feelings of hopelessness and fear of failure. By the time he had finished with her, Elizaveta would make the "suicide run."

~ ~ ~

Addressing the gallery more so than his seventh witness, Boris Toliskorn delivered his final series of questions. "And, Comrade Horowitz, did you receive a copy of the manuscript?" Toliskorn held the subject article outstretched in his left hand. "This manuscript which directly suggests that the Capitalists could best protect their imperialistic ambitions by a refusal to make credit available to the Soviet Union? Did you receive it?"

Horowitz answered clearly and strongly, "Yes, sir."

"From whom?"

Glancing at the judges, Horowitz replied, "Dr. Mraisky himself."

Toliskorn turned at the name. "Dr. Mraisky, himself? You mean the author of this perfidy?"

"Yes, sir."

"And what did you do with it..."

"Dr. Mraisky told me to pass it on to other members of the Moscow Group."

The senior judge rolled his eyes. The other two men hastily jotted notes.

"Do you know where the article ended up?"

Horowitz appeared reluctant.

"Well?"

"The London Economic View and the Washington Post, I believe."

Shaking his head in disgust, Toliskorn said, "Thank you, comrade. Your government and the workers appreciate your return of patriotism. You may go back to your work."

The senior judge cleared his throat loudly. "The court may, just may, have a question or two, Procurator."

Smiling easily, Toliskorn stepped back to his table. Leafing through his copy of the article by Mraisky, the old man asked, "Have you read this, Mr. Horowitz?"

Gulping with nervousness, Horowitz nodded.

"Do you agree with the Procurator's summary of the work?"

In a small voice, the witness said, "Yes."

"On page three, is there not a full paragraph quoted from the then Chairman of the Communist Party, Leonid Brezhnev, which makes exactly the same point as Dr. Mraisky's article makes?"

Stuttering, Horowitz managed to admit, "I don't remember."

"And does not Dr. Mraisky's concluding sentence state, quote, 'The Party correctly perceives this problem of potential exploitation of the Soviet government's social and economic consciousness and, as I have noted, is taking steps to avoid the same' I won't bother to quote Izvestia in its praise of this particular article. That is all I have."

Nonplussed, and uninterested, the junior judges waved off further examination.

Toliskorn spoke quietly, yet forcefully. "The court has made a powerful point, but our next witness will place Comrade Horowitz' remarks into the proper perspective, as well as those of the witnesses testifying earlier."

"Go on," the senior jurist said.

With the gallery hushed, Toliskorn brought forward his next witness. Two KGB witness assisted an immediately recognizable figure to the stand. Even Mraisky watched in suspense as Kanin Choirnoy was lowered into a chair provided for his benefit. All three judges leaned forward to hear his weak address.

"I am Kanin Abram Choirnoy, presently residing at Aznolov Hospital near Taizhet."

Dramatically raising the pitch of his deep voice, Toliskorn stated, "Professor Choirnoy appears as a volunteer, in spite of his condition. Since his trial last summer, Comrade Choirnoy has been serving as a volunteer staff physician at Aznolov Hospital and is now considered completely rehabilitated."

Choirnoy's eyes maintained a blank expression but his mouth twisted downward. Slowly he turned his head toward Mraisky standing in the "accused box."

"Do you know the accused, Dr. Choirnoy?"

"Yes," he said clipping the word.

"Was he not a colleague of yours in the so-called Moscow Committee for the Monitoring of Violations of the Helsinki Accord, the 'Moscow Group?'"

"Yes." Choirnoy's gaze held Mraisky coolly and steadily.

"You and he worked together on several projects?"

"We wrote articles. Circulated them among ourselves."

"And got them to the foreign press without authorization?"

Choirnoy did not even pause. "Yes."

"For which you were convicted last May?"

"Of course."

Toliskorn breathed in a burst of refreshing air. The tension had cracked as the convicted dissident admitted his transgression. The Procurator proceeded, more relaxed. "You circulated these articles, including the one just discussed by Comrade Horowitz, for a purpose, didn't you?"

"Yes."

Mraisky returned the unwavering stare of his former mentor.

"Why?"

"To let the West know how to deal with…" Choirnoy had to pause to gather strength. "…with the Soviet government."

"For what reason?"

For the first time since he had begun. Choirnoy transferred his eyes to the Procurator. "To force changes in policy. Toward an observance of minimum human rights. As set forth…"

"… in the Helsinki accord," Toliskorn said, finishing the statement with the same beat as Choirnoy's. "In other words to assist the Capitalist Powers in pressuring your country's government." Toliskorn's well-trained voice boomed in the chamber. "To subvert the policy of the Party and the government. Correct?"

"Absolutely," Choirnoy agreed resolutely.

"That sounds treasonous."

The senior judge interrupted. "Please, Mr. Procurator. It is either treasonous or not. Its sound is of little value. If my comrades have no questions...?" He looked to each of the silent junior members of the tribunal. "I have one. Dr. Choirnoy, did the Soviet government sign the Helsinki accord?"

With a painful, slow motion, Choirnoy turned from the Procurator to the chief judge. His face held a fearful expression as he hesitated.

The judge answered for him. "I believe it did. Although not with your interpretation in mind, Dr. Choirnoy, nor perhaps, Dr. Mraisky's. I'm finished."

Toliskorn brought two men forward to help Choirnoy out of the courtroom. When he pivoted back towards the bench, he said evenly. "The state will now establish the accused's undeniable link with the American intelligence agency. Again, I beg the indulgence of the panel, for the process of proof is one of steps."

Looking askance at Toliskorn, the senior judge admonished, "Try not to skip any steps this time, Procurator Toliskorn. I recognize that you are dealing with a great many witnesses, but this is an important crime. We must not take it lightly."

"Of course not, never."

The Procurator turned again to the gallery, to begin some prefatory remarks. Despite the uncooperative nature of the chief judge, he was smiling broadly. He let his eyes scan the gallery as he began to speak. "The American spies are in our country in many forms, many seemingly harmless guises."

It was disconcerting, Greenwald thought, that Toliskorn's casual gaze had angled upward toward the press booth.

~ ~ ~

Anna Folenya saw that time was running out. Once Mraisky's trial ended, the subversives would undoubtedly give up their attempts to get the tape into the American Embassy. It depended on her. She had to tempt them into an overt action. With Bellin overseeing the operation, that would be impossible.

The appointment of Toliskorn, once her superior at the KGB, had been a major boost to her chances. The new Procurator had, as promised, made her Assistant Director of the Department of Investigation, but she remained under Bellin's official thumb. Coupled with her Party influence, of course, she could eventually undermine Bellin; however, right now, time sided with the Director, against her.

Watching the dramatic scene between the Jewess and her sympathizer friend, Volenko, she had formulated a bit of a plan. Bellin had missed the episode, convinced that the American and, therefore, the subversives had ceased to pose a problem. Folenya knew better. Volenko had cleverly manipulated the Krylenkev woman into a state of Zionist fervor. With minimal "encouragement" she would try Dunney one more time or act directly. Either way, Folenya, after providing some kind of encouragement, would be ready to make the final move. Actually, the beginning step...

"You wanted to see me?" Bellin demanded in a loud, unpleasant voice.

Startled out of her thoughts, Folenya jerked from her seat behind Radnik's old desk. She trembled at the sight of the angry Director of Investigation. "Yes," she said simply.

Bellin's narrowed eyes swept around the office. Hardly an impressive room–it was tiny and bare, as it had been since Radnik removed his personal effects–the office struck Bellin as far too good for Folenya. For him it retained some of the worth given it by its former occupant. He cursed himself for not filling Radnik's position immediately after the young man left it.

Sarcastically, he noted, "You moved in with your usual efficiency, Comrade Folenya."

Bellin's pause had given Folenya time to regroup. The first thing she had done was to grab onto the written appointment, signed by Procurator Toliskorn. "The Procurator asked me to assume my new duties as quickly as possible."

"Good, good. Then you'll be ready to take over case responsibility equally quickly." Bellin's scowl deepened, as he thought of her botching the work he, Radnik and the rest of the staff had so carefully nursed along.

"The Procurator..." she began.

"You work for me, Folenya," he snapped. "Not for the Procurator. Or for the Procurator General. Or the KGB. Is that clear?"

Defiantly, she replied, "I work for the Director of Investigation, whomever he may be at the moment. But I am guided by the Party and its..."

"And what does the Party suggest you do?" Bellin, of course, anticipated her answer and did not wait to hear it. "Are you guided to imprison every fool who speaks to an American or who had the misfortune to have Jews for parents?"

Again, Bellin did not allow time for a response. "Well, your duty, in this job, is to protect the State against those people, Comrade, and also against people like yourself, who lack perspective or brains and most of all, discipline. Do you understand that, Comrade?"

Aghast at his accusations, Folenya could barely speak and when she did, she shouted. "You are with the Party or against it, Comrade Bellin! And you have made your position clear enough to me!" She paused for a breath and calmed herself enough to reduce her shouts to a hissing whisper. "And I have made it clear enough to the Procurator. And to the Party."

Bellin stared at Folenya, his contempt for her mounting with each passing second. For a full minute, the two adversaries locked each other in hateful glares. He knew that Folenya had the power she claimed. He knew that he now had none. Except the power of responsibility, of duty.

Finally, she averted her eyes, glancing down at the appointment signed by Toliskorn. When she looked up again, Bellin had a smug grin on his face.

~ ~ ~

Returning to the Press booth after a stop at the men's room, Greenwald sat uncomfortably watching Boris Toliskorn blithely chatting with several upcoming witnesses. It should have seemed quite acceptable, in the circus atmosphere which the Procurator had fostered in the courtroom and, particularly, in the gallery. Yet, Greenwald was uneasy, without knowing why.

Given latitude by the bench, if occasionally rebuffed by the provincial senior of the trio, Toliskorn had woven his tale well. In the morning, Mraisky had come across as a writer and purveyor of seditious literature designed primarily to instruct the exploitative Westerners in how to bully the great proletarian brotherhood of Soviet Socialists. Greenwald knew the basic tenet to be true, however slanted the telling, and privately grieved that he had not assisted Mraisky out of higher motives.

Mraisky's own motive, as ably sketched by Toliskorn, was to promote religious freedom and thus of Judaism in the Soviet Union. The Procurator had stressed that Jews had a natural place in the forefront of capitalist exploitation and counter-revolution, turning Mraisky's Jewish heroism into Zionist treason.

Toliskorn had made a smooth transition into the CIA aspect of his case from the "publication" stage. He had raised the question as to how Mraisky got his manuscripts out of Russia and into the hands of the Imperialists. The answer, while slow in developing, was inevitable: The bevy of frustrated spies maintained by the United States in and around Moscow.

Greenwald thought, half amused, of Kyle caring enough about an economics article to risk one of his men to get it out to Stockholm or London. He could almost see Mac vigorously denying such a thing and Washington restating the President's insistence that the Moscow Group and its fellow dissident organizations not be compromised by CIA complicity. He chose to remember as well the three or four short pieces which he himself had smuggled out...

Almost before he knew it, the three judges were reseated, impatient to proceed. Toliskorn. his deep voice seemingly even stronger, began speaking and stopped abruptly. For an instant he appeared to have forgotten something, or to be uncertain. Before he started again, he made a gesture to indicate the need for water.

As the Procurator made a show of pouring a glass of water, he half turned and, in a motion that hardly any person noticed, shot a glance at the Press Booth. Then putting the glass to his lips, he proceeded to, as Greenwald could clearly see, drink absolutely nothing.

~ ~ ~

"A message? Yes, Mr. Dunney," the clerk said.

Dunney, just returned from a tiring day of "site-seeing" as Sarkat insisted on referring to it, leaned with his back against the desk. Through the giant windows, he thought he saw a familiar figure...

"Sir."

He turned and took the paper from the clerk. Still trying to see out the window, he unfolded the note. All it said was, "Good-bye. Andy."

Swinging his briefcase up on the desk. Dunney ordered, "Watch this," and strode across the lobby. By the time, he had reached the square, Andy was being inspected. "Andy!" he called.

Though she heard, Andy did not intend to show it. She submitted to the search, which began casually and then, after a brief call for instruction, intensified. One of the senior soldiers reached down to her skit checking the inside of her thighs. She started to protest, but the pair of experienced hands was almost immediately running up her waist, breasts and back. Hearing Dunney's running footsteps, she quickly stepped through the gate.

When she was admitted, Dunney stopped frustrated and, he had to admit, breathless. The guard, only twenty feet away, eyed the panting American suspiciously. For a long moment, Dunney stood debating whether to follow her inside. Concluding that he had no reason to pursue Andy further, Dunney turned away. What was done was done, he decided.

Before he moved, one of the militiamen called out to him in English. "Mr. Dunney."

Hearing his name. Dunney pivoted to see a guard with a handheld radio walking up to him. Scanning the area in front of the embassy, Dunney spied at least one TV camera. Bellin, that bastard, he thought with a laugh. "What can I do for you?" Dunney asked in English.

"You may go through."

Dunney stared at the guard in amazement. "No inspection?"

"Not for you, Mr. Dunney. Director Bellin said you would know why."

"No, thanks," he snapped. Then, thinking again, he caught the guard by the arm. "I changed my mind. I should speak to the young lady. Give Director Bellin my regards."

"Yes, sir." the guard said.

The other members of the Militia platoon stepped aside, making a clear path for Dunney. It galled him, of course, to be so manipulated by Bellin, but he had little choice. Andy would undoubtedly leave directly from the Embassy, by the kind invitation of a Senior Staffer, Harmon Kyle.

Two buzzers at the gate signaled that the locks had been electronically deactivated. Dunney pushed the heavy wrought iron gate open just far enough to slide through. The front door, at least, was opened by a real person, Kyle himself.

The bemused Kyle shook Dunney's hand. "So nice to meet a celebrity. How did you manage that little trick, Dunney?"

Looking past Kyle at Andy, Dunney replied, "Their puppeteer likes the company I keep." He gave Kyle a quick smile and moved past him. "Andy?"

Andy sighed in resignation, accepting the final confrontation. She had deliberately left two hours early to avoid seeing him again. "You're back early. No luck?"

"Passable," he said with a shrug. "Mr. Kyle, could we have a room for a minute?"

Kyle showed them to the room in which they had once met John Winker. The memory nagged at Kyle: Winker's death had not been right. What they intended to do to him now, too, was not right. He shook off the feeling. "Use it as long as you like."

When they were alone, Andy back-stepped and stood with the firm feel of wood against her back. "You didn't have to say anything."

Dunney let his fondness for her show. He tried to conjure the more intense feelings he had had not very long ago. He found it bothersome that he could not.

"Andy, I have made you bear the brunt of... well, things. I can't explain everything and it wouldn't help."

"Are you," she asked, looking at her shoes, "in love with her?"

"It doesn't matter, Andy. For a number of reasons, Elizaveta and I are no longer an 'item', shall we say." He cleared his throat and took her hand. "I'm afraid I took advantage of both of you and I am very sorry."

Suddenly looking up, examining his eyes, Andy found herself caring again. He averted his eyes, but not before Andy sensed something new, however indefinable, in them. Less penetrating. She resisted a surge of warmth and kissed his check. "Good-bye, Chris."

His look running up and down her, Dunney smiled lightly. "I can't even think of how much I'll miss you, Andrea. You know how cold the winters are here."

She pulled at the door. "It's July."

"By the time I get out of here," he added lamely, "who knows." Dunney squeezed her shoulder. "So long, Andy."

Without any further exchanges of either words or glances, Dunney followed Kyle out the front door. Kyle stopped Dunney just after he unlocked the gate. "You'd better be ready, Dunney."

"Pardon."

"All hell will break loose stateside today," Kyle warned. "We don't know what effect it will have here."

"Thanks, Mr. Kyle. Good-bye."

Dunney shook the Senior Embassy Secretary's hand and walked back through the guard. He nodded to the one with whom he had spoken and the guard replied in English, "Good day, Mr. Dunney. Compliments of Director Bellin."

It wasn't like Bellin, Dunney thought, to be so heavy handed. Not like him at all.

~ ~ ~

Hanging up the phone, Folenya glanced toward the monitoring room door. Bellin still had not visited the station and, so did not know what she had done in his name. She intended, firmly, that he would not know. Until it was all over.

~ ~ ~

Bellin stormed into the courtroom. Having waited, at Toliskorn's command, until the court granted a brief recess, Bellin wasted no words, letting his scowl convey his displeasure at the Procurator's curt summons.

"Director Bellin," Toliskorn stated, "I have a delivery for you to make. Now, don't take offense. It is very important."

Sharply, Bellin replied, "I have a brand new assistant for such important matters as deliveries, Procurator."

Amused by Bellin's attitude, Toliskorn said mildly, "When this trial is over, I promise to review that appointment, Director Bellin, but for now, I require just one thing." He handed Bellin a subpoena. "Deliver it."

~ ~ ~

Greenwald watched as the Director of Investigation for the Moscow Procuracy angrily stalked off the courtroom floor and Toliskorn indicated his readiness to proceed. Greenwald then focused his attention on the third senior judge.

The old man, breathing labored and eyes heavy, waved Toliskorn on. The judge had depleted himself in the course of the day by reining the Procurator's tendency to stretch the evidence beyond common sense and shaping it to rather odd conclusions. By the late afternoon, he had worn himself out.

Toliskorn studied the judge, also. "I request the court's patience. The treachery of a man cannot be lightly proved. I have the obligation to convince not only the court, but the Russian workers, of Dr. Mraisky's guilt."

The Procurator turned and continued spouting rhetoric as he fixed his eyes off to the right of the Press booth.

Greenwald and the other reporters relaxed. Toliskorn, stalling for time, had nothing to say of any printable value. Having observed the Procurator for eight hours, Greenwald and his colleagues knew that he would gesture to them when he was ready. After all, as one reporter had pointed out, this trial was for public consumption, not private justice.

The tension had worn on Greenwald more than the others. Too often, he felt the sharp eyes of Toliskorn boring into him. The others wrote the stares off to showmanship, but Greenwald could not.

Toliskorn raised his voice suddenly, fortunately, for the sound of footsteps outside the booth would have drowned him out at his normal volume, to Greenwald's ears at least.

"And so, I have laid the foundation. That is where we should stop for today. Tomorrow, will bring the..."

"Shit!" Greenwald snapped, missing the word due to the loud opening of the door. He quickly looked toward the door, Who the hell?

"... a witness who will complete the connection of Dr. Mraisky with the American intelligence..."

Greenwald's eyes met the newcomer's. "Oh, my God." Bellin! He turned back to Toliskorn to see the Procurator looking back at him from the floor.

"... and there will be no mistake about his guilt!" Toliskorn concluded, his voice thundering through the Press Booth.

Chapter Eleven

Dunney skipped dinner. He had no appetite. After two short bourbons, he skipped the third. His restlessness would not allow him to sleep or even daydream.

Turning instead to work, Dunney sweated out drafts of clauses covering the six agreed-upon sites in both English and Russian, the later requiring twice the time. Finally, when he needed Andy... The five hours of pen and paper drafting left him exhausted and stiff from sitting on the floor with his legs stretched out under the coffee table.

Before beginning the proposed language for the twelve-site contract–a speculative matter, of course, but Sarkat had insisted–Dunney decided that exercise was a necessity. Sliding out from under the table, he shook out his limbs, donned a suit coat and headed for the square.

The clerk stopped him just as he reached the hotel door. Dunney had told the desk to hold any calls and take messages. There were three, two left by Elizaveta. Those two went directly into the wastebasket. The third was from Steven Klein. Reluctantly, Dunney unfolded the note.

The words staggered Dunney. "Considering climate in U.S., we are satisfied thus far. B.B.R.I. is better off if we do not appear to forsake elements popular in U.S. Sarkat's call helpful. Klein."

No mention of Andy's call, Dunney thought. Sarkat's call? He had Bellin to thank for that. Damn him.

And now Klein was more worried now about a backlash in the US market, Dunney mused. It made perfect sense, considering the ridiculous pro-dissident craze apparently sweeping the country. If only his fellow Bostonians knew that their high-minded dissidents pimped a little to accomplish their purposes.

Folding the note, Dunney rebuked himself for his naivete Was Elizaveta a whore? More than anyone else? He knew very well that he had overreacted mostly because she had fooled him. It hadn't occurred to him that she was using him, which was stupid of him. And fair of her. Hadn't he used her as well?

It served no purpose to examine things too closely, he decided. No one cared a lick about you anyway and the motives meant nothing. Even the means... Judged objectively, any one means to an end was the equal of another. Subjectively, each person had to make up his, or her, own mind as to how far to go. Elizaveta had left no doubt that her "end" was everything to her.

Was his important enough to him? Important enough to trade hers for it? To trade her?

Dunney was spared further reflection by the sudden appearance of Clinton Thomas and one of his running mates winding up their nightly jogging routine. Both young men slowed as they approached, settling into a slow walk. Dunney noticed immediately that Thomas stared at him with open hostility. "Nice night for running," Dunney said.

George "Whitey" Smith, the lightest-skinned member of the relay team, eyed Thomas for a moment and then said to Dunney, "Any night is fine for running."

Thomas managed a smile. "Not used to seeing you alone, Mr. Dunney. Where's your lady?" In spite of his best efforts. the words came out sarcastically. Thomas had flipped opinions on Dunney. Because of Andrea Wards. "That Russian babe."

The special mocking tone did not escape Dunney; the justification for it did. The change in attitude struck him. He and Thomas had been very friendly initially though upon reflection he realized that Thomas had pretty much avoided him all week. Not that made much difference.

He kept his reply short. "She's gone. So's the American one."

"Well, shit, you noticed." Clinton picked up his pace and trotted right past Dunney.

When Dunney shot a questioning look at Smith, the lanky boy said. "Hey man, forget it. Clint fucked himself up, bad, with your fox."

"Andy?"

Smith nodded seriously. "Happens."

Looking after Clinton, waiting nervously for Smith at the desk in the hotel, Dunney felt depressed suddenly. Andy and Thomas? Where the hell was he? "Yeah. Goodnight, George."

"'Night."

He walked aimlessly, unconsciously taking one step after another. He tried to think of Andy and Thomas together, but the picture did not focus. She had betrayed him in one way and, now, in a second. God damn! Was he so wrapped up in Elizaveta that he did not even notice? If so, Elizaveta was more to blame than Andy. No, completely to blame. Andy's betrayal was merely an extension of Elizaveta's. God damn her, he thought, agitated to the point of... What?

What was it when it all came down to just one person?

~ ~ ~

As Bellin carelessly swigged vodka, Folenya paced the floor. "Why doesn't he come back?"

Still able to smell the sulfurous odor of gun powder on his hands, Bellin found the vodka increasingly harsh. He had, fortunately, consumed over eight ounces in the four hours of surveillance and really did not require any more. It had taken some doing to restore his calm, his perspective.

Oh, they had made inroads, yes indeed. But as long as he remained Director of Investigation and in charge of the dissident containment program, Bellin had to carry out his responsibilities.

That was why he decided to take the surveillance watch that one last night, though he doubted Dunney or the others would try anything. He had come not to watch them but to watch Folenya. Watching over her was now his only duty.

"Why did he go there in the first place?" Folenya demanded of him. As a sympathizer, Bellin, she assumed, understood the American better than she could.

"Back to the Shashlik?" Bellin asked rhetorically. He had asked the same question originally. "Why should Dunney go back to the Shashlik? Perhaps he's hungry." Bellin allowed himself the luxury of hoarding his real opinion.

He suspected that Dunney had experienced, after his hours of incredibly diligent work, a feeling of emptiness. With no other means of addressing it, he had to confront is cause. The Shashlik was the logical, if indirect, way to do so. Little could Dunney have imagined that the true confrontation awaited him back in the hotel.

For an hour, Elizaveta had sat expressionless on one of the settees in the lobby. It had been her third visit of the night, the first two coming during Dunney's feverish working session. Each previous time, she had waited until she could sit no longer and had left messages begging Dunney to see her. As Bellin watched her, he knew that this third time, Elizaveta would stay is long is necessary. She held herself with a resolution that impressed Bellin. Each time she had come, she conveyed increased determination.

"Here he is!" Folenya cried.

Bellin took a moment to refocus his eyes on another monitor, one trained on another pit of the lobby.

Indeed, Dunney had slowly come through the door, preoccupied and disturbed. He went directly to the desk without so much as a glance to the side. When the clerk pointed in Elizaveta's direction, Dunney did not turn right away. First, he dropped his head slightly for a couple of beats and then raised it a bit more than level. Turning, he did not move toward her, greeting her with a long-distance, unconvincing smile.

"Sound," Bellin ordered.

The background noise of the nearly deserted lobby became discernible as the technician increased the levels.

Dunney and Elizaveta were fifteen feet apart and yet she whispered, "Hello, Christopher."

Dunney's voice was nearly as quiet. "You shouldn't have come. Elizaveta."

Folenya let out a groan.

The scene on the monitor seemed so posed to Bellin, so staged. yet he could feel the charge of tension. He felt it inside of him.

"Christopher, you don't have to talk to me."

Smiling sardonically, Dunney said, "That wouldn't be very polite, would it? Refusing to talk to a girl just because you're in love with her."

Elizaveta blinked, started to smile and pulled her mouth downward.

Quickly, Dunney added, "Don't get the wrong idea, Elizaveta. I haven't changed my mind. I just have a better idea of what I've decided."

"I see."

"My room?"

She nodded and joined him as he walked toward the elevator. They did not touch, or even come very close together, but unless Bellin was mistaken, it took considerable effort on each one's part.

"Do they never tire of sex?" Folenya demanded.

"Sex?" he asked, as he watched the elevator monitor. Ironic, he thought. They were making their most passionate physical statement standing side by side and inches apart in an elevator. It made sex seem like a card-party by comparison.

~ ~ ~

Dunney glanced up at the camera as he let Elizaveta enter the room. He wanted Bellin to know that he was taking the surveillance into account. "We may as well sit down, Elizaveta. What I have to say won't take long, but I don't know what you have in mind."

When she chose the couch, Dunney intentionally sat on it as well. He intended to show her and Bellin that he was in control, not they.

She was not surprised that Dunney sat stiffly within reach of her. It would be an appropriate test for them both. "I'm sorry if my coming here is a problem, Christopher."

"It will be all right."

"Since last night," Elizaveta began, "I have had to work very hard at not thinking about you... and me. Finally, I realized that I never dared to talk to you about what my... well, about me. You couldn't possibly understand what I had to do, and what I have to do. That was not right of me. I came for that reason. Nothing else. Not to convince you to help me or to make love to me again."

Dunney almost missed her last remarks, preoccupied with the earlier ones. They struck him very deeply, generating a gnawing sensation in his stomach. They had not talked about themselves, not in any depth, during their week of complete intimacy. He had thought, or rather felt, that he knew her, but how could he? And how could she know him? Had their week been so shallow?

His disturbance showed clearly on his face, but Elizaveta misinterpreted it. "I shouldn't have said that."

"No, no..." Dunney shook his hand at her disclaimer. "Say whatever you have to say." Before she could respond, Dunney restated his demand. "No, I mean, tell me. I thought I knew. Instinctively?" He shrugged, forced to admit that he had, in fact, relied on instinct. He had seen her only as a woman trying very hard to be a good lover, unsure of how exactly to please him, physically and emotionally. Trying hard, yet always holding back.

Elizaveta grew anxious about Dunney's unusual pensiveness. She suspected that he was examining her mentally, finding her wanting. "How can I make you see?"

"Try."

"Christopher, you have to live here to know. You have to be a Jew in Russia to understand. I know," she said sighing, "Because, I wasn't really a Jew until a few years ago. My mother was a Jew. After living through the pogroms–the organized attacks on Jews–she decided that it was easier to be a Russian. From the age of eight, all she wanted was to forget what she was."

"The war let her. People died or left the cities and villages, were lost, hurt, sick. The chance came for her to become a good Russian and she took it. She found a nice Russian to be her husband and they had a frail, premature Russian baby. Their only one. Christopher, you have to understand: I grew up Russian. My mother wouldn't even tell me what I was until I was eight years old. The same age when she had made up her own mind." The telling proved more painful and draining than Elizaveta had anticipated. "No one has ever heard this before, Christopher. I've always been too ashamed.

First, because I was really a Jew and then because I really wasn't. Isn't that foolish?"

She looked away from him, able then to stem the tears.

Tentatively, Dunney reached for her shoulder, yielding finally and brushing her cheek. As he did, she coked off a sob and shook her head.

"Elizaveta..."

Her voice cracking, she objected, "No. I want you to hold me. But if you do, I won't finish. You mustn't touch me until then. If you still want to."

Dunney pulled back, struggling to reassert his own reserve. When he was satisfied, he said, "Go on."

Sniffing twice, she continued. "She taught me little things; a few prayers, sayings, some history. But she would never go very far. She and father warned me never to tell, never. To them, my being a Jew was a horrible burden, for them and for me. It was a part of me they simply rejected."

"Pogroms come periodically in Russia, though we don't call them that any more. Things were very bad ten years ago. Twelve, it is now, I guess. The 1967 war." Elizaveta shuddered at the memory. "She was proud, but very worried. 'Now is not the time to be a Jew in Russia' she said. And Father agreed."

"They were very right. It was awful. Jews were threatened, called 'Kikes', bullied. One of my classmates, who was Jewish, was beaten unconscious. All this time, I knew that I would have been treated the same way if anybody knew. I didn't say anything. But I nurtured the good part, the feeling of success that comes with being on the winning side. I was willing to take the good, then, but not the bad."

"With the Seven-Day War behind me, I literally forgot all about it. I was only fifteen and stating to feel like a woman and that seemed important. Like all the other girls, I wanted to be liked. I wasn't pretty the way my mother was, so I had to try very hard. And I wanted to go to the University, which meant lots of work. My mother, of course, wasn't educated, but Father was an engineer."

"While I was first at the University, the Yom Kippur War came," she said grimly. "At the time, I was studying economics from Dr. Mraisky. I admired him tremendously, he was so brilliant and had just won the Lenin Prize, as a Jew no less. He had made me one of his favorites, because he knew. He told me that later."

"The attack on Israel stunned all of us, Russians and Jews. When the Egyptians did so well at first, all of my friends cheered and celebrated. I didn't have any Jewish friends, since they... Only Dr. Mraisky. And I could see that he was terribly sad about it. As it got worse, I began to feel it, too. I couldn't cheer with the others, but I couldn't cry to anyone either. It was like before, only the reverse. I had to share the bad part, the losing, the threat of extinction."

"When it looked worst, Dr. Mraisky called me to his office. He wanted to know why I had become so quiet in class. He knew, of course, but he wanted to help me admit it. He taught me what it meant."

"It meant, among other things, that I can't be a Russian anymore," Elizaveta concluded. "I am a Jew and I have to try harder than most because I denied it for so long. Our Group will make it possible for others to discover what they are, Christopher. That is why I have to..." She let the sentence die.

"... why do you have to help Mraisky." Dunney finished for her, as affected by her intensity as she was. There was too much for him to digest at once, but the feeling with which she revealed everything forced complete sympathy on him. No, the sympathy was not forced: His resistance to it was forced.

Breathing unevenly, Elizaveta fell back into the cushions. From there, she gazed at Dunney, wondering what he now thought of her. "You said before that you loved me," she said quietly. "I don't hold you to that."

Dunney got off of the couch and fixed them both a long drink. "You may not need this, Elizaveta, but I sure as hell do."

Disappointed by his failure to respond as she had hoped, Elizaveta accepted the glass without comment. It would have been wise for her to leave, she felt, but she could not move. Not without a smile from him, a touch.

He drank half of the glass at once and swirled the rest around en the glass for a moment or two, trying to frame his thoughts. "I don't have a long story to tell, Elizaveta. Mine is short, and quite simply not worth telling. Where I come from, it's easy to be in the background, because there's always someone who wants to be front and center. My family was like that, school was like that, business, law are like that. Think of it this way, you're trying hard to be a successful Jew. I'm trying hard to be a successful lawyer. It's what I have to be, because there isn't anything else to be, except nothing. Okay?"

"Yes, Christopher," she replied despondently. The word "successful" made them both sound cheap. "I understand."

Staring at his glass, Dunney added, "I don't, not really. I just know."

It was over, then. "I think I should go," she said, in an unintentional whisper.

As she moved to rise, Dunney seized her wrist. "No!" Almost as suddenly, he released it. "There is something else to say, Elizaveta," he said earnestly looking into her sad eyes. "it may not mean anything, but..."

Her fingers intercepted the words. She knew what he wanted to say and what she would say in return. There was a better way. She let her eyes drift toward the bedroom. "Christopher, it well mean everything to me."

Taking her hand, Dunney smiled sadly and said, "The camera."

"Bellin knows us well enough, Christopher," she replied, "by now."

~ ~ ~

When Dunney and Elizaveta reached the bedroom, Folenya clicked her tongue. "It never ends."

Bellin sighed heavily as he watched Dunney lay Elizaveta on the bed with loving gentleness, as if less care would break her heart. Scanning the other monitors, by now two dozen of them including a new one for Dunney's bathroom, Bellin smiled grimly. It was over.

He stood up, stabbing out his cigar against the back of the chair. "Turn it off."

Folenya started. "What?"

The technician turned around, shocked at Bellin's command. "I beg your pardon, Director Bellin."

Without looking at either of them, focusing instead on the rhythmic caressing of the two lovers, Bellin said again, "Turn it off."

"But..." Folenya fumed.

As the picture went out, Bellin turned his attention to Folenya. "It's over, Anna. All they can do is make love and it's over." He crossed in front of her and turned toward the door. "Tonight, I am going home. I have to get to know my wife again."

When she was certain Bellin had left the building, Folenya told the technician, "Go ahead."

The screen came to life again and Folenya cried in dismay, "They're under the covers!"

~ ~ ~

Nikolai Torlas stretched each one of his fingers in sequence. They were tired and stiffening. When he had begun writing, as a fifteen year old, five, six, seven hours had seemed nothing. To write longhand for seven hours, he thought, good God! Now, he had a typewriter, albeit manual, and he could take only two or three hours at a sitting.

He tore out the page he had started half an hour before, centered the carriage and covered the machine. Since Volenko's departure an hour and a half ago, he had gotten nothing done. How could he be expected to write? And why in Georgian, if it would not be published anyway? Why not German? Why not Basque?

Instead, Torlas took out the script that he and Mikhail had worked on all evening. The exact words, though unnecessary, had a certain appealingly evil sound to them which he liked, particularly the sniveling, "you must promise that I won't lose my Union membership." He reread with special interest the detailed description of Elizaveta, pleased with his usual flair for conveying physical presence.

The plan had, after all, a chance. Elizaveta was to phone Volenko when she was ready to meet him. Volenko, having retrieved the tape from Elizaveta's hiding place, would "pass it" to her in the form of a sealed, economics book, which she could carry along with the others Volenko would bring without arousing undue suspicion. Suspicion, he chuckled would hardly prove necessary.

The new Assistant Director of Investigation, a former KGB liaison to the Department of Investigation, was the perfect choice. Dull, ambitious, fanatically anti-dissident, Anna Folenya would react perfectly upon receiving Torlas' intelligence. Unless, of course, he botched the job.

Volenko had already prepared Elizaveta. She had agreed to the last ditch effort to carry the message. Their final hope for saving Mraisky. God, how far they were willing to go for that little Jew, Torlas thought. How does one man command so much love and respect, even from anti-Semites... Like himself.

Poor Elizaveta. When they caught her not ten meters from the hotel, her whole world would collapse.

~ ~ ~

"Settle down, Sy," Kyle growled, as he put the finishing touches on the final draft of Greenwald's statement. "The Procurator has kindly agreed to this compromise. They can't reach you in here and besides, in a few hours Mac will have landed a couple spies for exchange purposes. Arkilonov may not go for Mraisky, but he won't hold you back."

Greenwald sipped brandy, saying nothing. How innocently people destroyed themselves, he mused. Innocent of mind, that was, not innocent of motive.

Kyle read quickly over the writing. It had come from McDeamon, in code of course, and he had had to translate it to Russian. "At least it is the truth, Sy," he said lightly, "which is a rarity in this business. Disclaimer and all, the Ruskies will twist this just enough to fry Mraisky. Fuckers. And wait until the Senate gets a hold of this. Christ. And the public."

Handing the paper to Greenwald, Kyle poured more brandy. "Read it over and I'll get it typed in the AM." He checked his watch. "Shit! It is two o'clock in the morning."

His eyes scanned the page without reading. Greenwald already knew what it said: He was with the CIA; he had tried to enlist Mraisky; he had offered money, support, channels to the west. It was just what the Russians needed to destroy not only Mraisky, but the entire dissident movement, the Moscow Group and all of its regional satellites. Who would even read the last line... "Mraisky systematically rejected all of my overtures." Nobody. The Procurator might just omit it entirely.

It was such a short, unemotional thing, a betrayal in under two hundred and fifty words. And come tomorrow morning, he would sign it.

~ ~ ~

Glowering at the clock as if it were an enemy, Bellin closed the dossier. Four twenty! And he had not slept in two hours. Marta continued to sleep, restlessly without him at her side. How many nights had she, and he, spent so restlessly? In his career, many; the past week, six.

Dunney's dossier weighed heavily on his lap. It had grown fat in that week, since the American's arrival. Despite the unflagging efforts of the Boston Detectives Agency, Bellin had learned nothing he had not already surmised about Dunney. All the details of Dunney's strangely one-dimensional life simply fit the pattern he had seen early on: A man obsessed with his own version of success, willing to sacrifice everything for it, except his pride. Egocentricity, so typically American, dominated Dunney to a mystifying extent.

All his life he had maintained an ultra-low profile, while steadily moving toward his goals. Academically, the pattern consisted of generally solid marks interrupted by well-timed excellence at school–or job-application periods. In activities, sports and professional matters, Dunney had always lain low until a peak performance had been called for. Typically, his legal work, while strong, had never been spectacular. The Moscow trip was to be his burst of brilliance, timed to get him what he wanted most: A Partnership.

And yet, there were the inexplicable aberrations. The in-class humiliation of a student-teacher had gotten him a short suspension in high school. He had suddenly quit his freshman track-team in college, over an argument with the coach. He had chanced an affair with Steven Klein's wife, according to confirmed rumors, shortly after joining Klein's department at the firm.

Of all Dunney's aberrant streaks, however, his actions in Moscow impressed Bellin as the longest and broadest. Dunney had undertaken his affair with Elizaveta

Krylenkev in spite of the certain knowledge that it would destroy his otherwise perfect career opportunity, possibly the zenith of his life. In one night, Dunney had risked everything by defying Bellin's directive...

But now, Dunney had returned to his usual course, discarding the apparently deep relationship with Elizaveta–with a bit of "help" from Bellin–in favor of a renewed chance at success. It was this adherence to pattern which had induced Bellin to relax, to conclude that Dunney had been neutralized, despite this last, final moment with the girl. In that sense, it was an empty, if heartfelt, gesture on Dunney's part.

All was in hand and Bellin did not have to worry significantly about the last day of the Mraisky affair, as he had earlier told Marta.

Bellin looked over at the clock. Four thirty-one. What in God's name was wrong?

Chapter Twelve

At eight o'clock on the morning of the second and last day of Dr. Alexander Mraisky's trial, the two militiamen posted at the entrance to the Procuracy of Moscow's headquarters barred the door to an agitated, rotund man who spoke with a thick Georgian accent. The fat man looked from one to the other and announced, "I have come to see Assistant Director Folenya of the Department of Investigation."

"Your name?"

"Nikolai Torlas."

The guards shrugged indifferently, but one called down to Folenya's post in the monitoring room. Her sharp command shook the young guard. "You're to go with me."

~ ~ ~

Procurator of Moscow Boris Toliskorn sat quietly at the desk in his office awaiting the delivery of the statement from Seymour Greenwald. The short, stocky man with him paced the floor nervously. It was an idiosyncrasy peculiar to the man and very familiar to his former assistant, who interpreted it correctly: Pacing, for Vasili Arkilonov, was a thinking mechanism.

Toliskorn's phone buzzed and both men concentrated their complete attention on it. The Procurator kept it brief and shook his head. "It's just one of the judges," he informed his chief. "We'll have the two-to-one split we want. They're sure that our senile cow–the one trucked in from the provinces–won't go along."

Without acknowledging the expected information, Arkilonov returned to his pacing. And his thinking.

~ ~ ~

Still half in a dream, Elizaveta reached for Christopher Dunney. She started awake. He was not there!

Elizaveta sprang to her knees and looked anxiously around the room. Dunney. was nowhere to be seen. Only one thought raced through her mind: He had left her! "Christopher!" she cried once. Her own voice frightening her into silence, she slumped back on her heels and buried her head in her hands. She was fully awake now, to reality.

Dunney pushed the bedroom door open and stood stiffly, looking at her. "I couldn't sleep, Elizaveta. I was working."

To her, they were the three most brutal words ever spoken. She managed a smile and a quiet, "Of course."

Elizaveta's reaction did not make Dunney feel any worse than he had since dawn when he had finally gotten up. He had wanted to stay with her, but the work I hadn't finished last night when I... when we..."

Too hurt to protest, she ended the momentary silence. "I understand, Christopher."

"Explain it to me," he joked unhappily.

Explain it to him, she thought, how? "What time is it?

Reluctantly, Dunney went to the dresser for his watch. He had let the travel alarm go the night without winding. Had he thought that a stopped clock would arrest time? "A little after eight." He sighed. "Do you have an appointment?"

Thinking of Volenko, she nodded. "But the time of it is up to me." Upon an impulse, she added, "I'm to call Mikhail when I'm ready."

The name Mikhail sounded an alarm inside Dunney. He associated Volenko with Mraisky and with that side of Elizaveta which haunted them both. "Volenko? Why?"

Lying obviously, she said, "It's not important."

"Then don't go to him."

Holding out one hand to him, she said, "Come here, sit beside me."

Dunney grabbed his shirt from the dresser and threw it on the bed. "Put something on, Elizaveta. We can't talk politics with you like that."

Clutching the light blue shit to her breast, Elizaveta thought of their first night, their first morning. And the others. The shirt was so full of his smell, she wanted to cry. She did not.

"All right, all right," Dunney relented. "But don't expect me to listen. Or sit on my hands."

Firmly in his arms again, Elizaveta looked down over her own body. Would it ever feel that joy again? The cruel question stayed with her only a moment, forced out by its equally cruel answer. No. "Before I tell you, you must promise me something, Christopher."

"I'm not sure I can."

"Please. Promise, at least, to try."

Squeezing her lightly, he agreed. "That I can do. I can always try."

Carefully choosing her terms, she continued, "You must try, very hard, not to distrust me, or look for a motive I do not have." She waited for him to respond.

"Yes?"

The constant pressure of his body reassured her. "I am going to meet..." Suddenly she remembered the camera. "I can't."

"Elizaveta!" Dunney began to suspect that she intended to manipulate him. When his eyes followed hers and he understood. "Is it so bad, sweetheart?" he asked before kissing her softly on the neck. Close to her ear, he whispered, "Distract him."

Grateful and yet miserable, she nodded. Then she blurted, "Mikhail and I are lovers."

Dunney feigned shock and then resignation. He stood up and started to unbutton his shirt. Without comment, he went on to unbuckle his belt and slide his pants and briefs off together. As he climbed onto the bed with the startled Elizaveta, he said, "Let him wait." Half on top of her he whispered, "Go ahead."

She faked a hum of pleasure as he worked on her ear. The second one was real. His hands consumed her tingling skin making the act difficult to contain. "Oh no, Christopher."

"Come on," he encouraged her, pressing her mouth to his ear.

Her breath coming in bursts, Elizaveta was afraid to whisper. Only when Dunney rested his hand on her breast did she dare to try. Kissing his ear first, she told him. "I'm going to take it to the Embassy."

Dunney did not move, but every muscle in his body tensed. For an instant he refused to believe that he had heard it. She could not have been serious! When he was able, he pulled himself back to study her face. The look of agonized earnestness convinced him. Falling over onto his back beside her, he demanded, "My God, Elizaveta, why?"

Quickly, she swung into position above him, her face hovering over his. "There is no one else," she stated softly.

"It's goddamn fucking impossible and you know it!" he exclaimed through clenched teeth.

"Mikhail will try to bribe the guards."

He could not even look at her. Was she that foolish or just that treacherous?

"Look at me!" She knew what he was thinking. She could not leave him with that thought in his mind. "Christopher!"

Dunney began to throw her off of him.

Angrily, she resisted. "No. You must look at me first."

Complying, Dunney saw in her outrage that he was wrong.

"I love you. You don't have to do anything for that."

"Then don't go, Elizaveta."

If only she had a choice! It wasn't fair for her to be so torn apart, Christopher on the one side, her duty on the other. "I must."

Dunney knew he had to stop her. He also knew that he could not. Not without taking the message to the Embassy himself. And that, that was one thing which, for many reasons now, he simply would not do.

He reached up and enfolded her in his arms, pulling her down on top of him. Their bodies touched coldly at first, but soon the heat began to flow from one to the other as if no barrier lay between. They both knew that it would not last, but for the moment they were together. They lay still, afraid to disturb the feeling of unity that would have to be their consolation.

~ ~ ~

Folenya had scurried up to her office to receive the Georgian novelist and dissident. Carefully arranging herself behind her desk, Folenya waited impatiently for Torlas. Her curiosity about his call devoured her every thought. He was, after all, one of the leading members of Mraisky's band of subversives, a direct companion of Volenko and, more importantly, of the Jewess, Elizaveta Krylenkev.

Torlas entered, his appearance living up to her low expectations. The man was inhumanly fat, obviously self-indulgent in his appetites, like most Georgians. Folenya mustered her coldest expression for him. "Sit down, Comrade."

Wearing a somber look, Torlas took the offered chair. He said nothing.

Leaning toward him, she demanded, "Well? You came to see me, Comrade Torlas. If you have something useful, I am prepared to listen. If not, I am busy."

"They told me that you...," he began before running out of steam.

"They? Who? Come on man!"

"At the Writers' Union." Every one of his words was labored. "They said that I might make a bargain with you."

"Bargain?" Folenya's body pulsed with excitement. Torlas, a leading cog in the Moscow Group, was looking or a deal! "Don't be a fool, Comrade Torlas. What have you to trade? And for what?"

Torlas inhaled, puffing himself up to an even larger bulk. He tried to measure his words. "My membership in the Union of Writers is under probation, subject to immediate suspension. Without it, I cannot publish."

Nastily, she said, "I am well aware of that, Comrade. Perhaps if you were more dependable, it would not be so."

"That is what I hoped," Torlas responded anxiously. "Now that the Moscow Group has been shown up as..."

"An American cell?"

He nodded. "All I have, Director Folenya, is my craft."

Folenya noted that he had used the wrong title for her. She did not correct his error. "You have, your loyalty to the Party, Comrade, and to your country."

"Let me prove it," he pleaded.

Feigning skepticism, Folenya examined Torlas. She saw that he obviously feared sharing Mraisky's fate. Perspiration had begun to gather on his forehead and to stain his shirt. The longer she scrutinized him, the more nervous he became. "We shall see."

"I can offer some useful information."

"Perhaps."

"Do you agree to endorse me to the Union?"

Haughtily. Folenya replied, "if I find it worth my while."

Torlas deflated. "There's no point in trying to bargain with you, Director Folenya. I am at your mercy."

Without saying anything, Folenya signaled her agreement with a sneer.

"My former colleagues in the Moscow Group will try to run the US Embassy guard this morning." he admitted quietly.

"What?" Folenya rose halfway out of her chair and held the position for a moment, asking, "Who?"

"The Jew, Elizaveta Krylenkev, volunteered. Mikhail Volenko will create a diversion. I was to have bribed the head guard." In disgust he added, "And all to save a CIA infiltrator!"

Her eyes brightened with the sight of herself personally arresting the depraved Jewish slut. Folenya could feel the tape in her hand. "You are very wise, Comrade Torlas."

"Wise? If I were wise, I would never have thrown my lot in with the American CIA."

"Mistakes are correctable, Comrade."

"I want them caught, Director Folenya!" he growled suddenly. "I want you to show the Americans that they cannot use Nikolai Torlas!"

Vengeance, she thought, was a very healthy motive. Coupled with Torlas' fear of losing his livelihood, it convinced her that he had not lied. "When?"

Settled down, he said, "Volenko is to call me. It will be soon, any moment. If I confirm that I was successful, he will get word to Elizaveta. She will come out of the hotel..."

"The International?"

"Yes. She is to cross the square, while Volenko prepares his diversion to give the guards an excuse to leave the gate unattended."

"What is the diversion?"

Torlas shrugged. "That is up to Mikhail. But he often uses young boys to act as his decoys."

On her feet, Folenya said, "You will come with me."

"But I have to take Volenko's call," he objected.

Suspiciously, she eyed the fat man. Georgians were born to lie, she recalled. And this Georgian was an intellectual pig! "Where?"

Reluctantly, he answered, "The Writers Union."

"One, no, two of my men will accompany you," Folenya stated.

"But I have told you…"

"I will make the decisions, Comrade. My people will be in touch with me at all times. That way I will know when to pounce on your 'friends'. And," she added ominously, "I will know how accurately you have your facts."

"Director, I assure you…"

"Get up and come with me," she commanded. "Now!"

~ ~ ~

The technician had his feet up on the console when Bellin walked in. Folenya was nowhere to be seen. The scene made him uncomfortable. Surveying the monitors, he saw that of the various locations, only Dunney's rooms promised any interest. Dunney and Elizaveta were making themselves quietly presentable. When Dunney opened his briefcase without the customary clicking sounds, Bellin said sharply, "Sound. If you don't mind."

Swinging his feet to the ground abruptly, the technician knocked his earphones on the floor. "Yes, Director."

When the level increased enough to reveal the sound of shuffling paper, Bellin stopped him. "Enough. Have you been recording?"

"Yes, Director Bellin. Comrade Folenya ordered recording late last night, after you left. Both video and audio."

As Bellin had expected, Folenya had not resisted tuning in Dunney and Elizaveta's "fornication", as she insisted upon calling it. He moved forward, picking up the direct line to the head militiaman in the US Embassy guard. "Anything to report?"

"No. Director."

"How many men do you have?"

"Eight, all together, Director."

Bellin paused before ringing off. Certainly, he should double the posting. It was the last day of Mraisky's trial. If anything were to happen, it would have to happen by late afternoon. Beyond that time, nothing would save Mraisky. "Do you have a back-up unit available as ordered..."

"Back-up... Yes sir." The guard's voice revealed his awareness of the situation. "Should I call them up?"

Pondering the question, Bellin's eyes went instinctively to the television screen displaying Dunney, who at that moment was standing near the window. "No. No, but keep them on call."

"Yes, sir."

Bellin hung up the phone. What had told him not to post a double guard? He continued to watch Dunney as he racked his mind, searching for the impelling sense of restraint.

The American stood, tying his tie, his shoulders slumped. His eyes were glued on the bathroom door behind which Elizaveta nervously showered. Dunney's agonized expression touched Bellin, but also worried him. Dunney, for the first time, seemed oblivious to Bellin's intrusion!

His tie done, Dunney carefully centered the knot and settled the collar into a comfortable position on his neck. He sighed and, suddenly, turned to look out the window. With the left panel of the drapes in one hand, Dunney gazed out into the square. His posture still had not returned to normal. For a full minute, he just stared out the window, in the direction of the US Embassy.

What was he thinking? Bellin wondered, feeling an uncertain chill creep in on him. Did he contemplate helping Elizaveta? Bellin shivered the feeling away as Dunney turned slowly around, resignation showing clearly on his tired face. He could have decided then, Bellin knew. He could have chosen the girl over himself!

"Good God." Bellin mumbled, the internal exclamation spilling into public.

And then he knew. He understood just how close they had come. The doubling of the guard would have added a crucial element, the kind that would have tipped Dunney toward a suicidal decision to aid Elizaveta. It was the trigger of the one essential characteristic of Dunney's character that had until that moment eluded him.

He knew that Dunney had come to respect him, and to resent his authority over him. His doubling of the guard would have provoked Dunney to defy him outright. And in defiance, Dunney would do anything.

~ ~ ~

"Proceed, Procurator Toliskorn," the Senior Judge called, beginning what he intended to be the final day of the trial of Dr. Alexander Mraisky. "Yesterday you were talking about the accused's connection with the Americans."

"Indeed I was, and today I will continue along that line." Toliskorn ran his index finger gently along the edge of the paper sent over from the US Embassy only minutes before. He had not yet decided how, or even if, to use the document. Its contents had rather surprised him. He had constructed his case around proving that Greenwald was what the statement admitted he had been: A CIA agent. His task had been so simplified that he was somewhat taken aback. What was he now to do with all of the witnesses he had summoned...

Resigned to scrapping his entire plan, Toliskorn returned the Greenwald statement to his file. "I would like at this hour, with the court's permission to dismiss my various witnesses and proceed directly. There is no point in temporizing. I will question only one more witness." Toliskorn stared at the defendant. "Dr. Alexander Mraisky!"

With Toliskorn's announcement booming over the closed circuit hook-up in Feuchinko's office, Arkilonov stopped his pacing. He looked at Feuchinko. "Is he good enough to handle this?" The Procurator General set down the Greenwald Admission. It was a startling complication in the carefully planned trial sequence. "I don't know.

"Greenwald was your idea."

"I acknowledge that, but your boy could have just forgotten the statement and proceeded with our original series of witnesses," Feuchinko reminded the KGB Director. "This maneuver is hardly necessary."

Pacing once again, Arkilonov said nothing. Words were worthless to him at that point. The Americans had, minutes before, seized two senior KGB agents attached to the Embassy in Washington. They had taken a final, overt, public step. It was up to Toliskorn now.

Feuchinko watched his rival's feet. Where was the usual easy pivot at the end of each course? The gentle swaying from side to side? Good God, he thought suddenly. Arkilonov was nervous!

~ ~ ~

Her hand hovering over the telephone, Elizaveta returned Dunney's stare. Answering his final, understated plea in the negative, she picked up the receiver. "I will call from downstairs if you'd rather."

 Dunney remained by the window, rejecting his urge to seize the phone away from her. "If Bellin doesn't mind, I don't."

As intended, his words reminded her that Bellin and the KGB would overhear the conversation with Volenko from his phone. Elizaveta, however, had a harmless code prepared and knew full well that even the phones in the lobby were tapped, always. "An outside line, please," she said in her best English. The choice of language would tell Volenko if she were ready: English for "yes", Russian for "no". Carefully, she dialed the number of the university's Psychology Department. The secretary, who spoke both Russian and English, answered in Russian.

Unable to look away from Dunney, Elizaveta hesitated, one last time. Would he really allow her to do it? Dunney did not move. "Good morning," she replied, in English. "I would like to speak with Professor Volenko."

"He's not in," came the response. "Would you like to leave a message…"

"Be sure to tell him that I hope to see him tonight. This is Elizaveta Krylenkev."

She did not listen to the secretary's good-bye, cradling the phone directly after she had spoken the meaningless words. Only the language counted. When Volenko called in, as he was to do every fifteen minutes, he would know. "Will you say good-bye to me, Christopher?"

Turning, Dunney said, "What choice do I have?"

Unwilling to ask him again to carry the taped message, Elizaveta said nothing. He would despise her again if she tried to use him. And she would despise herself. The cause was hers.

Dunney regretted his question. He crossed the room in four seemingly endless strides and kissed her lightly on the lips.

For both of them, that was enough.

Without further hesitation, Elizaveta opened the door and left.

~ ~ ~

Bellin sighed heavily and walked out of the monitoring room. That was the end of that.

~ ~ ~

When Anna Folenya saw Mikhail Volenko turn into the International Hotel, she signaled the Embassy guard to be prepared for the diversion. Folenya visually checked her own four, hand-picked KGB officers, two on either side of the Hotel entrance, out of view from the inside. The traitors would not suspect.

~ ~ ~

By walking through the hotel door, Volenko set off his diversion. Four adolescents rushed across the square with anti-American signs straight at the Embassy gate.

Inside the lobby he greeted Elizaveta warmly and handed her a pile of economics books. She kissed him on the cheek, and fearfully, resolutely, headed for the door.

~ ~ ~

Having tried vainly to avoid the window, for fear that he would tip Bellin off, Dunney decided that the contrary might be more true. Would Bellin believe that he would not have to watch her go, forever...

Not that the rationale mattered. Dunney knew that he had to see.

~ ~ ~

When the four boys reached the guards at the Embassy gate, and the militiamen ran to intercept them, Folenya gloated over her pending success. She would now show Bellin up for the incompetent he was!

~ ~ ~

The comic chase at the other side of the square did not reassure Elizaveta as she began her deliberately casual walk across the square. The idiotic boys had remained right in front of the gate! And she saw no one from the Embassy. How would she get through? The books, one of which had the tape inside, weighed increasingly heavily in her arms.

It wasn't working! Involuntarily, she looked back over her shoulder, up at Dunney's window. He was there...

Then, off to one side of the gate, Elizaveta detected a sign of movement. Another contingent of boys was raising a ladder against the Embassy wall brandishing paint brushes. Volenko had come up with a double diversion! Reflexively, she picked up her pace, angling away from the source of the second diversion.

By the time she had crossed half the square, a guard had discovered the boys on the ladder. The police, whistle was loud and the response immediate: All of the guards moved in the same direction at once.

~ ~ ~

"Go!" Folenya ordered.

~ ~ ~

Dunney saw it happen, at first unbelieving. The flow of the Embassy guards seemed to draw Elizaveta into the trap at the very moment it began to close on her. From either side of the square, the KGB men ran in, while Elizaveta's eyes never left the gate. As they grabbed her, she did not react, except to try pulling them along with her.

Suddenly, Elizaveta understood, her knees caving in under her, her arms losing control of their precious cargo. In that instant of her agony, she twisted completely around. Dunney could not see the expression on her face, or the look in her eyes, but he knew it was meant for him. For the first time, he understood what it meant to have your blood run cold.

~ ~ ~

Elizaveta fought her urge to call out to Dunney. Not for rescue, but for the last comfort of his touch. She heard a woman's voice, but not the words. Thrown into a car from out of nowhere, the books torn out of her arms, Elizaveta heard her own, seeming distant cry of pain. Her head falling back, she felt strangely tranquil, almost sleepy.

~ ~ ~

Volenko had no time to watch the scene in the square. The gasps of the spectators in the lobby told him all he needed to know, as he flattened himself against the side of the elevator. Even when the doors closed, he knew that he could not relax. The KGB, fresh from seizing Elizaveta, would have to pursue him.

The elevator climbed too slowly. It whirred to a stop on the fifth floor, stopping Volenko's heart with its lurch. The door opened. It remained open too long. The elevator rocked slightly, the direction indicator went out and the doors began to slide together. Thrusting out both arms, Volenko squeezed through the opening before the unresponsive doors snapped shut.

The blood seemed to rush through his arteries with a roar, but Volenko could not afford to worry about that. He ran, nearly breathless, up the stairs, one agonizing flight to the sixth, Dunney's, floor. By then, his eyes had so blurred that he had to count the passing rooms rather than rely on the brass numbers on the doors.

His heart shuddered as he pounded on the door he hoped would be Dunney's. He let the door support him during the terrifying time it took to get a response. When the door gave way, Volenko fell forward. Only Dunney's arms prevented his collapse.

Mustering all of his fading strength, Volenko slid a note into Dunney's shirt pocket. Straightening unsteadily, he looked the American in the face and, still aware of the cameras watching them, handed Dunney a small envelope. "It's from her," he said in a labored whisper. From behind he could hear the noise of the elevator doors.

Dunney stared at him, expressionless. The American's chalk white face turned toward Volenko's left, just as the powerful arms of the KGB men encircled him. Dunney looked from one agent to the other and then back at Volenko. Spending his last bit of effort, Volenko kept his head raised enough to vaguely see the sneer as Dunney said tersely. "I don't know what this is. I don't care." With that. Dunney handed over the envelope Volenko had, only seconds before, pressed into his hand.

The KGB agent on Volenko's right released one hand to open the paper. Scanning it quickly, he wedged it into his belt. In brutal Russian, he said to Volenko, "You're beyond hope now, old man." To Dunney he said, "You were wise."

Coldly, Dunney replied, "Ask Director Bellin what else he wants of me." Without pausing to elaborate or to await a reply, Dunney spun back inside and slammed the door.

Volenko, unable to offer resistance, tried to walk to his fate. He felt a distant amusement as he felt his rubbery legs give way. No, he would, as usual, have to be dragged.

~ ~ ~

Bellin, in his office uneasily puffing his cigar, made two calls. One was directed at the technician in the monitoring station, the other to the KGB officer in charge of the Embassy guard. He asked each man the same questions: "Anything happening? Anything to report?"

From each he got precisely the same answer: "Nothing at all, Director Bellin."

~ ~ ~

Flushed with triumph, Folenya stepped out of the car carrying the one economics book which was sealed shut. Despite her efforts during the drive to the Procuracy, the adhesive had held. After giving instructions concerning the Jewess Krylenkev, Folenya set her full attention on the false book.

She proceeded surreptitiously down the darkened stairs to the firing range, which served Bellin as his sanctuary.

There she could work in confidence, she thought. No one ever even came down there, except, of course, Bellin, and she half welcomed the idea of his interrupting her.

Using the sturdy hunting knife Bellin used to dig spent lead out of the target walls, she forced the pseudo-book open. It had a thick wood interior with a central compartment. Folenya slid the veneer back...

The target range was well shielded. No one heard Folenya wailing.

~ ~ ~

"Isn't that so, Dr. Mraisky?" Toliskorn demanded.

The battered Mraisky bowed his head. For three hours, the Procurator had come at him, from every angle, with facts, with lies, with endless statements positioned somewhere in between. How could he know what was true? "The money came from friends." He had never even taken money for his articles published in the West. Had he?

Scornfully, Toliskorn announced, "The accused suggests that the thousands of rubles came from, what he calls, friends. Friends... Do you consider members of the Capitalist propaganda machine 'friends' you poor deluded man?"

The Senior Judge cleared his throat. Toliskorn, getting the message, relented. "Friends. Then you deny that the American CIA ever supplied you or your Group with money?"

"Yes," Mraisky responded tentatively, fearing what the Procurator would spring next.

Toliskorn made a gesture of frustration. He felt the harsh, hostile eyes of the Senior Judge digging into him.

"Procurator Toliskorn, have you nothing to follow with?" the old jurist demanded, incredulous. "When you accuse a citizen of this Union with taking money from foreign governments, you should have a little proof of it!"

"I have shown that the accused received money regularly from the United States and that..."

The judge thumped his hand on the bench. "I myself have a cousin who still gets money from his grandson in Cleveland, Ohio, Procurator."

"In compensation for seditious writings?" Toliskorn asked innocently.

"Comrade Toliskorn, you have not tied the two together."

Throwing up his hands, Toliskorn turned toward his table. The old provincial judge continued to amaze him. Where had Feuchinko found him? Still facing the rear of the courtroom, his eyes on the Press Booth, Toliskorn asked, "Dr. Mraisky, several of your articles, informing the West on how it might pressure the Soviet Government, several of these were deliberately passed on to American reporters, were they not?"

"Americans. English. The French," Mraisky replied. "Whoever had interest in economics."

Toliskorn picked up a list of names and began to read them off one at a time, allowing Mraisky time to hear each but not to respond. "Stuart. Dole. Bernstein, Greenwald. Parkinson. Weiss. Do you recognize these names?"

The names whizzed through Mraisky's mind, in conjunction with a jumble of faces. He could not put the two rosters together. "I recognize some..."

"Which ones?"

"Dole." Short, pudgy...

"Yes?"

"Weiss, I believe." A good Jew, who wrote for...

"Is that all?" Toliskorn questioned evenly.

"Parkinson. And Greenwald, yes, Greenwald."

Inwardly, Toliskorn laughed. Greenwald? Of course, Greenwald. "Did you ever pass your manuscripts to these American journalists?"

"Perhaps, if they..." Mraisky dared not finish. He sensed that something was wrong.

"At least, you knew these men."

"Yes," was all Mraisky said.

Finally, Toliskorn turned around, facing the accused. "Let's concentrate on just one, shall we?" He made a show of studying the list. "Greenwald. Let's concentrate on Greenwald."

~ ~ ~

In the hour since he had first read Volenko's note, Dunney just sat on the bed, the bed where he and Elizaveta... He had read the note over a dozen times, careful to shield it from Bellin's camera. Volenko's hasty scrawl had taken five attempts to decipher.

The Russian scribbling read, "I saw Bellin's men waiting. I had to hide the cartridge. Elizaveta did not know. There was no chance to tell her."

She was arrested for nothing. That much he had readily understood, if not fully comprehended. Dunney knew that he had let it happen, let Bellin take her. For nothing! She was his responsibility, if he loved her...

"Before we hoped to save Mraisky. Now, you must save her. Only the taped message can." Barely legible, the note went on to describe the hiding place Volenko had improvised. At first, Dunney had refused to believe that the opportunity was being forced upon him. It was a sham. No. Volenko and, perhaps, Elizaveta herself had manipulated him. As Bellin had manipulated him.

Dunney concentrated on the final passage, the part telling him where to find the tape cartridge. The final word definitely meant "box". The rest of it had something to do with the hotel, a desk.

Oh God, he thought. Volenko had left the cartridge for him in the most obvious place for a message: His hotel message box! Dunney laughed at the irony. An item important enough to die for, perhaps to kill for, worth risking everything for; and it sat innocently down in the lobby right under Bellin's all-seeing video eye. As if it didn't mean a damn thing.

He picked up the phone next to the bed, one eye on Bellin's watchful lens. "Desk? This is Dunney in room 618."

"Yes, Mr. Dunney." The clerk's usual civility encouraged him.

"I would like some lunch."

"Ah, yes, Mr. Dunney. The menu includes..."

"Just a pitcher of Bloody Mary's if you don't mind." What would Bellin expect? Bloody Marys were a good compromise. And one other touch. "How about a bottle of champagne?"

Skeptical, the clerk replied. "Of course, sir."

Making his voice as somber as possible. he added, "Two glasses for the champagne." Symbolic. Bellin.

"Two glasses, yes, Mr. Dunney."

Carefully, Dunney made the critical comment. "I'm expecting some important messages later today. I may have to phone in..."

"Certainly, sir. By the way, you have a..."

Cutting in quickly, he said as casually as possible, "Have them bring it up with the, uh, lunch. Okay?"

"Of course. Mr. Dunney."

"Thanks." Carefully, Dunney returned the receiver to its base. He could not afford to let the hand shake; they, or rather Bellin, would see. Right now, Bellin was the only one he had to worry about.

~ ~ ~

The KGB technician merely shrugged when Bellin asked about Folenya. Her unexplained absence bothered him. Something was wrong.

Bellin did not take a seat. The monitors covering Dunney's room showed him that the girl was finally gone. It was better for both of them... But, there was something... Dunney sat stiffly on the couch, working, but occasionally glancing at the door as if awaiting something. Did he expect her to come back? Foolish...

No, not Dunney. "Have you been recording Dunney's room!"

The technician started at Bellin's question. "Recording?"

"Yes, damn it! You were supposed to record." Bellin felt the hair on his neck stir. "Well?"

"Yes, Director," he replied hesitantly.

Annoyed with the technician's reluctance, Bellin snapped, "I want to see the recording."

The young man seemed puzzled. "Comrade Folenya just ordered them erased, Director Bellin."

"She what?"

"Shortly after she got back."

Bellin glared at the technician, stupefied by his words. "What are you talking about?" he demanded harshly. "Came back from where?"

Lying, the technician replied, "I don't know, Director. I haven't seen her. She phoned in the command."

"Internally, then?"

"Yes, sir."

"You called back to confirm, I trust," Bellin said more calmly.

Proudly, the KGB man said, "Of course...," before realizing that he had fallen into Bellin's trap. He gulped and tried to make the best of his mistake by volunteering the information. "Extension 188."

The target range! Bellin started to go, but turned back. With one motion he tore the intercom phone from the wall. "You record everything Dunney does, is that clear?"

The technician nodded.

"And if you erase one inch of tape," Bellin warned, "I won't even bother to bring you up on charges."

Without waiting for a response, Bellin bolted for the stairs leading to the target range. If it was as bad as he suspected, he might have only minutes to act.

~ ~ ~

Harmon Kyle listened abjectly as the Russian Foreign Secretary said quietly over the phone, "My government does not believe you have any cause to hold the men in question."

"Mr. Secretary," Kyle said as calmly as possible. "We can't hold this from the press for very much longer. Once the news is out, we well have to hold them. You must make your government understand."

"Mr. Kyle, I am sorry, but...   I will try again."

"Please do, Mr. Secretary. The relations between our countries cannot stand this kind of blow, as I am sure you are aware."

The Russian laughed. "I will try. Good-bye, Mr. Kyle."

"Good-bye. Mr. Secretary. I appreciate your efforts." Kyle hung up and stared past Greenwald. "God damn bastards. They aren't buying. Now what?"

~ ~ ~

"And so finally. Dr. Mraisky," the tired Toliskorn said, "we can agree that you were well acquainted with the American reporter named Seymour Greenwald."

Beyond his endurance, Mraisky nodded.

"Is that a yes?"

"Yes."

"And that you transmitted four separate articles or interviews through Mr. Greenwald to the American press?"

"Yes."

314 | John Nicholas Datesh

Striding back to his desk, Toliskorn picked up a sheet of paper. He moved over directly in front of Mraisky, bending over the exhausted defendant. "What I have here is a sworn statement from that same Seymour Greenwald admitting that he was, in fact, a CIA operative and that he actively solicited your involvement in seditious activities."

Mraisky's eyes and mouth opened wide at Toliskorn's staccato statement.

Leaving Mraisky, Toliskorn handed the paper to the Senior Judge. "You will note that the CIA agent denies that the accused participated in any direct activities. But I ask the court to consider the worth of such a CIA denial."

The three judges leaned together to read the document. The senior Judge finished first and asked Mraisky, "Do you have any response to this?"

All Mraisky could say was, "I didn't know. I didn't know." Working so nicely together, the CIA and KGB had damned him.

"Do you wish to call witnesses or address the court?"

Beaten, Mraisky hung his head. Why jeopardize the lives of the few brave souls willing to speak for him? "No."

"Procurator? Have you any final statement?"

Toliskorn. looking from one judge to the others, replied, "Mr. Greenwald's statement is summation enough in this case."

The senior judge stood, followed by the others. "The court will now retire to consider the case."

The silence of the still-stunned court room held Toliskorn in suspension for several moments. He found himself wondering what it would have been like if a man's life had really hung in the balance.

~ ~ ~

Arkilonov had already left the office by the time Feuchinko turned off the closed-circuit picture. The Procurator General stood over the television and thought how perfectly it had all come off. The verdict, of course, was not worth missing his lunch for.

When Dunney saw the size of the cassette package lying on the room-service tray, he finally realized the impossibility of the task. Even a mild frisk would betray him. He was hopelessly over his head. For an instant, he balked when the tray was offered by the room service attendant. He positioned himself to block the door. He could not afford to let the attendant enter into camera range.

"Your order, sir." The boy tried to move inside. "Let me set it..."

Dunney dug into his pocket, giving the attendant a tip. "I'll take it. Thanks." The tray in hand, he kicked the door closed and, keeping his back to the room, shifted the package to the underside of the platter. Having deliberately piled the coffee table with work papers, Dunney set the package and the tray on the couch. That maneuver completed, he turned to make his phone call.

"Front desk?" he asked in Russian. After the acknowledgment, he said. "I'd like to speak to the US Embassy, please."

"Of course. Mr. Dunney."

After several rings, the receptionist answered.

"Hello, this is Christopher Dunney. I would like to speak to Mr. Kyle."

Dunney waited on hold for what seemed an endless minute before Kyle answered. "Well, Mr. Dunney. Good afternoon."

Making his voice sound worried. Dunney asked. "I saw that business in front of the Embassy this morning..."

Subdued, Kyle interrupted him. "It's bad, Dunney. We've got demonstrations all over the place in the US, and it's still early morning. The FBI just picked up a couple Soviet embassy people. That little incident may be the beginning. We've been lucky so far."

"That was luck?"

"You're damn right!" Kyle snapped. "It could have been a whole hell of a lot worse. I've seen it much worse."

"I'm thinking of," Dunney began, acting nervous, "coming over there, to the Embassy, until it blows over. What do you think?"

"Good idea," Kyle responded. "Excellent idea. By the way, you might check with other people over there, especially those kids with the track team. I warned them against going out today, but I don't think they listened. They'd be safer over here, safer than running around the streets of Moscow in red, white and blue."

Dunney was speechless. His mind was too busy.

"Dunney? Are you there?" Kyle demanded.

"Yes."

"The sooner you get over here the better. Mraisky's trial is pretty much over. Only the verdict is left. An hour at the outside, and that's if they decide to make it look real."

Shaking inside, Dunney controlled his voice. "I'll go talk to the boys, Mr. Kyle. You just keep your eyes open for us. I want that gate opened when I get to the guards. Okay?"

"You got it. See you in a few minutes."

Minutes, that was all he had left. According to Elizaveta, the message's impact depended on its reaching the Embassy before Mraisky's trial ended. Mraisky. He didn't give a good God damn for Mraisky, for Russian dissidents or for Russians Jews. He had never cared. That was all Elizaveta's business.

He had his own now. And somehow, he had to make Clinton Thomas help him.

~ ~ ~

The Procurator of Moscow sat quietly in the empty court room, drinking coffee. He felt no pleasure in completing his job. When it was all over, his role would prove to be the least satisfying; he had known that from the beginning. Still, it did not sit well with him.

"Congratulations, Procurator Toliskorn," Feuchinko's voice echoed from behind him.

Toliskorn sighed, not looking around. "You may have it. Comrade."

Feuchinko laughed, saying, "I intend to have some of it, young man. We will all have our shares." He checked his watch. "How much longer?"

"Two hours, fifteen minutes were agreed upon."

"Less than an hour, then." Feuchinko straightened the chair behind Toliskorn. "We won't have too long to wait."

Toliskorn twisted around. "We?"

Winking, Feuchinko replied, "Do you think I would let you bask alone in this triumph for the Soviet legal system, eh?"

~ ~ ~

The familiar stairs creaked noisily as Bellin descended swiftly to the firing range. With the light already burning in the hallway, he ran at a half-trot into the target room. On the floor lay a box... His closer inspection chilled Bellin: It was a false book, one with an inner space for holding valuables. It wore the bogus cover of an economics book.

Beside the shattered book lay the knife Folenya had used to pry it open. He could tell that the knife itself had done a clean job. The smashing of the book had come after its opening. Whatever she had found inside had not satisfied Folenya, had indeed enraged her.

Folenya herself was nowhere to be found.

Bellin threw the broken book aside and walked slowly to the cabinet in which he had left his pistol the day before. He had nothing particular in his mind as he unlatched the old fashioned door, just something impelling him to look.

Its old wooden container lay on the shelf, the hook lock dangling open. He did not have to look inside, but he could not resist the impulse. The gun was, of course, gone.

~ ~ ~

Not knowing whether Bellin had bugged Clinton Thomas' room or not, Dunney hesitated when grudgingly asked to enter. Thomas and "Whitey" Smith were in the middle of a game of chess, both in track shots and no shits.

Catching Dunney's eyes on the chess set, Thomas remarked sarcastically. "I can do more than run the hundred and fuck, man."

Dunney just said, "I need a favor."

"You need a favor?" Thomas replied immediately. "I already did you a favor, man." If Andy had used him, Dunney had made it happen.

"Jesus!" Smith cried, hammering the chessboard. Thomas had been an ass for days over the white girl. He gave Thomas a hard stare. After a pause, he said. "You got yourself bent, man, eyes open."

The jab hit its target squarely. Smith had refused to sympathize with Thomas about Andy Wards. Thomas had wanted her and taken up with her knowing that she was vulnerable, needing a man. Why not? He had not expected to be vulnerable himself.

Reading his friend's face, Smith added quietly. "You owe the man one, Clint."

Dunney interrupted. "Listen. Clint. You don't owe me anything. Except maybe a chance to talk. Okay?"

"Okay." Thomas knew that Smith was right. Not because of the girl, but because he had tried to lay the blame on Dunney instead of where it belonged. "I can listen."

With a glance toward Smith. Dunney suggested. "Just a couple of minutes. In the hall. All right?"

Reassured by a nod from Smith. Thomas led the way. He then followed Dunney as the latter walked to the end of the corridor. There, Dunney hoped, Bellin would be least likely to have a microphone. Facing back toward the center of the hall. Dunney said conversationally. "Kyle thinks we all should get our asses over to the Embassy."

With a relieved sigh, Thomas asked, "Is that all? I mean, the man already keeps us off the streets."

Trying to look as natural as possible for any cameras Bellin might have had, Dunney turned toward the window. "No. Clint. That's not all. That's not even the beginning."

Dunney looked back at Thomas. "I don't know what Andy may have told you..."

"Enough."

"About the Russian girl?"

Thomas waited for a second unable to see Dunney's face. "Yes.

"She's been arrested, Clint," Dunney said, allowing a touch of emotion to color his voice. "She's a Jew and one of Mraisky's people..."

"I know that."

"Did Andy tell you that I was in love with this girl?"

Surprised, Thomas said, "No. She was sure you weren't." All that Andy had told him was that she loved Dunney. God, that had hit him from nowhere.

"Andy couldn't have known, I suppose," Dunney acknowledged. "I wasn't any more honest with her than I was with Elizaveta or myself."

"Is that the girl?"

"Elizaveta? Yes."

Every word rubbed Thomas raw. "You say they arrested her. You mean the KGB?"

Dunney nodded. "This morning. She had asked me to do something for her and," he explained, his voice more emotional than intended, "I have to do it."

Tentatively Thomas asked, "And you want my help?" He suddenly got the idea. "This is something dangerous, isn't it?"

"I sincerely hope not," Dunney replied. "but I'm afraid it could be. There's no question that I will be arrested."

"You're crazy, man!" Thomas was shaken. "You know that and you'll still do it!"

The crucial moment had arrived. Dunney looked straight into Clinton Thomas' widened eyes and said firmly. "Yes."

Backing away, Thomas shook his head. "Hey, I'm sorry, man. 'Go Soviet Jewry' and all that, but her cause don't play with the Muslims in my neighborhood..."

"I don't do causes," Dunney said quickly. "She's my cause. Just her. I've got to help her and I'm asking you to help me."

Held by Dunney's intense, demanding stare, Thomas accepted the responsibility imposed by his own guilt. For his own less-than-heroic ends, he had put himself into Dunney's game. He just had to have Andy, didn't he? "What will happen...?"

"If you get caught? You were just carrying a package for me. You won't know what's in it." Dunney did not release Thomas' eyes from his, pulling the cartridge, still wrapped, from the inside of his belt. "All you have to do is go out jogging to the Embassy. If you tape it securely in the arch of your back and pad it, no one will notice."

"The guards...?"

Dunney looked away, afraid his face would betray his own anxiety. "Someone out there will have to arrest me." He turned back with a smile. "If you make it, I'll be released. I won't have anything on me."

Thomas did not believe him. He knew that it could not work. He also knew he could give Dunney his best shot. "If we're caught. man, you're on your own. Believe it."

"Fifteen minutes?"

"What about Whitey? He'll have to be with me."

"If you don't tell him, he won't know, but that's up to you, Clint." Dunney shook his young courier's hand and, as he patted him on the back, slipped him the tape cartridge. "Be careful. They have TV cameras all over the God damned place."

Thomas could only mutter, "Jesus shit."

"I'll be in the lobby. When you walk out the door, you should call to me 'come on over' or something. They'll already know I've talked to you about going to the Embassy for safety purposes."

"Safety? We could get shot at!"

Dunney had thought of that more than once. He had visualized Bellin pointing a huge revolver at him. "If they do, you run like hell for the Embassy." Looking away he explained, "Because if they do shoot, they'll be shooting at me."

~ ~ ~

As she watched the guards casually melt away from the gate of the US Embassy, Anna Folenya settled back into the KGB car. Bellin's powerful service pistol felt reassuringly heavy in her purse. From where she had ordered the car positioned, she could easily see the front of the Hotel International and the Embassy entrance.

The radio-phone in hand, she spoke to the KGB officer in charge of the Militia guards. "That is fine. Leave just the two in the front."

"The others will move in on your signal."

"I don't expect the American to be any trouble," she said confidently. "Just keep them out of range."

"Yes, Comrade Folenya."

Bending toward the front seat, Folenya looked up at Dunney's window. She knew he had the tape. He had to. In a few minutes, he would make his pitiful attempt. And she would be the agent to stop him.

They had tricked her the first time, she admitted angrily. But that did not matter. It was better this way.

~ ~ ~

"Director Bellin?" the interrogation division deputy asked, stepping up behind him. "What should we do with the three prisoners Comrade Folenya brought in?"

His mind on Dunney's picture, Bellin did not react at first. Dunney was jamming something inside his shirt as he tucked it in. Cleverly blocking the view, yet...

Suddenly, Bellin pivoted to study the young man. "Prisoners! What prisoners?"

"Those three subversives..." He held out preliminary reports on each.

Bellin froze rock solid. Folenya had done it! Of course she had. Why hadn't he admitted it to himself? Grabbing the papers, Bellin threw aside the first two. There it was! Stupid Anna had fallen into... Stupid? No, it was what she wanted, what the fanatics in the KGB wanted! An excuse to wipe out every dissident, every mildly objectionable man and woman in Russia.

There was no way Dunney had not seen. They had taken her right out from under his nose. That kind of challenge Dunney could not refuse. He had the tape, tucked into his pants so artlessly, and now he had the resolve. God damn it! How could he stop it?

"I need a car," he declared, as he watched Dunney set his jacket on his shoulders and walk out the door.

"Assistant Director Folenya canceled the KGB requisition," the deputy said. "She said we didn't need them anymore."

"What about our own?"

"They're all assigned."

"Pull them all back in," Bellin ordered. "Every damned one. And get outside. I want a cab if you can get one."

The young man raced out of the room.

Dunney had started down the corridor, his swinging coat occasionally revealing the bulge of the package. Self-consciously, Dunney buttoned the front button and then unbuttoned it several times.

Bellin turned and ran.

Bellin had only one hope: That he could make Dunney see reason!

If the Folenya's won this round, too...

~ ~ ~

Inside the judges' conference room, Mraisky's three jurists debated his fate. The vote had, to that point, repeatedly been two to one.

"Unanimity would be better," opined one of the younger men. "A split in the panel implies doubt."

"I have no doubt," the Senior grumbled. "How can you?"

The two young judges exchanged glances. One of them had to suppress a smile. "We have none."

Stubbornly, the old man said, "Then let's go."

The third spoke abruptly. "No. Not yet. We must not seem too hurried. Especially with a divided court."

"We wait," the other agreed. "This trial is far too important. Far too important."

~ ~ ~

His stomach churned as Dunney stepped out of the elevator and into the lobby. It was so empty for mid-day, so empty that he could have been arrested without anyone even noticing. That dreary prospect held far less danger, of course, because Dunney had nothing incriminating on him, but it also held no satisfaction. Dunney wanted it known...

Recalling that the cameras gave Bellin a first-hand view of everything. Dunney found himself smiling. Bellin would know. No matter what happened, Bellin would know.

And, if Bellin knew, then Elizaveta would find out, though perhaps that was not necessary. She loved him, after all; he did not have to prove anything to her. You never had to prove anything to someone you love, he thought, only someone you despise.

"Mr. Dunney," called a woman's voice in heavily accented English, jarringly cutting off his thoughts.

He turned, too quickly revealing his nervousness for Bellin's cameras. "Yes?"

It was a desk clerk. "A call for you, Mr. Dunney."

"Tell him," he began to say, before realizing that, if it were Bellin. he would know that Dunney was in fact there. He said instead, "Tell whoever it is I'll be there in a second." Dunney took that second, collecting his wits.

As ready as his increasingly shaky nerves allowed, Dunney took the phone. "Dunney," he said, summoning a touch of bravado.

"This is Kyle, Dunney. Where the hell are you people?"

A squeeze of tension gripped Dunney. The Embassy, he thought, what was wrong? "I'm on my way, Mr. Kyle. I don't know about the others."

"Something may be up," Kyle said anxiously. "For some damn reason, they've cut down on the guard. Right when we may finally need it!"

Automatically, Dunney spun around toward the front of the hotel. Though he could barely see them, he knew that there were fewer men out front of the embassy than usual.

Bellin was daring him!

"If you move it, Dunney, you can probably get in easier now. But in a few more minutes, who knows?"

"I'll be there," Dunney assured Kyle grimly. "There isn't anything that'll keep me in here now." Dunney hung up and walked up to the large window beside the door.

Only two God damned guards! So Bellin wanted him to try. And, of course, to fail. "We'll see," he said to himself. "We'll see, Bellin."

~ ~ ~

Bellin's car skidded around the corner and swerved as he hit the brakes. Leaping out of his seat before Folenya could react, Bellin tore open the door of the KGB automobile. When she tried to reach for the purse, Bellin's arm slammed her into the back of the seat while his hand locked on hers. He froze the driver with a sharp glance.

For a moment, he glowered at her, saying nothing. Then he pulled the bag from her limp hand, removed his revolver and threw the purse on the floor. "If you move, even just get out of this car," Bellin said, his voice shaking with rage, "I will personally show you how well this thing works."

Rubbing her chest at the point of impact, Folenya stumbled over her words, "You'll answer, answer to us for this."

Bellin had to hold back on an urge to slap her unconscious. "I answer to the Russian people, Comrade."

Tucking the gun inside his belt, Bellin punctuated his statement by slamming the car door.

Striding toward the hotel and his certain confrontation with Dunney, Bellin desperately worked over in his mind what he would say to the American. He knew that his own plan was working against him now, not for him. He hoped to God that Dunney did not identify him with everything that had happened. If Dunney did...

As he broke into the square, Bellin looked over in the direction of the Embassy. What he saw shattered his hope. Folenya had pulled most of the guard. The uninterested pair of uniformed KGB officers looked like an invitation. It was an invitation which Dunney would have to accept.

"Come on, Mr. Dunney!" he heard someone yell, as if to verbalize the challenge.

As he twisted toward the hotel, Bellin felt the hardness of his pistol press against his groin. How would Dunney respond to it? His thoughts jumbled, Bellin heard another question: How would he himself respond?

He saw Dunney's face in the far lobby window. In front, two of the American track men, brilliantly dressed in their glossy blue, white and red uniforms, waved at Dunney, signaling him to follow.

Dunney spotted Bellin, as if he had been waiting for him all along, and stared dead at him. Absently, while still looking Bellin in the eye, Dunney waved to the two young blacks. They shrugged and jogged off, taking the long, roundabout route to the Embassy.

Once they had left the periphery of his field of vision, Bellin ignored them. As Dunney stepped away from the window, Bellin covered the remaining ten yards between him and the hotel entrance in quick, hard strides. Without his thinking of it, or even noticing it, his hand touched the butt of his gun. That part of his mind understood that Dunney had become only the instrument of the paranoid mania bottled up inside of the Folenya's. That part of him had to stop Dunney. At all costs.

~ ~ ~

Bellin's arrival had only spurred him, Dunney knew. It was what he had expected, even hoped for. He wanted Bellin there, in person, not behind a video monitor. Success, he had learned long ago, wasn't worth a damn if a man like Bellin, like Klein, like his brothers, did not see it for themselves.

He had no confidence in his chances. But the anxiety that had so often filled him in the past had left him completely. His thoughts of Elizaveta were stirring but oddly abstract: As Bellin doubted him, Elizaveta believed in him.

At the door, he paused both to be sure that Thomas and Smith had enough of a lead on him and, yes, to be sure that Bellin was in position. He satisfied himself that all was ready and pushed the entrance door open.

Bellin stood off to one side, careful not to move too close to Dunney. His sole intention at that point was to convince Dunney to surrender. If that failed, he would... try something else. When Dunney pulled even with him. Bellin fell into step with him. It was an easy, almost casual pace.

"Good afternoon. Director Bellin," Dunney said in a mockingly cheerful Russian. "Nice day for a stroll, don't you think?"

Bellin looked at the sky, preserving the fiction for the moment. "Yes, Mr. Dunney. And a bit of a talk."

Dunney could feel his step falter, as he glanced over to Bellin on his right. "Do you and I have anything to talk about? You've got everything you want, don't you?"

Earnestly Bellin replied, "Dunney, I didn't want the girl. I didn't arrest her. The KGB did."

Dunney laughed. "So? You've got her. What the hell."

"You know as well as I do that the KGB botched it. She didn't have the tape."

Involuntarily, Dunney stopped. "They what?"

"They don't have anything on her," Bellin explained. "She didn't have the thing the KGB thought she had."

"How much did the KGB have on Mraisky?" Dunney demanded, walking away again.

"I promise you that she will be released if the Americans do not get the tape." Bellin started after Dunney, still staying several feet away. "If you turn around now."

Dunney controlled his urge to check on Thomas' progress. A wrong look would give them away. He had to play innocent until they came into his front view. "Me? Why...?"

Framing his words carefully, Bellin said, "You're such an obvious suspect. Mr. Dunney, that even if you didn't have the tape, I would be compelled to believe you did."

"And you do?"

Bellin checked their location in the square: They had not yet reached the halfway point. "It doesn't matter if you do or not. If you don't, there is no one else."

Where the hell were they? Dunney's mind cried. "I see. Unfortunately, the Embassy has demanded my presence."

"Dunney, please," Bellin responded before he knew it. "If that tape gets into American hands, or if I have to arrest you and you have it, either way, Elizaveta could be executed. And that would just be the beginning. It's a license for the fanatics in the KGB to eliminate anyone, anyone. Including you and me."

Scornfully. Dunney dismissed Bellin's plea. "You are worried about the KGB, Bellin? You're the one who has monitored my every move. You're the one who followed me everywhere. You're the one who damned near climbed into bed with Elizaveta and me every night. Don't talk to me about the KGB."

Aroused by Dunney's accusations, Bellin retorted, "I have to fight them with their own weapons!"

"Good for you."

"For God's sake! I'm trying to save your life! And hers. And hundreds, thousands of others." Bellin saw that they had passed the halfway point. In glancing over to his right he saw something else, something which meant that his time was very much shorter than he had hoped: Folenya, backed up by two senior KGB officers were bearing toward them. "Please, before it's too late."

Thomas and Smith jogged into Dunney's view as Bellin spoke. He felt his leg muscles flex and his chest tighten in anticipation. Kyle appeared at the Embassy gate, pushing it open and calling to the boys. Simultaneously, the two guards prepared to search the oncoming runners. The time had come.

Bellin saw that it was already too late. The KGB officers striding in behind Folenya had their hands on the pistols in their coats. He lurched for Dunney's arm, only catching the sleeve as Dunney began to break stride. With the other hand Bellin pulled his gun out of his belt.

The force of Bellin's hand on his coat combined with Dunney's first running thrust twisted him around toward Bellin and his gun.

"Oh shit," he blurted.

The gun looked very much larger and more deadly than he had visualized. He glanced from the gun to the Embassy gate and then back into Bellin's eyes. Their expression told him that Bellin had no choice. He had to shot if Dunney ran.

Dunney broke away from Bellin, sprinting straight for the guards just as they started to search Thomas and Smith.

The last look in Dunney's eyes, Bellin saw, was not defiance, but acceptance. Quickly. Bellin glanced off to his side. The KGB agents, startled by Dunney's action, were recovering, stating to move.

Bellin had no time left. He had to be the one. He had to bring Dunney down. He had to beat the Folenya's to the kill, if he were to have any chance against them.

"Dunney!" he shouted. "For God's sake Dunney! Stop!"

Dunney heard Bellin's words at the same moment that the guards began frisking Thomas. If he stopped, they'd find the tape and Elizaveta would, as Bellin said, be dead. If he didn't...

Bellin set himself in the sharpshooters' crouch, slowly leveling his gun. He heard the KGB men's running footsteps mingled with Dunney's. Somehow he could not shoot. He had to. but he could not.

The guard had patted down Thomas' legs when Dunney accelerated forward, finding more strength, more speed. With every ounce of his breath, he screamed some kind of incomprehensible battle cry. In the blur of his vision, he could tell that the guards reacted, standing, looking towards him. Both started to swing their rifles around.

"Shoot, Bellin! Shoot!" Folenya screamed, as Dunney sprinted ever closer to the gate. Her own cry caught her up short. Not Bellin. She couldn't want Bellin to do it!

Bellin heard Folenya call his name. It strengthened his will to act, began beating back his reluctance to kill a man, a man he knew well. A man he liked.

Suddenly, the scene in front of Dunney erupted. Thomas and Smith rushed the guards from behind. Other guards raced toward him from either side of the Embassy. "No!" Dunney cried, in a shout that had little wind behind it. He could still stop, still surrender. Dunney felt his legs turn rubbery. "No! Get in!" he shouted, with one last burst of breath.

The boys heard him. They left the guards and bolted for the Embassy gate.

"Dunney!" Bellin tried one more time, still poised. The KGB agents whisked by him, one crying "Shoot, you foul!"

Dunney was nearing the gate. Bellin's mind was whirring, his consciousness jumbled with his subconscious. This time he had to...

The jolt numbed his arms, the roar pummeled his ears.

Dunney felt his feet leave the ground, but he felt nothing after that.

In a daze. Bellin watched as Dunney pitched forward, driven by the force of the bullet, and then jerk his back in a horrible arching spasm. Hitting the stone of the square. Dunney slid on his chest for several feet. Then he, and everyone else, was still.

Bellin moved first. He tucked his gun into his belt and slowly walked toward Dunney's outstretched form. When he arrived, he did not feel for a pulse, or breath. He patted the body down quickly, expertly, only vaguely aware of the touch. He removed the small package from Dunney's belt and slowly opened it.

It contained nothing. Nothing but crumpled work sheets.

Bellin looked toward the Embassy, his emotions banked. The two black Americans, with Kyle standing next to them, looked on in tear-stained horror. One of them held a small package, absent-minded in one hand.

He looked hack down at Dunney and his own blood-drenched hand. All that mattered to Bellin now, was whether Dunney were still alive.

~ ~ ~

Somberly accepting the opportunity to read the decision of the court, because the senior judge refused, the younger

on the left of the bench addressed the accused. "By a two-to-one decision. this court finds the accused, Dr.

Alexander Mraisky, innocent of all charges. He is to be released immediately."

The shock silenced the expectant gallery and stunned Mraisky himself.

Feuchinko tapped Toliskorn on the shoulder. Affecting a frown, he whispered, "Congratulations, Procurator."

Chapter Thirteen

"You'll live," Klein said.

Dunney let the savage pain in his left shoulder die down a bit before saying, "So I'm told. But this damn thing will keep me out of bed for months."

Klein laughed alone. The Soviet doctors had forbidden laughter on Dunney's part. Dunney, with a smashed clavicle, a fractured cheek bone and ripped lower back muscles to remind him of Bellin's bullet, had come a long way in four weeks. For the moment, Dunney was the prize patient of the Russian doctors and they wanted him healthy.

"Have you seen Sarkat, Steve?"

Troubled. Klein brushed the question aside with a lie. "Only once, a social thing." He could hardly tell Dunney the truth: Sarkat refused to see him as long as Dunney remained with the firm. And Bingo Williams had refused to even entertain that suggestion. Klein, himself, was working on a compromise. "SALT'S the big story now anyway, Chris. We don't want to be scooped by a mere arms-treaty."

"I haven't been reading the newspapers."

"Suffice it to say that now it's the Russians who don't want the original treaty," Klein explained grimly. "Not unless we agree not to interfere with internal affairs. Since that God damned trial, we're looking pretty stupid anyway. I think the foreign press has settled on the word 'humiliated.'"

"What happened!" Dunney demanded. "At the trial, I mean."

A bitter laugh prefaced Klein's answer. "You didn't know? They found Mraisky innocent."

Dunney tired to move. "Innocent!" The pain almost knocked him out. "What about... the others?"

His hand in Dunney's right arm, Klein replied, "I've asked several times. I don't know."

"Bellin. He knows."

Klein shook his head. "He's too busy being a hero. You've made quite a success of him. Obviously shooting an American spy is a big deal in Moscow."

Closing his eyes, Dunney awaited a hostile reaction. Bellin alter all was usurping his glory, for he, not Bellin, had succeeded. Where was the tape, he wondered. Why did he feel that it didn't matter?

"Are you all right, Chris?" Klein asked in a concerned voice.

Dunney opened his eyes and gave Klein an appreciative smile. "No. I'm fine. I was just trying to remember what I used to think mattered so damn much."

"Don't worry about it."

With a sigh, Dunney changed the subject. "Are those two kids, Thomas and Smith, all right?"

"They went back to the United States the night after you..." Klein let the statement hang.

"I made a damned fool out of myself, yeah. Well, that's something anyway. No one gave them any trouble?"

"No. Should they have?"

For the first time, it struck Dunney that Klein did not know! Did anyone know? Calming himself, he asked, "What does the Globe have to say about me? Anything?"

"Only that the Soviets accuse you of being a CIA agent, while the CIA says nothing. But after that Greenwald business," Klein added. "the world presumes that you were. American lawyers are rarely shot down in broad daylight, even in the streets of Moscow."

"Watch yourself," Dunney warned lightly. "It could be the beginning of a trend."

As he finished the sentence, a nurse walked in and hustled Klein out of the room with the admonition, "You are not the only visitor."

"I'll come back tomorrow, Chris." Klein said, going out the door.

Dunney felt cheered somewhat by Klein's solicitude. Perhaps, their former antipathy had been shown up for the pettiness if had always been by the events of weeks before. Perhaps, it was something else.

Before he had much chance to consider the change. Dunney found Kyle standing at the foot of his bed. The Embassy Staff Secretary looked drawn and depleted, his formerly crisp professionalism worn thin. "Well. Mr. Dunney. You are a remarkable man."

"Thank you. Mr. Kyle." Dunney replied, noncommittal. "I had just decided the contrary."

"When I got to you," Kyle said, "I thought you were already dead. Of course, I was still wondering why, at that point. But here you are, well enough to travel. So they tell me."

"They have good doctors in this country. Good doctors and good marksmen."

Kyle pursed his lips. "If you hadn't had your head tucked down to run, he'd've blown it off." Kyle reran the entire sequence in his mind, seeing Bellin's too-natural crouch, the long delay, Dunney jerking into the air, Bellin's cold, hurried search of the body. More than anything else, however, he remembered that Bellin had stood over Dunney the entire time he was being given first aid. "It got to him, Dunney. I can tell you that much."

For a long moment, Dunney stared at Kyle. "Now he's a national hero."

Raising an eyebrow, Kyle shrugged. "Arkilonov himself presented Bellin with a citation. He's supposed to be promoted to an all-Union job. He gets a better apartment. God knows what he would have gotten if he'd killed you?"

Dunney said nothing. Perhaps, it would have worked out better for all of them.

Taking a cue from Dunney's silence, Kyle got down to business. "The reason I'm here, Dunney, is official. We're getting you out of here in a couple days."

"Where the hell do I go?"

"Mass General, for starters."

"Boston". Dunney's heart sank.

"All around it." Kyle set his tired shoulders. "We're working a spy trade. We've got a couple of theirs and they've got a couple of ours."

With these things swirling around him too fast, Dunney barely managed to ask, "Two?"

Kyle laughed. bitterly. "Two. You and a guy named Greenwald. We'll be sending another one back, too, but the Russians don't know about that one."

"Who?"

"Me."

Appalled, Dunney just said, "Shit."

"My bureau fucked up. We didn't know what was going on. We still don't." He made a gesture of resignation. "At least, I'm not being demoted, just shipped off the our embassy in music-free Iran. And I'm lucky. The President is up in arms because we supposedly tampered with the fucking Moscow Group–the one thing we didn't do–Director McDeamon resigned yesterday."

The Moscow Group, the dissidents, Dunney thought absently.

"I guess someone has hang for it. God knows, enough of the dissidents will after this."

"What about the girl?" Dunney asked abruptly.

"What girl?"

"Krylenkev. Elizaveta Krylenkev. She was arrested..."

Scornfully, Kyle replied, "Forget it. She's done. They're all done. The calls are already going out to liquidate the dissidents, my boy. Mraisky's discredited, innocent or not. The US doesn't dare open its collective mouth," he snorted. "The KGB's got carte blanche. I don't think anything can stop them."

Dunney understood. "It would take a God damned national hero to stop then." A Havana-smoking hero.

~ ~ ~

Bescel Radnik jotted down notes as Dunney talked. Having recently rejoined the Department of Investigation as Bellin's Deputy Director, Radnik had been assigned the delicate task of interrogating the American within the narrow guidelines established under the exchange. He had gotten almost nowhere, with the American lawyer Klein objecting to any pertinent questions.

"From whom did you receive the tape, Mr. Dunney?" Radnik asked again.

Klein cut in before Dunney could answer. "Mr. Dunney has not admitted receiving this tape, Deputy Radnik. And under the guidelines, he will not have to discuss it."

The pain in his shoulder growing by the minute, Dunney was becoming frustrated. "Don't you have it on tape, Radnik? Why badger me?"

"Your testimony is important in constructing the ease against the three conspirators," Radnik replied casually.

Dunney started, rising out of his wheel chair. "Where is she?"

"An obscure little town, quite a way from here," Radnik replied. "Where the trial will get no international attention. It was part of your government's demands regarding the exchange."

Crushed by the revelation, Dunney fell back into his chair, immune to the pain. "My government?

"To avoid embarrassment. Further embarrassment."

"I see." Dunney looked at Klein, who returned the glance with a nod of his head.

Standing, Klein said. "I think Mr. Dunney has told you everything he can, Mr. Radnik."

"Just one more question, Mr. Dunney." Radnik waited for an objection but got none. He wanted his own curiosity satisfied. "What you did was foolhardy in the extreme, nearly fatal. I don't know what possessed you to do it, but... Would you do it again?"

"Now, just a minute," Klein objected.

Calmly, Dunney held up his hand, stilling Klein. "Is this for the record?"

"Under the guidelines, everything is for the record. Mr. Dunney," Radnik replied, disappointed that he would not get an answer. He wanted to know if Bellin was right.

Dunney stood up. ignoring the pulses of pain generated by the pressure on his shoulder. He looked hard at Radnik and said. "Yes..."

~ ~ ~

The Russian plane sat quietly in the dawn mist, awaiting the boarding of the American passengers. It would fly to Frankfurt, exchanging its Americans for two Russians and return to Moscow. At the moment, it was taking on luggage and a coffin.

Klein pushed Dunney's wheelchair around the corner and into a holding area, separately designated for the American prisoner. The large gate area was, aside from Klein and Dunney, completely empty.

Dunney had said nothing since leaving the hotel for the airport. He had not slept the last several nights–not since his interview with Radnik–and felt curiously numb about returning to the United States.

Overcoming his reluctance to disturb the obviously preoccupied Dunney, Klein said. "Andy sent flowers. Unfortunately, they got to the hospital after we'd left."

Andy. "That was very nice of her."

"You don't hold that call against her?" Klein asked.

"No." Dunney preferred not to think about it. "Good luck with Sarkat, Steve. He's a bastard, but he wants those restaurants. He's particularly keen on the African impression."

"They'll come around as soon as you're back in Boston, Chris," Klein said, withholding the terms of the compromise he had already worked out with the Russians. It was hardly the time to tell Dunney that he had to leave the firm. Klein felt guilty about not telling Dunney, but he simply could not. "You've done all the work. It'll move quickly."

Reflecting fleetingly over his ambitions for the Moscow trip, Dunney found himself more amused than disappointed. He had almost forgotten what he had been after. "Don't settle for six."

Klein had read Dunney's notes and drafts. He had also talked informally with Sarkat. "I won't have to." Behind them they could hear the door open. Klein turned, but Dunney could not, having only Klein's gasp to warn him.

"Mr. Dunney," the familiar voice said.

Bellin came into his view. Dunney felt more gratified than surprised. "Director Bellin. It's a long drive out here. Do I have to answer more questions?"

"For the record?" Bellin asked rhetorically. "No. Off the record, only if you will."

Continuing to look into Bellin's eyes. Dunney said, "Steve, would you wheel this thing?"

Bellin waved Klein off. "Allow me. I prefer this to be a private conversation, if you agree, Mr. Klein."

Dunney half smiled. "Director Bellin and I are old friends. Steve. There isn't a thing he doesn't know about me already."

"In that case, I will excuse myself for the men's room," Klein said, shooting Dunney a stern don't-say-anything glance. "I'll be back in a minute."

After pushing Dunney over to the window and taking a seat for himself. Bellin stared out at the plane. "You're mending well."

"You're a lousy shot." Dunney responded in Russian.

"That possibility occurred to me," Bellin admitted. He had, however, studied and restudied the tape recorded by the cameras near the embassy. That was not the case. He had missed Dunney's bobbing head only because the backward thrust of Dunney's arm had pushed his shoulder up as protection. "You were a runner."

Surprised by the statement, Dunney replied, "How did you know?"

Not wholly candid, Bellin said, "The way you ran."

Laughing, Dunney noted. "It's a long way to come for that. Especially for an All-Union hero."

Bellin became serious. "I have some information which may interest you."

Holding himself back, Dunney said nothing. When Bellin remained silent, he gave in. "Elizaveta."

"Her trial date has been set," Bellin said. "She will be convicted. As will the others. They are guilty."

Dunney almost lost control of himself. He deliberately shifted his body causing, a sharp pain. "No deals?"

"No."

"She wouldn't like that anyway."

Bellin nodded. "She turned down every one we've offered." He dug into his coat pocket and pulled out a wrinkled piece of paper. "Do not read it until you're on the plane. It's an official document."

Pocketing, the paper, Dunney smiled sadly. "Thanks, Bellin." He couldn't manage any more.

"That is not why I came." Indeed, he had intended to have Radnik deliver Elizaveta's note. Had he? No, he had not, not really. "There is something else you should know. I only recently found this out myself. About the message."

Dunney gripped the side of the chair with his free hand. "The message? You mean the tape?"

Bellin waited until Dunney had relaxed a bit. "The contents..."

"Good God, you're going to tell me?"

"Doesn't it matter to you?"

The question brought Dunney up short. He was curious. yes. But... "Matter, Bellin? I don't know. I don't think so." He smiled, adding "I'm curious as hell, though."

Leaning closer, Bellin dropped his voice to a near whisper. He felt it necessary to tell Dunney no matter what the risk, which he considered slight in any case. After all, the Americans had the tape. "The tape came from a dormant CIA agent in the Cipher Section of the KGB. Apparently, he came upon it when his section was told to encode the information. The tape, which is encoded as a top priority message, divulges a plan to manipulate the United States into an embarrassing position over human rights, to eliminate the question in the arms negotiations. The plan concerned a show trial of our most visible dissenter."

"Are you saying that the Mraisky trial was a hoax?" Dunney demanded, horrified. "That he was going to be found innocent all the time?"

"Yes," Bellin replied simply.

"Oh, my God. It was all for nothing!"

"It was a plan formulated at the highest level of the State," Bellin continued grimly. "The KGB was only in charge of its execution. The tape would have been an embarrassment to our entire government if it had gotten to the Embassy in time. Your government could have neutralized the plan by reacting more appropriately."

"Jesus! It was..." Dunney had to swallow his first words to counter a wave of nausea. He looked into Bellin's seemingly impassive face. The expression he saw was forced. "You didn't know either, did you?"

"Until a few days ago, no." The truth had come from Anna Folenya on the day of her transfer–with a promotion–back to the KGB. It had staggered him as much as it had Dunney. His unfocused rage had only recently abated. When he had recovered his senses sufficiently, and only then, he had agreed to accept Arkilonov's offer of the Medal of Merit. At the same time, he had demanded, and had gotten, a number of other things.

Dunney shook his head. "Then we were all suckers."

"Suckers?"

"Victims."

"Yes."

After a moment of relaxed, mutual silence, Bellin rose. He looked out at Dunney's plane. "It's time."

Wincing with pain, Dunney stool to go. "Bellin, I don't know what you can do for her..."

The Party, the Government, the KGB–even the American government–they all wanted her taken out of the way. "There is very little chance," Bellin told him. "Good-bye, Dunney."

""Good-bye, Bellin," Dunney said sincerely. "Good luck."

Pausing before he went, Bellin studied Dunney. He nodded in response, knowing that the American understood that he would try. He would try because, for different reasons, it mattered to both of them.

~ ~ ~

Dunney put his feet up on the empty desk, surveying the bare walls of the office. His mail lay unopened. He was in no hurry, since he had nowhere to go until a lunch date with his brother, Joe, at Dunfey's. After that, he had nowhere to go, period.

Standing in the doorway, Carl Abelson cleared his throat to get Dunney's attention. When Dunney looked up, Abelson said, "Good morning, Dunney."

"My last, Carl," Dunney replied matter-of-factly. "After twelve, you can have this crummy stall back. It's assigned, isn't it?"

Abelson nodded. "You don't have to, you know. Until you have another position."

"Carl, you guys bought me off, fair and square," Dunney said, bitterly. "And I took it. Okay? I got to be 'Partner for a day' I've got a nice chunk of partnership money in the bank and a bonus for my wonderful work in Moscow. All twelve units' worth. Why shouldn't I agree to pursue my career elsewhere? Anytime, Carl."

Drawn into the office by a desire to explain. Abelson began, "Chris. we had no choice..."

Granting him a brief, neutral stare, Dunney turned his attention to his mail, slitting open an envelope. Abelson, interpreting the message correctly, turned to leave. He stopped when he heard Dunney breathe in sharply. "What's the matter...?"

Dunney said nothing at first. still scanning the letter. He looked up at Abelson and reread it, aloud.

"'Dear Mr. Dunney. Your presence is requested on the Fourteenth Day of September for the purpose of a debriefing by the Agency. Please consider this as a routine matter and other arrangements will be made if necessary to suit your convenience."

Dumbstruck, Abelson whispered, "The CIA."

Dunney, feeling a growing excitement, if not the full impact, continued reading. "'I might add, however, that the Fourteenth of September is the Agency's choice so as to arrange a simultaneous debriefing with yourself and another party involved in the Mraisky matter. Under a Soviet Order of Expulsion, Elizaveta Krylenkev will also be available on that day and only that day. Please call my office directly if you have any questions. Sincerely,

Horace Washington, Acting Director, Central Intelligence Agency."

"My God," Abelson said softly.

Able to breathe again, Dunney said quietly, "That son of a bitch did it!"

~ ~ ~

Bellin finished his briefing paper with a cigarette. Yet another Afghan coup in the works. Embarrassing. Not his problem.

He carefully lit the Winston, the last of the pack. Through the smoke, he glanced toward the airport. A plane cut through the clouds, elegantly headed west. Bellin checked his watch. It was too early for her flight yet.

Returning his attention to the cigarette, he took a deep, satisfying draw. He had grown quite found of the Winston's. He checked his watch again. With all the Americans coming for the Olympics, surely he could get plenty more.

~

About the Author

Born in 1950, John Nicholas Datesh lived mostly in and around Pittsburgh, Pennsylvania until early 2009. At Brown University, he took many courses in writing as an institutionalized rationale for doing just that. Then, at Boston University School of Law, he learned to mix in words and phrases like *It Depends* and *Hereinafter*.

In Spring 2009, he moved cats Lila and Lucy Liu to a condominium one mile in from the east side of Naples Bay in Florida. He left his Pittsburgh career in law, business and product development in favor of concentrating on writing fiction, winging blogs and cultivating beach chairs, presumably in that order of dedication.

He began writing fiction with a pencil and published, on paper with actual ink, his first three books, the SF/Mystery novel *The Nightmare Machine*; the Soft-boiled Detective novel *The Janus Murder*; and the International Suspense novel *The Moscow Tape*. All three novels are currently *available* in virtual ink at e-book stores on the Web and in trade paperback.

Also widely *available* are the short stories *The Pro Station* (WWII), *The Final Equation (SF)* and *Reruns ad Infinitum* (SF/Fantasy). They join the author's definitive Christmas short story, *You Could Call It a Christmas Story* as works published after the move to Naples.

He concocted a humorous and/or satiric blog at EmptyGlassFull.com shortly after moving. His *Christmas Story* started out as post to the blog, and he has e-published a collection its other early posts, grandly entitled *The Very First Blog Posts of All Time*. As novel writing began to take more of his time, he sent blogging on long vacation.

His 2013 novel, *The Girl in the Coyote Coat*, came to ignore the boundaries of mystery/suspense genre for which it was originally intended. No one would call it a romance, either. With a real estate and finance backdrop, the novel exposes how love, sex, money, scams, drugs, house-breaking and -shopping and fur coats can affect the lives of complex and intriguing characters and even kill a few.

November 2016's *The Body in the Bog* is a Sunset Noir mystery novel. It is the first in the author's planned *Death by Condo* series starring prematurely retired lawyer Ian Decker.

His screenplay *The Last Three Minutes* was the first piece written partly on the beach and entirely in the Naples Bay scenery, though it is not set there. *The Last Three Minutes* has been adapted as a novel, if not a movie, by the author was published on December 1, 2016.

Author's Note: The novel
The Girl in the Coyote Coat
and A Need Apart

That heading is not an error. They are the same novel. So, why? To double sales? Not likely.

The novel *The Girl in the Coyote Coat* had a long, tortuous road to its final form, right down to the cover and the very title. It was published under that title after some serious consideration. The novel had gone through any number of working titles, as time allowed, from the 1979 original *The Real Estate Novel*. *The Girl in the Coyote Coat* was always my favorite, inspired, as it was, by an actual coyote coat on an actual model. In the end, that was the title I chose, in a close call (if only to me) over number two, *A Need Apart*, but I did not use the photo that initially inspired the title.

In 2016, I decided to try a little Amazon Kindle advertising. Amazon would not accept the somewhat racy cover. That rejection got me thinking. The novel had grown into what I must loosely call a literary novel, if only because it does not fit into any genre. Why not try a different cover for an ad? Then, I thought, why not try a different, more literary-sounding title. The result is the identical novel with a different name, *A Need Apart*, and a different cover.

Ironically, the *A Need Apart*'s cover uses the shot that originally inspired the working title *The Girl in the Coyote Coat*. Fortunately, I love both titles and both covers, equally. Oh, and both the coat and model, too, if not quite so equally.

www.ingramcontent.com/pod-product-compliance
Lightning Source LLC
Chambersburg PA
CBHW022151260626
47155CB00017B/239